THE BOSS

Charles Lambert has been a journalist for more than twenty years and has worked in all branches of the media – newspapers, radio and television. He is currently the BBC sports correspondent in the North-West of England, appearing nightly on regional TV programmes and covering football for Radio 5 Live at weekends.

Charles Lambert

THE BOSS

First published in Great Britain 1995
by Pride of Place (UK) Ltd
Specialist Sports Publishers

This Vista edition published 1997

Vista is an imprint of the Cassell Group
Wellington House, 125 Strand, London WC2R 0BB

All photographs reproduced
by kind permission of Colorsport.

A catalogue record for this book is
available from the British Library.

ISBN 0 575 60221 X

Printed and bound in Great Britain by
Caledonian International Book Manufacturing Ltd, Glasgow

97 98 99 10 9 8 7 6 5 4 3 2 1

To Dot

CONTENTS

APPENDICES

INTRODUCTION

Every footballer remembers his debut. Mine was Rochdale Reserves v Southport Reserves in 1971 – the first match I covered as a working journalist.

The game has seen many changes since then. Among them has been the way the job of football manager has turned into one described succinctly by Howard Wilkinson as 'a profession that always expects more than you can give'.

I have seen genial, cheerful characters become suspicious and defensive after a few months in the hot seat. The damage done by stress is becoming ever more obvious. Yet the vast majority of this remarkable breed consistently come back for more.

Seeing the effect of those pressures and the way the various managers cope prompted me to write this book. After talking to many of them I gained the impression that few had ever before discussed frankly the true nature of their calling. They spend hours answering questions about matches, players and formations, but how often do they have the chance to debate the real problems that the manager faces? So I am immensely grateful for the time and trouble taken by managers from Aberdeen to Exeter, from the foot of the Nationwide League to the peak of the Premiership, to tell me what it is really like being the Boss.

In the early years of my career I was in daily contact with various managers and am grateful to three in particular, both for their tolerance and for enabling me to learn much about the workings of professional football: Gordon Lee at Everton, Johnny King in his first spell at Tranmere Rovers, and Kenny Spencer, manager of Burscough FC, then in the Cheshire League, the first club to which I was assigned on a regular basis.

Acknowledgement is also due to the following reference sources: *The Breedon Book of Football Managers* by Dennis Turner and Alex White, the *Rothmans Football Yearbook*, *The Football Grounds of Great Britain* by Simon Inglis, and to the Association of Football Statisticians.

I am also grateful to Caroline North and Ian Preece at Victor Gollancz for their enthusiastic and professional support, and to my wife Dot and children Donna, Sallie and Russell for putting up with my lengthy absences on the road or at the keyboard.

Charles Lambert
Liverpool, January 1997

1

BEGINNING AT THE END

What happened at Arsenal was bad enough – but events at Doncaster Rovers beat everything. And Doncaster Rovers beating everything is hardly a common experience.

Four days before the 1996–97 season even kicked off came the first sacking. Arsenal fired Bruce Rioch. A little hasty, most people thought. Pre-season training couldn't have been *that* bad!

Then came the first Saturday. The only day of the year when every member of the managerial brotherhood feels optimistic at the same time. On day one there are new faces in the team, fresh grass on the pitch, and no defeats so far. This is the day for high hopes.

Sammy Chung began season 1996–97 as manager of Third Division Doncaster Rovers. Well, he began the opening *day* as Doncaster manager – but by the time the campaign actually kicked off, at three o'clock, Chung was out of work. At 64 years of age the oldest boss in League football became the victim of football's most cynical sacking.

'It was,' he says reflectively, 'the harshest thing that has happened in football, I think.'

Considering the height of its profile, football often shows amazingly low morals. Or maybe the two go together. Players have their spectacular collisions with the law of the land, fans complain about being ripped off, but the manager is the most frequent victim. Rough justice for the boss has become a way of life, and that stretches from the very top (Arsenal) to the very bottom (Doncaster Rovers).

On day one of the 1996–97 season Doncaster were at home to Carlisle United. Among the new faces at Rovers' Belle Vue stadium was Kerry Dixon, the former Chelsea and England striker.

It was the club's benefactor Ken Richardson who decided to sign Dixon. Sammy Chung made the arrangements and the deal was finalized two days earlier. What Chung didn't know was that Richardson wanted Dixon not just as a player, but as player-manager.

It was on the Tuesday of that week that Richardson first mentioned Kerry Dixon's name. Dixon was with Watford, his eighth club. Might he be available to come to Doncaster? Chung set the wheels in motion. He contacted his opposite number at Watford, Graham Taylor, who was willing to let Dixon go. The player arrived at Doncaster on the Thursday. Chung takes up the story: 'He came down at three o'clock and I spoke with him for a while and showed him the ground. After that I never spoke to him till after the match on the Saturday. Mr Richardson spent a lot of time talking to Kerry, about what I don't know.

'On the Friday I did my preparation for the game – my tactics, free kicks, corners, etc., and went home satisfied with what I had to do against Carlisle the next day.

'On the Saturday I arrived at the ground as usual at twelve-thirty. Mr Richardson and the general manager Mark Weaver and someone else were in an office and were not to be disturbed. Later I realized that Kerry Dixon was the other person in the office.

'Just after one o'clock Mr Richardson came and told me that he had appointed Kerry as player-manager.'

The appointment was with immediate effect. The rest of the football world was eagerly anticipating the first fixtures of the campaign, yet one of the most respected managers in the business was already out of work.

It didn't stop there. George Foster, Chung's right-hand man and coach, went too. Foster was in the dressing room, pinning up last-minute reminders of the tactics, when he was called into the manager's office. Richardson broke the news about Dixon, adding that the new boss would appoint his own coaching staff – so Foster was out of work.

'Doncaster Rovers,' says Foster, 'is a one-off place!'

Even to two men steeped in football's unpredictable ways this was a stunner. But there were no theatricals. 'I have been in the game a long time,' says Chung. 'I said to Mr Richardson, "OK, that is your prerogative. So long as you take care of my contract."'

And that is where the two men found themselves treading a path familiar to many a sacked manager. Each had the best part of a year left on his contract. Each says Richardson promised to honour those contracts and shook hands on it. In fact, neither had his contract paid up. George Foster: 'From being able to pay my mortgage on that Saturday, all of a sudden Doncaster stopped paying my wages and I never had a penny. That was a real shock to the system.' It was the same with Chung. Within weeks both initiated legal action to recover the money they were owed. Chung went home, played golf, and wondered whether he would find another post at the age of 64. Foster joined Chesterfield as head of their Football in the Community scheme. Despite their experiences at Doncaster, neither fell out of love with football.

'I'm a million miles bigger than Mr Richardson,' says Chung. 'I'm a very experienced manager and in my two years at Doncaster they had two of the best years they've ever had. Yes, I suppose I was hurt but the game itself is still so important to me. I had great relationships with the players at Doncaster and that's what it's all about, isn't it?'

As for that remarkable day, what do a sacked manager and dismissed coach do when they find themselves thrown out of work two hours before kick-off? Chung stayed and watched the game – sitting next to Richardson in the directors' box. 'I had done nothing wrong – I didn't see why I should run away and, after all, it was my team out there.' Foster, who was already in his tracksuit, had to send a youth trainee to rescue his suit from the dressing room and got changed in Chung's office. His car was blocked in by spectators' vehicles so he too stayed and watched the game – standing with the Carlisle supporters as the players he had prepared went to work without him. Doncaster lost 1–0.

'The great thing about football management,' said Tommy Docherty, 'is you know when you sign a contract that the only thing missing is the date of your sacking.'

Docherty knows about football and he knows about the sack. He's been fired four times – or five, if you count a double sacking by Queens Park Rangers. For the Doc the sack seldom came quietly: once after an eight-hour wait to learn his fate (Aston Villa); once to the accompaniment of lurid personal publicity (Manchester United); another time amid a row over a £15,000 loan (QPR). Rarely does professional football bring about change with dignity. The end of a manager's period of office is blunt, painful and very public.

Often the sack can be seen coming, as plain as a centre-half stranded in the wrong penalty area. Other times it sneaks up like a late run to the far post. When Everton fired Mike Walker in September 1994 they were at the bottom of the Premiership without a win from 12 matches. Hardly a shock. Yet the previous time Walker received his cards, his club – Colchester United – were top of Division Four. After he'd gone, he was named the Manager of the Month. Football's version of a posthumous medal.

Alan Smith could smell it in the wind long before Crystal Palace dispensed with his services at the end of season 1994–95. Coventry City's Phil Neal feared the worst from the moment Ron Atkinson reached a financial settlement with Aston Villa. Atkinson, available, duly moved in.

Fear of the sack haunts the dressing rooms and dug-outs of Britain. Andy King had a good season as manager of Third Division Mansfield Town in 1994–95 but had no illusions as he tried for a repeat. 'I think about the sack all the time. It's my biggest worry. Having a job like this is like loving a beautiful woman and fearing to lose her. Where would I go? Could I start again? If you're sacked by a top club you can drop down a division and try again. But from Mansfield, there aren't many places lower to go to.' A little over twelve months later the hypothetical became the reality. Mansfield sacked him.

Derek Pavis is a Nottingham businessman who built up a chain of companies in the plumbing and heating sector, sold out and made a lot of money. Two million pounds of that he has spent on a football club – Notts County. He stands guarantor of a further one million pounds in loans to the same club. Naturally, given that scale of personal investment, it's important that Notts County do well. Especially in a city where football is dominated by the team from the opposite bank of the Trent, Nottingham Forest –

a team which formerly had one D. Pavis on the board, until a difference of opinion with the then manager, Brian Clough, saw him depart.

Having thrown in his lot – and at three million quid it is a lot – with County, Pavis expected the team to leave Division One of what was then the Endsleigh League behind them. They did – but in the wrong direction, plummeting into Division Two. By the end of that disastrous 1994–95 campaign County had not only said farewell to First Division football, they had also seen off three managers. Pavis, the man who calls the shots at Meadow Lane, had claimed a hat-trick.

'Finding a manager who can accept all the problems, and be successful, is one of the hardest tasks I have had,' he says. 'I've built up companies. I've recruited and promoted people who can manage and people who can sell. But a football manager is something a bit special.'

Derek Pavis sits squarely behind a black desk placed squarely in a white-walled office. By coincidence or design, the colour scheme is that of Notts County, whose black and white stripes symbolize the oldest League club in England. On the walls hang pennants from County's European campaign – the Anglo-Italian Cup. A silver trophy rests in the window. One looks for the scalps of failed managers among the trophies; alas, in vain.

The man confesses he got it wrong. 'Hands up – I'm the first to admit it. I made three mistakes. Played three, lost three. But I know that with hindsight, and hindsight is a wonderful subject for discussion. We can all be wise after the event.'

'The event', so to speak, began when a man who had worked wonders for Notts County ran out of inspiration. Neil Warnock steered County out of the old Third Division in 1990, took them straight through the Second Division and into the First, in the last season before the Premiership was invented. Unable to live with the rich and famous, Notts slipped back down the greasy pole and Warnock paid with his job. That was January 1993, with the club in Division One of the Endsleigh League. Despite the unhappy ending, Derek Pavis still regards the Warnock appointment as a masterstroke.

'When Warnock applied for the job, I knew within two hours

of having a chat with him that he was my man,' he recalls. 'So I set him to work there and then. I was lucky. He had that flair of saying the right things at the right time during an interview. When you're looking for someone to manage a football club, you're seeking someone who can manage human beings. It's not like a racehorse trainer or a greyhound trainer. He's coming to manage between 35 and 45 human beings. He's got to get a team together that has the right attitude and in particular the right balance. And that's not easy, because you have some players who need a kick up the backside quite frequently, and others who need an arm round the shoulder. And some players who need both!

'So your manager has to have a knowledge of football – in terms of tactics, discipline and organization. But he also has to be a psychiatrist, to know how these 40 guys tick, because none of us ticks in the same way. People criticize managers, but it's not one of the easiest jobs. And you've got to be right when you select one.

'It's so easy to criticize, but at the end of the day it's not chairmen who sack managers. They pull the trigger, but it's players who get managers the sack. It's happened here at Notts County. Many good judges said we were too good to go down. By that they meant we had players who were of such a quality that we should never have been relegated. But somewhere along the line we either failed to find the balance or certain players failed to give 100 per cent.'

Neil Warnock had become the psychiatrist-cum-coach Pavis wanted. But with him removed from office, the chairman couldn't repeat the act.

'Season 1994–95 was a complete and utter disaster.' His words.

First through the revolving door was reserve coach Mick Walker. Hired January '93, fired September '94. Pavis's verdict: 'Mick begged me to give him the job. We knew his administration work was poor but he had done well with the youth team and the reserves for 12 years. Tactically he was aware of what was going on, so we gave him a chance. We appointed Russell Slade as his assistant and Russell was good at the paperwork. So the two worked well together.'

And for a time it seemed that the combination was a winner. County posted a strong bid for promotion, only faltering in the closing weeks of the season. The final placing of seventh wasn't bad. But it wasn't what the chairman required.

'Unfortunately Mick cannot man-manage, and the discipline – which used to be very good – dissipated altogether. We never won a game in the last six matches of the season and only one out of the first seven of the new season. The balance on the field had gone. The discipline had gone. When the team got off the coach they looked like Dad's Army. It was terrible, so he had to go.'

Next came Walker's assistant Russell Slade. Hired September '94, fired January '95.

'Another mistake. Russell had done a great job as Mick's assistant. The players seemed to respect him. So I thought I would emulate Liverpool – promote from within. But where Liverpool succeeded, Notts County failed. The players didn't look up to him because he had never played professional football himself. They seemed to respect him when Mick was the manager but when he became Number One they lost that respect – not as a person, but in football terms. So he had to go.'

Then came Pavis's boldest throw of the dice. He persuaded Howard Kendall to join Notts County – the same Kendall who, a decade earlier, had led Everton to two League Championships, the FA Cup and the European Cup Winners Cup.

'From employing two inexperienced managers, I then went for one of the most experienced – one who was at least in the top six in the United Kingdom. Which turned out to be 79 days of absolute disaster.'

Given Kendall's track record with leading clubs it came as a surprise to many that he took on the Meadow Lane assignment. 'He was out of work and like all managers he missed the smell of embrocation, the mickey-taking and the camaraderie. He was all for it. Couldn't get started quickly enough.'

Hired January '95, fired April '95.

'He cost us over £600,000 – four signings plus a goalkeeper on loan from Everton. On wages that this club couldn't – and still can't – afford. With the previous managers, I had sat in on negotiations with incoming players over their contracts, because I have put an awful lot of money into this football club and I feel I should be allowed to protect my own interests. And if a player has opened his mouth too wide – then it's have a coffee, cheerio and there's the door. But Howard didn't want that. He said he wasn't used to having chairmen around when he talked to players, he wanted to do it on his own. I thought – OK, if he saves us from relegation, so what? Let him get on with it. So I allowed him his freedom. And the salaries, signing-on fees and loyalty bonuses were frightening. The more I said to Howard that we couldn't afford it, the more he insisted that we had to have quality players if we were to get out of trouble. Well, we got these so-called quality players at great expense, and we still got relegated.'

Football is a game of partnerships. Think of Bobby Smith and Jimmy Greaves in Spurs' double-winning season, or Roy McFarland and Colin Todd in the Derby County defence; at managerial level Matt Busby and Jimmy Murphy at Manchester United, or Brian Clough and Peter Taylor at Derby and Nottingham Forest. In the nineties, the most crucial partnership is that linking manager and chairman. If those two individuals are not on the same wavelength, there isn't much chance of success. Howard Kendall's arrival at Meadow Lane confronted the chairman with a new type of personality – one who had been to the big-time, seen it, taken its photograph and acquired a lockerful of T-shirts. Kendall expected to do things his way, as tried and tested at Everton, Manchester City and Athletic Bilbao.

'I'm not saying Mr Pavis knows nothing about the game,' says Kendall carefully when invited to reflect on that turbulent springtime. 'He has done a lot of homework, football is his life and he wants the club to be successful. But he doesn't let the people he employs get on with their jobs. There is no way we would have built up a relationship, and no way would I have stayed beyond the end of the season.'

But he wasn't planning on leaving quite as soon as he did. Possibly the seeds of his sacking were sown on the day he was appointed. The arrangement, doomed, was heading downhill. Already the chairman was beside himself at Kendall's tactics.

'We played Southend, and they had a player sent off in the first half and a second player sent off within five minutes of the second half starting. So there we were, in front, playing against nine men. Southend put a midfield player called Willis up front.

And Howard kept five defenders back. I sat in my usual seat which was dead in line with our defenders, and I couldn't believe what I was seeing. I was so needled I felt like picking up the phone to the dug-out and saying to Howard: Do you realize you've got five defenders and they've only got one attacker? But it was nothing to do with me. I felt I shouldn't interfere. Then, in the 92nd minute, our full-back cocked it up and they equalized.

'I went home that night and I started to cry. I couldn't believe what I had seen. And here is a man who the football industry regards as one of the most successful managers in the United Kingdom! The following week I must have had 10 to 15 letters from supporters pointing out the very same point. I said to my wife: "This isn't the manager everyone thinks he is." I knew from that day he wasn't the manager for this club.'

The end came acrimoniously with both men on the ropes – Kendall accused of overdoing the drink; Pavis, taken ill while on holiday in Spain, needing an emergency operation. Back home, with the team struggling, the Notts County vice-chairman John Mounteney informed Kendall that he was no longer required. To the relief of both sides, no contract had been signed.

'It was,' says Kendall, 'a disgrace the way they treated me. They got so much bad publicity over my sacking that they had to come up with something to keep the local press off their backs. So they made a big deal out of me taking my staff out for lunch at a restaurant and not reporting back to the ground. So what? My secretary always knew where I was.

'I wasn't planning on staying there long-term, but no way would I have walked out before the end of the season. I had gone there to try to keep them up, and leaving would have been against all my principles. But this is the way clubs are going – hands-on chairmen who want to do everyone's job and keep an eye on the pennies. They are paying experts and paying them good money – they should let them get on with what they are qualified to do. Of course the man at the top has to have the final say on the major financial decisions – but not on minor matters like whether the team stays overnight before a match at Tranmere Rovers. They'll complain about that, yet they'll spend a fortune on signing a Nigerian player who has never produced the goods!'

County appointed a triumvirate of three senior players to pilot them through the closing weeks, but the team still went down. At the end of the season Pavis embraced a change of policy and hired a general manager, Colin Murphy, to handle the business side of the job, with a team manager, Steve Thompson, to look after the team.

They nearly delivered the goods. In their first season they took County to the Second Divison play-off Final. But defeat at Wembley was followed by a poor start to '96–97 and two days before Christmas Murphy and Thompson paid with their jobs. At Notts County of all clubs, this was hardly a surprise. When a chairman puts both his money and his reputation into a football club he expects success. If he doesn't get it, the manager is shown the door. It's that simple. That's football.

But then, it doesn't automatically follow that success keeps the manager flavour of the month. Alan Smith traces the start of his decline and fall as manager of Crystal Palace to the day he steered the club to promotion to the Premiership. A 3–2 win at Middlesbrough on May Day clinched it, but Smith travelled home on the team coach in morose mood.

The reaction of the chairman, Ron Noades, troubled him. Noades, always a high-profile, controversial figure in football, had seemed reluctant to join in the general spirit of celebration. Smith, himself an articulate voice with an open attitude to the media, sensed the turning of the tide of support. 'That trip home from Middlesbrough was one of the saddest times of my life, when it should have been the happiest,' he recalls.

In fact that season, his first as Palace's manager, had been a fulfilling one – not least because Noades was seldom around. The chairman had been ill and couldn't put in the time around the club that he liked to. Smith enjoyed himself. 'I loved every minute. I was running the club from top to bottom. There was a great team spirit – everyone was pulling in the right direction.'

But Noades, restored to health, quickly reminded him of who was really the boss. 'In the summer he dismissed two youth coaches while I was on holiday. He appointed replacements with instructions to report direct to him instead of me. I should have resigned then. The training ground is a very small world, it's like being in a submarine. If the players see coaches reporting directly to the chairman there's a crack in the structure. It was clear to the players what was going on. Mr Noades would come to the training ground for meetings with the coaches, which I strongly resented.'

Restored to Premiership status, Palace should have been looking ahead with optimism. Instead the team laboured all season, handicapped by a widening rift between chairman and manager.

'The chairman watered down my position. He brought in his brother (Colin Noades, a director) to do some of the things that I used to do. I used to type up my notes for board meetings. The chairman didn't like that. He didn't like it to be written down. But football is a great game for hearsay, and it's amazing the number of decisions that are taken yet no one is quite sure by whom – because so little is written down. In my last year we had four board meetings, of which I only went to one. That meant there was no continuity at the club.'

Smith suspected his chairman was jealous of his own high profile in the media. Whatever, life was getting increasingly hard. Even the traditional wheeling and dealing in the transfer market was becoming a problem. 'Signings were very difficult. We bought Ray Houghton from Aston Villa on deadline day. I felt sorry for Houghton. He was kept waiting for three hours in my office while the chairman made up his mind. Eventually we signed him with two minutes to spare.'

Long before the end of a doomed campaign, according to Smith, the directors were staying away en masse. 'When we played at Liverpool in the semi-final of the Coca-Cola Cup, no directors were there. At Newcastle, on the last day of the season, no directors were there. I was represented in the Newcastle boardroom by Jack Pearce, the manager of Bognor, a friend of mine for 20 years.'

Palace battled to the last but a 3–2 defeat at Newcastle confirmed their relegation. And Smith's departure. 'I think the chairman knew I was a lucky person and he expected us to finish fifth from bottom and survive. But whatever happened, he wasn't going to renew my contract.'

What happens behind those closed doors when the manager receives the order of the boot? The fanfares, the press conferences, the champagne toasts that welcomed him on arrival day are noticeably absent now. The sack is usually delivered in terse conversations, followed by the fervent desire for the displaced person to vacate the premises as quickly and as quietly as possible. What happened within the walls of Manchester City's Maine Road stadium on an August morning in 1993 was typical.

The two men were uniformly grey on top, one with the experience of his 60-plus years, the other, at a mere 37, ageing before his time. 'So you've got your things in a black plastic bag,' said the older man grimly. 'You are now qualified to call yourself a football manager.'

It was less than a month into the 1993–94 season. The campaign was barely breaking sweat. But already a manager's desk had been cleared, and the kit suppliers would have no further need to stitch the initials 'P.R.' on the training gear.

Peter Reid, the twelfth manager to fail to make Manchester City champions since Joe Mercer did it in 1968, had been sacked.

Ian Greaves was one of the few people to see Reid before he left. Greaves, the taller, older man who has seen most of what football can throw up, was manager of Bolton Wanderers when Reid began his playing career. Now employed by his former protégé as a talent scout, it was Greaves who provided words of consolation as the younger man vacated his office for the last time.

Rumours had been rife that Reid was facing the barrel of a gun from the moment the City chairman Peter Swales had created the new post of general manager and appointed a personal friend and former journalist, John Maddock, to the post. The general impression in Manchester was that Swales – a graduate of the Henry VIII school of fidelity when it came to tiring of relationships – had lost his stomach for wielding the axe and had employed a surrogate headsman to swing the blade on his behalf.

On that Thursday morning there was an uncanny atmosphere around the stadium. Reid and his assistant, Sam Ellis, had desks side-by-side in the manager's office. Desks that both faced the door. It was the day before a match – a Friday night fixture at home to Coventry City, yet the phones were unusually quiet, the habitual passage of visitors through the door non-existent. Word among the media was that today was the day. A knot of cameramen began forming outside the main entrance.

The two men in the office had both heard the rumours. Ellis, convinced that the end was nigh, was already clearing his desk. Reid, not so sure, picked up the phone and dialled the chairman's house. The message was that he was on his way to the stadium. Reid did not regard that as reassuring news. He glanced out of the window and spotted the pressmen. 'I'd better have a shave,' he joked. Then he instructed Ellis to arrange trays of coffee for the media men.

Peter Reid was a popular man with the supporters. He had taken over at a difficult time, following the resignation of Howard Kendall in the autumn of 1990. Kendall, wooed by his former club Everton, was deemed by the fans to have left City in the lurch. Reid, also a former Everton man, had rejected the chance to go with him. He had picked up a club in shock and restored its dignity – until results began to go wrong towards the end of season 1992–93. The club had suffered embarrassing publicity over misbehaviour by players. Then the new season began with three defeats in the first four games. Enter Mr Maddock.

John Maddock made up his mind almost as soon as he took over that Reid would have to go. 'The record from the previous February was appalling. I was told to sort the situation out as I saw fit, and although it wasn't my decision to sack Peter it was my recommendation to the board. Everyone I put it to agreed with me.'

Shortly before midday Reid and Ellis were told they were being dismissed. It was Maddock who delivered the news.

Soon afterwards, the man Peter Swales once described as 'City's best-ever signing' walked out of the main entrance and held an impromptu press conference in the car park. Getting into his car, he was distracted by a television cameraman tapping on the window. The man wanted the window lowering so he could get a shot of Reid without the reflection created by the glass. Taking media co-operation to its limits, Reid obliged, then drove away. The coffee never arrived. The execution squad got there first.

'The pressure on a football manager is intolerable. Success is everything. The demands are crazy.' The words, ironically, are those of John Maddock, yet he didn't flinch from carrying out his recommendation to the Manchester City board. 'I felt terribly sorry about sacking Peter and Sam. I had been with them on tour in Japan as a freelance agent and I had enjoyed their company. But it had to be done for the good of the club. If you believe something to be right, then you have got to do it.'

For a football manager, the end of the line is a uniquely lonesome place. Its isolation is magnified by the rush-hour confusion of life up to that point. In all walks of life people lose their jobs, but none has the intensity of commitment and high public profile of the man who picks the team on a Saturday afternoon. An exception might be a Cabinet Minister losing his post in a reshuffle. But the ex-Minister still has his constituency to occupy him, and even in defeat at a General Election an MP has his local supporters to dust him down and stand him upright again. The sacked manager is suddenly, completely and unrecognizably alone.

Peter Reid, out of work for the first time in a football career that began as an apprentice with Bolton Wanderers on the Monday after he left school, was on his own. He retreated behind the protective curtain of huge rhododendron bushes which circle his house and reflected on the downside of his profession.

'As a football manager you are constantly thinking about things. How to improve this or that. For the first couple of days after I left City I didn't think of anything at all. My mind was a void. Then, when you are not taxing your mind, you feel idle. I began to miss my problems. I didn't feel hurt. I knew it was coming. It was inevitable. I had known through the summer when I was trying to sign new players and couldn't do so. Manchester United had won the title that year and that caused added pressure at Manchester City.

'Gradually the relationship with the chairman got worse during the summer. But I was lucky – I was still fit enough to play, and I joined Southampton and then Notts County (under the ill-fated Mick Walker, though at that time Notts were going well). I was out of management for 18 months before I got the job at Sunderland. I did turn down some jobs that weren't right for me. But I was desperate to get back in – just to have those problems back. I suppose I must be some sort of masochist.'

In professional football, the sack is a way of life. When it happens, it enables the club to clear the air and start afresh, dust down the clichés for a new beginning, deflect criticism from the directors, and placate unrest among supporters. Doing away with the manager buys time and promises better days ahead.

At Manchester City, even with Peter Reid dispatched to the rhododendrons, it didn't quite work out like that. The following day City were held to a 1–1 draw at home by Coventry. After the match Maddock unveiled the new boss – Brian Horton, of Oxford United. The supporters were not impressed. Crowds gathered outside. Security men hurriedly closed the tall iron gates guarding the directors' entrance. The crowd became increasingly hostile. Abuse, followed by missiles, was thrown at the office windows. An attempt was made to rush the gates. Police on horseback clattered across the tarmac to quell the riot. It was an ugly upsurge of frustration and anger. The police restored order, but it took a lot longer for peace to break out within the football club.

Reid's ousting merely served to fuel public resentment of Swales and Maddock. Within weeks both men were themselves out, as Swales bowed to the pressure and handed control to former City favourite Francis Lee. Lee inherited Horton and the alliance was fraught from the start. Ironically, Maddock's choice was remarkably similar to the man he had fired – honest, industrious, and deserving of better results than his team provided. The threat of dismissal hovered like an incoming depression on the weather chart. After 21 months dodging the lightning, Horton too was packed off to the rhododendrons.

Peter Swales had promised Peter Reid that he would honour his contract, and he was as good as his word. The deal still had some two years to run and every month Reid continued to receive his salary as if he was still at Maine Road. It meant that his sacking was cushioned by the absence of financial worries. Even when he returned to management with Sunderland he continued to receive a manager's wage from Manchester City.

Swales died in 1996, a controversial figure whose love for his club was never matched by achievement. As for City, things went from bad to worse as Lee appointed his close friend Alan Ball to the manager's job, only to be rewarded with relegation from the Premier League and even more problems than Peter Reid had to handle.

But anyone seeking a consistent approach to problem-solving will look in vain at professional football. The policy of one club can be poles apart from that of another. Everton dismissed Mike Walker with the best part of three years remaining on his contract, and with the same assurances ringing in his ears. But the cash flow quickly dried up.

Everton's dalliance with Walker proved costly in more ways than one. He joined them in January 1994, quitting his post at Norwich City where he had created a stylish team on a shoestring budget. The trouble was that Norwich paid shoestring wages and Walker eagerly accepted Everton's offer to move to Goodison Park. The three and a half year contract was thought to be worth £150,000 a year, plus bonuses – over £100,000 more, annually, than he was getting in East Anglia. Norwich, outraged, complained to the FA that Everton had made an illegal approach. The FA agreed and Everton were duly fined £75,000 and ordered to pay £50,000 compensation.

But with a struggle for power in the Everton boardroom turning into a war of attrition that lasted many months, Walker hardly had the right support for his task. The team almost went out of the Premiership and looked even worse at the start of season '94–95. By now the boardroom crown had been won by Peter Johnson, a wealthy businessman who had achieved great things as chairman of Tranmere Rovers and was keen to flex his ambitions on a bigger stage. Johnson was already ploughing personal millions into Everton. Yet the team was incapable of winning. In the first three months of the 1994–95 season Everton achieved one win, six draws and nine defeats. They were bottom of the table. Walker was out.

'I got a phone call to go into the ground and see the chairman. It was after we drew 0–0 at Norwich. We had gone three games unbeaten. I went in. He said, "Well, that's it. We are terminating your contract." There was no song and dance. I said I thought he was wrong, but he's the guv'nor and he can do what he wants.

I asked about the rest of my contract. He said that was no problem to a big club like Everton. It would be paid up. A week later it was a totally different story.'

Walker was forced to go to court to persuade Everton to honour their agreement. The court ruled in his favour. 'I am more annoyed about that than I am about getting the sack. One of the things that attracted me to Everton was that they did things with style. They had that reputation. But I sued them because I realized I wasn't going to get anything. Even after the court ruled in my favour they still delayed paying me anything. It's stupid, because it cost them more in the end.'

At least the sack was no shock. Mike Walker, like all managers, thought he deserved more time to turn things round, but the potent mixture of new blood in the boardroom, the team's abysmal form and the particular threat that in the '94–95 season no fewer than four teams would be relegated, combined to lead him to the scaffold.

Seven years earlier it had been the same result but a different scenario. In his first managerial post, at Colchester United – then in Division Four – Walker had coaxed his bargain-basement players to play attractive football, a style which had taken them into the promotion reckoning. 'We were top of the table and the chairman, Jonathan Crisp, sacked me. That was my biggest shock in football. I didn't have a contract at Colchester and when the chairman asked to see me I thought I was going to get a contract.

'Instead I got the sack. It blew up with a difference of opinion over a player. The chairman thought the only way to get out of the Fourth Division was to kick our way out. Chairmen listen to what other people are saying. They hear whispers and allow their heads to be turned, and aren't as strong as they ought to be. I don't think I said anything for a few minutes; I was just stunned. Then it sank in and I went home and thought about it.

'I was fortunate in that within four days I was offered a job as reserve coach at Norwich City. But after that experience, even when things were going well for me as manager at Norwich, I wouldn't have batted an eyelid if the chairman had told me I was sacked. Something like that toughens you. It made me believe the old cliché: "Anything can happen in football."'

The thorny problem of 'compensation' is now as much a part

of the game as sponsors' names on shirts. But clubs are beginning to wise up. A contract lucrative enough to tempt the man they may want may not seem such a sound investment if he fails to deliver.

When Coventry City appointed Phil Neal, it was with a deal similar to one of those pre-marital pledges beloved of wealthy Americans, whereby the divorce settlement is finalized before the marriage has even taken place. Neal, the former Liverpool defender and England's most-capped right-back, took over when Bobby Gould resigned in October 1993. Coventry were still paying off a previous manager, Terry Butcher, sacked some 18 months earlier. Neal was asked to agree that if he was also dismissed, he would accept three months' compensation and waive any rights to the full value of his contract. Enthusiastic to take the job, he agreed. Fifteen months on, he was made redundant.

'Chairmen move the goalposts. The Coventry chairman said they didn't want another Butcher situation. I said, "OK, give me the job and I'll only a take a three-month pay-off." I bet they paid Ron Atkinson and Gordon Strachan five times more than they were paying me and Mick Brown, my assistant. But did they do five times as well?

'It was wicked after I was sacked. I felt a lot of anger. It hurt, and it was frustrating because we had finished 12th in my one full season there, we had obliterated the club's debts overnight by selling Phil Babb to Liverpool for over £3 million, and we had started building for the future. But it wasn't going to be allowed to happen.

'I think politics came into it. I could see it coming as soon as Ron Atkinson cleared up his affairs with Aston Villa. Ron was sacked by Villa in the November. I rang his wife one day and she told me they had negotiated his pay-off following the sacking. I smelt trouble then, and the reason is that Coventry's vice-chairman, Michael McGinnity, is a close personal friend of Ron Atkinson. In fact he was the best man at his wedding.

'The weekend after I heard about Ron's pay-off we played at Crystal Palace with an injury-hit team and won 2–0. I went up to the directors' room and Mr McGinnity in particular could hardly speak to me. I got home and said to my wife: "I've got to speak to the chairman." I spent the weekend chasing the chairman (Bryan

Richardson) on the phone. Eventually got hold of him. He said: "Can I see you?" And told me they were making a change of manager.'

Neal left Highfield Road with the team in 17th place and with an astonishing commendation from chairman Richardson. In a fulsome public statement he praised Neal's management skills, emphasizing what a sound job he had done in reorganizing the whole club.

Three months later, the compensation deal had run its course and Phil Neal was still out of work, a state of affairs which lasted a full year. Neal then returned with Cardiff City before moving to Manchester City as number two to Steve Coppell. For a few weeks the prospect of becoming City's next manager was dangled in front of him as he stepped into the breach following Coppell's abrupt departure – only for the arrival of Frank Clark to leave Neal again out of work.

Of course the real start of the domino effect which led to his departure from Coventry was not Ron Atkinson's pay-off in February, but Atkinson's sacking by the Villa chairman Doug Ellis three months earlier. Every club in the bottom half of the Premiership that season was looking for a knight in shining armour to lead them away from the relegation inferno. Atkinson, lurking in the backwoods, was a threat to any other leader whose troops were in retreat.

Had Brian Horton not achieved a useful string of results at Manchester City in the run-up to Christmas, Atkinson could well have ended up at Maine Road and that in turn could have bought Phil Neal a few more weeks. The tactics of football are not confined to the coach's blackboard. The game is played to even more deadly effect in the boardroom.

Doug Ellis has presided over affairs at Aston Villa for 26 years, 'apart from a three-year absence caused by a difference of opinion with fellow directors. His office high in the North Stand is a trophy room in its own right: behind him as he sits at his desk is a showcase boasting a miniature of the Coca-Cola League Cup, won by Villa in 1994. On the wall is a framed photograph of Ellis the fly fisherman, conqueror of a 27lb salmon in the River Tay. And on the desk, exhibited perhaps in fun, perhaps not, is a notice reading: 'Beware, my mood is subject to change without notice.'

Ellis has outlasted nine managers, six of whom he has sacked, in a reign which has seen Villa slide into the Third Division (1970–72) and rise to the pinnacle in Europe (Champions, 1982). His reputation is that of a ruthless dictator, sentencing his managers to the darkness like fallen heroes of the Politburo hustled off to the Lubyanka. The nickname 'Deadly Doug' has stuck – unfairly, he believes.

'I am impatient for success,' he agrees, 'but I am not impatient with individuals. There are many reasons why one gets the sack, and it is not necessarily because of what happens on the pitch. I hate sacking people. It's a terrible job; I have sleepless nights. I go through all the deliberations, and when it happens it has to be a unanimous decision of the board, not just me.' (There are four men on the board at Villa – Doug Ellis, his son, his doctor, and his lawyer.)

'The fact is that in 26 years, minus the three I was off the board, six managers have been sacked by Doug Ellis – that works out at almost four years on average to each manager. Certain other clubs have had many more managers in that time – Manchester City, for example, have had 15. We are not too bad when you analyse it. But it's no excuse – I would like managers to stay with Aston Villa for the rest of their lives, because it would mean they were being successful.'

Yet even by the standards which football, however unfairly, has come to expect of Doug Ellis, his dismissal of Ron Atkinson in November 1994, seven months after Atkinson's team had won the Coca-Cola Cup, seemed particularly harsh.

'It was absolutely the right decision, but I can't tell you all the reasons. I shook his hand and wished him the best of luck in whatever job he took next, and he ended up at Coventry and I'm delighted for him. Let's leave it at that.'

Doug Ellis has been hiring and firing managers for over a quarter of a century, a restless quest for perfection at Villa Park. An early victim was a man who was himself one of the game's turbulent characters, Tommy Docherty.

Docherty had been in charge at Villa Park just over a year. 'I was sacked four times in my career and the Villa sacking took me most by surprise. I took over when the club was bottom of Division Two. I got them halfway up the table and they gave me the sack. Dumped.

'They called me into a board meeting. I waited eight hours to go in. I was summoned at lunchtime and it was 8 p.m. when I finally went in. They had obviously been debating whether to keep me or not. It's all politics. As soon as he sacked me, Mr Ellis asked me: "Who do you think we should have as the new manager?!" I couldn't believe it. But I put it down to his inexperience. I think he was prodded by people who we called the "junior board" – people who were directors but knew nothing about football. I was disappointed because it was a great club and we had done all right. Nothing spectacular but I had only been there just over a year and I'd signed promising players like Bruce Rioch, Brian Tiler and Chico Hamilton.

'But the chairman wanted success immediately. He didn't want it next year. He wanted it last night, like a lot of chairmen. They don't want to wait.

'I just went home. They can take your job away from you but they can't take your ability away. You're still the same person – but a bit wiser. And you roll your sleeves up. You play musical chairs again. The band starts playing, the chairs come out, a vacancy occurs.'

Apart from a four-month curtain call with non-league Altrincham, the music ceased for Docherty over a decade ago when he collected his P45 for the fourth time, courtesy of Wolverhampton Wanderers. Now he sits, relaxed, in the stylish living room of his converted cottage in the Derbyshire foothills. Two small tan terriers jostle for space on the sofa. Tommy's wife Mary, herself once a prominent player in the saga of Docherty dismissals, supervises gardening activity outside. Yes, there are rhododendrons in bloom.

Football managers have one thing – and, perhaps, only one thing – in common: an unquenchable love of the game. Apart from that they are as varied as away strips in the Umbro factory. Where some managers protest bitterly and others bleed silently after a sacking, Tommy Docherty took his in his stride. Nowadays he capitalizes on it. The ups and downs of over 40 years in the game have provided him with the raw material for his present career as media pundit and after-dinner raconteur.

If Villa, 1970, was Sacking No. 1, Manchester United, 1977, was No. 2. Docherty had just seen his team win the FA Cup when news headlines blurted forth details of a blossoming relationship between Docherty and Mary Brown, now Tommy's wife, then married to the United physio Laurie Brown. With a hue and cry reaching manic proportions, the board fired their manager.

'I laugh about it now when I think what I got the sack for. And I keep thinking there must have been another reason, but I haven't come up with one yet.'

No. 3 was QPR, 1980. There had been a preview the previous year when the chairman Jim Gregory fired but reinstated him. This time there was no reprieve. 'The good thing about Jim Gregory is that he promised you nothing and he kept his promise.'

The club owed Docherty about £60,000 on his contract. The chairman offered him £15,000, minus the sum of £5000 which he had loaned Docherty to help him and Mary buy a house. Instead of handing over a cheque for £10,000, as might have seemed logical, Gregory demanded the Dochertys produce the £5000 first. Only then would he part with his £15,000. Even so, he was surprised Docherty settled for £15,000 when he was claiming £60,000. 'If I don't accept the £15,000 I'll end up with nothing,' explained Docherty. Clubs' eagerness to settle their contractual commitments in full hasn't improved much since 1980.

Rangers required the club BMW back on the spot. 'With £15,000 you can afford a taxi home,' were Jim Gregory's parting words.

Sacking No. 4: Wolves, 1985. 'After Wolves I had had enough. And probably the game had had enough of me. I had lost some of my enthusiasm. For about a year after I retired I found it very difficult. In hindsight, perhaps, I should have packed up when I left Manchester United.'

Football management is not a job for the faint-hearted, nor for those who bank on fair play. As Mike Walker observed: 'When 50 per cent of the staff get sacked, there's something wrong with the industry. That's what happened in the Premier League in season 1994–95. They can't all have been doing a bad job.'

Superficially, things improved the following season. Only thirty managerial changes occurred. Amazingly, the Premiership produced just one casualty – Bolton dispensing with Roy McFarland.

Was it a question of club chairmen learning to be patient? Hardly. More significant was the sheer extent of the carnage the previous year, which meant most clubs were under new management for '95–96. And most clubs will give a man one year at least. Though not Swansea, where Bobby Smith's departure in December ushered in the pantomime season: Jimmy Rimmer, Kevin Cullis, Rimmer again and Jan Molby all took charge in quick succession. Molby, confirmed in the post, was helpless to prevent the Swans' relegation.

When season 1996–97 got under way the dismissal notices began to flow once again: Alan Ball relieved of his command at Manchester City after just over a year, Alan Smith 'released' by Wycombe Wanderers after a similar span, Terry Bullivant surviving barely two months at Barnet. In Scotland, Raith Rovers acquired their fourth boss of the year when Iain Munro was appointed – Munro becoming their third manager in the space of two weeks. In fact Munro gave the clubs a taste of their own medicine. He resigned as boss of Hamilton in early September in order to take over at St Mirren, then changed his mind and returned to Hamilton, only to abandon the unfortunate Accies a second time to move in at Raith.

But the directors and the fans are the ones who usually have the final say. Not even winning the League Championship for Leeds United was enough to save Howard Wilkinson when he failed to produce another trophy in the following four years. Robin Launders, the club's recently appointed chief executive, blamed the supporters. 'You need them to be supportive towards the manager. They have not been, and it is they who have driven him out.' The chairman, Bill Fotherby, was the man who delivered the news. 'Maybe Howard has been here a little too long. We must have success at this club and we have not been getting it,' he said.

As for Wilkinson, he pronounced himself 'very disappointed, very sad and very shocked'. But evidently not surprised. No one is surprised when a football manager gets the sack.

So how was it for you?

BRIAN HORTON (sacked by Manchester City, 1995):
'I had been to a managers' meeting at St Albans on the Monday. Next morning all the papers were saying I had been sacked. I rang the chairman, Francis Lee, and he said: "You'd better come round and we'll sort it out." I went to his house and he told me they had made the decision. It shocked my family more than it did me. That's the unfortunate part of this game – how it affects other people and reading about it in the papers. The sack is still a shock when it comes. It's hard to take. Your pride is hurt. You want to do well, and I thought I had done well.'

RON ATKINSON (sacked by Manchester United, 1986 and Aston Villa, 1994):
'I've been sacked twice – I don't count Atlético Madrid; that was fantasy world. Both times, at United and Villa, it happened on a Thursday early in November. I'll have to watch out for Bonfire Night in future! But each time I left them with trophies on the table.'

BRYAN HAMILTON (sacked by Tranmere Rovers, 1985):
'The club had been taken over by an American lawyer. He put in his own people, including the chief executive, Ken Bracewell. The end came when we weren't good enough to win every game. As soon as we lost a couple the atmosphere changed. It was never quite explained, but it seemed the time had come. Ken Bracewell met me at a game one night, asked me to go in the next morning, and said they had decided to make a change. So I walked away. At Tranmere I had given a lot, over and above what was expected. I still feel I left a little bit of me there that day.'

MARTIN DOBSON (left Bristol Rovers 'by mutual consent', 1991):
'I left after I, in effect, called a board meeting one Sunday. I told the directors what I thought needed changing. They didn't back me so there wasn't much point in staying around.'

EMLYN HUGHES (fired by Rotherham United, 1983):
'I gave Rotherham the best team they've ever had and loved every minute of it. Then the chairman said he had sold the club and

the new chairman didn't want me. So that was that.'

LOU MACARI (sacked by Celtic, 1994):
'I was at Manchester Airport, about to go to America with my family. There had been disagreements with Fergus McCann, the managing director. I rang the club to leave a contact number for the time I was away and he sacked me then and there, over the phone.'

2

MEN OF MAGIC

Aston Villa v Coventry City isn't normally a fixture to set pulses racing outside the Midlands. When the teams met at Villa Park in March 1995 it was different. It was a Monday night match, live on Sky TV, so the teams had the stage to themselves, but there was more to it than that. This was Ron Atkinson's return.

Villa had fired Atkinson, suddenly and chillingly, four months earlier. This was his fourth match since taking over at Coventry and the fact that the fixture schedule brought him back to Aston Villa so soon meant that the attention of crowd and cameras alike was concentrated more on his reappearance than the outcome of the game.

The Villa Park layout was perfect for the occasion. The players' tunnel exits on to one corner of the pitch, so managers and coaches must walk half the pitch length to reach their seats on the halfway line. The players were already out, warming up, when Atkinson emerged. They were forgotten as all eyes watched him making his way along the touchline.

Atkinson is not a figure you would miss. Six foot tall, tanned, smartly groomed, clad in a bronze-coloured coat, he was given a standing ovation as he made slow progress to his seat. Autograph books were proffered from the crowd, hands were thrust forward to be shaken. 'It was,' wrote the *Daily Telegraph*'s reporter John Ley, 'like watching a once deposed dictator returning to his former territory.'

Most of the reporters were only too pleased to write about Atkinson's grand entrance. The match, failing to live up to the preamble, was a disappointing goalless draw.

Football management has come a long way since the duties

were performed by the club secretary in tandem with a trainer. Pre-war, most managers were low-profile figures, stronger on administration than tactics, although the Arsenal secretary-manager George Allison appeared in the 1939 film *The Arsenal Stadium Mystery*. Since 1960, however, managers have become as famous as their players, many of them achieving celebrity status far beyond the confines of sport. Ron Atkinson is of that ilk. No great shakes as a player, he has never won the League Championship as a manager, has never threatened to win a European trophy, yet he is as familiar as football itself. His public persona is sunny, cheerful, enjoying the good things, exemplified by metallic green Jaguar XJR, Gucci watch, and an educated palate for champagne. On the phone in his office at Coventry City's training centre, back in 1995, he was busy monitoring plans for a celebrity golf competition. 'See if you can get Botham, Gower, people like that.' The phone rang again. It was the England manager Terry Venables, chewing the fat about players. Mick Brown, assistant manager under the club's former regime and still on the coaching staff, briefed Atkinson on the opposition's likely tactics for the next day's game. Gordon Strachan, then Atkinson's assistant, reminded him he was due to meet the coaches. Atkinson took it all in his stride, just as he does the public appearances and the stints for TV in England and abroad.

The word is charisma. Some managers possess it in bucketfuls, and make full use of it. Others, joining a new club, take time to establish their personality, time to get the players on their side, time to establish a rapport with the supporters. With some of them it takes so long they're out of a job before they've achieved anything. When Ron Atkinson takes over, the atmosphere comes alive from the moment he walks through the door.

'Yes,' he admits, 'that can be helpful – up to a point. It's like big-time players taking a job in management. Their reputation helps, but only so far. The players will then judge you on what you can and can't do.' Atkinson thinks his public characterization as a 24-carat Mr Bojangles is an exaggeration. 'I see things written about me and it's usually by someone who I know full well has never met me and I think, Well how the hell do they know that? They've never been in my company, they're going very much on hearsay. But it doesn't bother me. I know what I am, I know what I can do. I've always considered myself very fortunate to be involved with football. To me, it isn't a job, it's a way of life. If I wasn't doing it, having a good lifestyle and being well paid, I would still be doing it for nothing anyway. So I consider myself fortunate and anyone coming into this game should consider themselves fortunate.

'I've always made up my mind that, whatever I do, I will enjoy it. It's not easy to enjoy it when you're taking a right good hiding. But you have to make sure you don't have too many of those in your career. There is no bigger football nut in the world than myself. I'm totally immersed in the game. But I don't believe in football clubs being prisoner of war camps. I like to see people work professionally, but I like to see them work with a bounce and an enthusiasm. If you can get that into your teams, you don't half get a good start.'

Coventry was Ron Atkinson's ninth command, following Kettering, Cambridge United, West Bromwich Albion, Manchester United, West Brom again, Atlético Madrid, Sheffield Wednesday and Aston Villa. The training centre on the south-east fringe of the city is a long, two-storey, gabled building in red brick, on which ivy is gaining a sturdy foothold. A clock tower is topped by a weather vane featuring three blue-shirted footballers. Downstairs are all the usual accoutrements of a football camp: boot store, sauna, changing rooms, and a notice pinned to the wall reminding the players that 'Items in the cafeteria must be signed.' The cafeteria, apart from storing footballs and birthday cards waiting to be autographed, is the players' meeting point before training. A plaque recalls the formal opening of the complex by Graham Taylor in 1990. The laundry lady chivvied two young players on YTS schemes to get the water bottles filled ready for the morning training session. The kitman was on the phone, checking an order for 40 pairs of purple shorts.

The playing staff reflected the manager's personality. This was now a Coventry squad full of dash and adventure – John Salako, the articulate winger from Crystal Palace, was bought by Atkinson, typically backing his own judgement, after Newcastle, worried about an injury, pulled out. Isaias, the Brazilian midfielder signed from Benfica, 'could be anything', said Atkinson. Unfortunately, he didn't turn out to be a hit in England. The 56-year-old boss played in a lively practice match – 10-a-side on a pitch less than half normal size. The emphasis was on control and passing at speed. And shooting. Atkinson's team won a penalty. The manager took it left-footed and scored. The crowd of onlookers loved it. The public are welcome to wander in and enjoy the fun. Long after the first team players had retreated to the showers, Atkinson remained outside – supervising abdominal exercises being worked through by Nii Lamptey, the brilliant Ghanaian forward who was with Atkinson at Villa and rejoined him from Anderlecht. The youngsters with autograph books were still waiting for the manager, who was last off the pitch.

'Wherever I've been I've had a rapport with the crowd. A lot of that is because they've enjoyed what they've seen on the field. I've had teams which have played in a way which has been pleasing to myself. If I enjoy watching them, I know the crowd will too.' Atkinson's teams have captured the FA Cup twice, both with Manchester United, and the League Cup twice, first with Sheffield Wednesday, then with Aston Villa – beating Manchester United in the final and denying them the domestic treble. His sacking by Villa came eight months after that success. 'The reception I got from the Villa fans when I went back there with Coventry was brilliant. Brilliant. In fact when I went to Villa Park again for a Rod Stewart concert the reception was just as good. I was sitting behind Andy Townsend – he said he thought Rod Stewart must have come out because of all the noise! I was angry about getting the sack, but the correspondence I had was phenomenal. I had so many supportive letters it was quite touching. I'd always got on well with the Villa fans. The same with the Sheffield Wednesday fans, and here at Coventry they've been the same. They want to see football that's pleasing, and that's what we try to give them.'

Things happen when Atkinson is around. Life is rarely predictable, and that adds to the public fascination. His career has changed direction as if ordained by the throw of a dice on a Monopoly board. How many other English managers would move from West Bromwich Albion direct to Atlético Madrid? Or walk out of Sheffield Wednesday immediately after winning promotion to the Premier League? Or be fired a mere six weeks after guiding Villa to victory over Inter Milan in the UEFA Cup? You also know with Atkinson that what you see is what the manager gives you – no chance of rule by consensus here, no possibility of compromising on decisions to please the boardroom.

'When I started off at Kettering the chairman, a very well-off man named John Nash, said, "There's a football club. Go and manage it." At the time Kettering was the leading non-League club in the country, and everything was very professional. I've always tried to do things the same way wherever I've been. When people take me on, they do so for that reason – they know that's my style, and that's what I'll do.

'Circumstances are always different. I went to Sheffield Wednesday originally for three months but stayed for nearly three years. I was three and a half years at Aston Villa. Normally at that club the manager is entitled to a testimonial when he's been there that long! What does please me is that wherever I went, the club enjoyed some of the best times they'd had for a long time. My big regret was only lasting four months at Madrid. But then, I recently looked through a list of the managers they'd had, and it was something like 26 in four years. I was about the fourth-longest serving. So perhaps I didn't do too badly there!'

Typically, Atkinson still enthuses about his time with Atlético and his relationship with the club president, Jesus Gil. 'Absolutely brilliant. Players had a great attitude. Public were smashing. Press were OK. I didn't even have any problems with the president. One or two others I did, people who had their noses pushed out. It was different. I always knew there was a likelihood of getting the push, although I was never told directly I was being dismissed. I heard about it at third hand while I was on a trip back home. I honestly thought that Spain is where I would finish up – that I would go back there. But circumstances changed so I never did.'

Circumstances always change in football. Ron Atkinson has proved that, whatever the game throws at him, he survives. At Coventry he failed to deliver the silverware – but was still able to choose his own successor in Strachan, even though the changeover came a few months ahead of schedule. Atkinson planned to step up to the post of director of football in 1997, but poor results through the autumn of '96 persuaded the club to make the change early. Atkinson, though, gave Coventry new ambitions and a higher profile. He was a manager who attracted players and publicity, personified the value of flair, and who, even when the team struggled, could never be confused with a loser.

There is a Continental fanaticism about life at Newcastle United. Not only is every game a guaranteed sell-out, training sessions at their Durham base pull in crowds by the hundred. Replica strips are everywhere. Football on Tyneside is a shared experience. Club and public have the same belief, the same ambitions. They hope for the same destiny.

It wasn't always thus. Prior to Kevin Keegan's arrival as manager in February 1992 the club and its support were on different tracks. The board was impoverished and going nowhere. The fans were irate and going crazy. Then came Keegan. Sir John Hall gained control of the board. The team improved, the Endsleigh Championship was won, and the team became one of the top cats in the Premiership.

Easy with Sir John's wealth? Not as simple as that. The catalyst for Newcastle's revival was Keegan himself.

Like Ron Atkinson, Keegan is a man with a vibrant magnetism. As a character, he is a different type, but the impact when he took over at Newcastle was similar to an Atkinson arrival. He is here; in consequence, things will get better.

Keegan's reputation was built on an outstanding playing career: Championship honours in England with Liverpool and in Germany with SV Hamburg; English Footballer of the Year, 1976; European Footballer of the year, 1978. More relevant to Newcastle supporters were his two seasons as a player at St James's Park, helping the club win promotion from the Second Division to the First before being hoisted into retirement by helicopter from the playing surface. For eight years he distanced himself from the professional game, living mostly in Spain. Then, suddenly, he was back as manager.

The turning point of Newcastle's recent history came not with the appointment of Keegan, but an episode soon afterwards. Seeking the funds he had been promised to strengthen the team, he was given the message many a manager had heard before – no money available. Keegan interpreted that as a promise broken and, along with his assistant, Terry McDermott, he quit. The directors hurriedly located some bundles of sterling and the twosome returned.

'Kevin was honest with everyone at the club, and he expected them to be honest with him,' says McDermott. 'He said, "Right, if that's how it is, I don't want to work for you."' The firm stand established Keegan as the guv'nor, someone who wasn't afraid to stand up and be counted, someone who would do things his way or not at all. The result was a period of dramatic and exciting success, in which adventurous players moved to Tyneside and the club became established as one of the best in England.

Keegan's enthusiasm and honesty were tailor-made to appeal to the public. McDermott thinks his playing pedigree was a significant factor with the players. 'If players see a manager has performed at the highest level and won things, they show him respect. That applies more today than ever before.'

Keegan had a single-minded self-confidence which, outwardly at least, betrayed no doubts. McDermott attributes that to the education both of them received with Liverpool. 'Kevin was there six years, I was there eight years, and we knew nothing but success. In the end, you expect success. We also learned that only 100 per cent effort was acceptable. Kevin gave that, and expected it back.

'When we first came to Newcastle things were chaotic. It's on an even keel now, but what we learned at Anfield stood us in good stead. There's nothing complicated about football; that was instilled into us at Liverpool and it's what we have brought into the coaching here. The big thing is, we understand players and their highs and lows – not just in football but in domestic situations as well. We try to help them. Years ago, that would never happen – you were left to get on with it yourself. Players are more high-profile now and you have to protect them. For example, it was a big shock to Andy Cole when he came here from Bristol City.'

The departure of Cole to Manchester United in 1995 showed that Keegan's personality was still the dominant force. Many managers would have quailed at the prospect of selling the club's leading scorer. Keegan not only did the deal, but went outside to take the fans' anger on the chin. It was a remarkable confrontation. Supporters, who had gathered outside St James's Park to protest, were nonplussed at Keegan's readiness to meet them. Having listened to his explanation that the move would benefit the club long-term, and heeded his appeal for trust, they gave him the benefit of the doubt. Most other managers would have had to endure weeks of contagious protests from the stands. Keegan confronted the issue head-on, and triumphed.

It was typical of Keegan to surprise everyone with the timing of his departure. He resigned as Newcastle manager barely a week after his team had thrashed Tottenham 7–1. Typical, too, that the human factor was present. The devastating impact of that result on his opposite number Gerry Francis upset him. As suddenly and dramatically as he arrived in 1992, Keegan was gone. The legacy of a unique character remained, evidenced by the astonishing footballing revolution on the banks of the Tyne.

Kevin Keegan played for two managers who themselves had that extra something – Bill Shankly at Liverpool and Lawrie McMenemy at Southampton. Shankly's mystique stemmed from the man's passion for football, his simple tastes founded on a frugal Ayrshire background, and his concern for people. He was an inspirational character, a natural psychologist and leader whose achievements were only partially counted in terms of trophies. His greatest legacy to Liverpool FC was the structure that maintained the club's position at the top of the English game for more than 15 years after he retired, and still has an influence today.

Lawrie McMenemy emerged on to the public stage in the seventies, as the media began to put managers under the spotlight. His playing career – a youngster who didn't make it at Newcastle and a Gateshead player who quit through injury a year after the club was voted out of the League – hardly provided a launching pad for fame. But success as a manager with Doncaster Rovers (Fourth Division Champions, 1969) and Grimsby Town (Fourth Division Champions, 1972) proved his man-management capabilities, and he moved to Southampton where his impact was immense.

Under McMenemy Southampton won the FA Cup, beating a surprised Manchester United in 1976. The Saints were in the

Second Division at the time. Promotion followed two years later, then came a return to Wembley for the 1979 League Cup Final, regular finishes in the top 10, and forays into Europe in the UEFA Cup. It was a romantic, heart-warming story, personified by McMenemy, whose image as the gruff Geordie with the twinkle in his eye was perfectly suited for the part.

'Until the seventies the players had been the personalities, which is how it should be,' he says. 'But then came a public demand to see and hear more of the managers, and TV began looking for those people who could handle it. Brian Clough and myself used to be on the box a lot. Then the interest waned – in fact these days it's turned again, and we have chairmen emerging as the personalities.

'It helps, if you are in charge of any group, to have an outgoing personality. Like Sir John Harvey Jones. Television either takes to you or it doesn't, and if the public like you and want to see you again, other things spin off. Like *Desert Island Discs*, *Parkinson*, *Wogan*. Once you get on that treadmill, people outside football tend to want to know more about you. Then you get encouraged to write a book. One thing leads to another. You have to be careful not to let things get out of context, and be aware that your main job is to obtain football results, and not let your ego get too big. We've all got egos – that's what got us into the job in the first place.'

McMenemy, a former Guardsman with height and straight back to match, came across as a genial giant with a down-to-earth approach to a high-flying sport. His personality was an attraction in itself – to the spectators, who enjoyed the best of times at the Dell, to the TV producers, and to the players. It's hard to believe that Keegan would have signed for Southampton, as he did in 1980, had the club not had McMenemy or someone like him in charge. Keegan then was in his prime, having had three successful seasons with SV Hamburg. The transfer was a genuine coup.

'With Keegan it was helpful that I could talk to him. He would pick up the phone to start with. I had handled quality players, and players talk about these things. He knew I was never going to tell Kevin Keegan how to kick a football, but I could understand his way of life, how he lived much of it in a goldfish bowl. All these things helped when it came to convincing him to join Southampton.'

* * *

The most dramatic example of the big-name manager having something about him which others lack is Kenny Dalglish. Blackburn Rovers had Jack Walker and his millions before Dalglish came on the scene, but the previous boss, Don Mackay, had limited success persuading players to move to Ewood Park. The club was stuck in the old Second Division, and no one outside North-East Lancashire had heard of Jack Walker. Gary Lineker was a target with Walker putting up £2 million for the transfer, but the deal never got off first base. Walker realized that money itself wouldn't be enough to tempt players who could have their pick of all the top clubs. He needed a manager who would himself be an attraction, and in Dalglish he found the perfect choice.

Unlike Keegan and Atkinson, Dalglish is not a great co-operator with the media. His public profile has been fashioned from a scintillating playing career which merged with a dramatic managerial baptism, appointed Liverpool's player-manager in the aftermath of the Heysel disaster. By taking Liverpool to three League Championships and two FA Cup wins (1986 witnessing the Double), Dalglish assumed immortal status. Any player would have more than a passing interest in joining a team headed up by Kenny Dalglish. Thus a group of players good enough to hoist Rovers out of the Second Division hastened to Ewood – Bobby Mimms, Tim Sherwood, Mike Newell and Colin Hendry. Then, having qualified for the inaugural Premiership via the play-offs, Blackburn had more success in the transfer market than any other promoted club. Alan Shearer, Graeme le Saux, Stuart Ripley and Kevin Gallacher all chose to throw in their lot with Rovers. Of course, the money spoke. But it was the manager who was the crucial factor.

The change of roles in the summer of 1995 was an interesting development. Ray Harford's promotion from coach to team manager, with Dalglish taking the title of director of football, was a move which could only have come once Dalglish had established a high level of success. It is doubtful if Harford could have revolutionized a slumbering outfit the way Dalglish did. Sixteen months later Harford was gone, handing in his resignation with the team bottom of the Premiership. The club's failure to attract major signings since the change of manager was cited as a significant factor.

Harford liked the limelight even less than his predecessor. At a pre-season media function at Haydock Park racecourse he was asked by one journalist: 'Will any of Kenny's reticence towards the press rub off on you?' He replied: 'I hope so.' It was said with a grin and drew a laugh but was probably not far from the truth. Harford was sacked from the Luton job in 1990 with the then Luton chairman claiming that he 'didn't smile enough' – remarks later denied, but the point was made. No matter how good a coach a man is, these days many people place value on his ability to handle press and public, and portray himself in a certain manner. Indeed, Mel Machin lost his job at Manchester City in 1989 with his chairman Peter Swales complaining that he didn't have a good enough rapport with the supporters. Harford is a respected coach, who was duly recruited to manage West Bromwich Albion, but it's hard to envisage him settling down to select eight gramophone records for *Desert Island Discs*.

'My Way' would probably be on Graeme Souness' list. At Rangers, where he was a brilliant success, and at Liverpool, where he wasn't, he deferred to no one and did the job exactly as he saw fit. But in failure as well as success, Souness carries with him a charisma which hints at drama, in the past and in the future.

Smart and stylish with no desire for flamboyance, Souness could comfortably slot into the role of the corporate executive. It is easy to picture him prowling the boardrooms of the business world, amassing companies with the same determined desire that inspired him both as a football player and a manager. In the midfields of Middlesbrough, Liverpool and the Genoese club Sampdoria, Souness was an inspirational orchestrator. A fierce tackler, skilled distributor and ferocious marksman, he was a player who commanded respect rather than affection.

Management began with Rangers in 1986, initially as player manager. He was sent off on his debut at Hibernian and the team lost 2–1, but by the end of that first season he had gained a measure of success which only enhanced his reputation as one of life's achievers. Rangers, 10 years without a Scottish League title, were the Champions, and also collected the Skol Cup on the way.

'The first Scottish Championship was the trophy that meant most to me,' he says. 'It was rewarding for the club to win it after a 10-year gap.' The financial resources of chairman David Murray were an obvious advantage, but Souness also had to cope with learning the managerial trade while still a player, and under a fierce spotlight. 'It was difficult. I had to train with the lads and deal with their problems, and do all the other work that goes with the job. It was hard to get the rest I needed. On the field I was a target for some players and, being the character I am, of course I took the bait.'

Souness brought to management a blazing self-confidence, an equally hot determination, and the experience of life with two of Europe's leading clubs, Liverpool and Sampdoria. He quickly took Rangers by the scruff of the neck, reversing the trend whereby the best players in Scotland left for England, or elsewhere, by bringing in some of the best talents from south of the border – Terry Butcher from Ipswich, Chris Woods from Norwich, followed later by Gary Stevens and Trevor Steven from Everton, Mark Hateley from Monaco, and a string of others, including the repatriation of Richard Gough from Spurs. Souness became a manipulator of men in a style never seen in British football, keeping the door to Ibrox revolving as players came and went in a restless search for the perfect blend. The most controversial by a distance was the 1989 recruitment of Maurice Johnston from the French club Nantes. By taking to Rangers a former Celtic player, and a Catholic, Souness confronted all the traditions of Glasgow football. Many were outraged, regarding the move as a betrayal of the club's Protestant history. Souness was unmoved, and at the end of the season he could point to another success story – the Championship was retained and Johnston was the club's top scorer.

Souness shook up the football establishment with a vengeance, though he denies he was aiming to sweep away the traditionally conservative approach to football in Britain. 'Our football is different from football in any other part of the world,' he says. 'You can't introduce things that are foreign to the players or, more importantly, to the public. Arguably, ours is the most entertaining game in the world, and the reason is that the public don't want lots of play in the midfield area – they want to see things happening in the goalmouth, and that's what makes us unique.

'At Rangers I wanted to introduce what I had learned with Liverpool and Sampdoria. In Italy I saw how much the players looked after themselves, in terms of rest and diet. In Britain, diet is a national problem, not just a footballing problem. It's definitely something we can improve upon. At Liverpool I was taught that the game should never be anything but simple. You shouldn't try to complicate things. The trick is to get good players doing the simple things well.

'When I was a player there, coaches from foreign clubs used to come to see us training, to find out what our "secret" was. They would watch us all morning, then we would leave at lunchtime and so would they. At the end of the week they would say, "I know what you do – you come back after lunch and do your real work then!" But of course we didn't. I heard that time and again. They couldn't believe that what we did was so straightforward.'

Souness returned to Liverpool as manager in 1991, after the resignation of Kenny Dalglish. In Scotland, he had won three Premier Division titles and left Rangers on their way to a fourth. He had also picked up the Scottish League Cup four times, proving the success of his juggling skills. But at Anfield his style didn't complement the habits of the club. Again he tried to wheel and deal in the transfer market, while cajoling an ageing squad to reproduce the form that had made them winners in the past. It didn't work.

'It was disappointing. I wanted it to work more than anyone, but it didn't happen and I have to live with it. I went into a dressing room that was a minefield. I had always been a strong personality as a player and as a manager at Rangers and I thought I could handle it. But unless you get the kind of back-up you need, you're not going to succeed. The signs were there early on that it wasn't going to work out.'

It was a Liverpool squad which included men like Bruce Grobbelaar, John Barnes, Steve McMahon and Peter Beardsley – men who had seen it all and won everything. They were not likely to be impressed by the fiery unpredictability of life under Souness, while the atmosphere of suspicion was not ideal for younger players to settle down and give their best. Were the players frightened of him? 'The only times I shouted at players was when they didn't give 100 per cent. I shouted a lot at Liverpool.'

It wasn't a barren time. The team won the FA Cup in 1992, beating Sunderland 2–0 in the Final, but by now the Souness story had taken an even more dramatic turn. Days before the semi-final against Portsmouth at Highbury, Souness was diagnosed as having a severe heart complaint that required immediate surgery. He kept the news secret until after the Portsmouth match, immersing himself in the game with as much passion as ever. The operation took place the following week, and Souness was just about fit in time to take his place on the bench for the Final. The experience, though, led him to reassess his priorities.

'I am totally different. I now realize that in the bigger picture of life, football is quite insignificant. Football will never again dominate my life. I will never get myself so immensely involved as I used to be. Nothing is worth that.

'At that semi-final I just treated it as a normal day. Got up at our hotel near St Albans, went to the gym, went to the game. I never thought about having to avoid getting excited. That's what I was like in those days. Then things happen in life which make you rethink, and that's one which has changed my whole outlook on life.'

Souness battled on at Anfield till January 1994 when he resigned. 'It would have been nice to have had a bit more help from certain people. But I have no bitterness. Liverpool FC is still the place which holds my fondest memories.' He was out of the game for the best part of 18 months before agreeing to join the Turkish Champions Galatasaray. 'Nothing was offered to me that I found attractive in England. Where do you go in Scotland or England after Rangers and Liverpool? I fancied a move abroad and when this one was offered to me I met the people and thought it an attractive proposition.'

Between leaving Anfield and accepting the Turkish job, Souness 'used the time to do different things – like getting married, travelling, attempting to take up golf, and attending to some business interests which had been neglected.'

But he returned and immediately made an impact, reinforcing the Galatasaray squad with imports from Britain, stirring up the locals by provocatively planting a Galatasaray flag in front of rival Fenerbahçe supporters after winning the Cup Final, getting sacked, and resuming domestic management with Southampton. A 6–3 win over Manchester United less than four months after taking over was proof that Graeme Souness was back in business, and whatever else took place, life on the Solent would not be boring.

Football management is made for men like Souness, Keegan and Atkinson. It gives them the stage, the lights, the colour, the actors, the special effects and the crowds. All they have to do is write the script.

3

IN AT THE DEEP END

Steve Coppell sucked in his cheeks, thought for a long moment, and gave up trying to decide on one single phrase. 'It was the blind leading the blind, a painful learning curve in which every week was difficult. I was totally unprepared for it.'

Coppell became manager of Crystal Palace at the age of 28, his career with Manchester United and England foreshortened by injury. He was a classic example of a big-name player being handed a manager's job and discovering that being a star footballer meant nothing.

Well, next to nothing. Alan Smith, then on the coaching staff and later Coppell's assistant, recalls how the new chief was 'like a little boy wandering around the place. But then he would pick up a training bib and go and play with the lads – and his talent as a footballer won him respect.'

Day One for a rookie manager is a daunting experience. Suddenly you are on the other side of the fence. Often – too often – the transformation comes with no preparation. And there you are, confronted by two dozen professionals, challenging you to put right what your predecessor fouled up.

Steve Coppell inherited a team in the Second Division and an office renowned for spitting out its occupant like an ejector seat. Only one of the five men who preceded him at Selhurst Park lasted more than a few months. The senior players weren't exactly overjoyed to see him. 'Just my luck,' grumbled one, 'here I am in my thirties and I'm going to have the last few years of my career handled by someone who hasn't a clue what he's doing.'

'That was one of the toughest parts,' admits Coppell now. 'Dealing with players who were older than myself. It was hard to find anyone to ask for advice. There was no money to buy players. All that first season (1984–85) we were in trouble. We weren't safe from relegation until the last Saturday – I'll never forget it, away to Cardiff. We won 3–0. We finished seventh from bottom and that was the highest we had been all season. Afterwards, travelling back, there was a great feeling of relief that we had survived. It was a good, warm feeling. All the heartache and pain had been worth it. I thought, If I can handle that, I might have a chance.'

The challenge of Manchester City was yet to come, with more heartache and more pain, but for the time being Coppell absorbed his lessons, won the respect of his club, and piloted Palace back into the old First Division. But football management is amazingly careless as to where it finds its recruits. Considering the complexity of the job, the tortuous hours, lonely decisions and unique pressures, you would expect headhunters of high repute to be employed. But the rule of trial and error, the principle of hit and miss, tend to be the guidelines.

'The crazy thing about football,' says Tommy Burns, 'is that there are so many millions of pounds coming into the game yet it is possibly the only industry which doesn't offer its managers any training.'

Burns is the man entrusted with the fortunes of Celtic FC. Bespectacled and thoughtful, he can change so dramatically on a matchday that he often gets into trouble with the authorities. On one occasion in 1996 he had to be restrained by the reserve official as he voiced his opinions to the linesman during a home defeat by Rangers. Afterwards he fined himself £3000 and apologized to the fans for letting them down.

Burns had no fierce ambition to become a manager. A former Celtic player he went to Kilmarnock when his Parkhead days ended, with the vague notion that he would eventually turn to coaching and one day, perhaps, management. It all happened much faster. Kilmarnock made him assistant manager to Jim Fleeting. When Fleeting resigned with six games left of season 1991–92 the board asked Burns to look after things until the end of the season. The stand-in boss saw his team win five of the six matches and the job was his for the taking. 'The opportunity was thrust upon me. I thought,

Well, at 35 I can't go on playing for ever, so I had better take it.'

Alex Ferguson was so uncertain that he would be a success in management that he bought a pub as a safeguard. The man who reached the peak of his profession by steering Manchester United to a unique double Double had his first taste as boss of East Stirling while also running Fergie's, his pub in Glasgow. 'In many respects you work on instinct in your first job,' he says. 'I got my coaching badge when I was 23 and it was always my idea to stay in the game. But you never know what will happen. East Stirling were in the Second Division, in the days before the reorganization of the Scottish League and the forming of the Premier Division. It was the first job I was offered and I grasped at it because it was a great opportunity.'

The first few months are make or break for many managers. Survival often depends on circumstances beyond their control. Luck, says Tommy Burns, is not to be underestimated. 'The longer you are in the game the more you realize that a huge part of it is down to luck. Injuries and suspensions can disrupt everything you have worked on.'

Alex Ferguson says the circumstances of the club can decide the fate of the manager. He started at a small club but doesn't think there is anything wrong with a manager going straight in at a big club – providing he has proper resources. 'If you go to a big club without resources, like Wolverhampton a few years ago, the timing would be wrong because the club lacks the means to fulfil its ambitions.'

Howard Wilkinson, former Championship-winning manager of Leeds United, now the FA's technical director, shakes his head wearily. 'I think the whole process of training and hiring managers in this country needs to be overhauled. Not just for the benefit of the managers but for the benefit of the game.

'I would love to play the concert piano. But I won't ever get a job with the Philharmonic because if I turned up they would say, "Well, what have you done? Where have you been?" But in football, I can say, "I want to be a manager," and I can get a job. Somebody will employ me, just on the basis that I have said I want to be a manager. Obviously other things come into it, but whether or not I'm telling the truth when I say I want to be a manager, whether I'm any good at it or not, I have actually got a chance of becoming one. Given the high degree of special ability required, that's crazy. That's no good for anybody. No good for those who really want to be managers, those with the talent to be managers, and no good for football, because it waters down the effectiveness of the management pool.

'Management turnover is unavoidable. Even in Utopia they are going to be fired, so that means other managers and coaches are going to be hired. Therefore, the availability of people to come into management is limitless – which facilitates change on a whim.'

Howard Wilkinson learned his trade step by step. Non-League with Boston and Mossley, coaching amateurs with the FA, a spell as a teacher, eight years coaching England teams from non-League level to the full international side under Ron Greenwood and Bobby Robson, club management with Notts County, Sheffield Wednesday and Leeds United, he wonders about the incoming generation of managers. What steps have they taken to prepare for the trials and tribulations? What calibre of individual is being given responsibility? How do chairmen know what to look for?

'A lot of chairmen I talk to – and as chairman of the League Managers' Association I spoke to a lot of them – admit that they don't really know what criteria to apply. As one chairman put it to me, in his own business he can hire a salesman and if after a month it isn't working he can get rid of him without too much damage to the business. If he's looking for a chief executive, he has come through that business himself so he knows what is needed. But in football, there's so little to go on other than a superficial assessment which might be based on six months' results, or someone's reputation as a player, or even his appearances on television.

'It can also be based on economics. Five on the short list and X wants the least money. Or, we'll appoint a player-manager and that saves us one wage.'

Alan Smith agrees. The former Palace manager, fired at the end of 1994–95, found himself on the job market for a few weeks before landing the Wycombe Wanderers post. 'I don't think chairmen have any clear idea of what they're looking for. I went for one job and the chairman complained because I hadn't submitted a CV. I know I'm not the biggest name in the business, but I have been manager of a team that's won promotion into the Premiership and reached Cup semi-finals, and I felt he should at least have known that.

'Chairmen look for the wrong things. They need people who can coach and motivate, but they tend to say, "Oh he's played 25 times for England, we'll have him." Directors, like all of us, are football lovers – and they like to meet famous footballers. That doesn't mean you should give them a job.

'It isn't always easy working out how to go about applying for jobs. Some clubs don't advertise, some do. You feel some don't contact you because they don't want you to turn them down. If you ring a club you don't really know who to speak to about the vacancy. It's very difficult.'

Much depends on the club. If you rang Aston Villa, the only person to talk to would be Doug Ellis, the chairman. He has a clear idea of what he wants from a manager. 'Honesty, integrity, principles and ethics, added to which, as an ex-professional who has played at the highest level, he will have the respect of the senior players and an opportunity to influence the younger ones in their approach to the game.

'I also look for a man who, during the season, is a workaholic – as I am. No one will work harder than me, and if I employ anyone they don't work for me, they work with me, and I work with them. I believe the manager and chairman have to be like blood brothers – no inhibitions between them at any time. They must say what they think at any time – as long as it's confidential.

'The ideal manager is one who lives right, has lived right in the past, has a wife and family, lives in the area – a condition I make, he must be part of the community. He must have man-management skills. That is a very important quality. At this club, as of now, we have nine coaching staff and 41 players. He is the team manager, following the Continental pattern – in charge of playing affairs while the rest of the activities are my responsibility.'

Ellis has worked full-time at Villa Park since 1982. From his desk it is a short walk through the office complex to the executive boxes in the North Stand, and a commanding view of the newest development, the huge Doug Ellis Stand which towers to the left. It is a fitting memorial to a man who has put heart and soul into his club. But his ambition has not been satisfied yet, not by a long chalk.

'Brian Little is our manager now, subject to success. He knows he stays if he is successful; he doesn't if he is unsuccessful. Every manager knows that.'

So what is his definition of success? 'Producing a winning team, preferably a team which will entertain the public as well. A team that will enable us to be in the Premier League the next year, preferably to win something during that year; to be in the top half, always fighting to be in the top five so we can qualify for Europe. Trying to win the trophies the supporters want, because we must never forget that football cannot progress without the support of the public.'

For many players, having coped with the application, the interview is the worst hurdle. Being confronted by a semi-circle of directors is a new experience. Andy King scurried through the midfields of Luton, Everton and Wolves before drifting out of the game, returning as Luton's commercial manager, and deciding to tilt at a team manager's job.

'I couldn't stand not being involved with the lads on the pitch. It was killing me. There was a managerial vacancy at Scarborough, so I went for it. The interview was frightening – nine people interviewed me! The lad before me came out looking really dour so I went in and tried to create a lighter atmosphere with a few jokes. I wanted the job so badly. The people on the other side of the table were nine individuals who stood between me and a dream – a dream of becoming a football manager.'

Either the nine didn't enjoy King's sense of humour or another candidate, Steve Wicks, made a better impression. Wicks got the job. King's dream was realized soon afterwards, though, at Field Mill, home of Mansfield Town. There was a different procedure this time. Following a one-to-one meeting with the chairman, Keith Haslam, King started next morning, with six months of the season to play.

'My first day was daunting. It was the first time I had met the press at management level and words of responsibility and respect came into play. I didn't know Mansfield, but I was impressed with the stadium. The size of the place surprised me.

One unfortunate thing was that the caretaker-manager hadn't been told beforehand, so that was a bit awkward. The hardest decision was to work out how to approach the players for the first time. Kicking the dressing-room door open wasn't my style. So I just said: "I've got no great ideas at this stage. Let's get to know each other. I'm a simple man. I love football and that's what I want from my players. I believe you come to your work for enjoyment – if you don't feel the same way, let's sort it out."'

The new boss quickly realizes that there's more to this business than geeing up the players. Bryan Hamilton, now manager of Northern Ireland, strapped away valuable experience as player-coach of Swindon Town before taking his first command, with Tranmere Rovers. 'I thought I was well prepared but that was a mistake. All the unforeseen problems landed on my desk.'

An experience echoed by many, including Peter Reid, who was Howard Kendall's player-coach at Manchester City before taking charge himself. 'I was with Howard a lot, seeing how he operated. But I don't think anything could have prepared me for going in myself. It was a different ball game.'

When Roy Evans became manager of Liverpool in 1994 he had the benefit of an entire career spent within the most envied club structure in the business. As player, coach and assistant manager Evans had explored every nook and cranny. Yet the transition to the manager's office still had a forceful impact. 'There is no preparation for a top job in football management. You need all your experience when you get there, and fortunately I had been through almost everything. All the same, you don't realize how big it is till you sit in the chair yourself. That is when the real responsibility hits you – not just to yourself and your family, but your responsibility to the fans. You feel everything you do is for them.'

Evans admits his nerves 'jangled' at first. It was a high-profile takeover, following the resignation of Graeme Souness whose turbulent three years had turned the normally stable Anfield into a volatile crucible. In his first full season, Evans' team won the Coca-Cola Cup Final – an achievement which any manager would welcome, but which this one accepted with a degree of relief as well. 'Winning that Cup at least meant I wouldn't go down as the only manager since before Bill Shankly not to win anything,' he says. 'With this particular job you are a victim of your predecessors' success. Standards have been set that are difficult to match. Liverpool teams have to be challenging in every competition.'

As baptisms of fire go, Roy Aitken's managerial christening was a veritable inferno. The former Celtic and Scotland captain was handed the task of halting Aberdeen's free-fall descent from the Premier Division in the spring of 1995. He had a handful of matches in which to prevent the Dons being relegated from the top flight for the first time since the Premier League was founded. It didn't help that the team's plight was being watched with macabre fascination across the whole of Britain. Aberdeen had been runners-up the previous season. The prospect of their being relegated was like a long-serving government being voted out of office.

The count hung on the last ballot box. A play-off against the First Division runners-up, Dunfermline, over two legs. The first leg at home. 'Before the match I didn't vary what I had been saying to the players throughout the previous weeks. By then we'd had four or five games unbeaten. I told them to be mentally strong, be positive in your approach, don't let yourselves down by coming back in here thinking you could have given more. I was looking for 100 per cent effort – OK it's a cliché, but I got it and that's what pulled us through.'

Aitken also concentrated on his own bearing and attitude. 'I wanted the players to see that I had confidence in them.' Team selection was vital. 'I had to recognize which players I could rely on and which I couldn't. The bottom line is that you have to pick a team that will do the job. So it's a question of identifying their strengths and weaknesses.

'You might not pick the most gifted player because you might feel you couldn't rely on him. Of course, footballing ability is the main factor. That's what got the player there in the first place. But at the top level you also need attitude, desire, and hunger. A good pro looks after himself – all you do as coach or manager is fine-tune the players. We pass on information on diet, training, coaching – how to play possession, whatever – and it's up to the player to take all that on board.

'When I took over the pressure from the public was intense. It was unheard of for Aberdeen to be in that position. But I looked on it as a challenge. That's what football is. It doesn't matter if you're at the top or the bottom, it's a challenge and a chance to silence the critics.'

The first day of Tommy Docherty's managerial career was in September 1961, when Chelsea split with Ted Drake, the man who had guided them to the 1955 Championship. Docherty, whose appointment as player-coach hadn't met with Drake's approval, was surprised to be put in charge. 'From the start the players began calling me Boss instead of Tom. I didn't ask them to – it just happened. Mind you,' he added with a chuckle, 'it's not what they call you but the way they call you it that counts! They can talk to you with respect or they can talk to you with malice. I found that all the young players in the club loved me – until I picked my first team. When they weren't in it they didn't like me as much. And the older players – they didn't like me because we had so many good young talented players at Chelsea, players like Harris, Hollins, McCreadie, Bonetti. The older ones could see these young lads would soon take their places, and they didn't like that.'

Surprisingly, for someone who seemed to revel in the job, Tommy Docherty had no driving ambition to become a manager. His playing career with Preston, Arsenal and Scotland was winding down to a natural conclusion with the player-coach's role at Stamford Bridge. Beyond that, he hadn't given the future much thought.

'I didn't particularly want to be a manager. I wanted to coach for quite a number of years and was looking forward to it. Then Ted Drake got the sack and the job was thrust on me before I was ready for it. It was a difficult transition. From working alongside players like Terry Venables and George Graham, overnight I was their boss. But the job looked interesting, I thought I could do it. And I had enough friends in the game – people like Bill Shankly, Matt Busby, Bill Nicholson, people who I could talk to if I had a problem. It was all trial and error. I made a lot of mistakes, but I was fortunate that I had an understanding chairman, Joe Mears. He let me get on with it. I think that's the biggest problem today – chairmen of football clubs don't let the manager manage.'

It isn't just a question of the buck stopping with the new manager. It's the number of bucks, and the sheer variety of shapes and sizes which makes it such a challenge. There is so much more to it than coaching the team and deciding the tactics. The manager has to dovetail with his directors, the rest of the staff, the media, and supporters' groups; he must travel long distances to assess potential signings and upcoming opposition. He is a father-confessor to many of his players. Depending on the size of the club he may well end up like Mike Walker at Colchester – washing the kit after a Saturday match and checking that it's dry in time for Tuesday.

Steve McMahon began season 1994–95 as a first choice midfielder in Manchester City's Premier League team. His daily routine was preordained by the club, the hours not too onerous, and if things went wrong the flak was not particularly aimed at him. Four months later he was player-manager of Swindon Town, running the show off the field as well as on it, taking responsibility and struggling to halt the team's slide down the First Division of the Endsleigh League into the open jaws of the Second.

That was the kind of appointment that had experienced managers shaking their heads. The Wales manager Bobby Gould saw his name written on the door of four different club managers' offices (Bristol Rovers, Coventry, Wimbledon and West Bromwich Albion. Bristol Rovers and Coventry have seen him come and go twice). Gould is adamant: 'I admire Steve McMahon's commitment but he was not ready for the Swindon job. He was thrown in. The job is colossal.'

McMahon, who failed to prevent Swindon's relegation, agrees with the last comment. 'The job is bigger than people think,' he admits. 'The difficult part is being responsible for everyone else's game as well as your own. The clubs where I played (Everton, Villa, Liverpool, City) had high playing standards, so you've got to be careful not to judge everyone here by the standards I've been used to. Obviously, they wouldn't be playing for Swindon Town if they were up to the standard of the Liverpools and the Citys. Your aims should be just as high, but you have to adjust your expectations according to what you've got.'

McMahon, an England international on 17 occasions, is now climbing the same learning curve that gave Steve Coppell so much trauma. While he and many others endure the traditional British form of football education, Bobby Gould warns that the game really cannot afford to let loose unqualified, inexperienced ex-players on the wider plains of management.

'The standard of English football is dropping because people are going into jobs they are not ready for. We have got no students, no disciples. People are not aware of the pitfalls. It's 24 hours a day, 10 days a week.'

One of the biggest obstacles in the way of preparing young men for a managerial career is the reluctance of those young men to commit themselves to a future in management. Many play cheerfully into their thirties with little realistic planning for the future, especially those at the top whose earnings have been so high that they don't need to worry about paying the mortgage when they hang up their boots.

Joe Royle is a prime example. The man who has become one of the game's most successful bosses, proving himself at a medium-sized club – Oldham Athletic – and a big club – Everton – had laid no proper plans for a switch to management by the time a knee injury ended his playing career at Norwich City in 1982.

'I had nothing apart from 16 years in the game and a little bit of coaching with the kids at Norwich. I never seriously thought of going into management until the last minute. I was quite happy running a little shop in Norwich where I sold catalogue surplus lines. Within 24 hours of announcing my retirement as a player I had four separate offers of jobs in insurance, and I also did a bit of work for TV in East Anglia. But I thought I would give management a try, and a job became available at Oldham. I had two interviews up there and after the second one I was offered the job on a one-year contract. As for preparing myself better – I can't think what sort of things I would have prepared for, because every day is different and so much in football is down to the individual.'

Royle took to management like a duck to water but no would-be manager should be fooled. Royle is probably as near as they come to being a natural for the job, driven by an unusual supply of common sense plus an even temperament. But he was also lucky that his first employers were Oldham. The club was then in the old Second Division and the directors were not the sort to work themselves into a frenzy if the Latics failed to win the

European Cup within three years.

'Oldham,' says Royle, 'are different from other clubs. When Graeme Sharp took over from me he was only their third manager in 25 years. They are not a sacking club. They are always realistic. We had some great times – good Cup runs and promotion to the Premier League. When we were relegated again it wasn't treated as a great disaster. The club only gets gates of 6000 to 8000 so they knew they probably couldn't afford to be in the Premier League. Their attitude was, "Let's just enjoy it." Other clubs could learn from Oldham's approach. They have been a beacon of stability. Three managers in 25 years? Other clubs have had 25 managers in three years! They change managers like the chairman changes his vest. So they have no stability, no growth, everything is stop-start.'

It's the misfortune of all too many rookie managers to dip their toes in the water at a club answering that description. Royle was able to learn his trade in a supportive environment, and the results were seen when he salvaged Everton's fortunes – escaping relegation and winning the FA Cup.

Ian Branfoot, in contrast, was always heading for a manager's job. He didn't quite understand why, but almost from the start of his career as a player there seemed to be influences pushing him towards an eventual appointment as a manager.

Branfoot, the man from the North-East who became a lightning conductor for discontent on the south coast during a controversial stint as manager of Southampton, started his playing days at Sheffield Wednesday. There he worked under Alan Brown, one of the most respected managers of the sixties and a man who both discovered and inspired a generation of young footballers.

'At the end of my first year as a player at Sheffield Wednesday, Alan Brown told me I was booked on a course at Durham to gain my preliminary coaching badge. I have no idea why he put my name down, but you didn't argue with Alan Brown so I went on the course and passed it. Then he said, "In two years' time you'll take your full badge." I did, and at the age of 21 I was a fully qualified coach.' Brown must have spotted something in the young Branfoot's character, because he was the only player dispatched from Hillsborough to complete those courses.

Equipped with the qualifications he began making use of them, working with youngsters at boys' clubs and doing other coaching assignments for the Football Association. He became a regular visitor to Lilleshall, the sports complex in Shropshire where the FA runs a variety of courses. Branfoot studied physical conditioning and the treatment of injuries, and continually freshened up his awareness of coaching techniques.

So when football's version of the Grim Reaper began checking Ian Branfoot's availability for transfer from the dressing room to the scrap heap, he got a disappointment. A playing past which had taken him from Sheffield Wednesday to Doncaster Rovers to Lincoln City was already merging into a managerial future. At Lincoln, under Graham Taylor, Branfoot became player-coach and after quitting as a player he moved to the coaching staff at Southampton, on to Reading as coach and then assistant manager before taking over in his own right in 1984. With some justification, Branfoot is able to make the unusual claim for a football boss: 'I was extremely well prepared for management.'

But like all the rest, he found his outlook on the game shifted significantly. 'When you cross from being a player to becoming a coach, your whole philosophy is different. You view the business in a much less selfish light. For a player, it's a very selfish profession. If you don't look after yourself no one else will do it for you. As a coach your outlook is wider, and when you move from coach to manager it's another big step.'

Branfoot had 17 years' coaching experience and seven years as a full-time member of the backroom staff before he had to take responsibility for picking the team. When he did so, the results were impressive. He quickly steered Reading to promotion from Division Four; and two years later the club easily won the Third Division Championship to reach the Second Division for the first time since 1926. But, this being professional football, the upward curve couldn't continue. Relegation followed, the sack tagged on behind, and Branfoot, like most of his colleagues, with or without 17 years of preparation, was another casualty of the industry. It was by no means the end of his story – ahead lay a roller-coaster ride at Southampton and the challenge of the lowest division at Fulham.

Bobby Gould is another of the few men who made a decision early. He was still only 24 and a player at Arsenal when he began directing himself towards his future career.

'Arsenal were brilliant. They instigated a preliminary coaching course for the players, every Monday for 10 months. Only two players in the first-team squad declined to take part. One was Bob McNab, the full-back. The other was – guess who? George Graham! He said he had no intention of becoming a manager!'

Gould went on to gain his full coaching badge in 1972. 'So from my mid-twenties I knew where I wanted to go. As a kid I always wanted to be a professional footballer. As a young man, I wanted to become a manager.'

His education was continued as a player at West Ham, listening and learning from one of the game's most respected coaches, Ron Greenwood. 'In contrast to most other clubs we played no five-a-sides in training. Ron thought it created bad habits. Instead, we concentrated on keeping possession and passing the ball.' He attended a two-week course for potential managers run by the Football Association at Bisham Abbey, learning the basics of administration, media communication and finance. Fresh from the course he applied for a vacancy at Lincoln City. 'I was interviewed by 15 people and didn't get it.'

So it was among the fjords of Norway that the man who was to plot one of Wembley's most sensational results, Wimbledon's 1988 FA Cup win over Liverpool, honed his instincts. With West Ham, Gould had visited the coastal town of Aalesund in 1975, returning for a coaching stint in '76. In 1978, with his playing days ending at Bristol Rovers, he made a typically wholehearted commitment to return.

'When the season finished at Bristol, I loaded up my Ford Escort, two sons in the back, drove up to Newcastle, got the ferry over to Bergen, and drove up the coast to Aalesund. I decided if I was going there, we would live among the community. We rented a house opposite the football ground and I spent the summer coaching teams from age seven up. We won promotion with the first team and it was a lovely time.'

So did all that give Bobby Gould a painless transition into management in England? Not exactly.

'There are always nasty shocks in this business. In 1981 Bristol Rovers sacked Terry Cooper and brought me in. I met the directors at Oxford where Rovers had been playing. I said to the directors, 'Be fair and honest with me over my salary and that's all I ask.' They offered £12,500 a year and I agreed.

'I went into the ground for the first time on Thursday 22 October, 1981. In the evening I took all the players' contracts back to my hotel, went through the lot of them, and found that two players were on £150 more per week than I was. I phoned the chairman and told him he'd have my resignation in the morning because the board had been dishonest with me. I got an increase!'

Joe Royle had a different kind of shock when he took the Everton job. It was the night of the club's AGM. The shareholders convened in Goodison Park's 300 Club amid eager speculation about who was to succeed the sacked Mike Walker. Royle's name was on everyone's lips, but so far there had been no confirmation.

The chairman, Peter Johnson, addressed the meeting: 'Ladies and gentlemen, I am pleased to inform you that we have a new manager. And you will be able to hear from him before the meeting concludes.' And with that tantalizing prospect left in the air, the AGM continued with the dreary business of a year in the life of a none-too-successful company.

An hour later Johnson put them all out of their misery. 'Please welcome the man who is to be the new manager of Everton Football Club – Joe Royle!' And in came Royle, grinning from ear to ear, as the cheers rolled round the room and the flashlights sparkled. It was, or at least it appeared to be, the perfectly stage-managed entrance.

Except that at that moment, Joe Royle had not agreed to be manager of Everton at all. He had barely met the chairman, had talked no terms, had signed no contract. He had arrived at Goodison Park to be swept along by the board's need to give the shareholders something positive. After 10 years as a player with Everton he knew the place inside out but this was not quite the homecoming he expected.

'The whole night was a whirlwind. Oldham and Everton had been negotiating compensation for a couple of days. As soon as that was settled I was whisked to Everton, ushered up to the shareholders' meeting, walked through the doors and that was it. Lights on, microphones everywhere. I had no idea it was going to be like that. I thought I would have an hour first to sit down and discuss a contract. Instead I was in the midst of a media circus without even talking about terms or the staff I would have. To be fair to the club I knew they were desperate to produce something at the AGM because the club was in a bad way and the supporters were getting restless. But it was certainly a dramatic entrance and one that I was completely unprepared for.'

Small wonder that Joe Royle, once courted by insurance companies, has his own verdict on the job. 'If this was assessed as an insurance risk it would be Group 28 with the same rating as a nitro-glycerine juggler!'

The risk cuts both ways. The individual and the club can both suffer if things go wrong. Lack of preparation makes failure more likely, yet the football establishment has been reluctant to take seriously the way it prepares men for this the most crucial role of all.

The Football Association discontinued the management course Bobby Gould attended years ago, although they are now showing renewed interest by discussing the setting up of a new course in conjunction with Loughborough University. For now, however, the only option available is a two-week course run every other year by the Professional Footballers' Association.

A dozen players gather at a training centre owned by the electricity company Norweb at Chorley in Lancashire. Lecturers from the St Helens School of Management run the proceedings with outside speakers drafted in to help with specific areas.

Before they arrive the players have been asked to fill in CVs. One of the first tasks is to have those analysed and criticized. Week One continues with coaching in interview techniques – players are put through 'job interviews' with fake directors, every facial spasm studied by closed-circuit television for analysis later. On the first evening a manager who is still relatively new to the job discusses his experiences.

Day Two concentrates on finance – understanding balance sheets, organizing budgets, the AGM, the work of the commercial department. The week continues with such topics as information technology, referees, contract law, board meetings.

Week Two moves on to the management of coaching – organizing coaching and training, providing leadership. Group behaviour and how to handle it is discussed, as well as discipline and counselling, the media, marketing, statistics, scouting and youth policy.

'After the first three or four days they're absolutely shattered,' says Mickey Burns, the PFA's Education Officer. 'I don't think they have any conception of what it's really like. They don't realize all the areas in which a manager has to be involved, and the tremendous amount of work that goes on. In particular they find the interview sessions very difficult.

'I wonder sometimes how many of them will make it, how many of them will still be in a job in five years' time.

'We tell them when they arrive that the course won't help them win football matches, and that they will only keep their jobs if they win matches. But it might buy them a bit more time.'

Howard Wilkinson says the PFA course is fine but doesn't go far enough.

'The PFA course is an out-of-service course, not an in-service course. It's one which I can go to or not as I choose.

'What I would like to see is a training process established for managers – not so that it would guarantee that you were a good manager, but at least it would show you had sufficient interest to complete the course. Hopefully along the way it would also make you a better manager. It couldn't make you worse. So you would then have a boundary around the pool of available managers and coaches. And that would lead to less changing of managers by clubs.

'I would insist on it, as a condition of becoming a manager, that you had been through the course. The sort of thing I would like to see is a course to stretch over a longer period of time. Players in their late twenties or thirties could, for instance, spend three periods of study over three years which might, in units of time, take up a month. That's not too much to ask, but the main thing is that it tests their desire.

'Something along these lines will come, and I want to make sure it is as useful as possible when it does – so that it's seen as a positive advantage rather than a hurdle.

'It has to be run by the FA so that it gains recognition from UEFA and FIFA. Increasingly, anywhere across the world, internationally recognized qualifications are becoming a necessity rather than simply something that's nice to have.'

Wilkinson's words are the latest contribution to an argument that has raged for years. Traditionalists mock the quest for paper qualifications and FA badges. Liverpool's success is often held up as an example of how little such badges are needed – Bill Shankly and Bob Paisley didn't waste their time on coaching courses, they say, and it didn't do them any harm! But not everyone has the instinctive feel for the job that those two – in markedly contrasting styles – always possessed. And the game is changing, becoming ever more complex as the financial stakes are raised and agents from all quarters of the globe come knocking on the manager's door.

What the traditionalists perhaps overlook is that Shankly worked his way into the job at Workington and Grimsby before moving up to Huddersfield and Liverpool. Paisley had 35 years as player, trainer, physio and assistant manager before taking over.

Ian Branfoot reflects on the numerous courses he attended and sums up: 'You can't say that qualifications are any guarantee, but if you do these things you are better prepared for management when the time comes. I went on the PFA course and found it extremely helpful. It provided the groundwork for the job.'

Alan Smith is adamant. 'To take a player and stick him straight into a manager's job is unbelievable. Spain and Portugal are the only other European countries where this could happen, and even there it doesn't happen much.

'In Denmark and Italy it takes seven years to qualify. If you start at 28 you can be in the top flight at 35. In Holland and Germany they're disgusted with the way you can become a manager in England. The FA have tried to take a lead but I don't think the clubs take any notice. Whereas in Germany's Bundesliga or in Italy, there's no argument – you don't get your licence to coach unless you have qualified.

'And of course it all depends on how realistic the qualification is. I don't think you can attend a two-week course and go and manage Everton. It's scandalous. But the clubs are very anti the FA so nothing gets done.'

Smith himself started in non-league football – first as assistant manager to Wimbledon, in their non-league days, then as manager of Dulwich Hamlet in the Isthmian League. 'The problem in non-League is that the players are all part-timers and you spend half your life prising them away from the building site or the bank. And you can't kid those guys because they're streetwise. With full-timers I found it a bit easier because they had never been out in the big wide world.'

Aberdeen's Roy Aitken says man-management is a more important attribute than coaching skills and admits he has had no formal training in the former. 'I learned through my own experience of working with quality managers. I do think there are skills and techniques you can learn from attending courses or seminars, but football is slightly different from business. There are a lot of variables – suspensions, loss of form, injuries, plus the different personalities in the club. I try to treat people the way I want to be treated myself.'

Lennie Lawrence, who chalked up eight years as manager of Charlton Athletic before heading north to Middlesbrough and Bradford City then returning south to Luton, says he feels sorry for young men moving into management in the 1990s. 'It's harder for them now. There's more pressure. We live in an instant society and people want instant success. At Charlton I wanted to build a club, not just a team, and I was able to do that. I doubt if managers are given time to do that today.'

Steve McMahon was invited to stop an avalanche. Swindon had risen up to the Premier League, had never looked like staying there, and sure enough had reverted to the Endsleigh League. The manager who took them up – Glenn Hoddle – had moved on; the manager who brought them back down – John Gorman – had been fired. The chances of a rookie romping to victory were about as promising as a three-year-old colt winning the Grand National. 'If anything could have gone wrong, it did. We nearly got to the final of the Coca-Cola Cup – but we lost in the semi-finals and got relegated.'

As player-manager, McMahon found no respite. He was in the front line before, during and after every game. His composure became stretched. Twice in a short space of time he was sent off.

'My disciplinary record until then had been good, but I think the sheer frustration got to me. Even so, the second red card was a bit harsh. The job is a hard one but I love it. It's a great chance to put my ideas into practice.'

Many of those ideas have been formulated from McMahon's time as a Liverpool player. The men who built the Anfield foundations may not have possessed formal qualifications, but they did provide any Liverpool player with the opportunity to observe a management system at first hand. Generations of players have left the club with a set of principles on which they base their own managerial style: keep it simple, don't shout the odds in public, attend to detail, don't let players believe their own publicity; plan for the future, don't be afraid to spend when you must, but never throw money away carelessly. Remember that the club is bigger than anyone and that without the supporters none of us would be here.

Like a graduate reflecting fondly on university days, Phil Neal looks back on his 11 years as a Liverpool player with affection buttressed by appreciation. 'I was always aware of the knowledge I was gaining through working with Bob Paisley, Joe Fagan and the other people on the staff. I had the privilege of working alongside England managers as well – Ron Greenwood, Bobby Robson and their coaches – and I was always enthralled at being in their company. At Anfield the people were so solid. One of the things that I learnt from Bob Paisley was how good he was at getting the balance right throughout the team. He collected a team that could run itself. It is the epitome of a good manager when you can achieve the right blend, with the right characters. There were a lot of captains within that unit. There might only have been one with the armband, be it Emlyn Hughes, Phil Thompson, Graeme Souness, whoever, but there were a lot of others who were willing to take responsibility. Another thing was observing the number of people Bob had as backroom staff. People like Geoff Twentyman, the chief scout. It isn't until you go to another club where they can't afford a chief scout that you realize how well off we were at Anfield. They are one club which gives the manager very good support. They give you a real chance to manage, and they rarely want change, preferring to bring people through from within.'

But then, does that sort of experience equip a young man well for the future? Or does it give him unreasonable expectations? If an Anfield Old Boy thinks the down-table club he's just joined is run on the lines he's been used to, he might be in for a shock!

It was Bolton Wanderers, then in Division Three, who gave Phil Neal his first chance, as player-manager. 'Bob Paisley warned me that being a player-manager takes a lot out of you. He was right, and I didn't really have the experienced backroom staff that I needed.' Neal took with him a former Liverpool team-mate, Colin Irwin. The two had grown up together at Anfield, but the combination didn't work. They were two of a kind, both rookies together, neither covering the other's weak spots. After 18 months Irwin left and Neal brought in Mick Brown, formerly Ron Atkinson's assistant at Manchester United. Older, more experienced, Brown had handled all the problems several times over and the result was a better management combination. His arrival steadied the ship which was floundering after being relegated (through the play-offs) at the end of 1986–87. Neal and Brown brought them back on the bounce and went close to taking them up to the Second Division (the play-offs were once again Bolton's downfall).

There were more shock-waves in those early days at Burnden Park. After life at Anfield, where nothing was spared, the switch to the lower divisions was an eye-opener. The Wanderers had no training ground. In fact they had very little by way of training kit. Shirts and socks were ripped and tatty, towels had holes in them. 'We had lush grass kept in immaculate condition at Liverpool's training ground at Melwood. At Bolton we used to train on parks pitches. Now that's OK, but when you work out your training routines and the quality of the ground is bad, it just destroys you. It brings you right down to earth.'

Neal began working on plans for the future, setting up a school of excellence, bringing his Anfield background into play, even though he had no guarantee that he would still be around to reap the rewards. He had an early taste of the politics of football following Bolton's relegation to the Fourth Division. The chairman, Barry Chaytow, wanted Neal out. The other directors disagreed. The battle raged for several weeks before the Neal camp carried the day. In due course, it was the chairman who left. But the episode reminded the young boss still further that he was in a different world. Like Judy Garland on the way to Oz, this sure wasn't Kansas, Toto!

'You felt that people at Liverpool would never have to face that kind of situation and there I was, in the early part of my managerial career, having to put up with pressure from the chairman, through the media as well, on a weekly basis.'

Lou Macari is from the same playing generation as Phil Neal – they were on opposing sides in the 1977 FA Cup Final. Macari also dropped down the football pyramid to find his first job in management. Like Steve McMahon he was welcomed aboard by Swindon Town and found the County Ground a valuable nursery.

Macari went straight into management with little preparation. He didn't even give the preliminaries much thought. 'I had been a footballer with Manchester United and Celtic, and nothing else. After a 20-minute interview they decided, for some reason, that I was someone who could pull them out of the Fourth Division. I went into the interview with no advice on how to conduct myself, and maybe that is what got me the job. I was just myself so perhaps I was different from everyone else. I didn't really know what they were looking for. Apparently afterwards they thought I was frank and honest and said what I believed. I believe that tickled a few of them and frightened one or two, but I got the job and cracked on with it.

'Like anyone else in their first job I didn't have a clue what it was all about. In my first year I did so many stupid things. The most stupid was expecting players at that level – the Fourth Division! – to have the same quality about them as players I had been used to with Manchester United. I was asking them to do certain things on the pitch and getting uptight when it didn't happen. I had to realize that the reason why they were playing at this level was because they weren't good enough to play at a higher one.

'But it was a good start for me because it was a laid-back area. Not a lot was expected, there wasn't a lot of pressure, and I was very comfortable there and stayed five and a half years.'

During that remarkable time Macari's team showed their quality could indeed rise to a higher level. Swindon won the Fourth Division with a record 102 points in 1986, won promotion from the Third the next season, and nearly went straight up through the Second as well. In the ceaseless duel between sink and swim, Macari showed an impressive tendency to stay afloat.

His former Old Trafford team-mate Bryan Robson had a dream start – from helping United achieve the League and Cup double in 1994, Robson became player-manager of Middlesbrough and guided the club to the Endsleigh League Championship. To the outsider, Robson seemed to take it all in his stride, and he admits as much himself. But the secret was in the people who moved in with him.

'Having Viv Anderson as my assistant has been invaluable. Viv had already done a year as manager of Barnsley and knew what to expect. He has taken a lot of pressure off me in handling the media and the office work. John Pickering organizes the training. Without that back-up I would have found it very difficult as a player-manager.

'I knew there would be small matters which you have to help the players with and I don't find that a problem. I had good advice from Ron Atkinson, Alex Ferguson and Terry Venables. As for the matches, once I am on the pitch I don't think about being the manager. I just get on with my game.'

Moving to an ambitious club which was already building a new stadium meant Robson could apply some of the strategies learned at Manchester United. 'The best decision I have made was to fly to some of the most distant away games like Portsmouth and Charlton, instead of going by coach. It made the difference between a two-hour round trip and a 12- to 14-hour round trip. United tried everything to rest the players and make it as easy as possible for them, and that was something which paid dividends. At Middlesbrough we can't do everything United do, but I am trying to adopt the things that we can afford.'

Howard Kendall can identify with any young player-manager grappling with the dual chains of office. He began assimilating knowledge and experience relatively early – as club captain under Freddie Goodwin at Birmingham City, as player-coach to Alan

Durban at Stoke. Then came his first solo command – player-manager of the then Third Division Blackburn Rovers.

'It was really enjoyable – but hard at first. When things weren't going right on the field, all the players would look at me as if to say: Well, you're the manager, you put it right! It took time for them to realize that we were all level on matchday. I had a tremendous disciplinary record as a player but I must have become a right pain in the butt to referees as a player-manager. I didn't swear at them, but I couldn't stop moaning when they gave decisions that didn't go for me, or the team, or the club. Because I was responsible for the result.'

Occasionally lack of experience can be an advantage. Mike Walsh, once of Bolton, Everton, Blackpool and the Republic of Ireland, began his first managerial assignment at Bury, with the club in a financial crisis. 'I don't think an experienced manager could have done it. When you're told you have to sell all your experienced players and bring in part-timers, it isn't a situation that an experienced manager could have taken on.'

Few managers active in the game today have enjoyed a smooth transition into their first post. There is one man, however, who took on his first job and and went straight into the business of winning Championships and competing in Europe – Walter Smith.

Smith was in the right place at the right time, but he also had the foresight to equip himself to take advantage of opportunities when they arose. He also demonstrated a valuable appetite for handling players.

His playing career terminated through injury at 29 when he was at Dundee United. He turned to coaching, working with the club's youngsters, and made such an impression that the manager, Jim McLean, upgraded him to work with the senior players, then to assistant manager. From there he joined the staff at Ibrox, working as assistant to Graeme Souness for five dramatic and successful years. When Souness left to join Liverpool in 1991, the Rangers chairman David Murray avoided the big names being touted as a replacement and asked Smith to take over.

'I was very fortunate. My experiences with Dundee United and then as assistant to Graeme Souness stood me in good stead. If I had gone straight from playing to being manager of Rangers it would have been entirely different. I had a much better idea of what the job entailed.

'Rangers is a big club with a lot more outside activity than most others – the media attention is massive, for example. But the hardest part of the job here is just the same at any other club – winning games.'

That's true, but the settled background at the club has also been to Smith's advantage. He came into a system already running on effective lines thanks to the commitment of the chairman, and the set-up has remained more or less the same since. Not having to cope with the political upheavals of, say, Celtic, has been a major advantage for the manager of Rangers.

Since taking over from Souness Smith has maintained Rangers' grip on Scottish football. The team has won the Premier Division every year. He is the only manager in the business who doesn't know what it's like to be beaten. Yet even here the football industry hasn't exactly created a Garden of Eden. The flipside of life as boss at Ibrox is that you tend not to be judged by achievements at home, but by achievements in Europe. Because Rangers are always in Europe, and since 1989 always in the European Champions Cup, their peers are not Motherwell and Aberdeen but Milan and Ajax.

'Yes,' admits Smith, 'it is an extra curse we have to bear, constantly being judged on European results. Competing against the Continental teams has not been quite as easy as people think, especially when we had the three-foreigner rule. The preparation of the team is different and over the last few seasons injuries have been a major contributory factor to our not doing as well as people expected. But a few years ago we were the most successful British team in the European Cup, going ten games without defeat and nearly reaching the Final, so we have had our successes.'

Bruce Rioch began at Torquay United in the Fourth Division and nearly failed to make it anywhere else.

Rioch stepped up after a year working as player-coach under Frank O'Farrell. As a player he was an upright, hard-tackling, hard-shooting midfielder whom put the bite into the midfields of Luton, Villa, Derby, Everton, and Scotland, whom he skippered in the 1978 World Cup Finals. As a manager he was hard-tackling too. In his own words: 'I was very intense, lacked tolerance, and saw everything as black or white. I had come from an environment which included Roy McFarland, Colin Todd, Charlie George and Francis Lee, and found myself working with players who had the same desire but less talent. I ran into arguments and created storms which weren't necessary.'

Fourth Division football has a way of ushering star footballers into management, much the same as Gordonstoun School welcomes princes to education. Torquay was the typical tough test, with menial tasks waiting to be done by the dozen. Rioch and his assistant Alan Slough swept the dressing rooms, cleaned the bathrooms, acted as physiotherapists, and even copped the blame when too few turnstiles were opened for a youth match.

For someone who demanded a lot but was never going to get it at Plainmoor, it was a relationship laced with frustration. By season 1983–84 Slough had left and Rioch was doing everything. One night at an away game against Tranmere he was standing on the touchline when the former Manchester City boss Joe Mercer called out to him: 'Bruce, come and sit up here in the stand – you get a much better view.' Rioch picked up the bucket and sponge and shouted back: 'I can't run on to treat the players from there!'

Not long after that there was a skirmish during a training session and Rioch landed a punch on one of his own players. It accelerated his downfall at Torquay – he resigned in January '84. 'I regret that deeply. It had all built up through the very frustrating situation I was in, but I am the first to admit I was wrong, totally wrong.'

In a way, it might have been the making of him. He had to endure a two-year exile from English football, taking a job in insurance, then joining the Seattle Sounders in the USA as coach. It was a much more mature manager who returned to Middlesbrough in 1986, possessed now of the boss's most priceless asset – experience – and astute enough to benefit from it.

Not every manager makes it through the uncharted territory of his first posting. Peter Reid sums up what it is like going in at the deep end: 'Management courses are fine. But when you actually do the job you come across more problems than anyone theorizing about it could possibly make up.'

Howard Wilkinson has a response to that: 'A course would

make a number of basic statements at the start. One would be: "You are going into a profession that always expects more than you can give."'

4

CRISIS

On matchdays they were routed through the players' entrance; any other day in the final years of Stoke City's 119-year occupation of the Victoria Ground – the club were, at the time of writing, due to move to a new stadium in late 1997 – the footballers would enter via the main reception area. Glass doors opened off a narrow street which had changed but little since the club's most famous son, Stanley Matthews, was in his prime. A bust of Sir Stanley, with the title 'The Wizard of Dribble' watched the professionals of the modern age as they passed through the inner doors leading to the dressing rooms.

Exactly what the world's most famous winger – a teetotal fitness fanatic – makes of the nineties crop is something his likeness isn't giving away, but the man now charged with getting the best out of Stoke City's footballers is more forthcoming. Lou Macari, an eager midfielder-cum-striker with Celtic and Manchester United, is now in his second stint as Stoke's manager. It's his sixth managerial appointment since starting out at Swindon in 1984, and there is an unmistakable air of disillusion about him. Not with the club – clearly, Macari has an affectionate regard for Stoke, who hired him when he resigned from Birmingham City and who welcomed him back after a brief, controversial and disappointing return to Parkhead as manager of Celtic. No, the manager is becoming impatient at what he sees as a lack of dedication on the part of today's professional footballers. The time has come, Macari has decided, to speak out on the evil which he believes is seriously harming the game – drink.

'One of the biggest problems any manager faces now is a

disciplinary problem connected to drink. Whenever I get reports of some problem involving players, the first thing I say is, "Where did they get the drink?"'

Macari isn't alone. Other managers are increasingly angry at the tendency of their players to attack the bottle. Macari, however, is scathing.

'The biggest problem in football is alcohol,' he says, and repeats the words as if he can hardly believe it. 'We went to Sunderland last season. Played all right. Needed the points. A long way to go but somewhere between 500 and 1000 Stoke supporters travelled. They stood in the corner amongst all the Sunderland supporters, cheering us on for 90 minutes. In the 88th minute we lost a goal from a free kick which we were stupid to concede and even more stupid to allow them to score. But 15 minutes out of Sunderland, as we headed back down the motorway on the bus, the players are laughing and joking, while me and the staff are sitting there wondering what to do next, tearing our hair out. All right, people will ask why shouldn't players have a laugh after a football match, but I can't remember Manchester United players joking on the team coach when we had lost a match and disappointed the Manchester United supporters. United might have had 10,000 fans at an away game but I don't see it as being any different. I don't think the 500 or 1000 who followed us to Sunderland were sitting on their bus laughing and joking on the way home.

'We get back to Stoke and you find that on the way back the players have had a few drinks, which you don't realize at the time. So where are we going? There is nothing right about that. We have had another day in which nothing has happened that is right. We've been involved in a football match and we've lost it. Fair enough, everyone loses, but nobody else seems to bother. There have been so many incidents off the field with footballers getting involved with assaults, even stealing a bus, and everything you hear seems to have drink surrounding it.

'The time has come when people have to acknowledge that drink is a bigger problem than the drugs issue. There's a campaign to stop use of drugs in football, but the chances of many people in this sport being involved with drugs are slim. There are not that many, no matter what they might want to write in the newspapers.

'I have never been a drinker so it's easy for me to talk, and I know that in my playing days there were players who enjoyed their drink. But in those days I saw the downfall of great players. Maybe "downfall" is too strong, but their careers could certainly have been better, and longer. The difference is that these were naturally great players. When I read people like Peter Osgood and Alan Hudson saying that drink didn't do them any harm, they forget that they had, in the eyes of nearly every football supporter, a talent that very few players have got nowadays. And people like Alan Hudson were not even the very top names in their day. Now, with their ability, they would be the main men. The modern-day player hasn't got that natural talent like George Best to cope with being out all night, and come in next morning and allow his magic feet to perform. These days, especially at the level I'm at, their feet aren't magic.

'It is becoming harder than ever for a manager to exert proper discipline, and if you can't be the boss the way you should be, then it isn't good for the game.

'This year, I had something outrageous happen here that was a sackable offence. In the eyes of anyone with a scrap of decency about them, it was sackable. But the Professional Footballers' Association didn't see it that way. They said it was just a prank. I won't say what the incident was, except that in any profession it would be a sackable offence.'

The offender was not sacked. Football's business structure means that if Stoke had fired him, the biggest losers, by a disproportionate margin, would have been the club itself. The player, who might have cost the club half a million pounds, would be able to join another club on a free transfer. The new club would be so pleased at picking up a signing on the cheap that they would award him a better salary. Only Stoke would be the losers. The same quandary is confronting managers throughout the country, hamstrung by the ruling agreed between the Leagues and the PFA that the maximum punishment for disciplinary offences is a fine totalling two weeks' wages.

What makes Macari even more steamed up is that he cannot stomach defeat, and therefore can't understand why anyone else can shrug it off. 'I only worry about one thing in football, and I worry too much about it – the result on Saturday. When I was a player, Saturday was my whole life, and if we lost there was no Saturday night out.

'Of course, that's changed for most footballers today – defeat doesn't really matter. My wife, in all the time I have been in football either as a player or a manager, has never even suggested that we might go somewhere on a Saturday night. She knows that there is not a cat in hell's chance of us getting there if the team has lost on Saturday afternoon.

'It is crazy, I know. I go home sometimes and think, I am off my head. Why am I like this when no one else cares? If we lose I sit in the house, tear my hair out, watch *Match of the Day*, go to bed, don't want to get up Sunday morning, read the papers, sit in the house all day, and wait for Monday morning to come.

'I wonder how some managers can look as if they haven't a care in the world. I'm trying to change, and the way the game is going it's helping me because when you see that everyone else is only motivated by money you wonder what you are doing, busting a gut, running up and down motorways, sometimes watching three games a day. You see the game changing – in my opinion deteriorating – every year, so why am I sat at home worrying about Saturday's result when everyone else is out partying?'

The Wales manager Bobby Gould is pleased that, being out of club management, he doesn't have to cope with the problem. 'I became less tolerant with the players. The professionals *are* the game, and they have to realize they can't go out drinking as much as they do. Modern-day players aren't fit to tie the shoelaces of players of my era. We played for £20 or £33 a week, and we played because we loved it. Now, players are different. If they're on £15,000 a week they have to accept responsibility. In the end, I didn't want to take teams away on tour because I expected to have problems – and the media were always out there waiting for trouble.'

Lou Macari also sees the alcohol problem as symptomatic of a general decline. Players in the nineties, he believes, lack the dedication of their predecessors. 'The game is changing and everyone is thinking about only one thing – cash. It's unfortunate for the supporters because they are becoming disillusioned. It's all about money. Years ago when we wanted to play at the highest level or play for a certain club, that is what motivated us. That has all gone. Players will go anywhere now for a bigger salary – even to a lower level of football.

'Not even Manchester United can keep their best players. I used to think I would love to be manager of Manchester United. But the game is so different, I would have no desire to do the job now. The final straw for anybody who likes their football is that you look at Old Trafford and you see the place is wonderful, the stadium is fantastic, everything is getting better, but still that is not enough to keep a player like Paul Ince. If that is a sign of the times, it shows you what counts.

'I will encourage a player to move on from here if it's a footballing move – one that's good for his career. Like Mark Stein who came here from Oxford Reserves and got the opportunity to move to Chelsea. But the days have gone when people would move because they always wanted to play for Manchester United or Arsenal. If we are now in an environment where players are not knocking the door down to play for Manchester United it's a bit disheartening.'

Alex Ferguson was awarded the CBE in the New Year Honours for 1995. The day he went to Buckingham Palace to collect it, resplendent in tartan kilt, was the day one of his players, Eric Cantona, was sentenced to two weeks' imprisonment.

Alex Ferguson took his team to Wembley for the FA Cup Final. Four days later he appeared in the witness box in Number One Court at Croydon Magistrates to give evidence on behalf of another of his players, Paul Ince. Such is the scope of a football manager's responsibility.

Managers of famous clubs, with profiles higher than the grandstand roof, have learned some hard lessons since the power-crazed nineties spawned a new style of football club. No Premiership team is content to remain a small-town outfit. The emphasis is on the wide horizons. To stay at the top, clubs must maximize their income. That means promoting themselves as never before. Manchester United's merchandise operation alone turned over more than £14 million in 1994.

But having courted wider attention, the club reaped a punitive backlash when the very star who had inspired them to the heights self-destructed. Eric Cantona, the extra ingredient that was crucial to the team's Premiership Championship in 1993 and League and Cup Double in '94, succumbed to the red mist when abused by a fan at Crystal Palace, launched a kung-fu style attack, and found himself banned from all football for the next eight months and staring a custodial sentence in the face. The two-week term was reduced on appeal to 120 hours' community service.

Ince, joining in a mêlée that mushroomed around the area of conflict, spent two days in court defending claims that he had punched another supporter. He was cleared. Public interest in both cases was massive – inevitably, given the trouble United and their sponsors had taken to inflate the players' status.

Alex Ferguson, a football man whose life experience hardly equipped him to handle the consequences of all that, was required to pick up the pieces. Interestingly, his advice to the board was that Cantona should be sold. The directors overruled the manager and Cantona emerged from an eight-month ban imposed by the Football Association to inspire United to their second Double. The next season he was made captain.

A happy ending, but it was a salutary lesson. In football a crisis used to consist of having two internationals on the injured list. Now it's two internationals on a charge sheet.

The team's results continued to be good despite Cantona's ban in the latter part of the 1994–95 season, but the dressing room was not the same. Three top players were dissatisfied – Ince, Mark Hughes and Andrei Kanchelskis. At the end of the season United finished second in both the Premiership and the FA Cup – a blank season. Ferguson blamed the lack of trophies on the Cantona incident, with all its ramifications. And the consequences continued to haunt him. Mark Hughes left. Hughes had ended a lengthy wrangle over a new contract by accepting a two-year deal in February. He did not, however, sign the contract. At the end of the season his old contract expired and, as a free agent, he signed for Chelsea. Ferguson was taken by surprise. Like all United's supporters, he thought Hughes was safely tied to a new contract at Old Trafford. Only when it was too late did he discover the contract had never been signed.

Could that have happened in the old days, when life was simple and managers took sole charge of contract negotiations? Definitely not. Would it have happened if there hadn't been so much else for the manager to worry about? Probably not. At the same time Ince and Kanchelskis moved on too. In normal circumstances these defections from a club like Manchester United would have been unthinkable. But 1995 was no normal year. It was a year which, in its opening month, produced an unprecedented crisis that taxed the manager and the rest of the hierarchy to the extreme, and left all involved in a weaker condition.

In November 1994 the *Sun* newspaper printed allegations that the Southampton and ex-Liverpool goalkeeper Bruce Grobbelaar had taken a bribe to throw a match while with Liverpool, and had discussed doing the same at a future match with Southampton. For the Southampton management team of Alan Ball and Lawrie McMenemy the accusations had a huge impact. Instead of concentrating on the upcoming home game against Arsenal, they found themselves at the centre of an international media circus. Though Grobbelaar denied the charges the story spiralled into the hottest item of sports news for years, stretching tentacles as far as Africa, where an undaunted Grobbelaar played for Zimbabwe days after the story broke, and later to Asia, as speculation rose that a betting syndicate there was behind the alleged scam.

McMenemy, former manager of Doncaster Rovers, Grimsby, Southampton and Sunderland, has the title of director of football at the Dell, where he is also a member of the board. It was a natural decision for him to become the public face of Southampton FC for as long as the crisis lasted, leaving Ball, the team manager, to continue working with the team. It was impossible to carry on as if nothing had happened, but McMenemy's presence at least spared Ball many of the distractions he would have had otherwise.

'The news broke in the middle of the night,' recalls McMenemy. 'The *Sun* had kept the story out of their first edition to avoid alerting their rivals. I got a call from Bruce to tell me what was up. There had been rumours that a goalkeeper was going to be named but we didn't know who. I got what sleep I could and woke to find the press in my driveway. It wasn't the first time I'd experienced something like it – we had an incident in Sweden when some players were accused of rape a few years before. These days the media is a 24-hour phenomenon. I had the local radio stations ringing up – everyone wanting the same words. In between I had to speak to the chairman and try to come up with some sort of campaign. To us, it wasn't hard to decide that we regarded Bruce as innocent until proved guilty. It was obvious that I would be the one to handle the press, and I had to talk to them rather than hide away. But I had to get them away from the house so I told them there would be a statement at the ground.

'Then we heard that there were more pressmen and photographers at the training ground so we had to organize security there.

'We got through the first few days. Then Bruce came back from Zimbabwe and it was like the Keystone Cops with the media chasing around all over the place. These days it has become even more necessary for them to get that one picture or that one story. If it's a worldwide story you realize how much it can mean to them. I needed eyes in the back of my head. There were photographers up trees with long lenses pointing at the training ground. We had to call in the police. That was ironic – the police wanted our goalkeeper for questioning and we wanted the police to look after our goalkeeper!

'It would have been very difficult for Alan to have coped with all that as well as preparing the team for matches. When we had the rape allegations I was having to take training as well as deal with everything else.

'Some managers have the capacity to take a lot on board. Questions crop up day by day and you learn which mental pigeon hole to put them in, and which has the highest priority to be dealt with first.'

Southampton's answer to the crisis worked well. The club was portrayed as a loyal employer, defending the character of their employee with common sense and firmness, clearly concerned but reminding all and sundry that the allegations were far from proven. The playing department was able to get on with its job, distracted but not diverted completely from the game in hand. When play resumed, the team ran out 1–0 winners against Arsenal. Under the circumstances it was one of the best results by any team in the Premiership all season.

Most observers saw the whole of Brian Horton's 20-month tenure as manager of Manchester City as a crisis at some stage of the fermentation process. It was either brewing up or creating a hangover, as the action on the pitch was overshadowed by boardroom politics. But for Horton, the whole experience was put in perspective by his experiences before he even arrived at Maine Road.

Horton is now in charge of Huddersfield Town, taking over at the smart McAlpine Stadium on the heels of Town's success in winning promotion from Division Two under Neil Warnock. Warnock, for his own reasons, resigned and Horton moved in less than a month after being given his cards by City.

Even when he's relaxing behind his desk, Brian Horton appears to be on the alert. Fit, lean, with eyes that you would like to have on your side if you're on patrol in sniper country, he has come through some tough times with dignity intact.

Horton began his managerial career at Hull City, trading on his natural enthusiasm and an appetite for work. As a player he was active in the PFA, attending meetings as the union delegate on behalf of his colleagues. He went on coaching and management courses, and when he accepted the vacancy at Hull he made such an impression that the chairman Don Robinson made him a director. In this capacity Horton made decisions on financial and administrative matters as well as supervising the players. It was, of course, the results in the latter category that mattered most and when they took a turn for the worse Horton, director or not, was out in time-honoured style.

The next stop was Oxford United where his exposure to football's volatile brand of crisis-management was given its sternest test. It was the Oxford of the Maxwells. With Robert in charge at Derby, son Kevin was chairman at the Manor Ground. As at Hull, Horton was given scope to run things as he saw fit within certain budget limits, and life was ticking over reasonably well until November 5, 1991 – the day Robert Maxwell was found dead in the sea off Tenerife.

'People ask me about being sacked by Hull and Manchester City, but the most traumatic time I have had in football was at Oxford when the Maxwell empire collapsed. I was driving to a game with my assistant David Moss when we heard on the radio that Mr Maxwell was dead. Then we got a call from the club secretary to confirm it. Almost from that moment all the bank facilities stopped. Everything went. The cars we were driving round in had to go back because they were all part of the Maxwell deal. I had to sell my players in order to pay the wages – not just the remaining players' wages but the office staff too. Literally, the whole thing stopped. So it was my job to keep the club going. It was tough because people's livelihoods and careers were at stake. But fortunately I had made some good signings and we could sell them. If we had had no saleable assets in the squad the club would have gone out of business. Because of the situation Kevin Maxwell had to resign as chairman and the administrators took over until a new company was set up. So what with that and a relegation battle as well, it was difficult.'

With huge public interest in a high-profile story it was impossible for Horton to handle the affair the way most managers would want to: i.e. keep everything as quiet as possible and leave the players to concentrate on football.

'I have always tried to keep players away from any politics. It's their job to play football. OK, they do worry, and at Oxford they were right to worry because they didn't know if they were going to get paid or not. But usually I would try to keep anything like that away from them.'

With that experience under his belt, perhaps Brian Horton wasn't such a surprise choice for the Manchester City job as the fans thought! It was another crisis, though of a very different nature.

'I had been told what to expect. They hadn't won a game in the first four so a relegation battle was on already, and there was friction at boardroom level.'

Horton was ushered in on the August night when the fans vented their fury at the Peter Swales regime by assaulting the directors' entrance at Maine Road and forcing the mounted division of Greater Manchester police to give their horses a genuine crowd control opportunity. His appointment, far from lancing the boil of disaffection made it fester, as the fans identified John Maddock, the man instrumental in hiring Horton, as Swales' hitman. They believed that the arrival of Maddock as general manager made it more rather than less likely that Swales would hold on to power. Although Horton himself was never a target, the supporters' frustration contributed to a poisonous atmosphere at Maine Road, which in turn made it hard for the new manager to get the best out of his team.

'When things like that happen in football it always has an effect on players. People say it shouldn't make any difference, but it does. They read about it every day. They can't switch on and off – they're human beings.'

The team initially responded well to Horton's arrival. His first game resulted in a 3–1 win at Swindon, then came a convincing home victory over Queens Park Rangers. There were signs of progress, but against a constant backdrop of demonstrations in the stands and outside the ground, the crisis off the field quickly transferred itself on to the field. 'While all the demonstrations were going on – people shouting for Peter Swales to go, people shouting for Francis Lee to take over – the players were frightened of making mistakes. So we found ourselves in relegation trouble.'

At City's AGM in October Swales was voted out on a show of hands – but re-elected by the bloc votes of himself and his allies on the board. By this time it wasn't just the team manager who was feeling the strain – the general manager was in stormy waters too.

John Maddock, the man who sacked Peter Reid in his first week, is a pugilistic character who says what he thinks and attacks problems at their roots. A friend of the beleaguered Peter Swales, he aimed to transform the mood of the club in the hope that better results on the pitch would relieve the pressure and enable Swales – who, after all, held the majority of the shares and could not be outvoted – to see off the threat from Lee. Maddock thus became a target himself.

'I was abused and spat upon. My daughter was abused when she went out. I received all kinds of hate mail. I also received sackfuls of junk mail – things I hadn't ordered from mail-order companies. I got everything from porcelain plates to a lorryload of concrete, which was delivered to my house.

'I was physically threatened, away from the ground, and by people who had nothing to do with Manchester City. There were times when I wondered if it was worth it.

'People use football for their own emotional outlet. When they go into a crowd it's amazing what they will do once they are incited. We knew a company executive on something like £60,000 a year who joined the rest of them chanting "Swales Out". This was a man we knew and we challenged him about it. He denied it. So we showed him the security video and there he was. He explained that he had gone to the pub with his mates and had six pints, and this was his sport. But he was enticing other people to follow him – and I was his victim.'

In November Swales resigned. The following month, with the Lee consortium ready to move in, Maddock went too. Would he get involved with a football club again? 'Without a doubt. So long as the owner is prepared to give me the authority to do what I see fit. I like to think I could run a successful club. There is pressure and it is created by the phenomenal money. At Manchester City I went in knowingly, aware of the problems. It was as if we were 4–0 down with 15 minutes to go. We got back to 4–3 and lost to a last-minute penalty. But it was a tremendous time – I wouldn't have missed it for the world. I learned a lot – not about the game, but about people. How they react under pressure, and how a football club is a hotbed of jealousy.

'I probably went about things the wrong way, but the situation was such there wasn't time for anything else.'

Before going hands-on at City, Maddock was a football writer and an agent working on the commercial side of the game. Since leaving, he has resumed his commercial activities, but his four months as general manager of Manchester City were an eye-opener even to a seasoned watcher of the game. 'When I was in newspapers people told me you could count your friends on one hand,' he says grimly. 'When you're in football, you can chop two of your fingers off and what's left is the number of friends you can count on.'

The departure of Swales and Maddock left Brian Horton up the Eiger without an icepick. Francis Lee duly took over, amid speculation that he would install his own man in the manager's chair at the first opportunity.

'I tried to concentrate totally on the football,' says Horton. 'I've been a director of a football club and I've seen what it brings. I made my mind up to stay out of the politics and I think that will be the way I am for ever and a day now. I've always been quite a calm person. Pressure is what you make it. I was under pressure at Manchester City and in some ways I feel like a ton weight has been lifted now that I'm not there – but at the same time I miss it. I thrive on it.'

In an era when the cult of the high-profile manager has reached new proportions, Brian Horton had to co-exist with two high-profile chairmen. Lee formally took over on the day City entertained Ipswich, arriving in the directors' box to the sort of adulation the players might have expected had they won the Premiership. 'When Francis came in, it was always going to be a grand entry, and it gave us all a lift. The chanting against Peter Swales stopped, and things were on the up. We started building a new stand, but that meant in turn I didn't have money to spend on players. I understood that and sold a couple of players to help the club through that year. The economic realities apply just as much in the Premier League as lower down. Although at the end of the day it doesn't always benefit the manager to do that.'

Brian Horton was eventually dismissed in May 1995 after another flirtation with relegation. It was one of the least surprising developments that he found a replacement job more quickly than City found a replacement manager.

The politics of football are a convoluted creation, the more so since football clubs became desirable commodities to be traded like pork belly futures, or acquired like yachts in Mediterranean anchorages. The collision of old traditions, new money, demanding supporters and anxious players makes for an unstable cocktail of explosive elements, with one man doing his darndest to prevent the whole canister of grapeshot self-destructing: the manager.

It was into an environment not a million miles removed from

the above scenario that Lou Macari stepped when he took over as Celtic manager in November 1993.

Celtic, desperate to recapture the good times but lacking one useful weapon – money – invited Macari to try where Liam Brady had failed. Everyone Macari consulted advised him not to touch the job, that it was fraught with peril, but the lure of the old green and white hoops was too strong for an ex-Parkhead player.

'I was brought up a Celtic supporter. I used to go and watch them – players like Jimmy Johnstone and Billy McNeill were my heroes. Anyone who was brought up with a club, who went on to have good times with them as a player, and unbelievably was offered the chance to manage them, would take it.

'I knew that the problem I would have was that no one could match what Jock Stein had done for Celtic. His was a record that could never be equalled. I hadn't been back to Scotland since I left to join Manchester United as a player. It was a long time to be away – I wondered how much had changed, if the style of Scottish players had altered. The old board of directors were still in command, but a new consortium was campaigning to get them out.'

It was to be another interesting test for the man who had already come through a personal crisis. Having left Swindon to take over at West Ham in 1989, Macari found himself under assault as allegations surfaced of illegal payments and illicit betting during his time at the County Ground. The FA later dealt heavy punishments to the club and the then chairman Brian Hillier and fined Macari £1000 for what they described as 'a minor part in a foolhardy misdemeanour' – assisting the placing of a bet on Swindon to lose a Cup tie at Newcastle. Macari denied any wrongdoing but with the hue and cry at its height decided to quit the job at West Ham after only seven months. 'The story was making headlines every week for three months. The people at West Ham were magnificent but I told them the club didn't deserve the adverse publicity so I wouldn't stay. I had two and a half years left on my contract but I didn't ask for any money – I just left. Afterwards, I regretted leaving. Perhaps a more experienced manager would have ridden the storm.'

Macari was therefore determined to ride any storm that broke at Celtic. It was probably an even more tricky situation than that faced by Brian Horton at Manchester City. The old regime, personified by vice-chairman David Smith, was trying to find ways of refinancing a club which needed to modernize both its stadium and its team. A rival group headed by Canadian businessman Fergus McCann was trying to gain control. Public opinion was even more virulent than in Manchester, and the players were dragged into the crossfire.

'Players were publicly voicing criticism of the directors,' recalls Macari. 'People probably thought it was a genuine feeling. But what does a footballer know about boards of directors? Nothing. It was all being orchestrated by the people who were trying to come in. Matches were being boycotted by supporters. I had never known anything like it: it was bizarre. At board meetings I used to ask what they planned to do about it. "Oh, we don't think the players mean it," they would say.

'I was on television passing my opinions about the board who had hired me. So far as I was concerned they were all right. They had no money but that wasn't their fault, and I had doubts about whether the people wanting to come in had any money either. Of course, the new people seeing this would not want me as part of their plans if what I was saying was anywhere near the truth. But the big problem they had was that I and my staff were on three-year contracts and it would cost them a lot of money to get rid of us.'

Macari arrived at Parkhead in October 1993. Five months later the McCann takeover was complete, and an uneasy spell followed as the new owners and surviving manager rubbed one another up the wrong way. McCann accused Macari of refusing to move house from Stoke to Glasgow; Macari denied the charge and on one occasion his wife Dale angrily stormed into McCann's office to prove that the children's school had been given notice they would be leaving. None of it was conducive to producing the turnaround desired in the club's fortunes, culminating in Macari being fired over the telephone as he prepared to fly to America with his family for a summer break.

This time, he had handled a crisis differently. It was the directors who ended the relationship, leaving Macari to make the choice whether or not to lodge a claim for breach of contract.

* * *

Brian Horton and Lou Macari had no choice but to cope with the crises at Oxford, Manchester and Glasgow in the glare of publicity. Most football clubs, however, go out of their way to avoid attention when the going gets tricky. Doors which open invitingly when they desire publicity for new sponsorship contracts or transfer deals suddenly become watertight bulkheads.

So that made Alan Smith's handling of the Chris Armstrong case particularly intriguing. Armstrong was a notable absentee from the Crystal Palace line-up to play Watford in an FA Cup replay in March 1995. It turned out that the striker had tested positive for cannabis but while most clubs would have sheltered behind the excuse that Armstrong had some run-of-the-mill ailment, Smith declared that he was out 'on the advice of the club surgeon' and that his absence was 'an ethical matter'. With prompting like that, it didn't take long for the truth to emerge, duly confirmed by Smith.

Smith ignored pressure from the Palace board to keep things quiet. 'I asked if I was supposed to lie to people I knew well, like the TV commentators Brian Moore and Martin Tyler, who would both want to know why Armstrong wasn't playing. Was I to pretend he had a groin strain, or that he had been dropped from one of the most important games of the season? I felt it was right to speak about it, especially as the initial speculation was getting out of hand. The tabloids were suggesting he was on hard drugs and that women were involved. I found that honesty was the best policy.

'There are various kinds of reporter, but most of them are intelligent and those who aren't are streetwise, so I didn't try to cover it up. On top of that, the supporters had the right to know. They needed an explanation. Chris Armstrong had let them down.'

More typical was the response of Peter Reid when two of his Manchester City players were featured on the front page of a tabloid after a fracas involving a woman. 'I tried to dampen everything down. Once the initial 24 hours have gone you can put the lid on it. People asked for my comments but I said it was a private matter; the lads weren't on football duty at the time. Incidents happen at all clubs but don't get into the papers.'

Except for the times when the manager decides a cold shower of headlines might do more good than harm. Tommy Docherty shocked the football world in the sixties when he sent no fewer than eight members of the Chelsea squad home from their base in Blackpool for going out on the town. 'It wasn't a one-off incident – that was the sixth time they had broken the rules,' he remembers. 'The ringleaders were George Graham and Terry Venables. We fined them and sent them home. Afterwards the attitude of one or two of them changed towards me. They thought I should have handled it in a different way. But how many warnings do you get? Of course, now that they've become managers themselves it's a different ball game!

'Everything goes full circle. I used to catch players in the nightclub and they would say, "How did you know we were here?" I would reply, "Because I did exactly the same thing when I was a player." I met Lou Macari last season at Stoke. He told me the players were driving him mad. I said, "You used to drive me mad!" He did – he was a pest. A good player, but a pest.'

Docherty agrees that it's harder for today's managers to exercise discipline. The financial rewards are so high that fines scarcely bite. But he believes that suspending players from the team is a punishment that hurts. 'Players do not like missing games. They don't miss a few pounds, but they do miss it if they don't play. You've got to be seen to be a sensible disciplinarian today. Yes, there are fewer talented players about and you don't want to alienate them, but the club is always bigger than any player. As a player you never beat the Establishment.'

You know it's a crisis when the receivers put chains around the gates and lock the players out of the ground. You know it's a crisis when the phone rings when you are on holiday and someone tells you your salary has been stopped. You know it's a crisis when the coach and physio leave for pastures new and it's you against the world. It was that kind of crisis at Ayresome Park.

The manager was Bruce Rioch, a matter of weeks into the job. It was his second managerial post, and after his two-year absence from English football following the volatile end to his connection with Torquay, he needed to make a success of it.

Rioch had joined Boro as first team coach in January 1986. The next month the manager, Willie Maddren, was dismissed and Rioch took over as caretaker. 'At the end of the season there was a board meeting. I was there, and in came one of the directors, Steve Gibson, who is now the chairman, accompanied by some financial experts. He said, "We are going into provisional liquidation." That was the first I knew of the extent of the problems. The debts were estimated at a million pounds. When they sat down and worked things out the figure rose to 1.6 million, then 1.8, then 2.2. Who knows where it ended?

'The season was over and we were asked to carry on as normal. But no one knew what the outcome would be.

'I had a holiday arranged in Majorca, and the day I was leaving I got a call from Danny Bergara, my coach, saying that he had the opportunity to go to another club, and because of the doubts at Middlesbrough he would have to go. The physio, Steve Smelt, was approached by Sunderland, and again, because of the uncertainty over his position, he felt he had to go too. Obviously, I understood that. And there was Colin Todd, who I had brought in as youth team coach. Colin and the chief scout were the only members of staff that stayed. Colin didn't want to go back to his previous job, as a rep for Vaux Brewery – he thought he was better off staying put.

'I went on holiday, and all the time telephone calls were going back and forth with the three of us not knowing if the club was going under or whether we would still have jobs come the end of the summer.'

There was no escape from the uncertainty, even in Majorca. One day Rioch was halfway through a glass of beer when he was summoned to take yet another phone call. This time it was from a representative of the firm of administrators which was attempting to save the club. 'I am afraid we are going to have to cut costs,' said the voice. 'And you have two options. One is that we terminate your salary and you leave and find another club. The other is that we terminate your salary and you stay on.'

Rioch chose the latter, made the most of what was left of his holiday, and went back to live with the nightmare, unpaid. Ayresome Park was a dismal spectacle – mothballed by the administrators with chains across the gates. No one could get in, but the problems struck even deeper. The club's YTS trainees were without pay, the rent for their digs wasn't being paid. The kitman's wages had been stopped. There was no cash to run the club's cars. The manager realized that unless the rot was stopped quickly there would be nothing left for the administrators to save. So he paid the rent, the wages and the car repairs himself.

'I would think it cost me around £2000 during that period, just to keep the people we needed on the staff. It wasn't a hardship, and I did get it back from the club eventually, when a new company took over.

'Until that happened I told the players – who were mostly Middlesbrough boys – to concentrate on one thing: preparing for the start of the season. Regardless of what the newspapers or the radio might be saying, I told them that unless they heard it from me they should assume we were kicking off the season as normal. Of course there was all sorts of speculation in the media about the club folding, but it didn't, and in August a new board took over and as we all know the club has made good progress since.'

The new owners nevertheless had a surprise up their sleeve for Rioch when the reward for his loyalty was a paltry three-month contract. 'I turned it down. After all I had put in I wasn't prepared to stay on a three-month basis so they could assess me. Eventually I got a three-year contract. But they were great days, brilliant, and I had some great people around me plus some good players.'

With the crisis over, Rioch and a team built on emerging youngsters like Gary Pallister and Tony Mowbray prospered. Boro immediately won promotion from the Third Division and went straight through the Second to reach the First Division, in the days when the First represented the élite. But they couldn't consolidate, and when relegation entrapped them on the last day of the season, Rioch was on his way out. Not even two promotions and heroic efforts in the face of acute financial distress could stave off the inevitable.

'We know that it is part and parcel of the game. It's not necessarily the case in other walks of life, but football is an occupation whereby the results are paramount to the people who come through the turnstiles. If you have an unsuccessful team, fewer people come to the matches, you have fewer sponsors and less money is generated. The simple equation is that you can change three things at a football club – the directors, the players, or the manager. The latter is the easiest.

'Sometimes people find the circumstances irrelevant. When we came down on the last day of the season it was with a young side which had been hit by injuries after the transfer deadline, so they couldn't be replaced. But whether you like it or not – and generally you don't like it – you have to respect the fact that directors must make decisions. When they make their decision to part company, a lot depends on how they go about it. If they go about it in a manner which is proper and honourable then you can't have too many complaints, and Middlesbrough did it that way. Colin Henderson, who was the chairman at the time, broke the news to me and within half an hour he had resolved the remainder of my contract. I had the cheque in my hand. That speaks volumes for him and the people at the club. But in many cases that doesn't happen and the whole relationship degenerates into bitterness and arguments in court.'

5

TELL HIM ON A FRIDAY

How do you know when it's the right time to give a young player his debut? How much time should you spend with the press? How do you sort out a bad atmosphere in the dressing room? These are all questions which weigh on the mind of the boss. At the end of the season it will be only the broad picture that counts – did you avoid relegation, did you win at Wembley? But in between, day in, day out, the small detail is what taxes the mind most.

Winning, naturally, is the detail that matters most. But what kind of winning? Roy Evans inherited a Liverpool set-up desperate for success but scotches any impression that it might be success at any price. 'Winning has always been the most important thing but I like to win with a bit of style. If you play good football over the length of a season you'll win more than you lose. But it's still important to have a steely approach as well.'

It's a short trip from Liverpool to Crewe by rail, but a lot further in football terms. Nevertheless, the attitude towards winning is the same at Gresty Road. The club's manager is Dario Gradi. 'Winning is the most enjoyable part of the job – and the fact that we play nice football. I wouldn't get a buzz if we played nice football and lost, or if we played bad football and won.' But realism is seldom far away. Phil Neal, who has been dismissed by Bolton and Coventry: 'There's only one winner of the Premier League, one winner of the FA Cup. You can set up the best school of excellence in the history of the game, but you still have to win on Saturday. No one wants to know about anything else.' Sentiments echoed by Bruce Rioch: 'The most important thing I want to do is win. I want to do so with a bit of style and a bit of class, but you have got to win.'

And keep winning. Alex Ferguson has won three Scottish Championships and two English Championships, plus domestic cups and the European Cup Winners Cup with both Aberdeen and Manchester United. 'Even in the good times you have to make sure people are still hungry, because, believe you me, you don't win anything if you're not hungry. If you don't have the desire to do it, you will never win anything.'

Jimmy Armfield, who had his successes as manager of Bolton and Leeds and who was instrumental in the choice of Terry Venables as England supremo: 'If your team plays unattractively but wins, there will be a large percentage of people who will go along with you. Only a small percentage will say, "I'm not watching that rubbish." If you keep winning, keep getting the headlines and stay in a prominent position, the manager will be looked upon as a success.'

For Alan Curbishley, manager of Charlton Athletic, winning is part of the magic of football. 'During the week you're out in the fresh air working with the players, doing something you love. You are fit, and you stay fit. When you win on the Saturday it gives you a great feeling which carries you through the evening and all day Sunday. Then you start looking forward to the next game.'

Sheffield Wednesday's David Pleat: 'Winning a football match is a high that you can't experience in any other walk of life. The moment the whistle goes to tell you you've won a game is a marvellous feeling of achievement.'

PLAYERS

Sometimes, to the team manager, the players are a necessary evil. Like teachers who ponder the bliss of a school without pupils, there must be times when the manager reflects on the progress he could make without the players creating complications!

There is a romantic notion that all players pull together for the boss, and that a new manager can automatically rally the troops around him. Not so. Lou Macari has sampled life at Swindon, West Ham, Birmingham, Stoke, Celtic and Stoke again and vividly remembers the dressing-room welcome at West Ham. 'The problem was that there were older players there. If they are on their way out and they think you are the one who is going to move them on, they are not going to make your life all that comfortable. Your opinion is not going to be wonderful about all the players you inherit. There must be at least three or four who are not your type or who have had their day. A player doesn't want to accept that, and if he can hang on at your expense he will attempt to do so.'

Bruce Rioch went through something similar at Millwall. 'Players complained that I made changes too quickly, but the complaints were coming from those players of an age and type which meant they weren't going to be part of it. Their noses were put out of joint and, naturally, they weren't happy. It's hard to keep a contented dressing room in that situation.'

'There isn't as much loyalty as there used to be,' says Alan Curbishley, 'and I think that is a problem. In my playing days if you were left out of the team you tried your best to get your place back. Now players won't accept being left in the doldrums. If they don't get back in the team, they want to get away from the club.'

Bobby Gould and his coach Don Howe went into their first meeting with the Wimbledon players ready to show who was boss and got a surprise. 'We were expecting to lay the law down, but it was the players who did that. The likes of Lawrie Sanchez, Alan Cork and Dave Beasant ruled the roost there.' Many managers are concerned at the increasing influence of players. Peter Reid: 'Players have a lot of power. It's changed since my playing days. Agents have come in and the players earn a lot more.'

One of the guiding principles of Ian Branfoot's managerial faith is to sort out discontent in the playing squad quickly. 'If you've got any bad ones, exit them as rapidly as you can. Even if it costs you money. Get them out, because otherwise they will ruin your club. Decision-making is the hardest part of the job. That's why I think being a coach is the best job in the world, because you don't have to make those hard decisions. You don't have to hurt people and take the flak.'

That's where a manager's strength of character is put to the test, and how he survives that, according to Brian Horton, is the making or breaking of him. 'The more so with the massive media coverage of the game, particularly in the Premier League. You also need the ability to handle people. You can't please everyone. Someone is bound to dislike you and write you off as a manager or coach. We've all had that. You don't select certain players and that upsets them. Experience is a big thing today. I know some managers have success in their first year, like Bryan Robson, and as I did at Hull City, but generally, you need experience or an older colleague you can consult when you need to.'

For the most successful manager in Britain, Rangers' Walter Smith, dealing with players is one of the job's plus-factors. 'I have never had any problems. It's part of the job which I enjoy, and I've never been afraid of it. One of the big challenges is handling everyone who comes on board – they're all different and it's rewarding to bring the best out of the people working for you.'

Craig Brown, the Scotland manager, had added reason to feel a glow after his team defeated Austria in Vienna. 'Two of the players in the squad were Ian Ferguson and Pat Nevin – players who I signed as 17-year-olds with Clyde years ago. To see players like that come all the way through is one of the most rewarding aspects of the job.'

The job is big on decisions. Every teamsheet sparks off countless minor shockwaves through the dressing room. Who is in, who is out, who is in a different position this week. As Alan Smith observes: 'The life of a professional football club is such a small, parochial existence that everyone sees what's going on. Footballers don't miss a trick.' Andy King, when at Mansfield Town: 'I try to use all the good things I've seen in football and reject the bad things. Like telling a player if he's not in the team. Tell him on the Friday – don't leave it till quarter to three on the Saturday. Don't shirk the responsibility. If a player isn't in the team he'll work it out for himself anyway. If he's being used in the defensive wall when we practise free kicks in the Friday training session he'll have a good idea he isn't starting the game on Saturday.'

Even the top managers suffer when the time comes to whittle that impressive squad down to the 11 men who will line up for the kick-off. 'I find it very hard to leave players out when they don't deserve it,' admits Liverpool's Roy Evans. 'But sometimes you have to pick a team which you feel is best for that one match, and that can be hurtful to individuals who are not included. I have to accept that players will be upset, but the only way to handle the situation is to be honest and fair with them.'

Tommy Docherty thinks managers shouldn't worry too much. 'You can't keep them all happy – certainly not the ones who aren't in the team. They might not all be on the same wages, but they all want to be playing.'

Most managers agree that they are at their most contented when they are working with the players on the training ground. Howard Wilkinson sums it up: 'My biggest satisfaction comes from working with players, influencing them, making them better, helping them understand the complexities of the game, creating something better than what was there in the first place, and seeing that player gain his reward. It's knowing that in some small way, it's down to you.'

Paul Ince's transfer from Manchester United to Inter Milan had Lou Macari thinking back to his dealings with Ince at West Ham. Ince was the star man but Macari didn't take to him. 'Ince was desperate to move to United but I didn't like the way he handled the move. He missed a club trip to Norway and I had newsmen flying out to show me photographs of Ince posing in a United strip while he was still a West Ham player. I didn't think the West Ham supporters deserved that and I told him so. I told him that if he did get to United he would have to improve his stamina and his approach to the game or he would be just another player there. But if he improved, he had the talent to become one of the best. His stamina was pathetic at the time, and because he didn't want to train, let everyone down. He improved his stamina, his pace and everything about his game and I was pleased for him. He had listened, pulled up his socks, and made himself one of the best players in the country. So that is the sort of thing that gives you a lift.'

Bryan Robson inherited a stable dressing room when he embarked on his managerial career at Middlesbrough. 'I have to thank my predecessor Lennie Lawrence, because the players I took over were all good professionals. The players here haven't been a problem.'

Lawrence, now in charge at Luton Town after experiencing

promotion and relegation with both Charlton Athletic and Middlesbrough, says it's a question of character. 'You need players who are pleased and proud to be part of the club – not those who think they're doing you a favour.' As to the amount of work put in on the team's technique, Andy King reckons the further down the League you go, the more the manager has to concentrate on the quality of performance. 'Players at higher level don't need so much coaching. If they're being employed by a club like Mansfield it's because of bad habits, their state of mind, or limited ability. Players like David Platt and Roy Keane didn't always have the ability they have now – it comes with quickness of mind and how you are taught.'

A key moment in the career of every professional is the day he finishes his YTS scheme – or apprenticeship, formerly – and is awarded his first full contract. But for every youngster taken on, several more will be discarded. 'That is the worst part of the job,' says Peter Reid. 'Telling young players that they are being released. And changing your coaching staff. In effect, you are sacking them. If you confront it and do it face to face it's the best way, but it is definitely not a nice thing to do.'

Joe Royle has the same agonies at Everton: 'It is my biggest trauma. It's bad enough telling a seasoned player you don't need him any more, but when you tell a youngster that you are effectively denying him a profession, you are breaking his heart as well.'

And every manager has to work out how close he can get to his players when they are off duty. Rochdale's Graham Barrow: 'There are times when we are socializing that they clam up if I am there. So I know I can only go so far with them. It's the right way for it to be, but it hurts as well. Being a manager is second to being a player – there's nothing better than to be a player, 14 or 15 lads in that dressing room having a laugh. I miss that.'

LOSING

If there is one aspect of the game that brings home to a football man the different thinking between a player and a manager it is suffering a defeat. Bryan Robson identifies it succinctly: 'If you lose as a player and you did quite well personally, you tend to say, "Well, it's the manager's fault for not selecting the right team in other positions." As a manager, it's far worse. You selected the team and the tactics so you ask yourself if your decisions were correct. You run through everything in your mind far more.'

Tommy Docherty recognizes the symptoms: 'I would look at it to see if it was my fault – had I picked the wrong team or decided the wrong tactics. I never said anything to the players afterwards – I would wait till the Monday.'

But how often do managers wait till the dust settles before pointing out to the players the error of their ways? Peter Reid: 'There are times when you get stuck into people afterwards. Sometimes it's best to get it out in the open straight away, other times it's best to wait. I look for something positive after a defeat. You have to remember you are never going to win every game. So long as they give 100 per cent.' Andy King: 'I take it personally. We have 10 minutes of brutal honesty after a match. A lot of truth comes out in emotion. You can't kiss and cuddle them when they've done well and not bollock them when they've done wrong.'

Brian Horton of Huddersfield Town: 'By five o'clock it's done with. I might have a blast at the players but after five I don't sulk. I don't call off Saturday night. Come Monday you start again.'

But Saturday night can be a struggle if Saturday afternoon has strayed from the script. Phil Neal confesses: 'My wife would know all too well that our Saturday night out would be made if we'd won – but if we'd lost it might as well be pouring with rain.'

Roy Evans: 'I'm not good, but I don't think anyone is. I try to make sure that I don't go out on Saturday night with an attitude that will spoil the evening. The worst thing you can do is go into work on Monday with a gloomy face.'

Alan Curbishley of Charlton Athletic has it all worked out: 'I don't go overboard over a victory or a defeat. I certainly wouldn't cancel Saturday night if we lost – but I don't plan much for Saturday night anyway!'

Sheffield Wednesday's David Pleat: 'I try to smile but inwardly your pride is hurt. I tend to take defeat personally. You feel everyone is looking at you, watching your every movement. You hate the director who says, "Well, what did we do wrong today?"'

When Bruce Rioch was interviewed for the vacancy at Bolton Wanderers in 1992 he was asked the very question: 'How do you react straight after a defeat?' His reply was the same as his philosophy now: 'No straight answer.

'You can play well and lose to a penalty, or be abysmal and still lose 1–0. Personally, it isn't easy to take any defeat, but you can understand and accept it a bit more if you've played well. You might hit the woodwork four or five times, or you might have a shot which hits someone's body on the line and the other team goes up the other end and scores. When that happens you think there is no justice, but you can take it better if everybody's given everything they've got, played well as a team and worked well as a unit.

'When that happens, what do you say when you go into the dressing room? You can't go up the pole. No way. And I don't think you should go up the pole too often in management. I did when I was younger because I expected performances and results to be good all the time. But in my last year at Bolton I got really annoyed only a couple of times. And you have to know each player as an individual. To one I might have to be short and sharp, with another I might put an arm round his shoulder.

'Coming off the pitch at Burnden at half-time, I've often heard someone shout: "Get stuck into them, Bruce. Give 'em hell." Then we might come out and turn a draw into a win and people say: "I bet he gave them hell at half-time." But more likely than not it was the total opposite.'

Walter Smith makes a conscious effort not to allow a result to affect him too deeply one way or the other. 'I always try to take a middle line after a defeat. I try to be the same, win or lose. At a big club you shouldn't get carried away when things are going really well. That's as dangerous as the opposite reaction when they're going badly. You have to remain positive. Maybe I'm lucky in that I can be reasonably philosophical. I do get excited and I do get angry, but in public it's important that you're seen to be taking the situation in your stride.'

But how in the name of reason does a manager cope with a result such as that which the news agencies transmitted to their worldwide customers on 10 April, 1994: FA Cup semi-final (at Wembley)

Manchester United 1 Oldham Athletic 1 (after extra-time)?

That was the day when unfancied Oldham were one minute away from a place in the Cup Final, only for Mark Hughes to volley an equalizer in the 119th minute. Oldham lost the replay 4–1. Joe Royle was the Oldham manager. 'I was disappointed, obviously, but I was more disappointed with the consequences of that game. It knocked the stuffing out of a lot of the players. They never recovered and that is one of the reasons why we were relegated at the end of that season. But I have always believed that once a game is finished, the next game becomes immediately important. That's why we never sit in the dressing room throwing things around and shouting for hours on end. The game finishes at quarter to five – by ten to five I'm thinking about the next one, rather than harping on about what's gone wrong.'

To say that not every manager is like that is an obvious understatement, as many a player would testify! Royle, though, insists that the phlegmatic approach is in keeping with his nature, but he acknowledges a little help from the experts: 'I have spoken to psychologists about positive thinking, and that's something I've always believed in anyway. Particularly at Oldham, where we only had 14 players for 11 positions when I first went there. It didn't take a mathematician to work out that no matter how bad they played the team would be selected from the same players the next week. So there was no point in haranguing them because they had to do it again the following Saturday.'

TEAM SPIRIT

Team spirit is that vital commodity that makes a collection of footballers a force to be reckoned with. Sometimes it breeds naturally, other times the conditions are so hostile that it won't take root without serious fertilization. Howard Kendall experienced both situations at Everton – the upside with his squad that won two League titles, the Cup Winners Cup and the FA Cup in the mid-eighties; the downside when he returned to Goodison in November 1990.

'At Everton first time round I never had to worry about the team's mental attitude. They have sports psychologists coming in today – we didn't need them, we had Andy Gray. Players like Andy, Peter Reid, Adrian Heath and Kevin Ratcliffe were so full of confidence and personality they brought out the character in other, younger players. Once we became successful, the younger ones became characters in their own right. But of course players like Gray and Reid are not easy to find, and Everton only took them on because we were prepared to gamble on their fitness.

'When I went back the second time, I had never seen an atmosphere like it. It was the worst dressing room I had ever walked into. There was effectively an 'A' team and a 'B' team. The players who had been successful in the eighties on one side, and those who had been brought in later on the other. Players who had been brought in weren't achieving the success the older players wanted; the older players thought the new ones weren't good enough and the new ones thought the older ones were past it. So there was no harmony, and when it's like that mistakes are made.'

While Andy Gray has transferred his natural enthusiasm to the TV studio, Peter Reid is using his to revive Sunderland. 'The place and the players seemed down when I came here. But you need to have a smile on your face, and I like a laugh with the players. You work hard at your football; it's a difficult and very competitive sport, but you can still enjoy it.' Many managers announce their presence by reorganizing the day-to-day routine behind the scenes. Reid was no exception when he moved in at Sunderland. 'The assistant manager and the chief scout had desks in the manager's office. I didn't think that was right so I moved them out. The players were using the physio's phone and I didn't think that was right either, so there's a ban on that.'

The days when players would be part of the community are disappearing, and the same applies to managers. The professionals within the game move on so rapidly that many would need a permanent contract with Pickford's to keep up. Phil Neal retained his family home on Merseyside throughout his time as assistant manager, then manager, of Coventry City: 'Managers used to insist that players lived no more than 20 miles from the training ground, but I can't see that happening any more. People can't sell houses, and more and more players are renting places where the job takes them. It's the same with managers. It's so insecure no one wants to uproot his entire family because you can be blitzed by injuries, lose five games, and no one wants to know you.'

Stoke City's Lou Macari believes the supporters have a part to play. 'You get a feeling about a football club that things can happen. You need support not just to generate income but to create a real passion and enthusiasm, to help the team get off their backsides and start winning. I felt it at West Ham, Birmingham and Stoke – each club has a good basis of support. At Stoke I took the job because even in the bad times the attendances were 10,000, so you knew you had a chance.'

COACHING

Nathan Blake shivered in the shelter of the players' tunnel and pulled his blue woollen hat an inch lower over his eyebrows. It was a December morning, cold, wet and miserable. His club, Bolton Wanderers, had lost their last match. Today the players were to be shown the error of their ways. Blake – despite a perfect alibi, being on international duty with Wales when the Wanderers lost at home to Ipswich – was nonetheless required to slog it out in the teeth of an icy wind. 'You'll enjoy it when you get out there,' offered a bystander. 'Yeah, like a hole in the head,' muttered Blake. And he was off, to spend the best part of two hours being re-educated in tactical awareness.

The manager of Bolton is Colin Todd, a man who knows a thing or two about tactical awareness. Todd became a legend within his own career (winning 27 England caps and two League Championship medals as a centre-back) with the intuition to detect an attacker's intentions before the attacker had made his mind up. Now he is striving to rectify the faults which saw his team concede two daft goals the previous Saturday. Todd has Phil Brown, a former Bolton player, as his coach, but there's no doubt who has the real influence over the coaching – the boss himself.

'I am still out on the training ground almost every day. It can be difficult finding the time because management entails so many other things. People come to me about mundane things, like kit, which I don't want to know about. Being able to delegate is an important thing. But working with the players is vital. You've got to be careful – you can't do functional work all the time or they get bored. I always believe in keeping the players switched on mentally. They've just lost their way a wee bit and it needs to be installed in their minds again.'

Brown sorts out the teams – seniors against kids. It's 11-a-side on the main Burnden Park pitch, using mini-goals on the 18-yard lines. Todd takes over. His aim is to get the defensive line moving as a unit, so that one centre-back moves across to cover an attacking full-back, and that both full-backs don't go forward at the same time. The manager plays for the seniors in wide-left role. A flow of shouted commands penetrates the Lancashire drizzle. For a practice session this is reasonably competitive stuff, as the youngsters cheerfully attempt to embarrass the seniors. A knot of onlookers roars with delight as the young left-winger tricks his way past Gudni Bergsson. Todd halts play and instructs the troops. Blake and his attacking partner John McGinlay are not left out of it, lectured on the merits of running off the ball, but the main focus is defence.

It's sound, solid work but these defenders are no novices. The Bolton back four consists of Bergsson, Chris Fairclough, Gerry Taggart and Jimmy Phillips – all highly experienced players. Bergsson and Taggart are both internationals, for Iceland and Northern Ireland. It comes as a surprise to see solid veterans like this needing to be coached in such basics.

Todd, poker-faced, doesn't disagree. 'I would expect them to be able to use their voices a bit more. As a team, we are very quiet. Fairclough, Bergsson, and Phillips are all quiet. Taggart is aggressive but a team needs 11 leaders and maybe we haven't got enough. They all have ability, but how do you get certain other things out of them? Maybe you have to provoke them, and perhaps for some of these it's too late now.

'When I went to Derby as a young player I was very quiet and Brian Clough helped me a lot. He was always provoking me – calling me and kicking me. With youngsters you can do that. My players are a great set of players, otherwise we wouldn't be in the good position we are in, but they do look to a leader when perhaps they should sort things out for themselves.

'What we're doing today is helping the back four get their

starting positions right. But I can't teach them decisions: I can't teach them when to go and win a ball, when to go and win a header. They've got to assess that situation themselves, and they've all got a football brain. Sometimes you make a wrong decision and then it's up to someone else to cover.'

Todd played his best football for Sunderland, Derby and Everton. He used to read the game the way most players read *The Sporting Life*, his tackling as clinical as Frankie Dettori going for the finishing post. That ability, he says, is something which comes naturally, meaning there is a limit to what a coach can achieve. 'Players have said to me, "Well, it was easy for you because you had that natural ability." But if you don't try to make them reach the standards that you performed at then you're not doing your job properly. You encourage and help them, and I'm sure they've all made improvements. But it's how high they can go. Some of them might have reached their maximum now, in the First Division.

'At this club I sometimes believe we don't have enough defenders – they can play but can't defend as well as they should do and that's why we concede goals away from home. Away from home you've got to set your stall out to have more steel and be more disciplined. That's a word that creeps into football more and more. Discipline to keep your shape, discipline with the back four to keep their starting positions, discipline with the wide men to know when to go and when not to. Sometimes coaches can't put that there. But if you can organize them into a pattern of play then you've got a chance.'

TRANSFERS

You see them on the back pages several times a season, grinning with a mixture of relief and embarrassment, holding aloft one end of the club's scarf while the other end is clutched by the new signing. The manager is accustomed to posing for the cameras with a scarf borrowed by the local freelance from the club shop. Transfer deals are a major part of the job. At most clubs the manager recommends to his board the player he wants and the chairman or chief executive will work out whether they can afford him. At some clubs the manager has his transfer budget and looks after the whole deal. At a few, on occasions, the chairman does the lot and leaves the manager to make the best of it.

When Duncan Ferguson moved from Rangers to Everton it was one of the biggest deals of the year. Initially the transfer was a loan deal, but Ferguson eventually cost £4 million. The signing ceremony was hosted by the Everton chairman Peter Johnson with the then manager Mike Walker a peripheral figure on the edge of the top table. Was this a sign that Walker's days were numbered, that the chairman was doing the deals?

'I would have left the club a lot sooner if the chairman had been signing players – I would have resigned,' says Walker. 'We had been chasing around for a striker all summer – Martin Dahlin of Sweden, Muller of Brazil. Everton have always had a big centre-forward so I enquired about Mark Hateley of Rangers. They wouldn't let him go. So then I wondered about Duncan Ferguson. How was he going to get a game if they wouldn't sell Hateley? I recommended him to the chairman. We knew he had been in a bit of trouble in Scotland so I suggested we took him on loan to see if we could handle him.' Johnson was due to fly to Glasgow on business and firmed up negotiations with Rangers while he was there.

The Ferguson deal was typical of many high-profile transfers. The manager sniffs around till he finds a player who might be available and the chairman handles the finance. Some managers prefer to retain full control, as the Notts County chairman Derek Pavis discovered when Howard Kendall moved in at Meadow Lane. Most are content for the chairman to play a part. Joe Royle: 'The chairman knows the day-to-day cashflow situation at his club – how much can be released at any given moment and so on. Every transfer deal is different. If the club has a high-profile chairman it tends to be him who handles the financial side once the manager has done the basic deal with his opposite number.'

As manager of Crystal Palace, Alan Smith did have a high-profile chairman in Ron Noades. 'When I was negotiating a deal I always went through the other manager. Sometimes the chairman went out on a limb and did his own deals.

'Nine times out of ten I would bring the player back to my

house. It helped to get them on my side. I made sure there weren't enormous gaps in the salary scale. I would work out who was the best and set the rest of the scale in relation to him. Attackers would earn more than defenders, but the difference couldn't be too large because word quickly gets around the dressing room.'

At Sunderland, Peter Reid has a transfer budget – he knows what he can spend and is expected to stick to it. Phil Neal is proud of the way he kept Bolton Wanderers' transfer account in the black. 'I spent money very carefully, as if it was my own. Six out of seven years at Bolton we made a profit on my account. Now it's getting to the stage where a manager will decide to blow £8 million simply because the chairman has given him that amount to spend.'

John Neal is from the same school. He handled the affairs of Wrexham, Middlesbrough and Chelsea. 'There's no skill in getting out the chequebook and writing a cheque for £8.5 million. But there is a skill in looking for bargains when you've only got £15,000 to spend.'

It is during transfer negotiations that the agent plays an important part. Steve Coppell doesn't welcome their involvement: 'It's the deviousness of them. If you speak to a player individually you feel you have a relationship with them. With an agent, you never seem to get through to the real person. You feel there is a shield there – they have one, you don't.'

Doug Ellis shakes his head as he recounts how close his manager Brian Little was to signing Les Ferdinand for Aston Villa. 'Ferdinand sat in this office for three hours. He was very keen to join us but at the very last minute his agent said, "Les, remember you promised Newcastle you would at least talk to them." So we lost him.'

The transfer market can be an unpredictable place. 'Very frustrating,' says Bryan Robson. 'Players you want aren't available, then the ones who are available are priced at a ridiculous rate. I won't pay inflated prices for players.'

And at the lower end of the market, managers sweat on a different set of problems. When Graham Barrow assembled the team that would win promotion from the Third Division for

Chester City, it wasn't a question of whether the club could afford the players – they were all free transfers – it was a matter of whether the players would elect to join Chester. 'I was pleased when I saw the list of players available that summer. Among them was Colin Greenall, a good defender released by Preston. I spoke to Colin, told him what wages we could offer, and spent an agonizing few weeks waiting to see if anyone else would make him a better offer. But I was a bit of a pest – I kept agitating him and thankfully he signed.'

It isn't unknown for chairmen to become suddenly incommunicado when the manager is on the prowl for money. It's no new phenomenon. Tommy Docherty tells of his first stint at Queens Park Rangers in 1968. 'The chairman, Jim Gregory, promised me money to buy players. When I tried to buy them, Gregory was in a health farm which didn't receive incoming calls. The only way to get in touch was for him to ring you. Which he never did.'

The curse of the manager at smaller clubs is to see their best players move on. So long as they obtain a fair price they take it on the chin, but Martin Dobson felt cheated when he sold future England full-back Lee Dixon from Bury to Stoke City. 'We picked up Dixon on a free transfer from Chester. I told the board he was worth £100,000. When we sold him to Stoke the transfer tribunal – who hadn't seen him play – fixed his value at £40,000. My credibility with the board suffered. Yet when Stoke sold him to Arsenal, he was worth £440,000. Then the board said, "Can't you find another one like him and groom him?" But it takes 18 months to do that, and in the meantime you're losing games.'

The one stain on David Pleat's managerial record is his sacking by Leicester City in 1991. He went, he claims, because he was successful in implementing the board's requirements on transfers. 'I went to Leicester with the instruction to put things right at the bank. I had to sell players and I did so quite effectively. For example, it was excellent business to get £105,000 from Scarborough for Martin Russell. I did make mistakes and it was a setback when Russell Osman left under freedom of contract. But I did what the board wanted – the trouble was they couldn't carry the crowd with them. Often in football the next manager benefits from the groundwork done by his predecessor, and I feel that was the case when Brian Little took over from me at Leicester.'

Everyone is looking for value for money; few believe they get it. Howard Kendall: 'Ten years ago you could go into the lower divisions and pick up a prospect like Derek Mountfield, a centre-half from Tranmere, for £35,000. Now, you're being asked for £500,000-plus.' Kendall saw both sides of the transfer market when he moved to Everton in 1981. The club he left was Blackburn Rovers, whom Kendall had taken from the Third Division to the top of the Second. 'I went from a situation where Blackburn couldn't afford £30,000 for Brian Marwood, who might have made the difference in winning promotion, to one where I was instructed to go out and spend money. At Everton I was told to buy players in order to generate interest during the summer and stimulate season ticket sales. It was a totally different situation.'

One of the manager's pet hates is to have his hand forced when it comes to selling players. Not by the board – managers are realistic enough to know that will happen sooner or later – but by the player himself. At Bolton the Serb Sasa Curcic was a crowd favourite even in the club's relegation season, 1995–96. Just before the start of the next campaign Colin Todd sold him to Aston Villa. The fans were incensed but Todd insists he had no choice. 'Sasa wanted to move on and I was in an impossible situation. I didn't have to sell him – he was still under contract – but once a player makes up his mind that he wants to go you can't win. I'd already had a taste of that when Jason McAteer and Alan Stubbs decided they wanted to leave. You can make them stay, but it reflects badly on team spirit because they don't do what you want them to. You can't please everyone so you just have to do what is best for the club in the long run.'

But the transfer market, with all its frustrations, often gives managers their warmest memories. Steve Coppell signed a youngster called Ian Wright after three days of a two-week trial and later sold him to Arsenal for £2.5 million. And Dario Gradi blesses the day he convinced a youngster freed by Manchester United to join Crewe. David Platt went on to captain England and by the time he moved to Arsenal from Sampdoria in July 1995 he had attracted over £22 million in fees.

It was the day after he was appointed manager of Arsenal that Bruce Rioch inked the name of Platt at the top of a shortlist of players capable of achieving what he wanted in the team's midfield. He had a similar list of names for forward positions. At the top, Dennis Bergkamp of Inter Milan. Within three weeks, both men had signed for Arsenal.

The more illustrious the name, the more complex the transfer, the smaller the role of the football club manager. That is the direction the business is taking. Having delivered his wish-list to the Arsenal vice-chairman, David Dein, on the first Monday after taking over, Rioch's next involvement in the deal was receiving a call from Dein two days later to say the Bergkamp deal was likely to come off. The negotiations with the player's agents and with Inter Milan were handled by Dein and the club secretary Ken Friar. It was the same with the Platt deal. Rioch was on holiday in Portugal while the nitty-gritty was being sorted out. But a manager, having set the ball rolling, still has a part to play in ensuring the putt drops into the hole. At many Continental clubs players are signed solely by the president, leaving the manager/coach to fit newcomers into the team as best he may. British football hasn't reached that stage yet, and both Rioch's Italian deals could have foundered if the manager and the players had failed to hit it off at one-to-one meetings which took place at the end of the negotiation process.

In the case of David Platt, Rioch barely had time to unpack his shaving tackle after flying home from Portugal before he was airborne again, bound for Genoa.

'David Dein was in Sardinia, talking to Platt who was on holiday there, while I was in Portugal. The day after I got home Mr Dein rang me and said that David Platt wanted to come back to England, he wanted to sign for Arsenal, he was with him at that moment, and did I want to speak to him? I had a chat with David Platt over the phone for about 15 minutes. I asked him, "Do you want to join the Arsenal Football Club?" He said he did so I flew to Italy the next day and met him in Genoa.'

While Dein concluded the deal with the Sampdoria club, Rioch spent four hours with Platt at the England captain's home. 'His home, overlooking the Bay of Genoa, was magnificent,' said Rioch, with a shake of the head, as if he still couldn't quite believe that Platt had decided to give it all up. From the start, the Arsenal team had identified the enviable way of life enjoyed by Platt in Italy as the biggest hurdle they would have to overcome. For that reason as much as any other, Rioch had been determined on a face-to-face meeting with the player. It was not necessary in terms of the business deal, but it was vital to Arsenal to make Platt feel wanted at Highbury.

'I didn't talk to either player about the terms of their contracts. But when Dennis Bergkamp was at Highbury before signing, while the negotiations were going on, he sat with me in my office and we just talked about football. I didn't talk to David Platt about his salary, although I was available if the managing director wanted to refer anything to me. I think it is right to handle it that way these days.'

Even at Bolton Rioch had established a similar pattern. At first, he handled all the deals himself in the traditional manner – negotiating fees with the selling clubs, sorting out the individual contracts with players. By the time he left, the business side was the responsibility of the chairman, Gordon Hargreaves, and the chief executive, Des McBain – a reflection both of the progress Bolton had made and of the increasing complexity of transfer business.

'The reason this system isn't in place at all clubs is that there is a tradition in English football that the manager does all the work. In the past a club director wouldn't want that role anyway. They would appoint a manager and let him get on with it. These days the time it takes to put together a transfer deal is enormous. Even at Bolton it could take up a week or more of your time and that means you are not out with your players on the training field.

'The other reason why things haven't changed is that managers don't like to feel they are not in control of a situation. A lot of them still want the power to do the whole deal themselves. But if a chairman or another director can help crunch a deal with a director of another club, then let them do so. They know about the money side of it, after all.

'The only drawback is that sometimes directors come to me and say, "Well, we tried for that player but he's not available." So

I say, "Try again. And then again." That's when you do feel that you are not in control. If you are dealing direct and the manager at the other end says the player is not for sale, you will pick the phone up later in the afternoon and ring him again. And you ring him again the following moming. You exhaust all avenues until he says, "Maybe we will sell him." And then you dive in.'

At Ibrox it's a similar set-up, though not identical. Some deals are piloted through by the manager. The more complex ones are handled by the chairman, David Murray. Deals like the capture of Paul Gascoigne from Lazio, for example.

'I thought Paul Gascoigne would be a good acquisition for us,' says Walter Smith. 'The chairman set the ball rolling. He arranged a meeting with Lazio which both of us went to. Then the chairman did the financial deal with Paul's advisers. That took place in London. The following day I flew to Italy to meet Paul. I had already met him on holiday in Florida two years previously, so that was helpful. I spent a day with him renewing our acquaintance and establishing the start of a relationship which I hoped would prove to be a fruitful one for Rangers Football Club.

'The way we operate is that I am responsible for the football side and the chairman looks after the business side. If I want a player I will go to the chairman and discuss it with him. I do complete some deals myself – if another manager approaches me and I start the deal, I finish it. But, to be honest, it's a relief to have a chairman who is able to handle the major deals. The amounts of money are enormous and sometimes it's wrong for the manager to handle them – his responsibility is to liaise with the chairman to decide who would benefit the team.'

At Liverpool much of the wheeling and dealing is performed by the chief executive Peter Robinson, although Roy Evans does have an involvement in deciding transfer fees and salaries. 'I think it is important that I do that, in consultation with Peter Robinson. It works with Liverpool, but other clubs might not think our way is for them.'

And like Bruce Rioch, Evans thought it worthwhile making an unexpected airline flight to ensure a deal wasn't lost at the eleventh hour.

Evans was in the middle of a family holiday in the West Indies when Liverpool's lengthy stalking of Nottingham Forest's Stan Collymore eventually looked like paying off. Alerted by Robinson that Collymore and his agent were ready to sign, Evans flew from St Lucia via Barbados to Gatwick and on to Heathrow for a meeting with Collymore, which was over in two hours. The subject matter? 'Not finance, just football.' Nonetheless, it was another example of that important initial bonding between manager and player. 'I was impressed with him and hopefully he was pleased too.' With the deal done, and a record £8.5 million about to change hands between two English clubs, Evans flew back to his family in the Caribbean. A 28-hour trip for the sake of a two-hour chat about football.

'When something is as important as that you don't mind. We knew Stan had spoken to Everton. You can't take any chances if you are serious about signing a player. Always in the back of your mind is the thought that if you don't make the effort, even at the cost of more than a day in the air, you might be disappointed.'

THE LONG VIEW

When it comes to planning long-term, football tends to talk big but deliver little. Managers are all aware their days may be numbered, and short-termism tends to dominate. Rochdale's Graham Barrow: 'Long-term planning isn't really feasible. I have to listen to the youth development officer saying he's got the best 14-year-old, but sometimes I think, What use is that to me at the moment? It's hard to believe I will still be here to see him make his debut.'

The dangers of that philosophy strike a chord with the former Manchester United and York City boss Wilf McGuinness – hardly surprising, given his background as a former England youth coach: 'There should be money put aside that managers can't touch, to be spent on schoolboy and youth football. It could come from the PFA, from TV or a levy on transfers, and it could finance a youth development post with proper facilities – nothing to do with the first team.'

Peter Reid believes 'developing kids is an important part of the job. I will get a youth scheme going even though I may not be here to see it come to fruition.'

But Barrow still has his doubts. 'You can become too involved with youth development, because young players don't win you anything. It's not so bad if you bring one youngster in, but if I blooded half a dozen I would be putting my job on the line.'

Brian Horton: 'Some managers don't believe in youth policies because their philosophy is that they won't be there to see the good side of it. I disagree. I think you have to have a structure and it gives me a buzz when I bring someone through. In my last year at Maine Road Manchester City's kids had a great season, with a lot of success. I look forward to seeing some of those boys progress further and I will enjoy feeling that I had a part in that.'

All too aware that the sack may materialize at any time, managers stay on their toes. 'Some managers are driven by fear,' comments David Pleat. 'They go for the expedient way of playing football, get success as quickly as possible, and then move on.'

It takes stubborn commitment to develop a true youth policy. When a manager is granted enough time to make it work, the benefits can be staggering. Manchester United now make enough money to enable Alex Ferguson to bid for any star he wants but his success at Old Trafford has come from blending big signings with home products. The locally groomed youngsters are just as important as the classy imports.

It was at St Mirren, his second managerial post, that Ferguson first showed his belief in youth. 'I did start tinkering with a youth policy at East Stirling but I wasn't there long enough to get it going. But at St Mirren I had three years and that's where I learned to scout for players. The club had two scouts at the time, both experienced at watching junior football – in Scotland that's the equivalent of non-League football in England. In Scotland it was well-established that clubs would recruit from junior leagues, but I felt it was more important to get kids at a younger age and work with them as they grew up.

'Rangers and Celtic both had their boys' clubs. Celtic in particular were very strong at the time, bringing through boys like Dalglish, McGrain, Hay, Macari, Wilson, Connolly – an unbelievable crop. Celtic, without doubt, were the strongest in Scotland at producing young players at the time.

'But it didn't stop me from setting up our own boys' club at St Mirren, and going out on Saturday mornings to watch schoolboy matches. I used to learn a lot from the old scouts like Jimmy Dickie,' who worked for United and the others. After a while I realized just how cute they were. They would come and chat to me on the touchline, offer me sweets, anything to stop me concentrating on the game so I wouldn't know which boys they were following. Eventually I realized what was happening and I would stand by myself on another part of the ground.'

At Old Trafford Ferguson's faith in youth has spawned the most spectacular success. Not only have youngsters like Ryan Giggs, David Beckham and the Neville brothers made it to first-team level, they have been vital members of teams which have won trophies, and become established internationals in their own right. There used to be a theory that it was a waste of time for a youngster to join a famous club because, whenever a vacancy occurred, the club would always buy a ready-made player through the transfer market. Manchester United have disproved it with a vengeance.

The club had a school of excellence when Ferguson joined in 1986, but it was a shadow of its present size. 'We had Joe Brown, who was responsible for bringing in the players, Eric Harrison in charge of the coaching, and a part-time teacher. Now we have Paul McGuinness in charge plus eight part-time coaches and two part-time physios. We have a school of excellence in Durham and another in Belfast, with two coaches at each centre. We might start up in one or two other places. And we have youngsters coming in from the age of nine on a Sunday.'

When the Bosman case of 1995 outlawed the payment of transfer fees for out-of-contract players within the European Community, there were fears that clubs would abandon youth policies. Why bother when experienced internationals are available for nothing and much of the money saved on transfer fees can be diverted to the players' salaries and agents' commissions? But the reverse has happened. Clubs value youth development more highly than ever, knowing that the Bosman ruling only applies at the end of a player's contract.

And more clubs are stressing the importance of youth.

Liverpool have announced plans to build a youth academy on the fringe of the city, complete with residential accommodation and treatment facilities. The aim is to match the Dutch club Ajax, whose reputation for producing world-class players is legendary.

It will, of course, take time. And only the richest clubs have the time to allow young talent to flourish. At most clubs the quick fix is still the favoured option.

DISCIPLINE

The subject of discipline is rarely far from the boss's mind. Tommy Docherty has talked of his stand against the nightclubbing tendency at Chelsea in the sixties. Today, he thinks lack of discipline has got out of hand. 'Too many players are known for their antics off the field. I couldn't have handled that. A player who gets into trouble with the law for violence would never represent his country if I was the manager.'

Lou Macari pulled out of a move to Docherty's old club, precisely because discipline was still an issue there. 'After Swindon I more or less promised the Chelsea chairman Ken Bates I would go, but at the last minute I got the impression they wanted me because they thought I was a rigid disciplinarian. I had a reputation for keeping my players fit and strong, but it seems strange that if you don't want your players living it up till four o'clock in the morning or getting drunk every week that you are marked down as a disciplinarian. What is unusually strict about that? It appeared that Chelsea wanted me to be a really tough nut and knock all the players into shape. Well, if that was the job that needed doing there, I didn't fancy it.'

It is a dilemma for the manager when his most talented players turn out to be the least reliable. 'If we have three star players, and no decent cover for them, and on the night before a match they shin down a drainpipe and go out on the town, and the press finds out, what do you do?' asks David Pleat. 'Hush it up? Or expose everything and jeopardize the club's results? It's a tough one, and so many vital decisions like that have to be made in the course of a single season.'

THE MEDIA

The influence of the media on football has expanded immensely during the careers of today's managers. Most of them put up with the demands although their tolerance is tested to the limit. Howard Wilkinson sums up what many of his former colleagues think: 'Spending time with the media never helps me do my job better, and in a lot of instances it makes it harder because it impinges on my time to a point which is not really in my interest, the club's interest, or football's interest. Beyond a certain limit, publicity does not sell football.'

A new manager is usually stunned at the demands from the media. Newspapers (local and national), radio (local and national), TV (BBC, ITV and Sky), ancillary services like the Clubcall scheme operated in tandem with clubs themselves, all desperate for the latest developments, all hustling to be first in the queue. The nature of the coverage has intensified too. Lou Macari noticed it when he returned to Scotland to manage Celtic: 'When I was a player with Celtic, the Scottish press were as harmless as the Oor Wullie comic strip in the *Sunday Post*. When I went back to manage Celtic I wondered if they had gone down the same line as the English press, where everyone is trying to get in front of one another. They had changed all right. The *Sun* was selling in Glasgow and the *Daily Record* was competing with the *Sun*. It was a lot more competitive.'

'We don't have reporters any more, we have QCs,' observes Everton's Joe Royle. 'Quote Collectors. I always thought journalists were there to report or comment, but now there are a lot who want to make the news. At any time you can be frivolously connected with up to 10 players, and sooner or later they'll hit the nail on the head.'

'That is one of the most annoying aspects,' agrees Middlesbrough's Bryan Robson. 'If one paper speculates that you are going to sign someone, all of a sudden you've got to deal with 20 phone calls asking you about the same thing. That has happened to me quite a bit, because with a supportive chairman people know I have had money to spend.'

'It isn't the relationship with the press that used to exist when

I was a young player,' continues Royle. 'The reporters used to stand around in corners wearing trench coats, smoking their pipes and waiting for the odd snippet to report. There was always great trust between the players, the club and the journalists. Now there's a great distrust. It isn't always the soccer reporters' fault, but nowadays they aren't interested in how many goals a player scores but where he's scoring at night.

'I get on well with the press at Everton, as I did at Oldham. They're all good lads, but they are all in a race themselves and under pressure from their editors to provide scoops. But we all have to get on with one another and I have always been of the opinion that if you are honest with reporters they might be honest with you, and they tend to have been that way up to now.'

At neighbouring Liverpool the course of managerial history was changed when Graeme Souness sold the story of his heart bypass operation exclusively to the *Sun*. The tabloid was unpopular on Merseyside as a result of its sensationalist reporting of the Hillsborough disaster. Souness, who was in Scotland with Rangers at the time of the tragedy, was unaware of the extent of ill feeling, but soon found out. Public opinion tilted against him, so that when his team hit a bad patch he found little support from the stands. When the directors accepted his resignation there were no protest demonstrations in the streets.

With that episode still raw, Souness' successor Roy Evans decided the main block of his media policy would be to steer clear of exclusive deals with anyone. 'If you get too close to one newspaper you can give yourself problems,' he says, adding in an echo of his Everton counterpart: 'If you stay reasonably honest with the media, they will be reasonably honest with you.'

But it can be a fragile relationship, this Faustian pact. At Coventry, Phil Neal felt let down. 'I got to spend more and more time with the press, but it didn't do me any good. Three months later they were running polls asking if I should be sacked. There needs to be a press officer at every big club to build the right headlines. At Coventry, media demands were taking up too much of my time and I was missing going out training with the team.'

Howard Wilkinson sympathizes with Neal's suggestion but doubts if it would get off the ground. 'The media don't want to talk to a front man,' he says. 'They want the manager.' As Roy Evans knows all too well. 'Sometimes the phone never stops – you can live on the phone if you're not careful and the family get sick of it. But you have to accept it. I need to be in contact with other people in football and accessible to the media.'

Dario Gradi laid down ground rules in his early days at Crewe. 'I told the local paper they couldn't have it both ways. They couldn't be in the club all the time, enjoying full access, and then slag us off. I don't mind them saying the team played badly or Dario Gradi picked the wrong side. But it's out of order if they say something like: "One thousand five hundred people turned up for last night's match and those who stayed away must have known something because it was appalling."' The vocabulary of the press doesn't go down well either. 'They can be quite yobbish in their comments. I can't believe some of the headlines I read. I often think, What right have they to say that? The papers should be ashamed of themselves for the way they treated Graham Taylor when he was manager of England.'

'A lot of creative language has gone missing from the newspapers,' agrees Joe Royle. 'You can't pick up a paper without being hit by words like "shock", "blast" and "snub".'

Phil Neal believes the media treats the Premier League's mega-clubs more generously than the rest. With the experience of Coventry City still fresh in his mind he says: 'They report the big clubs completely differently. When Newcastle drew 1–1 at Coventry, much was made of the fact that Peter Beardsley was injured. Two weeks later we had eight first teamers out and it didn't get a mention. There is definitely a prejudice because Coventry haven't got a string of internationals. So it makes it hard when you are battling at a less fashionable club.'

Lawrie McMenemy recalls criticism from an unexpected direction. 'Years ago after one Southampton match I was in the press room, back to the wall, and one man kept asking awkward questions. I always tried to be accommodating to the press but this man kept on, so eventually I asked what paper he worked for. He said, "I'm from Hospital Radio." I told him to get out. He was an amateur who we had invited in and he was asking all sorts of questions which the national newspaper writers wouldn't have considered asking. Of course, the tabloid men were loving it. They didn't ask the questions but they all wrote down the responses.'

Tommy Docherty is part of the media himself now, as a radio reporter. His main complaint concerns players criticizing managers from TV studios. 'Players should not discuss managers or coaches on television,' he states. 'They are still only learning the game themselves. They get paid to play it and they should stick to that.'

The complaints about the media are so vocal that one wonders if managers take too much notice of what the media say. Shouldn't they treat them like a sideshow, instead of regarding them almost as a major player in the sport's lifestyle? Like Judy Collins, Tommy Docherty has seen it from both sides now.

'They only listen to the media when the media prints something outrageous. People say the media picks the team sometimes, but I don't believe that. Yes, they put pressure on the manager, but that is part of their job. I never looked on the media as an enemy. If you have got a good team, and you're playing good football, they will give you a million pounds worth of publicity. When things go wrong you can't complain if they reflect the other side. Especially if you are one of those managers who takes money from the media for writing articles. It's too late to get on your high horse.

'People in the game do get very upset when a reporter expresses his opinion – but it's only his opinion. There's no need to take offence at it. On the radio I have praised Alex Ferguson and I have also criticized him, constructively I think, but he won't speak to me. And there are a lot like that.'

Terry Neill, former manager of Hull City, Tottenham and Arsenal, is another who now follows the game from the press box. 'Managers have to accept being in the limelight more than ever. The downside is that the media will infiltrate every facet of their lives, turn up on their doorsteps, explore anything on the romantic side, whether they're mixing with the wrong people or having a few too many drinks. The bung allegations have surfaced. They are under the microscope. But the money has improved, so it isn't all that bad.'

Jimmy Armfield has been player, manager, newspaper writer and radio reporter. 'Ninety-nine out of a hundred managers don't understand the media. And ninety-nine out of a hundred of the media don't understand managers. Why should someone be an expert in someone else's profession? When I say they don't understand it, I mean that they don't understand it totally. It's like dentists and doctors. They do overlap, but they're different professions. I would say my IQ is average for a football person, but when you sit down behind a typewriter to write your first newspaper article it isn't easy. Managers think they can write but they can't – not if their programme notes are anything to go by!'

Alex Ferguson has had his volatile moments with the media. Now, he says, he avoids reading the tabloids. 'The praise is over the top and so is the criticism. As a person, it doesn't do you any good to read the papers. There are some people in the game who get carried away by all the praise – they don't realize that next day the same papers will stick the knife in.'

Wilf McGuinness has reservations about the extent of TV coverage in the nineties. 'Television has brought football into everyone's living room, but it has also brought the problems that go with it. Like the Cantona incident at Crystal Palace. Without TV the fuss would have died within a week. I remember a Manchester City winger in the late sixties punching a referee – everyone forgot about it. We had Best and Law who would retaliate first and others like Nobby Stiles and Pat Crerand who would sometimes go over the line. But now there is so much detail in the TV coverage that players can't get away with it, and when they are caught out it puts the manager in a difficult situation. He can't defend obvious wrong-doing, so it makes it much harder for him to support his players.'

THAT'S THE WAY IT GOES

If nothing else, professional football produces good philosophers. The peaks and troughs come faster than a storm off Cape Horn, so that if the man at the helm avoids being washed overboard he emerges with a totally realistic appraisal of what it's all about.

'The only job you can compare it to is the Prime Minister's,' declares Wilf McGuinness. 'You have to lead the way, make decisions, pick a team, and if it doesn't function there's always someone on your back.'

'You've got to be single-minded and have a thick skin,' says Joe Royle. 'You must be prepared for hard work. It's no good being slightly lazy because a footballer's life consists of around two hours a day whereas a manager works up to 16 hours a day. If you have an idea of what you want and you are tactically aware and player aware, then you've got a chance.'

Like navigating round Cape Horn, experience is invaluable. Tommy Docherty has his own definition. 'Experience is pitfalls, setbacks, failures, disasters, success, joy, winning, losing, injuries, illness, recuperating from injury, and yet getting back to top spot again. That's experience.'

Bruce Rioch: 'The mind is a wonderful thing. From experience it learns to handle things. That's why there are no 19-year-old football managers, because they lack any experience.'

Brian Horton: 'It's a tough game. You can't please all the players, like you can't please all the crowd. It's a very fickle business.'

Lawrie McMenemy: 'Management is about getting the best out of what you've got available. It's about knowing you can do all your planning at home the night before, and come in next morning, realize it isn't right, and change in mid-stream. You've got to be flexible and take on board the unexpected.'

Peter Reid: 'The job is like a drug. If you have three games in one week and you win the first, you're on a high. Then you lose in midweek and you're on a low. On Saturday you win again. It's a roller coaster, an amazing profession.'

Lou Macari sums up his philosophy of football's job market: 'I have a shop in Manchester which someone runs for me, but I still need football for my living. I have always taken career decisions based on whether I will feel comfortable in a job. If I don't, I won't stay there just for the wage. I would rather sit at home with no wage coming in. Every club I have gone to seems to have been struggling. Once in a while it would be nice to go to a club which was doing well – but then, I suppose that's why the job comes up in the first place.'

And when the job does come up, what on earth is a man to make of it?

Joe Royle: 'There are so many misapprehensions about the manager's job: what you should or shouldn't do to make a success of it. On the one hand you get managers who are strong on the coaching side, work all day with their players, are still out there at eight o'clock at night with the youngsters, and in the final analysis getting no results. And there has been the other side of the profession – managers who have barely been seen. The late Harry Catterick, here at Everton, was one of them. When I was here as a player we rarely saw him except peering through the slats of the blinds over the office windows which overlook the training ground. Yet he managed two Championship teams and a Cup winning side, always playing attractive football. So the answer is: whatever gets the job done. And when you stop to think about it, you will find that two of the most successful managers have had as their major qualifications the fact that they were physiotherapists – Bertie Mee of Arsenal and Bob Paisley of Liverpool. So there's no set formula. I see managers busting a gut to be the next Brian Clough or Kenny Dalglish or Ron Atkinson. But the answer is to do what comes naturally and hopefully get results.'

Phil Neal: 'You learn a lot of things without being fully aware of it. It's like a hypnotic trance, especially coming from a club like Liverpool, and being around the managers and coaches there for 10 years. For example, one thing I learned from Bob Paisley was to consider whether a player who has always played in one position might actually be better in another. Like Bob switching Ray Kennedy from striker to left-side midfield and turning him into an England player. Only Bob sussed that out.'

As for the managers who gravitate to the apex of the pyramid, Joe Royle thinks that has nothing to do with chance. 'You tend to find the managers with the top clubs are with the top clubs because they are single-minded people and get what they want.'

DIRECTORS

Directors tend to get a bad press from managers. It's probably inevitable, given that almost every manager has been fired at least once, almost every time believing he was the victim of rough justice, and just as surely blaming the men who fired him – the directors. Mike Walsh, who left Bury 'by mutual consent' after a 5–0 defeat in 1995, has not been sacked but knows plenty who have. 'Spectators have higher expectations than ever, and spectators do sometimes dictate to directors that the manager should go – when the directors know he's doing a perfectly good job but they just aren't strong enough.'

Tommy Docherty goes along with that. 'The hardest part of the job is placating supporters. Chairmen don't sack managers – supporters do. And players do. If players aren't performing, supporters boo the players. Then they boo the manager. After a few bad results they're out of a job. If you've got a good, understanding chairman it makes a big difference. Good players, good chairman, good luck.'

Brian Horton rates his first chairman as one of the best. 'Don Robinson was chairman of Hull and gave me the player-manager's job. I was lucky – he was a chairman who was different in many ways and had the foresight to do things differently. He had good ideas to get things going among the supporters and I learned a lot from him.' Horton also learned from him what it was like to be fired.

Jimmy Armfield recalls the director who took the gloss off his celebrations the day Bolton won the Third Division title in 1973. 'We had been presented with the trophy and we were in the dressing room afterwards. The players were all drinking champagne and I was taking it all in. One of the directors came up to me and said, "Jim, you've done a great job. This team will go straight through the Second Division next season." We had only just got out of the Third and he was already winning the Second! That was putting me under pressure, just when I was looking forward to a break.'

He has fonder memories of his chairman at Burnden Park, Jack Banks. 'A very good chairman. He used to call in every Monday lunchtime for a chat. He would turn up in sandals, open-neck shirt, smoking a fag, driving his Rolls Royce and bringing a flask of soup that his wife would make for us. When I went to Bolton the club had just been relegated to the Third Division and morale was bad. I told the chairman we couldn't turn it round in an instant, Rome wasn't built in a day. He said, "I know, but I wasn't on that building site!"

'In that first year we were fourth from bottom coming up to

Christmas and we'd lost on the Saturday. On the Monday he arrived at the ground. I said, "I thought you might come in today, Mr Chairman." He said, "Don't think I've come to sack you – I don't let people off that easy. When you go, I go with you because I'm the one that brought you here."' In the same conversation, Banks complained that Armfield had promised to blood some of the younger players but hadn't yet done so. 'They're not ready yet,' the manager told him. 'How do you know if you don't play them?' answered the chairman. The following week Armfield chose three youngsters. 'We won the game and never looked back.'

Lawrie McMenemy is himself a director, at Southampton, but spent long enough answering to various boardrooms. 'Tommy Docherty used to say the ideal board consisted of two directors, one dead and one dying. Sometimes I have understood what he meant! But directors are there to lend their expertise from their own walk of life. The chairman should have business acumen and an awareness that the football business is a bit different from most others. Then, ideally, you should have an accountant, a lawyer, a builder, and a football man.'

Bryan Hamilton reflects on his 18 months at Leicester City: 'I took over with the support of Terry Shipman, the chairman, and Gordon Milne, the chief executive – but not with the full support of the board at the time. Sometimes you get caught up in a situation in which you become a pawn in someone else's game.'

But Bobby Gould, with the imprint of Bristol Rovers, Coventry, Wimbledon and West Bromwich Albion on his backbone, weighs in with words of support for the men around the boardroom table – at least, for those with the financial clout: 'It's individuals' money that you're talking about now, and there's no greater example than Sam Hammam at Wimbledon. Some can afford it – well, one can, Jack Walker. The others have to bear the consequences. As a manager you have to understand the highs and lows of the chairman, and the criticism he gets. Mind, I wasn't too thrilled when I took over at West Brom. The chairman, John Silk, introduced me to the press and then said, "I'd just like to make it clear that Bobby Gould wasn't my choice." What chance did I have after that?'

Craig Brown, manager of Scotland, cut his managerial molars

at Clyde where he spent 10 years and was given a seat in the boardroom while still the manager. 'That day we were playing Morton and a supporter shouted, "Well, Brown, now you're a director are you going to get us a decent manager?"'

MATCHDAY

'It's a great job during the week,' says Mike Walsh, 'but sometimes the Saturday spoils it. You go to games and you can get so worked up because so much depends on it.'

Matchday for the manager is the weekly audit, the public rendering of accounts for inspection by the masses. It could be the day for a bold strategic ploy, or a desperate gamble on a half-fit superstar; it could be a day when the club's progress to the next round of a Cup is at stake, or its very survival in its league or division.

'The buzz on a Saturday kicks me off,' states Phil Neal. 'Particularly if it's a game in which my team is the underdog. Like taking Bolton to play Manchester United in the Cup. That way it's really pushing my skill to get the blend and tactics right against Alex Ferguson.'

'I find the last hour beforehand worse than the 90 minutes,' says Howard Kendall. 'Especially at an opposition ground where you aren't invited into the office for a cup of tea. It's OK at home because you have your own office. But you want to stay out of the dressing room so that when you do come in you make an impact. It only takes a couple of minutes to give them a gee-up. Someone once said to me, 'The last thing a manager says to a player is the first thing he forgets.' Because he's so hyped up. What sinks in is what he does during the week.'

Joe Royle agrees. Not for him the haranguing of players in the last five minutes before kick-off. One of the most impressive team displays of 1994–95 was Everton's 4–1 victory over Tottenham in the FA Cup semi-final at Elland Road. Everton were substantially inferior to Spurs so far as the League table was concerned, but grasped the initiative from the start and ran out deserving winners. It was a remarkable exhibition of mental fortitude allied to physical commitment.

The week's work on the training ground was important, but on this occasion what was said in the dressing room was also significant. 'With 30 seconds to go before they went out I switched off Neville Southall's ghetto-blaster and reminded them that these games are generally won by someone's mistakes or a lack of adventure,' Royle said. 'I told them, "Whatever you do, don't come back in here after the game cursing what we might have done, could have done or should have done. Go and enjoy it and seize the day." That was the longest team talk we had all season.

'We don't have team talks, as a rule. I have always preferred to walk round having a quiet word with individuals, telling them what I want. If everyone is sitting around quietly it creates the wrong vibes and makes them nervous. If you've been working on something for five days, the last thing they want is to be reminded of it all again, in front of everyone.

'As for that semi-final, it was easy to motivate them. The papers had been talking all week about how Spurs would beat us and Manchester United would win their semi-final to set up the so called "Dream Final". For me and my assistant Willie Donachie that was manna from heaven!'

If only every game went as smoothly! On the same day Alan Smith watched his Crystal Palace team take the lead twice against Manchester United in the other semi-final before being held to a draw and losing the replay. 'The 90 minutes of any match is a strain. It's the part of this job that is difficult. Matters are out of your hands. In the semi-final against United we were 20 minutes from going to Wembley for the Cup Final and time seemed to pass so slowly.' Smith, of course, lost his job at the end of the season.

Sunk into his greatcoat in the directors' box, hopping up and down off the bench, or standing like a sentry alongside the dug-out, the manager gets through the proceedings as best he can. 'I'm quite vociferous on the bench,' says Peter Reid, 'but the players can't hear you. It's just nerves, wanting to be involved.' 'The worst thing I ever did,' says Bobby Gould, 'was to go on to the pitch at Leicester to complain about a penalty decision when I was manager of Coventry. We lost the match 5–1.' The details of the incident still rankle, though, and he can't resist adding: 'Mind you, it was a diabolical decision.'

The aftermath of a game is now a ritual. The manager has little time with his players as the demands of the media, the directors and the sponsors take over. The pattern is the same from the foot of the Nationwide League to the top of the Premiership. Rochdale's Graham Barrow: 'I go into the boardroom but I don't really like it. Obviously if we've won they're fairly happy. But I can't wait to get out of there, and I don't make much of a secret of it.' Shouldn't he at least be diplomatic about it? 'Well, I give them half an hour,' he says with a smile. 'But I'm still wrapped up in the game myself, and I think they should respect that.'

Brian Horton took over at Huddersfield on the heels of a torrid time at Manchester City. 'In two years I only missed one press conference, before or after the game. Many times it would have been easy to say I wouldn't do it. Saturday is the pressure time. People tell me I look tired, which isn't surprising. It does get to you after 90 minutes – that's when it all counts. Many times I have watched myself on television later that night and thought, My god, you look bloody awful. But I would much rather face the music, whether it's good or bad.'

And occasionally it all works out fine. Phil Neal: 'When we won the Sherpa Van Trophy at Wembley with Bolton, all of a sudden I realized how many smiles you can bring to people's faces. It was brilliant to see the whole town at Wembley. People dismiss that competition, but it is a great day out for the two clubs.'

MOVING ON

'You know it is the right time to move on when you don't have to stop and think about it.' The words are those of Joe Royle, much courted during his 12 years with Oldham Athletic but faithful until he opted for the Everton job in November 1994. Among the clubs who had tried to lure him away from Boundary Park was Manchester City. Royle stayed put. 'If the City offer had come at the start of that season or the end of that season it might not have been a problem. But having been with Oldham all that time, and dealing with the people there, I felt that if the moment came for me to go it would have to be done nicely. It was the biggest season in Oldham's history. We were in the hunt for promotion and had two good Cup runs. I didn't want to be remembered as the fellow who walked out on the verge of something big.'

Royle duly saw Oldham through to the Premier League, survived one close call against relegation, but couldn't save them the following year. Then came Everton. 'The time was right, and it was right for Oldham too. They needed a change. It was going to be hard to change the team because of a lack of finance. So if you can't change the players and you can't change the system, change the manager.'

The timing of Royle's move to Goodison fitted in, more or less, with Howard Kendall's definition of the best time to move – though with Everton then bottom of the table they were not the best circumstances. Kendall rejects the theory that the summer is the ideal time to switch clubs. 'You have got players who are at the end of their contracts and you have to decide whether to keep them without properly seeing them in action. You are pushed into battling with your players before they have even kicked a ball for you. The ideal situation is to go a couple of months before the end of the season, with the team in a position of safety.'

Lou Macari joined Birmingham in February 1991 on 'a poorish wage – the club had no money and I agreed that if we won anything I would be rewarded then.' That agreement proved to be the catalyst for his departure three months later. 'We took 48,000 to Wembley and won the Autoglass Trophy. The board gave me a bonus of £1200. That wasn't what I had in mind. Any manager in the game will tell you that when they win something they are looked after, and it isn't £1200. Along with my assistant Chic Bates I resigned. They offered me another bonus then but I had taken the job in faith and it hadn't been rewarded so I didn't want to continue.'

It could be one single issue like that, or it could be a combination of circumstances. When Millwall parted company with Bruce Rioch in 1992 it was as if every sign in the astrologer's chart was pointing in that direction. The team was in the wrong half of the table, the ball was going into the wrong net – a 6–1 defeat at Portsmouth was the final nail – Radio 5's Danny Baker was leading a chorus of disapproval, good players had been sold to help the finances. But the manager's personal life was in turmoil too.

'During that time my father died. That was the main reason I left. My mother had passed away while I was at Middlesbrough and I hadn't seen much of her at all and I regret that deeply. You're so preoccupied with your job, but you only have one mum. The rest of my family was in the South; I was in the North-East trying to get Middlesbrough up from the Third Division and my whole energy was going into football. She passed away and when I look back I'm so sad. So when I moved to Millwall I lived in Hertfordshire, where I am now, and I had nearly 10 months with my father, which was priceless. When he passed away it was a real body-blow.

'At around the same time I went down with measles. And I just felt it was the right time to leave. There was nothing untoward. We had generated some decent players for the club – players who had a future, like Mark Kennedy who went to Liverpool and Colin Cooper who went to Forest. Reg Burr was a great chairman. There was a bit of barracking from the crowd and Danny Baker was doing pieces on the radio, but they weren't the real reasons. The fact was that I had lost my dad, I was ill myself, and I just felt it was time to move on.'

As did Steve Coppell when his first, nine-year stint in charge at Crystal Palace ended with relegation from the Premiership. 'The week before we got relegated we won 3–0 at Ipswich and everyone thought we were safe. But the next day, a Sunday, Oldham – who were also in trouble – won away to Aston Villa, who were going for the Championship. I just knew then that Oldham would win their last two games and stay up. We had Manchester City and Arsenal away – drew one, lost the other. After we went down, I thought my resignation was best for the club. After spending so long trying to get them out of the old Second Division, I just couldn't have coped starting all over again, trying to be enthusiastic about a new season out of the top division. And it worked out right. Alan Smith took over and steered them straight back up.'

Jimmy Armfield gave the Everton chairman John Moores one of the biggest shocks of his life when he declined the opportunity to take over at Goodison Park. It was in 1973, after Bolton had won the Third Division. Everton were seeking a successor to Harry Catterick. 'I went to see John Moores at his house in Formby. I rather liked him; he seemed a very honest man. He showed me his paintings. He was very interested in music – we spent more time talking about music than Everton. I promised to give him a decision within 48 hours. The following day I rang him back and declined. He couldn't believe it. I didn't think I was quite ready. I knew Everton quite well and I didn't think it was right for me at the time.'

Five years later his managerial career was over. 'My contract at Leeds ended in October 1978. That summer I told the board that if I was to move my family over to Yorkshire – we couldn't move before because the children were taking O and A levels – I would need more security than a two-month deal. The directors said they wouldn't give me a new contract but wanted to see how the new season started. There was a board meeting just before I went on my holidays and I said, "If you're not going to give me a new contract, let's call it a day." They had a chat among themselves and said, "OK." So I thought I might as well leave then and there. One of the directors said he thought I should have fought harder for my job. But after four years you shouldn't have to fight for anything, and I certainly wasn't going down on my knees to them. After I left they struggled to find a manager – eventually Jock Stein took it, but within three months he had left to take the Scotland job.'

When things are going badly many managers jump before being pushed. But Colin Todd believes it's in the boss's interests to wait for the sack. 'My first managerial post was at Middlesbrough, where my relationship with the chairman, Colin Henderson, went downhill in my second season. I resigned, but I wouldn't do so now because I think you are better thought-of if you get the sack. People think if you resign you might be too strong – too strong for the chairmen and directors. If you're sacked, people tend to think, Well, he's done a good job there. But when you resign they think there must be some problem. It took me a long time to get back into the game after Middlesbrough, and I honestly believe the reason was that I resigned instead of waiting to be sacked.'

And sometimes it is all out of your hands. Howard Kendall was all set to leave Everton for Barcelona in 1986. 'I had an approach from Barcelona – they didn't think it necessary to go through the "right channels", they were too big for that! I kept my chairman informed and signed a provisional agreement to join them because their coach at the time, Terry Venables, was thinking of leaving. Then Terry decided at the last minute to stay, so the move was off. But I still wanted to try coaching abroad and after we won the League for a second time at Everton, in 1987, I went to Athletic Bilbao. Everton made me a very good offer to stay, but it was something I had to get out of my system.'

The next time Kendall departed from Everton it was not so amicable. It was the autumn of '93 and Kendall was desperate to strengthen a struggling team. 'I was driving myself potty looking for players who were good enough but they just weren't there. I could see even my quality players dipping because nothing was happening on my side of the desk. Eventually I settled on Dion Dublin, then with Manchester United. I had done a lot of homework, I knew I would have to pay over the odds, but we needed him. At first Alex Ferguson rejected my approach but later he agreed. I told the chairman, Dr David Marsh. The payments were agreed, and I thought everything was settled.

'Then Dr Marsh came back to me and said, "We don't like the deal." I couldn't believe it. I thought they had pushed me into a corner – maybe they wanted me out? He was adamant he wouldn't sanction the transfer and I just felt my position was being undermined.

'That Saturday we were at home to Southampton. I saw him in the car park beforehand and said, "This is my last game." The only other person who knew was Colin Harvey, my assistant.

'After the game, which we won, I was called into the chief executive's office. I said I wanted my resignation to be handled properly, with a news conference on the Monday. They had already prepared a statement, very coldly, and decided to announce it then and there. So that was that.'

THE INTERNATIONAL SCENE

It is a common complaint among managers who take international posts that the lack of day-to-day involvement with the game is the hardest aspect. That same pressurized routine which drives them up the wall at their clubs becomes as much missed as a noisy relative. Bryan Hamilton won 50 caps for Northern Ireland. Now, after managing Tranmere, Wigan, and Leicester, he is in charge of his country's footballing destiny.

'The international job is more of a coaching job. You only have players with you for a short period of time, so you have to be very specific about what you plan to do with them, totally organized and focused. I have learned that there is only so much you can do so the job has taught me patience and understanding.'

That is put to the test when you experience a home defeat at the hands of Latvia. 'I die inside, but you have to be resilient and remember that the game is not all highs. You also have to remember the tremendous feeling of winning an international match – probably the best feeling I've ever had.

'In this country we are living through such a massive change. We have had so many lost years in Northern Ireland because of the things that went on that were nothing to do with football but affected everyone's lives. So we are trying to develop international players without having the time to do it properly – which isn't fair on the players, isn't fair on me and isn't fair on the country. But it has to be done.'

Working with a national team means there is no board of directors breathing down the manager's neck, anxious for a rapid return on their personal financial investment. Hamilton is answerable to the International Committee of the Irish FA. 'They are different. They come from all sections of the community and different parts of the country. There is no financial input but pride keeps them involved. It takes longer to change things at Association level, where there has been a long-established routine. It's not like a football club, where you make one phone call and it happens.

'The game is different. I have come in at a very interesting time because we have just had the break-up of the former Soviet empire and the emergence of the African nations, plus big developments in the Far East. Football is taking off all round the world, and changing in many aspects.

'The hardest part of my job is that I desperately want to win for Northern Ireland, but I know our limitations. I am very proud to be from Northern Ireland. It is a close-knit community and when we lose a match it hurts me more than anything I have known for a long time. I do know exactly where we are coming from but they have to realize where we are coming from too. Every country wants to be the best, and sometimes people don't want to understand that in a country our size resources are limited. To lose, say, six players through injury is a massive blow.

'I know the changes that I would like to make and the players I would like to bring in, but at international level you can't go out and buy them. You can't invent them. You have to try and make things happen around what you already have. So I have tried to make myself a better coach – become more aware defensively and of how to expose other teams' limitations. I have become more intense about coaching, the chess part of football. I watch a lot of videos, a lot of matches, and I study other coaches working. I almost find that better than watching matches.'

Craig Brown manages the Scotland team from the senior end of the managerial age-range. At 55 he accepts this will be his last job as a manager. His background was one of steady grooming rather than meteoric lift-off: 10 years as part-time manager of Clyde, combining the post with lecturing at a teacher training college. Three and a half years as assistant manager to Willie McLean at Motherwell, then an invitation to join the Scotland camp when Alex Ferguson took charge during the 1986 World Cup in Mexico, followed by the assistant manager's post to Andy Roxburgh and sole charge of the under-21 team. He also had responsibility for Scotland's youth teams.

'Yes, you need a different mentality as an international manager. You suffer withdrawal symptoms from the daily contact with players. Every Saturday is a nightmare because the adrenalin doesn't flow. You go to a game but you don't care who wins. You're there to check on players for the international teams. After a while you get used to it.

'Once, as a club manager, I watched 11 games in one week. These days I see as many as I can but the administrative side of the job takes up a lot of time.' As well as being national team manager, Brown is director of coaching and has 28 full-time coaches reporting to him. 'Without the coaching role I don't think this would be a full-time job. But as it stands, it certainly is. In some respects it's more relaxing when a week comes around which has an international fixture – apart from the media involvement.'

Brown's views on the preparation of players for international football will surprise those who believe the international game should be the showcase for the most sophisticated tactics. 'You try more complicated training routines with a club side than an international side. You don't ask international players to do complex things which might embarrass them, because they switch off. Normally, you only have a couple of days to prepare for a game. You have more time to develop sophisticated tactics at club level. It's a bit easier when you are involved in a tournament, like the Toulon under-21 competition in France each summer. You can do a lot more work in that environment. But the problem with an international team is ensuring the players have enough rest. They are coming from an arduous League competition, and your objective has to be to get them to peak on the Wednesday night – or, in the World Cup or European Championships, to peak three times in one week.'

Every manager knows the difficulty of keeping players happy when they're out of the team. Brown puts a different spin on that one. 'This demands more sensitivity. The guys you've got are not used to being substitutes, or left out altogether. They are international footballers. But I have never had a problem. I have never heard an international player being huffy or jealous.

'As for money, that is never mentioned. Gary McAllister set a superb example. Before the first match in the last European Championship qualifying competition I told them that they would each be given a sheet with the bonus money set out. Gary McAllister said, "I'm not interested in that," and put his in the bin. All the younger players heard that, and they all threw their bonus sheets away too.'

Bryan Hamilton sees himself as a missionary for the game of

football in his own land. He is aware of the irony that while the game lifts off from Cameroon to Japan, here in the cradle of the sport football is under threat from countless rival leisure pursuits, while in Northern Ireland in particular, the problems of living a normal lifestyle have also diluted the appetite of the rising generation.

He recalls with dismay taking an English League team to play the Irish League in Belfast. The English team included big names like Bruce Grobbelaar, Matthew le Tissier, Graeme le Saux, Nigel Clough and Gary Mabbutt. Yet the public response was minimal. Hamilton was shocked, remembering the queues at the turnstiles that used to accompany international occasions in the past.

'I want to give something back to Northern Ireland. I have done all sorts of presentations and coaching courses to stimulate interest and make people aware that we are their team.' The bottom line is his aim to broaden the base of the squad and bring through more talented youngsters like Keith Gillespie of Newcastle United. 'When I took over there had been a lull in the game's progress after the success in the 1982 and 1986 World Cups. So I have spent a lot of time working with under-16s and under-18s. Now I want to devote more time to monitoring the progress of young professionals on the fringe of Premier League teams, to let them know we are aware of their potential.'

He dismisses the notion of calling up players who might qualify for the team even though they were not born in the province. 'I firmly believe in the Northern Ireland team consisting of Northern Ireland players. People should play for the country they were born in. These days we see players allowed to switch their national allegiance because they might have won a cap in a non-competitive game. The game is losing something as a result of that. The one thing we have always had in the Northern Irish team has been spirit, and I want to retain that.'

So how realistic can he afford to be when things go wrong? Does he forgive a defeat because his resources are slender? 'My expectations are greater for this job than any other job I have had. In the dressing room, I have been mixed with them. If we lose badly I am very disappointed. I try to be understanding because the players are young and we have had so many changes. I talk to them more. I remind them they are playing for their country, that they must have pride in their shirt, and I remind them of the aspirations of the people of Northern Ireland. I have only got really annoyed with them on a couple of occasions.'

For an international manager, leaving it till the Monday is not an option. Players disperse almost as soon as an international is over. Hamilton may not see them for another two months. 'That is the big problem. All I can do is to talk to them afterwards on the phone. For example, I gave one young player, Pat McGibbon of Manchester United, his home debut and substituted him at half-time in favour of a slightly more experienced player. After the game I didn't have a chance to talk to him. I phoned him the next night to explain the situation to him, so that he wasn't too disturbed. That is the way you have to operate at this level – to work with players, rather than be the man with the big stick.'

Craig Brown has to cope with a fiercely partisan public and expectations that are often impossible to satisfy. 'One of my hardest decisions was leaving out Paul McStay for our match with Italy in Rome. I found it very difficult to tell him I didn't think he was playing well enough, having won 72 caps for Scotland. When the news hit the press you would have thought I'd killed my next of kin! I couldn't believe the reaction. There was great indignation. But it didn't bother me because I believed I was doing the right thing.

'The press keep pestering me to play Richard Gough of Rangers but I think the team is better without him. Sometimes you can get the full venom even when you win. We took a lot of criticism when we only beat San Marino 2–0. The sports writers can be quite vitriolic but, again, I don't get concerned about it.

'There's been criticism about my own appointment. It's fashionable to knock the governing body and there were plenty who would have preferred an appointment from one of the big clubs. But what we're trying to do is develop the Liverpool approach and groom from within. It hasn't been too unsuccessful. Andy Roxburgh was more successful as Scotland manager than the late great Jock Stein. There are so many facets of international football – for a club manager it's like starting from scratch.

'It helps that I am 55 years of age and could have retired if I wanted to. This isn't a career move for me. I am more philosophical than a younger man so I can take the pressures, but it's pride that motivates me. I feel accountable to the nation, and that is a far greater responsibility than developing your personal career. Pleasing the Scotland support gives me a huge thrill because it's so fervent and enthusiastic. They pay their money and are totally committed to the team. If you let them down you feel distressed. If I stopped to think about the responsibility I would start to worry about it. But I feel comfortable with what I'm doing – it's only afterwards that you sometimes think, If we'd lost that one there would have been people going home punching their wives.

'What you must be in this job is very single-minded. That's why I admire Sir Alf Ramsey – he felt England would be better off without Jimmy Greaves and stuck to his guns. Jack Charlton was equally single-minded when he left Brady and Stapleton out of the Republic's team.'

Brown believes international football no longer exerts the same hold on supporters worldwide. 'There is only one country which can attract full houses for its international matches – the Republic of Ireland. When we played in Rome, there were 20,000 unsold tickets. It's the same in Spain. In Amsterdam, Ajax will attract bigger crowds than Holland. Rangers pull in more than Scotland. The marketing of football at club level is very slick, big overseas stars are turning out for club sides and the whole emphasis has changed.'

The man now guiding Scotland's fortunes may not have played international football himself but he did experience one of the greatest odysseys at club level. Brown was in the Dundee team that rocked Europe by reaching the semi-finals of the European Cup in 1963. He points the finger at today's club managers for letting their country down when it comes to ensuring players turn up for international duty.

'The nature of the job makes some of them frightened. A lot of the withdrawals from international squads come from managers who are afraid they will lose their next game because a player is injured or tired.'

While Scotland have one man to head up both the international team and the domestic coaching programme,

England made the decision to split the roles when Terry Venables took over from Graham Taylor. The appointment of Venables came on the recommendation of Jimmy Armfield, hired by the FA as their Technical Consultant. According to Armfield, a man's ability to coach is not the decisive factor in such a decision – although clearly it is very important. 'You've really got to be able to handle the media on the large scale. And you've got to be able to live with everything else that goes with the job – it's life in a goldfish bowl. The other major qualification is that a man who runs an international team should have had experience of working in another country. Otherwise he's too insular in his thinking (Venables, of course, worked with Barcelona; Glenn Hoddle with Monaco). It doesn't mean he's going to be successful, because it is not about managers – it's about players. Alf Ramsey's success was not based on his ability to manage, but was due to having three world-class players (Banks, Moore and Bobby Charlton) who would have got into anyone's team, and another seven or eight who were pretty good.

'If you look back through the successful teams at international level, not many managers spring to mind – it's the players we all remember.'

Ramsey had the title of England manager. So did Revie, Greenwood, Robson and Taylor. Venables was England coach, the same title inherited by Glenn Hoddle when he took over following the 1996 European Championships. Armfield says the distinction is important. 'Graham Taylor and all the people before him ran the entire coaching scheme and all sorts of things. But they're only judged on one thing – the England team's results. So the coach should be given the chance to concentrate on that. It's no good people saying, "He did a fantastic job with the England coaching school." That isn't what counts. It's how the international team fares, and these days international football is all about winning, winning and winning.'

It was his spell in charge of Scotland that gave Alex Ferguson his least enjoyable experience as a football manager. Ferguson took over on a temporary basis after Jock Stein collapsed and died at a World Cup qualifier against Wales in Cardiff. Ferguson was Aberdeen manager and Stein's part-time assistant. He was beside him in the dug-out that night. 'Jock was ashen, and suffering from a chest infection, but you don't realize how serious things are till it's too late. He had a bout of angina the year before. There was a cameraman who was a real nuisance, lying in front of the dug-out taking photographs all the time. That didn't help. Jock lost his temper with him. It was not a very nice night.

'I had a really good relationship with Jock. I found him to be an immensely clever and powerful man who was unquestionably ahead of his time.'

Ferguson agreed to take temporary charge, to see the Scotland team through the upcoming World Cup finals in Mexico. 'I enjoyed it up to the World Cup itself. We had to play off against Australia, then played Romania, which was Kenny Dalglish's 100th cap, England and Holland. I felt good and in control, although I do believe that my main job as Aberdeen manager suffered. That season we finished fourth, the lowest in my time there.

'The moment I had to pick the squad to go to Mexico I stopped feeling comfortable. One of the problems was having to be fair-minded about the Aberdeen players in the squad – I had six of them, plus two ex-Aberdeen lads, Gordon Strachan and Steve Archibald. Trying to pick the right team and be fair to my own players was difficult. The one time I let myself down was when I selected Paul McStay of Celtic ahead of Jim Bett for the final match against Uruguay. I needed someone to take over from Graeme Souness and I should have picked Bett. He was a better player than McStay at the time, a more mature player. The reason I didn't pick Jim Bett was because he was an Aberdeen player. That was a silly one.

'The World Cup is supposed to be a festival of football, but Mexico was no festival. It wasn't well organized and the hotel was claustrophobic. Nice place, nice people, but I didn't enjoy it.'

Bobby Gould applied for the Welsh job after two years out of football because 'I started to feel hungry for management again. And my wife didn't object too much – in fact she was intrigued by the idea.' Having moved from a media job with Sky TV, Gould did not go through the withdrawal symptoms, described by Craig Brown, of a man stepping over the line from club management. 'This is a new venture for me and it's a wonderful opportunity to be working at international level. For a kid who was told at 15 he'd never make it to be handling international players – dream on!

'At a club, everyone wants a piece of you, and you find it very difficult not to come apart at the seams. Here, I've got the chance to put my feet under the table and run things the way I think they should be run, with proper time to organize things. I don't have to worry about paying a player £15,000 a week. I've got a shirt to give him, and the pride that comes when he puts it on. It's back to the old values of football, the way it ought to be.'

THE SECOND MAN

Some managers go it alone; most work closely with a trusted lieutenant who has the title of coach or assistant manager. Often, the lieutenant is the man who benefits when the manager gets the boot – promoted into his mentor's empty office.

Joe Royle's partnership with Willie Donachie is one which has stood the test of time. The two met as players at Manchester City where Royle led the attack while Donachie propped up the defence at left-back. They teamed up as a manager/coaching duo at Oldham and the pairing transferred intact to Everton. Royle is very much the front man, but he is quick to include Donachie in any assessment of success.

'There's no ego problem with either of us. There has never been a harboured thought or a massive secret. I have always said to Willie if he ever wanted to try his hand at a manager's job I wouldn't stand in his way. Knowing him the way I do I think he's happy working out there with the players, and all the peripheral matters which are also part of the manager's job aren't for him. He's a great coach. A lot of great coaches become ordinary managers, although I am not saying that would necessarily be the case with Willie. But it is a different job.'

Terry McDermott has the assistant manager's title at Newcastle United, working with Kenny Dalglish, and before that with Kevin Keegan. 'I tried to take on a lot of Kevin's workload. Any Premier League manager needs someone to act as a buffer. I got involved in every aspect of the job. We had no secrets from each other and we both approached the game in the same way. We liked a laugh – it's important to enjoy life and we tried to instil that in the players.'

Jimmy Armfield accuses managers of letting their employers down when it comes to appointing assistants – the implication being that they're frightened of being replaced by their deputy. 'I've always felt managers don't try to obtain the best staff. It suggests to me there's a degree of insecurity within them. And yet they have a responsibility to their clubs. If they are ill, who will take over? You should have the best staff you can find.'

The most bizarre appointment of a second man came early in the '96–97 season when Stewart Houston embarked on his career as manager of Queens Park Rangers. Houston impressed as assistant to Bruce Rioch at Arsenal before taking over as caretaker when Rioch was chopped. Now, having moved to QPR after the resignation of Ray Wilkins, he sought an assistant in the person of his old boss.

Even more surprising was Rioch's decision to accept. If ever there was a manager who seemed tailor-made for the job of number one, with the decision-making that goes with it, it was the man who now found himself part of a weird reversal of roles.

'It was the first start of a season that I'd missed since I came into the game as a player,' he explains. 'I did some radio and TV work, and while I was grateful for that I really wanted to get back into the game in an active capacity. So when the opportunity came along to join Stewart at Rangers it didn't take too much thinking about.'

The chance arose when Rioch travelled to Colchester to watch his son Greg in action for Hull City in a match at Layer Road. Houston lives in Colchester and the two men met for dinner. Houston mentioned that he was looking for an assistant and popped the question. Possibly to the surprise of both, Rioch said yes. 'I joined him because we'd had such a good working relationship over the past 12 months. We didn't know each other very well prior to my joining Arsenal, but over the 12 months we got to know each other extremely well. He's a very loyal, honest person, with tremendous integrity. There wasn't a problem over the reversal of roles because I knew what would be required.

Stewart was going into his first managerial job and would need as much support and experience as he could gather around him.

'Over the years you do get used to having the final say. But if you go into the job as assistant you know the manager is the one who will have the decisions. Your job is to advise, discuss, debate, give him the food for thought if he asks for it, but then the manager must make the final decision.

'I don't think coaches appreciate the difficulty of the job until they're actually in the seat themselves. Stewart has certainly found it enjoyable but demanding. As assistant it is less demanding. I like management. I always have done. But I would rather be working in football than sitting at home.'

The last word on coaches goes to Bobby Gould. 'When I went to Wimbledon I needed a coach so I went for the best – Don Howe. It was like being a wallflower at a Saturday hop and asking Miss World to dance.'

6

LIFE IN THE SLOW LANE

It had seemed a good idea at the time. A mid-season break in the Mediterranean resort of Magaluf was a reward for some good results, and a chance to gee the players up for the rest of the season. But arriving at the airport for the homeward flight the news wasn't good. The flight was delayed, and the management knew that every hour that passed would cost them dearly at the other end.

For Third Division Mansfield Town the fact that they were able to take a break at all was an achievement. But the budget was tight, and the chairman, Keith Haslam, had no choice but to accept a package which kept the squad in Magaluf until the Friday – the day before their next League fixture, away to Exeter. It was a tight schedule, but so long as nothing went wrong they would get away with it.

Of course, something did go wrong. Flight delays meant the party didn't arrive back at East Midlands Airport until 10 p.m. on the Friday night. There they embarked on the team coach for the long haul west to Exeter, getting to bed far into the small hours. Next day, going through the motions, they were lucky to win – lucky, perhaps, that Exeter were statistically the worst team in the League that season.

For Andy King, the then Mansfield manager, the episode was another example of the compromises a professional must make to survive in the lower divisions. Despite the 2–1 victory he was furious – with the players, the airline, the airport, and mostly himself.

'We should never have arranged to fly back on the Friday. I knew it was wrong but it was the only time the chairman could fix the trip. All right we got caught out at the airport but it was bad management on my part to allow it to happen.

'In the match the players were lethargic and lazy. Useless. We were lucky to win. I went mad at them. I couldn't shout at myself so I shouted at them.'

Mansfield Town FC hugs the hillside on the southern approach to the town. Field Mill is a rambling old stadium, with a main stand which was spectacular in its heyday and still impresses even though it belongs to a pre-Taylor Report era.

In the manager's office a framed photograph captured manager King and the Brazilian star Zico having a good time in New York. The offices, like the rest of the stadium, were in a timewarp and could have used some fresh paint. The one exception was the physiotherapy room which gleamed with high-tec efficiency, the result of a special grant which the club had to spend on medical facilities. Outside, a minibus awarded when Mansfield reached the Freight Rover Cup Final in 1987 rusted quietly. The chat between manager and chairman was about improving the training facilities. Keith Haslam thought he had reached an agreement to use a council pitch. 'But who's providing the goal nets?' King wanted to know. The impression was that the team had been caught out before by training on pitches with no nets.

The facts of life in the lower divisions hit you like a jammed turnstile – hard. Money is a constant talking point. Only a handful of teams pull in decent attendances. The majority struggle to stay alive, cadging sponsorship where they can, postponing bills for as long as possible, hoping for a good Cup run or the sale of a player to keep the ship afloat.

When Bury engaged the managerial services of Martin Dobson in 1984 he was told by the chairman that the club operated on a budget of minus £100,000 per year. It was up to the manager to bring in the difference, through transfer dealing or uncommon success on the field. In the nineties, things haven't changed in the Second and Third Divisions of the Nationwide League. If anything, the belt is being tugged a few notches tighter. The Premier League breakaway meant television and sponsorship money which used to be shared throughout the 92 clubs of the old Football League was scooped up by the 22 teams – now reduced to 20 – in the breakaway élite. The clubs on the wrong side of the tracks were left to fight for the coppers.

At the wealthy clubs like Manchester United, Blackburn and Arsenal the players have lunches cooked for them daily at their training headquarters, using the best nutritional advice. Each player has several pairs of boots provided. Many are paid £100,000 or more to wear certain brands. Travel is by air or luxury coach and overnight accommodation is in five-star hotels. At Mansfield the players bring packed lunches and eat them in the dressing rooms. They buy their own boots. Overnight hotels before away matches are rare. 'We might have got an overnight stay before the Plymouth match,' said King. 'But a lot would depend on where we were in the League. If we were bottom of the table and struggling we wouldn't get an overnight stay in a hotel. It would be an early start and straight there.

'These are all things that come with every club at this level. It might be a culture shock at first for a young player who joins a club like Mansfield from a Premier League club, but he's so excited at being part of a first-team squad that he forgets it. The one bugbear is the training facilities. You like to have a decent surface and we didn't have one. It was worse in the summer when the pitches are rock-hard. I like to work with the players on touch and control, but on a bad surface with a bad ball that's got no casing on it the session is ruined. They say the Brazilian players have such great skills because they practise on the beach, but I can't believe that. If you train on good facilities it does improve your standards.

'We are all very devoted professionals and we all strive to reach the heights of the Premier League, but the Premier League have cut us off. The media has done it as much as the game itself – the media are only interested in the Premier clubs. Some of the revenue coming into the game could be shared better than it is. I wouldn't ask for millions. But a few training balls that England kick away wouldn't go amiss. I don't think they realize the severe problems such clubs have. Mansfield's cashflow situation was so severe we trained at the end of one season with one single football. Our minibus was so bad that our youth team and reserves were travelling to matches in sub-standard travel.'

Outside football's magic circle the manager has to be even more of a magician. He lacks the support mechanisms his counterparts in the Premier League and the First Division take for granted. When a problem arises, the one thing that can't be thrown at it is money. Yet the demand for victory on Saturday is identical. 'The only thing that frightened me,' said King, 'was the effect a defeat had. The consequences of defeat if you're in a promotion place and have to keep winning, or if you're in relegation trouble and mustn't lose. You could only go four games without a win and the crowd would start calling for your head. But on the other side of the coin, I loved winning. I didn't get carried away by it, but there's nothing better.'

If football management is a test of character, in the lower divisions it's all that and more. The one man who cannot afford to be ground down by the poor facilities, the threadbare budget, the flaking paintwork, is the boss. And that is where the smaller clubs are usually better off than they realize, because the manager, almost without exception, is motivated by a passion for the game that defies rational explanation.

'Simply driving into a football ground gives me so much joy in life,' said King. 'Most people in work look forward to Friday night so they can have a weekend off. To me, Sunday wasn't a day off, it was something that got in the way of work – between a match on Saturday, and training on Monday.'

Andy King cajoled and inspired his Mansfield team to a memorable season in '94–95. They had some Cup glory and reached the play-offs. At the end of the season he said: 'I've created my own monster now. The club and the supporters want more success. But three of my best players have been sold, so whether I can produce the goods again is something that scares me. We need to win the first round of the League Cup, the first round of the FA Cup, and do well in the Auto Windscreens Trophy. The extra finance means survival.'

Sadly for King, Mansfield had no good Cup runs that year and the monster duly devoured him. The team subsided to 19th place and a few weeks into the next campaign he was out.

What he'd needed was a repeat of one of the most famous victories in Mansfield's history. In September 1994 his collection of free transfers and bright youngsters beat Leeds United in the

Coca-Cola Cup, 1–0 at Elland Road. In the second leg they held out for a goalless draw to claim one of the giant-killing feats of the year. Nights like that make a lot of frustration over training pitches worth while.

'The pleasing thing was that it was over two legs. If we had beaten them in a one-off game people could have said we had caught them on an off-night. In the first leg at Elland Road it was a case of 11 players playing beyond themselves, each man thinking it was the last game of his life. My talk to them in the dressing room was: "You may not get an opportunity like this again, so go out and enjoy it. Don't be afraid of them. Don't sit back and let them come at you or they'll kill you." I had watched Leeds and I felt that if we put their midfield under pressure we might have a chance. We did have a plan – we had a lot of pace in the team, and we played to it. We got a goal and for 75 minutes we gave everything to hold on to it. In the dressing room afterwards there were people being physically sick through the effort and the emotion. So that was good, but it was even more rewarding after the second leg. They knew what they were up against and we not only held them but created chances and could well have gone in front.'

That win over the two legs earned Mansfield not only a dubious trip to Magaluf but a third-round tie against Wolves of Division One. Amazingly King's team went into a 2–0 lead by half-time, only to lose 3–2. 'I had been to watch them, seen what I thought was a weakness – lack of pace at the back – and for 45 minutes we tore them apart. But at half-time I couldn't get them to believe they could win. I could sense it. If we'd carried on the way we were playing we would have beaten Wolves 5–0. But once they scored one goal, nine of our players dropped behind the ball and let them have the initiative. Sure enough Wolves scored two more goals to win the game.

'What you have to accept is that players are at that level for a reason. It may be because they can't handle the pressure. You can't expect them to sustain a certain quality of performance for a long period of time against higher opposition. They might do it for 45 minutes, but you can't expect it for 90 minutes.'

* * *

At a small club the manager is closer to the coalface than his counterpart in the upper echelons. The essential work is the same, but there are fewer people on hand to help with the digging. Like Mike Walker with his self-op laundromat activities at Colchester, the manager is always likely to chip in when the system breaks down.

Bryan Hamilton found the system close to meltdown while he was player-manager of Tranmere Rovers, then in Division Four. 'When you go to a smaller club you have to touch almost everything – commercial, PR, coaching, contracts. When I went to Tranmere I didn't realize all the problems they had, but I soon found out. There were difficulties regarding the finances, and that meant having to make decisions that would affect every part of the football club. It was a lesson to me, before taking any future appointment, to get to know more about the financial background of a club.'

Hamilton came in with ambitious plans but soon had to water them down. 'It happens in almost every job. Your ambitions are so high but unless you are with one of the top few clubs you have to limit what you can do. The problems at Tranmere actually stimulated me even more. It was difficult because I had to make a lot of decisions which I didn't feel were right for the football side of the club. For example, we had to cancel almost all the youth policy. We couldn't afford to run the teams, use the training facilities or employ the staff. We did away with two teams, and four or five part-time coaches and scouts, which was disastrous. But there was no alternative. Tranmere were nearly the first club since Accrington Stanley in 1962 to go out of the League because the money ran out. So decisions had to be made for the future of the club.'

One phenomenon the wealthy clubs will never know is how a community rallies round its football club in its hour of need. That was the case with Tranmere in the cash-strapped eighties, and, inevitably, it was the manager who was obliged to take the lead – putting on the brave face, rallying the public and keeping the players up to scratch at the same time.

'It got to the stage where we had sold three or four players and I told the directors we had to go public over our problems.

It was unfair not to tell the supporters exactly where we were at. So they did, and from there we attracted a lot of goodwill from the community. Clubs came to play fundraising matches for us – Liverpool, Everton, Manchester United, Wolves. A lot of people worked hard to keep the club alive and I'll always remember that as a special time in my management career because I felt there was a real unity about the place. They say that, in adversity, sometimes you surprise yourselves, and I felt that happened during that time at Tranmere. Now, I'm delighted to see the club doing so well.

'The other thing about a small club is that you have no money to buy players so you have to produce and groom them yourself. At Tranmere we did that with players like Colin Clarke, John Clayton, Dave Burgess and John Williams, who all went on to bigger and better things. I enjoyed that; it was probably one of the most exciting and rewarding parts of my career. When you take something as desperate as that and make something of it, you feel you have achieved something.'

But that reputation for making a silk purse from a sow's ear landed Hamilton in a situation that almost got out of control. It was the second of two spells at Wigan Athletic. The first (March '85 to June '86) was a success – the team went to Wembley to win the Freight Rover Trophy, then missed promotion to the old Second Division by a point. But when he returned to Springfield Park after a spell at Leicester he was given the post of chief executive. Suddenly, the business decisions were his.

'When I came back to Wigan the club was in serious financial trouble. I was more involved on the financial side without having real experience of it. That worried me. I never felt comfortable in the job. I had to get involved with ground safety and VAT. It was also the time when the Football League structure was changing, so I was involved in all that. There were all sorts of areas of the club that needed attention – the business side, the commercial side – and I didn't know enough about them. I used to go in and read reports and try to understand them, but quite honestly it got to the stage where it was all too much and I was running rings round myself.' So he stepped back from the administrative side of the job and concentrated on coaching footballers, happy to bring down the curtain on a sobering experience.

Politics are rarely far from the surface at a football club. Often it seems that the smaller the club, the more disruptive the politics. Graham Barrow discovered the truth of that at the very time when life should have been at its most settled.

Barrow took over as manager of Second Division Chester City in the winter of '92. The team was already at the foot of the table and he couldn't prevent them tumbling into Division Three. The following season, however, he brought them back up, an unexpected success. Instead of being fêted by the directors as the man who had achieved the impossible, Barrow found himself eased out. Unable to secure a new job, he signed on the dole.

'We went through some very strange circumstances at Chester,' he says, and you can sense the understatement.

It was a tricky time for everyone connected with the club. Yet another to suffer a cash crisis, Chester had been saved by the intervention of a development company, the Scottish-based Morrison Group. The company bought the club lock, stock and barrel, in order to demolish the old stadium at Sealand Road, turn the site into a retail park, and relocate the footballers on a greenfield site on the edge of town. The scheme duly happened, and with the new stadium open Morrison's wanted to offload the football club and concentrate on other projects. The problem was that candidates were not exactly rushing forward to take the now-solvent club off Morrison's hands. While the boardroom awaited new owners, Barrow got on with the task of winning promotion.

The players clinched their return to Division Two with two matches in hand. 'It was the best feeling I have had in football,' says Barrow. 'After going through the nerves of every Saturday it was a tremendous relief – especially as I had been the manager who took them down the year before.

'Nobody knew what pressure I had been under since Christmas, when the owners were trying to sell the club and none of the directors seemed really interested in anything that was going on. I couldn't allow the circumstances to get through to the players. It only came to their attention at the very end of the season when there were a couple of sportsmen's dinners and not a single representative of the club was there. Only the supporters, no directors.

'After matches I would spend time with the players, then go up to have a drink with the directors and find they had all gone home!

'There were problems from the start of that season. I spent the summer signing players on free transfers and felt quite pleased with the squad. The day before the first match, against Doncaster, we were training when the secretary informed me that none of the players had actually been registered with the club as I thought. Apparently the owners were expecting to offload the club but by the following summer the club still hadn't been sold. There were disagreements between the manager and the chief executive over new contracts for the players. Convinced that his position was being eroded, Barrow resigned.

'I had just signed a two-year contract and I could have sat there and picked up the money. But at the time when we needed more players they were trying to get rid of the ones we already had. I saw it as a matter of principle so I quit.

'It didn't seem such a great idea when July came and I was still out of work. My brother is a self-employed painter-decorator, and two months after winning promotion I found myself painting a ceiling at a social club in Chorley when I should have been supervising pre-season training. I put it off for as long as possible, but I had to sign on the dole eventually. The girl asked me what I did. I said, "I was a football manager last year, but I'm also a qualified central heating engineer." She said, "We've got no vacancies for football managers and there are 500 central heating engineers already on the books." So there was nothing.

'When the season started I didn't watch any matches, except for the odd non-League game at Chorley. I used to go and stand there by myself. I couldn't get myself up to go anywhere else. I was just living off hope that I would find another job in football. I was manager of a promotion-winning team, which was a good record. But it wasn't a long record; I had been a manager less than two seasons.

'All you can do in that situation is wait for someone to get the sack. I got an interview at Blackpool but it sounded as bad as

Chester. There were various conditions about reporting to other people and working with various coaches. I didn't like the sound of that.

'I remember I was at home putting up my son's Scalextric when I heard on the radio that the Wigan manager, Kenny Swain, had gone. Walsall's manager went on the same day. I know it sounds bad, but it took two managers getting the sack to lift my spirits. I thought I might have a chance. I had an interview for the Wigan job. Heard nothing and was about to apply for the Walsall vacancy when the Wigan chairman got in touch. He said, "We've got a game against Hereford tomorrow and we need a manager." I was back in business.'

Once again Barrow was asked to take over a club at the bottom of the table – this time, bottom of the entire League. He brought about another revival, steering Wigan to a mid-table position. In the meantime boardroom politics surfaced again as his new club was taken over. Again Barrow was the loser. The new owner, David Whelan, had dreams of the Premiership and recruited a former Premiership manager, John Deehan. Barrow was out of work for seven months before returning with Rochdale. 'I love the work, but in the boardroom, you never know what reaction you'll get. Win, lose or draw.'

There are times when it must be hard for a manager to decide if the job on offer is a proper challenge or a poisoned chalice. Exeter City had a nightmare season in 1994–95 – the team finished bottom of the League and would have been relegated but for the failure of the top non-League side, Macclesfield Town, to satisfy the Third Division's minimum entry standards. Not unconnected with the team's failings was a financial crisis which almost saw the club fold. The manager, Terry Cooper, decided he had had enough and the job was offered to the side's veteran goalkeeper, Peter Fox. Presumably on the basis that all goalkeepers are a bulb short of a floodlight pylon. Sure enough, Fox accepted.

It looked a reckless move but Fox went into the task with both eyes open. In addition to coaching certificates he had a diploma in sports and recreation management and was taking an NVQ in teaching adult education, 'which is proving very useful,' he says. 'I knew exactly what I was taking on because I had been here a couple of years as a player and reserve coach. Success for this club will be a mid-table position on the field – and still being in existence in 12 months' time. If I can achieve anything here, I should be able to achieve things anywhere!'

The Premier League clubs attract most of the money, most of the glamour, most of the media. But that doesn't mean everything of value is concentrated in the wealthy élite. Life in the slow lane can be surprisingly rewarding. Just as at the top, what matters most is that the partnership is right between chairman and manager.

Crewe Alexandra ceased to be the butt of anyone's jokes a long time ago. These days the club on the main line from Euston to Glasgow is envied as a rare point of stability in a volatile business.

Dario Gradi, Milan-born, London-bred, Cheshire-adopted, has transformed Crewe from a destination where ageing professionals tended to hit the buffers into an international departure hub. 'Crewe,' he explains, 'are a coaching club. We are in the business of coaching and improving players.' Gradi and his staff run an impressive youth scheme, operating teams from under-l0s up. The summer of 1995 saw the under-lls on a trip to America, the under-12s in the West Country, the under-14s and the under-16s in Ireland. Crewe have 150 youngsters associated with them, plus 23 trainees on YTS places and 25 professionals. The flow from the club's own scheme is augmented by crafty recruitment from elsewhere – players abandoned on free transfers by bigger clubs reappear within months showing a confidence and skill no one suspected they had. Rescuing David Platt after he had been rejected by Manchester United, and setting him up for a career that took him to Aston Villa, Juventus, Sampdoria, Arsenal, and the England captaincy, is a justifiable source of pride for the remarkable man at the helm. Nor is Platt by any means the only one. Crewe, over the years, consistently supply the Premier League with outstanding footballers.

There is a rare harmony at Gresty Road which stems from unity of purpose. 'Every club has to know where it's at, what its role is in life,' says Gradi. 'Unrealistic expectations are pointless.

When I first came to Crewe in 1983 I asked the directors what they expected of me as manager. They said that if we finished fifth from bottom – in the old Fourth Division – they would give me a contract for next season. If we finished in the bottom four they would probably give me a contract anyway. The aim was to keep them out of financial trouble, and that is still a major consideration. If we have some success along the way, that's terrific – and we have managed to do so.'

Gradi has stayed at Crewe for over 13 years – a remarkable stint. It is not coincidental that the boardroom has been unusually stable as well. The present chairman, John Bowler, was a director when Gradi arrived; the then chairman, Norman Rowlinson, is still on the board and is the club's president. 'The directors are all local men and they are fans of the club,' says Gradi. 'They are not of the breed that arrives from somewhere else, wanting to make a name for themselves as well as the club. So they are pleased to see the progress we've made.'

Crewe have given Gradi a stable, supportive environment and he has rewarded them. The team has risen from the Fourth Division to what is now the Second, missing out on a place in the First Division only in the play-offs in '94–95. Well-established clubs view a Cup tie against Crewe with trepidation (in 1992 West Ham lost 2–0 in the Coca-Cola Cup at Crewe after a 0–0 draw at Upton Park). And the club's reputation for polishing rough diamonds is now legendary.

So what are the tricks everyone else is missing? One is that the good relationship between manager and board is not left to chance. Gradi makes a point of dining out with the chairman once a fortnight – nothing special on the agenda, just a chance to talk football and iron out any problems. 'It's a useful way of making sure relationships don't get strained. They are bound to be stretched from time to time but you have to get on and it's up to both sides to be sensible.'

Money is rarely a cause of friction. Crewe's policy is straightforward. If there's money available, the manager can spend it. Anything he shells out, he has to recoup. 'It is ridiculous for a manager to go into battle with his chairman over money for signings. You have to get on with your chairman, see his point of view.'

Certainly Gradi's handling of his players is different. There are no laddish pre-season trips or mid-winter breaks here. 'I don't believe in things like that to foster team spirit. Team spirit has to take care of itself here. As soon as you go away there's a problem: what to do in the evenings? The players end up having a drink. Someone will buy a round, then someone else will. They go out nightclubbing. It's counterproductive. To make the trip pay you've got to play too many games in a short time, so you end up with strained muscles. So we stay here and work.'

Gresty Road isn't the lap of luxury, even by the standards of the lower reaches of the Nationwide League, but it isn't Bleak House either. Crewe are negotiating for 17 acres of land for a new training ground, and while Gradi cheerfully drives the minibus and helps stow the kit, he no longer has to help with the commercial department or the PR side. 'Even though we are a small club, we are getting bigger,' he says.

'This is a good way of preparing managers for the higher leagues. It surprises me that so many well-known players go straight into management jobs at the top level. They would be better off emulating George Graham and starting off as a youth coach, or Brian Little who began at Darlington.'

So why, comes the inevitable question, has Gradi been content to stay in the small pond when, by anyone's standards, he has passed all the exams to swim in the open water? 'I haven't closed the door on a Premier League job if the right one came along. But sometimes I see my name linked with a vacancy and I think, I wouldn't fancy that. To get on with players you have to respect them, and there are an awful lot of them that I don't have enough respect for, either as players or as people. Whereas if you develop your own players you can bring them up the way you want them. I would rather see our young kids coming through here than deal with the so-called superstars with their accountants and agents.'

Nonetheless, Gradi has an escape clause written into his contract. It specifies what Crewe's compensation will be if he moves up. The last major club to sniff refused the compensation, so Crewe's directors refused permission for the club to talk to the manager. Gradi was far from miffed. 'If they're the sort of club that won't meet a fairly modest compensation claim, why would I want to go there anyway?'

The slow lane it may be, but the journey is every bit as fascinating, the arriving even more rewarding.

7

IS THE PRICE RIGHT?

The day Kenny Dalglish resigned as Liverpool manager was the day I went to the Fleetwood Beer Festival. There is no link between the two events – except that the impact of the Dalglish resignation means I will always remember what I was doing when I heard the news.

It had a sobering effect.

Then came the two inevitable questions: Was it true? And if so, why?

The news conference relayed from Anfield answered both. Yes, it was true – there was Dalglish sitting alongside the Liverpool chairman Noel White as White read out the statement. Why? It was etched all over the man's face.

'This is the first time I have made a decision that is more to the benefit of Kenny Dalglish than Liverpool Football Club,' said Dalglish. His features were a mask of taut control. The eyes that had sized up a thousand half-chances were dull and lowered. Here was a man who had been driven to the edge of something, something that perhaps not even he could identify. Except that, wherever it was, it was also the end of the road.

As an example of managerial burn-out, Dalglish's abrupt exit from Anfield – 48 hours after a 4–4 draw with Everton, which had tested everyone's emotional stamina – was an extreme example of what can happen to a football boss when the strain really bites.

I am making no attempt to analyse the psychology of the Dalglish case. It is enough to know that he recognized the end of his tether when it came into view. But the build-up to that moment was not something which happened overnight. His entire experience of the manager's job was enough of a mental and emotional test to have wrung out a less resilient character ten times over. That experience also emphasizes how much our football clubs demand of the guy who gives the team its final pep talk. Dalglish took over in the worst possible circumstances – the day after the Heysel Stadium disaster. It should have been a relatively smooth transfer of power from the outgoing Joe Fagan, whose swansong was the European Cup Final between Liverpool and Juventus. Instead, with 39 spectators dead, most of them Italian, following fighting on the terraces, Dalglish found himself representing the public face of Liverpool FC on the one day in its history when no one else would have wanted the role.

At the same time Liverpool were facing up to a ban from European football, with the knowledge that other English clubs were being tarred with the same brush. And Dalglish was still required as a player.

Six years on, the date of his resignation found Kenny Dalglish a man drained by the soul-destroying demands of football management. It wasn't enough that his first season should see him inspire Liverpool to the League and Cup Double. It wasn't enough that they should add two more Championships and another FA Cup. Football had to throw at him the Hillsborough disaster as well.

Dalglish's position as manager of the Liverpool team on the day that 95 people (rising later to 96) died in the crush before the FA Cup semi-final against Nottingham Forest was taxing enough. But it was his role as front man for the grief of the entire city of Liverpool which really bit deep. Anfield became a focal point for bereaved families. Dalglish, sober-suited, usually accompanied by his wife Marina, was always there, available to share quiet moments in his office or alongside the field of flowers that covered the pitch. Trained counsellors and men of the cloth played their part, but it was the manager they all really wanted to see.

Nothing in his experience could possibly have prepared Kenny Dalglish for the demands that were made on him in the wake of Hillsborough. But he was the manager of Liverpool FC. He had a role to play even if he didn't know the lines. There could be no hiding even if he felt like declaring 'enough'.

Trevor Hicks, spokesman for the bereaved relatives, remembers the visible strain on the manager's face. 'I wonder whether the strain of Hillsborough wasn't a major factor in his decision to resign,' he says. Hicks lost two daughters, Sarah and Victoria, at Hillsborough. Like hundreds of other grieving relatives in the days following the tragedy, he was drawn to Anfield. 'The first person I met from the club was Marina Dalglish. Along with some of the other wives, she was running an informal coffee stall and counselling service. Marina, I thought, was an absolutely wonderful person, and that opinion hasn't changed. As daft as it seems, we were able to have a laugh and a joke. Her heart was completely in what she was doing.

'I met Kenny soon afterwards at a memorial service at the Anglican Cathedral. I don't know of a single reasonable request that he refused, from attending funerals to arranging for family members to be mascots at matches. He was involved in lots of little things which by themselves might not seem much but added up to a huge commitment. All that and running the team as well.'

Hillsborough showed how the manager of a football club has a role in the community that transcends football. He becomes the focal point for the town's hopes and fears, a touchstone of the good and the bad.

The disaster gave Dalglish an even higher profile, unwelcome for a man who dislikes the limelight at the best of times. Even as a player, Dalglish was uneasy in the media spotlight. Reluctant to give the interviews that his talent inevitably prompted, he was never one for the outrageous comment or the boastful prediction. The result is that the public often sees a dour and grim Dalglish when the real man is warm, humorous and intensely loyal.

His relationship with the media has often been testy. From the start he was driven by a determination that none of his players should learn information about his career from the newspapers. As a player himself, Dalglish saw how demoralizing it was for a player to learn he had been axed by reading it in the paper. He has always been fiercely protective of his players, and if that means giving the media short shrift, so be it.

But the pressures of rebuilding an ageing Liverpool team, against such a background of human tragedy, became too much for him in the end. It took him eight months to regain an appetite for the game. Then came Blackburn Rovers, another Championship – and another surprise resignation.

Dalglish's switch from team manager to director of football in June 1995 was far from the sensation of his Anfield exit. It was a logical move for Dalglish, for Blackburn, and for Ray Harford, the coach, who achieved his aim of returning to team management without having to move clubs. Significantly, Dalglish stressed at the time: 'I wasn't prepared to commit myself for seven days a week, which is what is required to be the manager of a football club. Anybody in any walk of life would like more leisure time. I am fortunate in that I'm in a position where I can say I can help, but I don't want to commit myself seven days a week.'

Kenny Dalglish has often appeared to have the Midas touch, whether as a player at Celtic and Liverpool, or a manager at Liverpool and Blackburn. But the cost was high. Football management took him to the edge of a nervous breakdown. Even the final parting from Blackburn left much to be desired. On holiday in Spain at the start of season 1996–97 he decided his role as director of football was going nowhere. He phoned the chairman, Robert Coar, to tell him he would like to quit, to be told that the club had already sent a letter to Dalglish's home informing him they had decided to dispense with his services.

It seemed a strange way to treat a man who was one of football's most talented players and most successful managers. But then professional football has never been an industry much given to courtesy.

It is also a game with the grip of a narcotic. January 1997 saw Kenny Dalglish return to duel with his demons once again. Becoming manager of Newcastle United would require something horribly close to commitment seven days a week.

Ask any manager how much time off he has and the answer is the same: 'Not enough.'

HOWARD WILKINSON:

'Executive stress, battle fatigue, or whatever you want to call it, is increasing in football management. Pressure is getting greater and it is taking its toll, both individually and collectively in terms of the family and quality of life. People talk about the rewards – fine, managers are paid good money, but money can't buy you health and you don't have to be on £200,000 a year to be under pressure. I know people on £25,000 who are under pressure.'

WILF McGUINNESS:

'I don't know one manager who hasn't neglected his home life. It's that kind of job. I would say – don't neglect your family. But they do, because they feel they must give everything to the job. When I look back, I know there were times when I was unfair on my wife and family because of the job, and that is wrong. Managers go away for a family holiday once a year and they think that's enough, but it isn't. The rest of the year the family is suffering. A manager can find time if he tries, but I didn't, and looking back that is the bad thing that came out of my time as a manager.'

STEVE COPPELL:

'You can be on a beach in Marbella and you'll be thinking about formations, selections and players. What you're going to do differently next time. What you should have done differently last time. It's always with you. Go to the theatre and you might be watching the most enthralling play, but I can guarantee any manager will be thinking about what he's going to do on Saturday.'

BRIAN HORTON:

'The toughest part of the job is the sheer time you spend doing it. I enjoy it – I love going to games on Tuesday nights, Wednesday nights, whenever. Some managers don't like watching other people's teams play but I enjoy it. That's when I sometimes have to be told that I'm spending too much time on it. It isn't just a seven-day-a-week job. It can be seven days plus four nights. All of a sudden you are not seeing your family, which is wrong.'

JIMMY ARMFIELD:

'It's a job for loners, and that's not me. That's one of the aspects that took me out of the profession. You're often left with your own thoughts. You can be sat watching the television at home, surrounded by family, and you don't see any of it. You're just thinking about what's going to happen in the next game. It does absorb everything else in life. The real reason I left management was because it stopped me doing anything else, and I felt there must be other things in life. And I've found them.'

[The way football can punch you on the nose at the very moment you hope it will plant roses in your lap came home to Armfield in cruel fashion in May 1975. His first season as manager of Leeds United ended in the team reaching the European Cup Final in Paris. They lost 2–0 to Bayern Munich in a match remembered for the sort of refereeing decisions euphemistically described as 'controversial' when you mean 'rubbish' – and, more vividly, for rioting by Leeds fans once it became clear they were destined to lose.]

'I could have been the first English manager to win the European Cup. We should have won it. We were better than Bayern. But the crowd reaction upset me a lot. It was a total let-down. I expected so much. It was the biggest club game I'd ever been involved in, but I sat for the last 15 minutes watching the police wading into our supporters. I was unhappy with the referee, unhappy with everything. By the end of the match I was thinking how horrendous the next three weeks were going to be. UEFA would throw the book at us. Everyone would say how bad English supporters were. The whole thing was flat.

'The Leeds players at that time deserved better. They were good – arguably the best set of players any club has had in my time. They peaked just before I got there, but they had been together for 12 years or so. I learned a lot from them. We had one or two little arguments now and again, but they were experienced players and strong opinions were only to be expected.'

JOHN MADDOCK:

'Some managers handle it well, some don't. Some turn to the

bottle. Some turn to women. Others just shut themselves away. Ideally, you should be very pragmatic. Level-headed. Even-tempered. Some are; many are not. But there's nothing finer than to be involved in the life of a football club. It's a drug. You can understand why people put so much of themselves into it, and why they're so reluctant to let go.'

DAVID PLEAT:

'You keep calm and try to enjoy it but it's very difficult. To do the job properly there are more demands than one man can cope with, so you have to hive some of it off to responsible and loyal people around you.'

JOHN NEAL:

'You get totally immersed in the job. It comes before anything and it doesn't half hurt at times. It nearly killed me.'

It was the last match of the 1983–84 season. Chelsea had already clinched promotion from Division Two. Now, with just 90 minutes of the campaign left, it was between them and Sheffield Wednesday as to who would be Champions. It was an honour that John Neal, the Chelsea manager, wanted desperately.

This was the Chelsea team of Kerry Dixon, David Speedie, John Hollins and Nigel Spackman – an entertaining, adventurous line-up that had been rolling over the opposition all season. A 5–0 home win over Leeds United in front of 33,000 at Stamford Bridge set up a barnstorming finale. But for the manager, simply ending Chelsea's five-year exile from Division One wasn't enough. He needed the Championship as well as promotion.

'I wouldn't relax. And I wouldn't let the players relax. Sheffield Wednesday looked favourites for the title. Then they lost at Shrewsbury. We had won 14 and drawn three of our last 17 games. In the end it was all on the last day – we were at Grimsby, Wednesday were at Cardiff.'

Chelsea fans painted the fishing port of Grimsby and the neighbouring resort of Cleethorpes blue and white. The Blundell

Park ground could barely cope with the influx. The match had to be halted while fans spilling on to the pitch were shepherded to safety. The atmosphere was electric. In the Chelsea dug-out, John Neal became aware that a familiar pain was intensifying.

'It had built up over the season. Even playing golf I was struggling to get 18 holes in because of the pains across my chest. In a match, I would sit and get tense, and the pains would come. After a while I would be OK and I could get through the rest of the game. But nearer the end of the season it got worse. So we came to the last match, and we were top on goal difference. We had such a good team – I don't know why I worried so much but I did!

'Kerry Dixon scored and we went 1–0 up. Then there was a stop for a quarter of an hour while they sorted out the crowd. There was no panic but they just had to sort things out and they did well. There were an awful lot of Chelsea people there. I was hoping to go in and find out how Sheffield Wednesday were doing at Cardiff, because we were only winning 1–0 and our game was now 15 minutes behind theirs. We couldn't find out. Then we heard they had won – so we had to win to become the Champions. And that made the pains come again. The club doctor knew there was something wrong with me. Well, we won the game 1–0. Forty-two games, 88 points and we were Champions on goal difference! After the match the doctor told me to see him the following week. He checked me out, sent me off to Harley Street, and they took me in straight away for a heart bypass operation. Two of the veins were 95 per cent gone, one 65 per cent, one 45 per cent, so the surgeon did the lot.

'It was the end of the season, everyone was celebrating, and I was in the operating theatre. But I had done my job. We had gone up as Champions, and I was a very proud man.'

John Neal's tale says it all about the crazy values of the football boss. He had driven himself to death's door, and was proud of himself!

The causes of the heart condition which could easily have killed him were various. He was a smoker (gave up the day before his operation, hasn't touched a cigarette since). There was a family background of heart trouble. But the profession was a major factor.

'There's no doubt about it. Football contributed to my heart problem. I talked it through with the surgeon before and after the operation. Smoking, hereditary, and stress. Doing the job the way I did it. It's like Bill Shankly used to say, "Football is more important than life or death," and I think it's right. It's the way you're made. It was harder than life or death. I used to play golf on a Friday and try to relax, but then on Saturday I used to worry for all the players. Try to take the pressure off them. You can only do that for so long. I used to get so churned up inside it would take me till the Monday to get my system settled again. I couldn't eat till late on the Saturday night. And that was when we were successful! So if we had been relegated it would have killed me, I'm sure. That's how it worked for me. Then, if we had a midweek match, I'd be off again.'

John Neal is not one of those managers who would relieve the tension by hurling teacups around the dressing room. It might have been better if he was. But anyone mistaking his quiet, reserved personality for a laid-back attitude towards sport couldn't be more mistaken. Even now, fully recovered from his heart surgery and content to be retired from the game, he is a mean competitor on the golf course, playing off a handicap of seven at Wrexham Golf Club and entering Seniors tournaments at every opportunity.

His is quite a story. He was brought up in the North-East pit village of Silksworth, County Durham. A quick and tenacious full-back, he was signed by Hull City at the age of 17 and played in the same team as two of the legends of English football, Raich Carter and Neil Franklin. 'Raich Carter was player-manager, and what a privilege it was to play in the same team. A great man and a great player. Neil Franklin was the best centre-half I've ever seen, along with John Charles. At 20 I was captain, with Neil Franklin in the same team!'

After Hull Neal moved to Swindon Town of Division Three (South). 'The bottom of the pile, scratching and scraping, where you had to be in early to make sure you got a jersey for training. Bert Head was the manager; he brought in a load of us for peanuts and finished up with a damn good team. Then to Aston Villa under Joe Mercer, and what an amazing, wonderful fellow he was. So I was blessed that I played under these people. I played alongside geniuses. And I played against some of the greatest – Finney, Matthews, Lawton, Ivor Allchurch, John Charles. I talked to them, listened to them and learnt from them.'

Neal went into the record books as a member of the Aston Villa team that won the first-ever League Cup Final, beating Rotherham. His managerial career began at Wrexham in 1968, stepping up from coach in succession to Alvan Williams. 'We were a good partnership. He was brash, I was quiet, so we complemented each other well. I would have been happy for that to continue but it wasn't to be, so I was thrown in. All the experiences I had with my various managers helped and it was a fairly painless transition.

'Looking back, you get so totally immersed it isn't until now that you realize what an influence the football club had on the town of Wrexham itself. They still come up to me and reminisce and it brings home to me how big a part we played in the life of the place.'

John Neal's tenure as manager at Wrexham was one of the game's bitter-sweet romances. He took over a team in the Fourth Division, guided them into the Third and on to the brink of the Second. At the same time, having won the Welsh Cup, the team reached the last eight of the European Cup Winners Cup. He gained a reputation for developing players who were quick of mind and nimble of foot – many of them going on to greater heights. The stadium was substantially rebuilt and began hosting international fixtures. Logically, the whole process should have culminated in promotion to the Second Division for the first time in the club's history.

The opportunity was there, as clear, as welcoming and as unusual as an empty motorway. With two games of 1976–77 to go, Wrexham were favourites to win the Third Division and needed only one point to secure promotion. Their last two matches were at home, against promotion rivals Crystal Palace and Mansfield Town. Neal's team were unbeaten at the Racecourse all season. His team lost both games. Palace and Mansfield went up. Wrexham stayed down. It was the most savage kick in the stomach; worse, probably, than relegation. At least the drop can be seen coming weeks beforehand and is almost always thoroughly deserved. This

Seventies men: Manchester United manager Tommy Docherty (*above*); and Ron Atkinson of West Bromwich Albion (*below*), at the 1978 FA Cup semi-final.

Kenny Dalglish took over as Liverpool boss the day after the Heysel Stadium disaster. He's pictured (*above*) at the old Den, four days before Hillsborough.

In the dug-out at Anfield, Graeme Souness, during his first match in charge of Liverpool, witnesses a 3–0 victory over Norwich City.

Roy Evans' first match at the helm was also against Norwich (*above*), a 2–2 draw at Carrow Road.

'I feel very uneasy about the way football is so motivated by money. Ultimately greed will ruin the game…we're losing the moral fibre.' Tommy Burns (*left*), manager of Celtic.

Casualties: John Neal (*above*) left the manager's seat at Chelsea to undergo major heart surgery; Mike Walker (*below*) set up his own waste-disposal company after dismissal from Everton.

(*Above*) Bruce Rioch and Colin Todd during their Middlesbrough days.

(*Left*) Currently the longest-serving League manager with the same club, Dario Gradi has been with Crewe Alexandra since 1983.

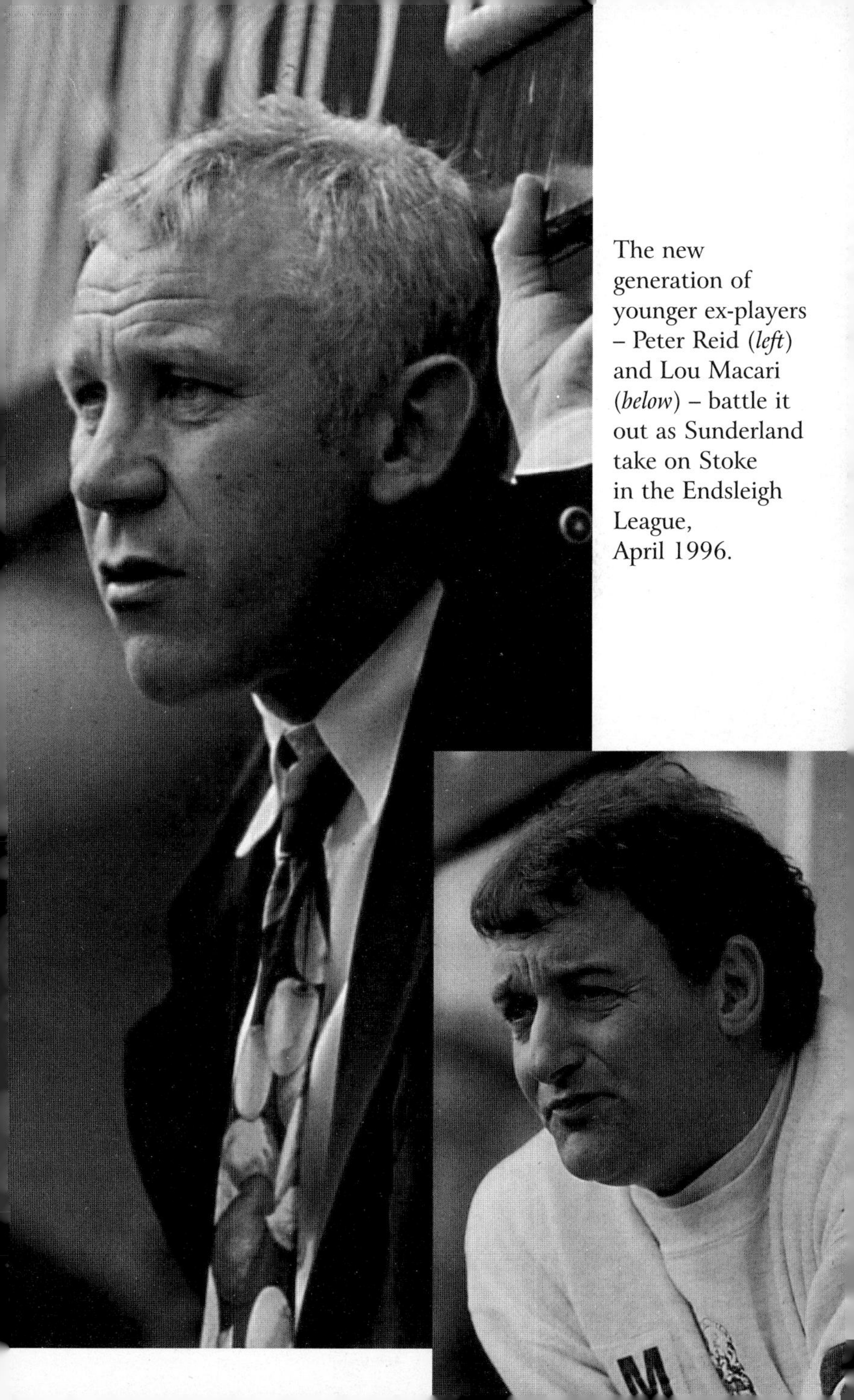

The new generation of younger ex-players – Peter Reid (*left*) and Lou Macari (*below*) – battle it out as Sunderland take on Stoke in the Endsleigh League, April 1996.

Currently the most successful manager in Britain, Manchester United's Alex Ferguson.

was a mugging on the steps of the Lord Mayor's Banquet.

After the final whistle of the last match players and supporters were in tears. Neal sat in his office, quietly drinking milk. Bill Shankly was there. The former Liverpool chief was a regular visitor that season. Not even Shankly, with his legendary command of the language, could find any words of consolation.

'I didn't cope very well,' admits Neal now. 'It hurt so much. But it wasn't to be, and I'm a great believer in that philosophy. If you're meant to win the Cup you'll win it. I'll give my lot and do my best but after that there's nothing more you can do. For some reason, that year, we were not destined to go up. It was unfortunate that one or two important players were missing from the last two games. Arfon Griffiths was our general – if he had been fit, I'm sure we would have gone up. But he wasn't, so it was destiny. It was my destiny that we didn't win it.

'I admit I wasn't as philosophical then. It was a very, very painful time. It hurt.'

Neal moved on after that season. Middlesbrough, of the First Division, liked his style and signed him on to galvanize the talents of bright young things like Mark Proctor, David Hodgson and Craig Johnston. Neal took over from Jack Charlton, inheriting a team strong in defensive organization. The change of clubs was a lesson for the newcomer. 'Jack's team was built of good defenders. They won a lot of games 1–0. I didn't like that – I would rather win 4–2. The team had a negative reputation, and it took a while to change it round. I thought, with all those good players, I could go in, get them superfit, and let them loose. But it doesn't work like that. I had a rude awakening. I got them fit, let them loose – but what they produced wasn't what I wanted. They needed help. Suggestions had to be made. Changes had to be brought in, and you couldn't do it overnight. You had to talk to them one at a time and gradually coax and persuade them to play a more attacking type of football. Graeme Souness was there when I arrived but he had his heart set on joining Liverpool. When he left we took off because I brought in young Craig Johnston who had been brought up in the way I wanted. I liked players who could go forward and attack without worrying about defending. That's a problem with some players – they go so far forward, but they can't get it out of their mind that at some point they must stop and go back. I wanted to get that fear out of their minds, and it took a while to get it through to them.'

Neal's philosophy was close to heresy, especially in the late seventies when the English game was going through a phase of repression. Even today, the notion of a manager telling his midfielders and defenders to cast off any defensive obligation is as alien as Jimmy Savile telling a car driver to forget about his seat belt. Middlesbrough signed a Yugoslav, Bosco Jankovic. Neal scoffs at any suggestion that Jankovic failed to fit in at Ayresome Park. 'He was one of the most skilful players I had at Middlesbrough. People say he took a long time to settle, but I disagree. We took a long time to settle in with him. It wasn't up to him to accept us, it was the other way round. Once we had sorted that out, he used to frighten the opposition.

'My second year at Chelsea, we were nearly relegated into the Third Division. We finished fifth from bottom and that was soul-destroying. I had a fair few downs, but I never got so depressed that it destroyed me. You bounce back. You get out in training, see the lads, and you realize that they are depending on you. They don't want you to bottle it. You can't throw the towel in. The highs I took, without going overboard – and I had a few of those too. When we did well in Europe with Wrexham, after the game, I would say to the players: "Right lads, have a good time and don't overdo it." And I would go off on my own. I didn't want to go round jumping all over the place. I just wanted to be left on my own with a job well done. It wasn't for me the drinking and going overboard.

'So if I suffered, I suffered alone. I didn't drag anyone else into it.

'With Middlesbrough, we played in the Japan Cup in Tokyo at the end of one season, and we won the tournament. It was tremendous. As usual I went off by myself, had a quiet drink, went to bed early, got up the next morning and went out having a look at the places of interest.'

After his heart attack Neal was moved upstairs at Chelsea. John Hollins was put in charge of the team and Neal fretted as the momentum slowed. 'In theory it was a good idea, John Hollins taking the reins with me as consultant director to keep him on the right lines. But Hollins blew it. He didn't want any advice and slowly destroyed my set-up.' Neal retired and disappeared for a while. He moved to Scotland, to St Andrews, the home of golf, and let two years go by. The psychological scars of a lifetime in football took slightly longer to heal than the surgeon's incisions. Now he is back in his adopted home of North Wales, burning up the fairways, keeping in touch with football, and every now and again is reminded how his team made an entire town hold its breath at the agony and the ecstasy of football played from the heart.

It takes all sorts to make a football team. It takes all sorts to make up the regiment of men in charge. John Neal nearly worried himself into an early grave. Others deal with the pressures with a bit more ease:

MIKE WALKER:

'I think I have coped all right so far. Obviously, no one likes criticism. Everyone keeps on about the pressure, but sometimes you bring it on yourself by worrying. I didn't go grey through worry! And I certainly won't have a heart attack because of football. I work as hard as I can, and if the chairman decides I am not the man for the job, whatever I do isn't going to change it. Even if you win the League – if they want to change you, they will. I know one or two managers who were suddenly ousted. They thought they didn't deserve it, but suddenly they were gone. You can't worry about it – you've just got to get on with it.'

PETER REID:

'You can never get away from football, but the only thing they can do to me is sack me, and worse things happen at sea. I am from Liverpool where a lot of people are unemployed and worse off than me. I may have some sleepless nights, but I doubt if I'll have a heart attack. When I took the job at Manchester City I knew the average lifespan of a manager there was short. While I was there the club finished fifth, fifth and ninth, and I am proud of that. I was disappointed we didn't win anything but my record wasn't bad. I didn't worry unduly over what might happen to me. I've been in the game long enough to know that things happen which are beyond my control.'

TOMMY DOCHERTY:

'I used to feel the strain. I tried to say, "Well, worse things happen in life every day. It's only a game of football." But a bad decision by a chairman, a few bad results, a bit of pressure from the media, friends of the chairman saying something on the golf course – that sort of thing can quickly turn your life upside down. It can have a bad effect on your family. Especially when you have kids at school. When we won the Cup at Manchester United my son Peter took the Cup to his school to show it to the other kids. They were mostly City supporters. A month later when I resigned those kids destroyed him. He was only 1 l.'

ANDY KING:

'Stress to me is sitting for eight hours in Stevenage, watching videos telling you how to sell insurance to people. My father died while I was on that course. The day I got the phone call I had been watching a video about someone dying and the family hadn't got his insurance up to date.'

ROY AITKEN:

'I always try to stay on an even keel, whether things are going well or going badly. I don't have difficulty getting to sleep at night, but I do find that when I wake up my mind is already attuned to what I'm going to do in the day. There's no chance of dozing in bed.'

DARIO GRADI:

'It's not a matter of life and death. If it was, you would be a long time dead. I do still suffer if we lose, especially if we hit a losing run. But it's only the stress I put on myself. I have conditioned my mind to enjoy the game and I do look forward to the matches.'

JOE ROYLE:

'I always believe in not transmitting stress, or nervousness or fear to the players, so sometimes you have to get yourself right so they don't see you that way. But there is a high rate of illness in the job. Managers suffer from heart problems and stress. Like any management job, that's what you are paid for and that's why the wages are higher than ever. It doesn't alter the fact that if you lose four games in a row there'll be some sections of the crowd shouting for your head. It's the same as any management job – if you are not successful you face the boot.'

HOWARD WILKINSON:

'Hopefully age has taught me restraint, control and perspective. If you don't get too high you won't get too low. Not every problem has an answer in football – I used to think it had. You have to accept that some problems just don't have an answer.'

BOBBY GOULD:

'The toughest part is having to win every Saturday. There's a leather case full of wind, and it doesn't always bounce your way.'

The tide had turned for Ian Branfoot as manager of Reading. Two rapid promotions, sweeping the club from the Fourth Division to the Second, with gates over 10,000 and a goal-hungry scrounger named Trevor Senior regularly on target, had given way to gloom. The club's Elm Park home had witnessed relegation 12 months after promotion, with every prospect of another relegation to follow. The supporters blamed the manager. Branfoot was growing accustomed to abuse. Then he came home one night to find a noose swinging over his front door.

Getting the treatment at Reading was ideal preparation for what was to follow at Southampton. Succeeding the sacked Chris

Nicholl in 1991, Branfoot launched upon three years of uncertainty twinned with hope. It was a Southampton squad containing not just le Tissier but Shearer, Ruddock and Flowers. In his first full season the FA Cup yielded drama aplenty – the Saints won a penalty shoot-out away to Manchester United in a fourth-round replay and progressed as far as the last eight before, anti-climactically, being held to a goalless draw at home to Norwich and losing the replay. The same year the team reached the Final of the Zenith Data Systems Cup, giving the fans a trip to Wembley to see a 3–2 defeat against Nottingham Forest. League form, though, was poor – 16th in '91–92, 18th in '92–93, and in the relegation zone when he quit in January '94. By now Shearer, Flowers and Ruddock were gone and le Tissier was out of the team more often than in it. Branfoot's departure had been seen as inevitable for months, with the fans seeming to put more energy into abusing him than supporting the players.

Branfoot insists that his time at Southampton was a happy one, but there is clearly a residue of bitterness towards those supporters who orchestrated the opposition. 'The press overplayed the hostility there. They made out it was a lot worse than it was. I'm not saying it was an easy time, but to me it was all part of the job. If you're not prepared to accept the bad times as a football manager, you shouldn't enjoy the good times.

'I had two great years at Southampton, working with smashing players and good people. Most of the supporters were top class too. The only ones who spoilt it were an insignificant bunch called the Southampton Independent Supporters. They were horrible. People like them don't go to football to give the team their backing – they go for the recognition. Of course, the majority of people will sometimes criticize, but the people who run independent supporters' clubs at any club require recognition. They love being on television, and seeing their quotes in the papers. It happened at Southampton and it's happening at other clubs now, even Manchester United.'

The experience didn't deter Branfoot from management – within two months he was back in the game, in charge at Fulham, buttressed by his own self-confidence and the support of his wife Jeanette who, it turned out, bore responsibility for the noose.

'Reading had been beaten at home and we were under pressure. I came home to find this noose swinging in the hallway, hanging from the banisters. I hit my head on it when I came in. Jeanette said, "The choice is yours – do you want to hang yourself, or do you want your dinner?" That put it all in perspective. If you let it get to you in this job, you don't recover.'

It's a Thursday night. It usually is a Thursday night when the football fraternity gets together for social frivolity. Thursday is the one night of the week when social secretaries can be reasonably sure that sought-after 'names' are available for after-dinner speeches or personal appearances.

The guest speaker gets to his feet. The audience is chuckling already. His reputation as a wise-cracking fast talker has preceded him. 'Nice to know I'm among friends,' he says. 'And family. That's my young son over there.' And he indicates a man who must be 60 if he's a day, as bald as a billiard ball, nodding appreciatively through the cigar haze.

Wilf McGuinness, once manager of Manchester United, trades cheerfully on his Kojak appearance to crank up the laughs on the after-dinner circuit. He'll make a point of chatting to anyone in the audience similarly short of thatch up top, and if he detects a shared sense of humour he'll include him in the act.

Matchdays at Old Trafford will find McGuinness mingling with sponsors and official guests, representing the club that has been a huge part of his life since he joined them as an eager young amateur in 1953. But his mere presence represents quite an act of reconciliation. McGuinness' experience of management in the very stadium to which he now welcomes the good and the great turned out to be so traumatic that he has truly never been the same since.

We pick up the story in the Greek city of Salonika where McGuinness, having been relieved of his command as United's boss in December 1970, is employed as coach by Aris, the town's top club. 'One day I woke up and there were chunks of hair on the pillow. I said to my wife, "I think you're losing your hair." She said, "No, it's you – you've got a big patch here." Inside a week, all my hair had gone. It did come back wispy and grey but it never grew properly. The doctors asked if I had had any particular upset within the last 12 months. I said, "Yes, leaving Manchester United." And that is what caused me to go bald – the hurt and the upset of leaving United.'

McGuinness was struck by a condition known as alopecia, baldness caused by shock or some other nervous reaction. To him, the sack from Manchester United was like severing an umbilical cord.

Wilf McGuinness was appointed team manager at Old Trafford when Sir Matt Busby retired in the summer of 1969. McGuinness was a local boy, on the staff since he was 15, and a wing-half of high quality, winning two caps for England, before a broken leg forced his retirement at the age of 24. After that he was guided by the club along the coaching route, and quickly showed himself well suited to it. He became trainer of the England youth team and worked with Alf Ramsey in preparing the full England team for the World Cup in 1966. When the preliminary squad was whittled down to the final 22, McGuinness was stood down, but recalled within hours of England's victory over Portugal in the semi-final. He was put in charge of the players' wives' outing on the eve of the Final; then worked with Ramsey and the other coaches, Harold Shepherdson and Les Cocker, in the Wembley dressing room. After England's victory over West Germany, Wilf was out on the town with Bobby Charlton, Nobby Stiles and Bobby Moore. 'It was magnificent. We were just floating along.'

Three years later, United having won the European Cup, came the moment football had been debating for months – the anointing of Matt Busby's successor.

'There was speculation in the press that Matt was going to retire, and names like Jock Stein of Celtic and Don Revie of Leeds were bandied about. Somehow, I thought I might have a chance, even though I was only 31. My name was mentioned a couple of times. Then someone said, "Come to work with a tie tomorrow." Matt Busby called me in and said, "I've chosen you, Wilf."'

It should have been the ideal solution. But it didn't work.

'I was confident I could do the job and it was a great feeling. There were a few uncertainties about who had responsibility because Matt stayed on as general manager. He said, "We'll call you Coach at first, and I'll take a bit of pressure off you," which I thought was all right, but that sort of pressure honestly didn't worry me. I knew the players and the club and I thought everything was great. I had had eight years on the coaching staff, working with Sir Matt, so there were no problems there.

'But there were grey areas. I didn't know when to go to him for something and when to keep away. Transfers, we did together, but there were a number of players I wanted who we didn't get. I brought in Ian Ure, the centre-half from Arsenal, but I also wanted Colin Todd and Malcolm Macdonald. I felt we could have picked up Mick Mills from Ipswich when Bobby Robson first went there. But we didn't, and with a bit more experience I might have pushed harder to get those players.

'The other thing that went against me was that – although I had played for England – coming from reserve-team trainer to taking on the first team was difficult. If I had had 18 months working with the first team alongside Sir Matt it might have been easier.

'Many managers will tell you that when things start going wrong the games seem to come too quick – "My God, we're playing again on Wednesday and I haven't got it right from Saturday yet!" You never seemed to have the time you needed to put things right.

'But the pressure didn't get to me, maybe because the press were very kind and the fans were magnificent. They understood. They wanted one of their own to come through and hoped I would succeed.'

United under McGuinness – with Busby still very much a presence – failed to regain the European heights of the class of '68. In his one full season United finished eighth, reached the semi-final of the FA Cup (beaten by Leeds in a second replay) and the semi-final of the League Cup (beaten by Manchester City, who went on to win both that and the Cup Winners Cup, doing the manager of Manchester United no good at all).

This was still the United of Best, Charlton and Law, plus all the other big names, but the magic only worked up to a point.

'People say the players let me down in the end. I felt they all worked very hard in training, but some of them were getting old. Several of them were in their thirties, and my plan was to bring in younger players to support the great names. But the youth policy was a bit ragged at the time and you can't update something like that overnight.

'When I left senior players out, the logic was right but the players weren't happy about it, which was inevitable. One time I dropped Bobby Charlton and Denis Law for the same game – it was away to Everton. We went to Everton a fortnight after they beat us 2–0 at Old Trafford. It was the year Everton won the League and their midfield of Harvey, Kendall and Ball ran our midfield ragged. So I thought we had better put an extra man in. Denis wasn't quite 100 per cent fit, so I decided to leave him out and Bobby too. The headlines were so huge you would have thought I'd dropped the atom bomb. It was as if I'd killed them, not dropped them! Even now I believe the logic of that selection was right, but perhaps, if you're leaving out popular names, you might be better off doing so at home where you've got more chance of getting a result.

'That sort of decision didn't trouble me, but it might have been unpopular with the board. I didn't attend board meetings – the only one I ever attended was when they sacked me. Matt Busby took that sort of thing off me, thinking he was reducing the pressure. Looking back, I would have preferred to go to the board meetings so they could understand what I was trying to do.

'I still see many of the players and from talking to them now it's clear they thought I said certain things to them in a bad way, which isn't me. I thought I was being honest and straightforward – they thought I was stabbing them in the back. That's one of the things about being a manager – when you have to say something critical to a player it hurts him more than you realize. It feels like a dagger, when you're trying to be a gentleman about it.'

United's form showed little hint of improvement as season 1970–71 got under way. By December, the directors were showing signs of anxiety. One Monday, McGuinness was summoned to Sir Matt's office at Old Trafford. The meeting lasted two hours, as the realization dawned that the board and Sir Matt had decided to relieve him of first-team responsibility. He wasn't being fired from the payroll. But he was having his job taken away.

'It upset me that I was being demoted. I had a three-year

contract and it had only run for 20 months. I wanted it to go all the way. I felt badly let down. And I felt bitter about it. I was in a state of shock for a while. I went to the training ground, had a look for the whisky bottle – it wasn't there so I had a go at the sherry bottle. I remember phoning my family and saying, "It's all over." To me it was the end of the world. I was nearly broken for a few weeks. It was Christmas-time, which made it worse. A lot of other things were happening; my father-in-law was in hospital dying of cancer. It all seemed to come at once. The club tried hard. They asked what I wanted to do, did I want to go on holiday. We talked it over and I agreed to most things at first. I was asked to go to a board meeting to finalize a statement saying I was resigning. One or two directors had tears in their eyes. I went home and thought, No, I won't resign. I won't ask to stand down. So I rang Sir Matt's home and told him they would have to sack me. The next morning I had to go in while they re-wrote the statement. After that I stayed on the payroll till February, even though I had been demoted in December. That was wrong. I should have gone straight away, because I was in an aggressive mood and wanting to harm people. I hired a solicitor to represent me while the club sorted out my contract. They wanted to resolve it between ourselves but I was so angry I said, "No, you've let me down, why should I trust you?"

'So I was pretty hurt at the time, but I suppose that's part of life. Looking back, doing the job wasn't too difficult, except that certain things came too quickly.'

Leaving Old Trafford meant far more than giving up a job. For McGuinness it was the end of a lifelong connection, one which was every bit as intense as a family relationship. In 17 years he had witnessed the birth of the Busby Babes, the brilliant team of the fifties; the Munich air disaster which wiped out many of those young men, his own friends and team-mates; the rebirth of the club and the glories of the sixties, culminating in European triumph against Benfica at Wembley. Suddenly he was no longer part of it, and like a deposed prince he was obliged to voyage into exile.

Every time Wilf McGuinness looks in the mirror he sees the legacy of his sacking by Manchester United. What the alopecia would have done to a lesser man heaven only knows, but Wilf has survived, and survived in some style. How did he cope at the time? 'I thought, Life can be a bit cruel at times!' Then the chuckles rumble forth in the infectious fashion, instantly recognizable to his after-dinner audiences. 'In Greece, I wanted to cover it up so I told my interpreter to get me a wig. I didn't know what that would achieve, because everyone knows you've got a wig. But I just wanted to cover it. I only kept it for a week or two and then I thought, What the hell am I doing with a bloody wig on? So I got rid of it. But at first you do wonder what's happening to you. I said to the players, "You can make jokes for the first week. After that you'll get fined." And we got on with it.

'These days, with the after-dinner act, it helps me. If I see a whisker I shave it off. I'm an extrovert, a fun-loving person, and going bald was no bother once I had got used to it. I've never been frightened of getting up and saying something, with or without hair.'

McGuinness stayed in Greece for three years. Returning to England he served York City as manager, then Hull City as coach. He almost quit the game when he was fired by Hull, and began training to take on a pub. Eventually he gravitated back to the Manchester area and embarked on a long and happy connection with Bury. Then came retirement and the chance to concentrate on his public speaking, and his ambassadorial role for Manchester United, the club that broke his heart but couldn't break his spirit.

In less time than it took the leaves to turn brown and fall from the trees Steve Coppell came and went as manager of Manchester City. Appointed as successor to Alan Ball he inherited a team in decline, a business lacking financial clout, and unrealistic expectations from chairman and fans alike. Within 33 days Coppell was so stressed that he quit.

With the benefit of hindsight observers described a significant change in Coppell's physical appearance: they said he had lost weight and become gaunt in the month he was in charge. But Coppell has always had a pinched appearance. Whatever changes there might have been they weren't enough to alarm even those working closest to him. Phil Neal, brought in as his number two, had no idea his boss was struggling.

Coppell's departure represents one of the most spectacular victories that stress has yet achieved. His statement to the media said: 'I am not ashamed to admit that I have suffered for some time from the huge pressure I have imposed on myself, and since my appointment this has completely overwhelmed me to such an extent that I cannot function in the job the way I would like to. As this situation is affecting my well-being, I have asked Francis Lee to relieve me of my obligation to manage the club on medical advice. This is the hardest thing I have ever had to do and I can only say the decision I have made is an honest one made in the best interests of the club as well as myself.'

His very departure was not without its strain. The Manchester media were told at around 11 a.m. that a news conference would be held at 11.45 at Maine Road. On the dot of 11.45 a small procession, consisting of the chairman Francis Lee, Coppell, chief executive Colin Barlow and the club solicitor, filed into the executive restaurant where chairs were arranged in rows for the reporters. But the conference had been arranged so hurriedly few journalists were there. Coppell, clutching his resignation statement, was ushered away to wait for a further ten minutes until enough reporters turned up to record his downfall. It was like seeing a condemned man taken to the electric chair, then being told to take it easy until the witnesses showed up.

Coppell's departure was a stunner. It was the brief time he had been in office which caused most queries. How could stress become such a problem in only 33 days? Part of the answer was that Coppell, like Kenny Dalglish, is a quiet, shy person, who didn't share his worries, even with his assistant Phil Neal. And at Maine Road the scope for worry was endless. The manager was told by Francis Lee, on day one, that his brief was to restore City to the Premier League that same season. Yet the playing staff was plainly inadequate for the task, and with debts of some £12 million, cash for quality replacements was not available. Add the desperate fanaticism of supporters suffering agonies from Manchester United's success and you have a fair description of British football's Mission Impossible. The best decision Steve

Coppell made was to recognize that this was not, after all, the way he wanted to spend the next few years of his life. The mission to restore City to greatness may not be impossible, but it does require a manager with a tough exterior, and unlimited self-confidence.

But then Coppell, of course, returned to the fray for a third spell at Crystal Palace, stepping into the shoes of Dave Bassett ...

The departure of Steve Coppell from Maine Road was watched with an unusual degree of understanding north of the border. Paul Sturrock, once a lively striker with Dundee United and Scotland, reckoned that Coppell saw the danger signs somewhat more clearly than he did.

Sturrock succumbed to stress in a spectacular manner when he collapsed midway through a match in the 1995–96 season. He had been in charge of St Johnstone for 19 months when the strain caught up with him during an away fixture at Dundee United. The doctors attached to both clubs hurried to treat him in the dug-out before he was taken away by ambulance. Paul's wife Barbara was watching her first match of the season. As she climbed into the ambulance with her ailing husband she was less than impressed to hear him telling the doctors what substitution the team should be making. They both feared he was suffering a heart attack, although the doctors were able to reassure them that it wasn't the case. This must be one of the few occasions when a football manager was relieved to find he was 'only' suffering from stress.

So what brought it on, this 'wee hiccup' as Sturrock now smilingly describes it? 'Not sleeping, too much work, not eating at the right times – and trying to change players' mental approach to things, which is very, very difficult.' Sturrock and St Johnstone had suffered an unusually tight relegation in his first season, 1993–94. Level on points with Partick Thistle and Kilmarnock, Sturrock's team lost their Premier Division status by just one goal. The next season failed to produce an instant return. 'I was trying to change the personnel and at the same time gain promotion, and I found it very frustrating as results didn't go the right way.

'I think sleep is a problem to all managers because your mind is always on what you've got to be doing – team selection, buying and selling players, negotiating new contracts. If you wake up in the night, and I've got young children, you can never sleep again. A lot of managers go through that.'

Through the autumn of 1995 he felt pains in his chest, but other than that he suffered no more. 'It just caught up with me on the day.'

The upshot was that Sturrock went away for a week's holiday in Spain, came back to serious discussions with the medics, and resumed work with a new attitude. 'I changed the whole structure of training at the club, and changed the way I operated, delegating a lot more work.' He had valuable support from the club's managing director, Michael Stewart-Duff. The signs were encouraging. Twelve months later St Johnstone approached Christmas 1996 top of the table with a healthy run of unbeaten matches behind them. The manager reported himself feeling much better – but added quickly: 'You are only as good as your last game and you have to keep everyone on their toes. No matter how much you delegate, the pressure will always be on you at quarter to five on a Saturday afternoon.'

In his eyrie at Villa Park, chairman Doug Ellis wonders what the fuss is all about. 'I think there are more strains and stresses on a chairman than a manager,' he grumbles. 'The job of a football manager is the best job in the world. You get the sack, you get money for being sacked, then you go to another club and get paid more money again. Wonderful!'

8

OVER THE ASYLUM WALL

'Being in football management,' said Bobby Gould, 'is like being in the mental asylum.' When he made the comment Gould had been out of the asylum and living happily in the community for the best part of two years. Two months later he accepted the job as manager of Wales. Clearly, it's the sort of asylum where the inmates can check back in when life on the outside becomes too predictable.

But what is the verdict of those who rub along with the managers of the nation's clubs on a daily basis – the people who are close enough to observe exactly what takes place on the other side of the asylum wall?

THE PLAYER

Duncan McKenzie played under more managers than most in a career that embraced Nottingham Forest, Leeds, the Belgian club Anderlecht, Everton, Chelsea, Blackburn Rovers, and wound down in the USA and Hong Kong. If beauty is in the eye of the beholder, so were the talents of McKenzie. He had the ability to delight and annoy at the same time, depending on who was watching. Magical ball-control and outrageous risk-taking thrilled spectators, but dismayed his managers when he chose to display his penchant for living dangerously too close to his own penalty area. When Gordon Lee took over as manager of Everton in 1977 and inherited McKenzie in his squad, he was dumbstruck after the first away game, at Aston Villa, when McKenzie produced a tape recorder and started interviewing his boss for his programme on Radio City, Liverpool's commercial station. McKenzie was a showman who played to the crowd. Signed by Brian Clough for Leeds in 1974 he earned lasting if bizarre fame by demonstrating his ability to jump over cars and throw cricket balls enormous distances, the legacy of a career as a promising athlete in his schooldays. More significantly, he was never fooled by the tinsel trappings of professional football, carrying a lively sense of humour and an element of scepticism through all his various clubs.

He witnessed how different managers handled their relations with players. They were all different, but mostly fell into one of two categories – the remote men, and the men who mingled.

'When I started it was with managers like the late Johnny Carey and Allan Brown at Nottingham Forest. They were people who largely distanced themselves from the players. I would never dare call Johnny Carey "Boss". It just wasn't what you did. It was always "Mr Carey". Matt Gillies was another manager at Forest who kept his distance. It was a working relationship only.

'The other side of the coin came with people like Dave Mackay at Forest, Brian Clough at Leeds and Howard Kendall at Blackburn. They would all spend time socializing with the players – but you knew they had a cut-off point. It was a closer relationship with the more modern managers. The breed of manager who would turn up wearing pork-pie hat and overcoat disappeared and the tracksuited manager replaced them. The first tracksuit manager I had was Dave Mackay. Things were less formal at the club and it made for a better relationship. You had easier access to the manager and it was simpler to get things off your chest. If he was out there on the training field with you – which wasn't the case with the old-style managers – you could talk through any problems with him. With the old school, like Johnny Carey and Matt Gillies, it was almost rule by fear. If anyone told me "Mr Carey wants to see you," I'd think, My God, what have I done wrong? It was like being summoned to the headmaster's study.

'I think things have moved on again now. There are so many areas in which a manager has to be involved that we are getting closer to the way it's always been on the Continent. The demands of buying and selling are taking the manager away from the training ground so he will become a specialist in doing business deals. In the future the man who handles the players will be the coach and he'll tell the directors, or a middle-man, what players he wants to sign and leave them to get on with it. Ultimately, players will have their wages negotiated elsewhere.'

So what of that bonding which some present-day managers feel they establish with players by handling negotiations directly? If the days are numbered whereby the manager argues with his directors to get the best deal for his players, will some of that personal loyalty be lost? McKenzie thinks there is little to lose in the first place.

'There wasn't one manager who I believed had my interests at heart. In fact I don't believe there's a manager in the game who has his players' interests at heart. They pay you as little as they possibly can. When I used to negotiate with managers it was as if they were shelling out their own money. I was sold from Blackburn by Howard Kendall, so I was told, because they couldn't afford to renew my contract – which was a basic £200 per week. But they had written into my contract a signing-on fee which would have more than doubled the wage structure at the club, and they couldn't afford it.

'One manager who did have the players' interests at heart was Don Revie at Leeds, but he nearly bankrupted Leeds to do it. He saw the need to keep happy the players who weren't always in the team – the likes of Mick Bates and Terry Yorath, and the way he did it was to constantly to improve their contracts. The problem came when those players wanted to move elsewhere but couldn't find anyone to match the wages.

'The best negotiations I ever had were with Anderlecht. It was very businesslike. There was no need for agents or anything like that. Why do players have agents now? It's because they feel it's made so uncomfortable for them. They don't want to face the manager directly because they don't trust him.'

McKenzie emphasizes that the mistrust only applies to the financial side of the relationship. 'Once the deals are done you put it all to one side and get on with the football.'

Motivation is a prominent word in the managerial vocabulary: the need to galvanize players who are depressed by defeat, to inspire players who are overawed by celebrity opposition, and to persuade them that the tactics they've worked on all week really will do the trick on Saturday. 'The poor managers,' says Duncan McKenzie, 'were the ones who condescended to everyone, and I had one or two of those.' Even now, some 25 years on, he recalls life as a youngster trying to gain a toehold at Forest. 'Matt Gillies would only play the senior players. And if you'd been bought by the club, you got more than a fair chance. It's the same at many clubs. If you haven't been bought you're often made the scapegoat. I was probably the best striker at Nottingham Forest for three or four years before I became a regular in the first team. That's not being big-headed – it's a matter of fact. Martin O'Neill didn't become a good player at the moment he was put into the first team – he had been just as good for two years beforehand. It was the same with John Robertson – another player who was held back by the older brigade.

'One of the few managers who isn't afraid to bring through young players is Alex Ferguson. He did it at Aberdeen and he's doing it at Manchester United. He has never been afraid to leave out the big names and put in the kids.

'Managers by nature are quite conservative. They aren't as bad as they were in the eighties, when the game was consumed by fear, but they still hedge their bets.

'Dave Mackay, by a mile, was the best motivator I played for. He lacked in many areas of management – he knew he wasn't a great coach, but he was a great motivator. Of the top managers at the moment, Joe Royle is good at motivating players. Tactically, Howard Kendall was the best, if a bit negative at times. The only one who wasn't at all negative was Cloughie. He used to look at his team as if it was a jigsaw puzzle. If a piece didn't fit, he would get rid of it straight away. He signed Asa Hartford but sold him after three pre-season friendlies. It wasn't because the lad wasn't a good player – he just didn't fit in with the pattern. Cloughie wouldn't stop to think about getting the best price for him – he would simply sell him.

'Bill Shankly was the one we were all in awe of. Soon after I signed for Leeds we met him at a function. He told my wife, "He belongs to football till he's 35 – then he's yours!"'

Unlike most of his contemporaries, McKenzie never flirted with the notion of becoming a manager himself, preferring to maintain his links with the game as a media commentator and after-dinner raconteur.

'I wouldn't swap places with any of them. I don't think they're equipped to cope with the way the game is changing. We've got billionaires coming out of the woodwork to take over clubs. Transfer fees are so vast they've lost all credibility. Millions of pounds are being spent as if they don't matter. Football has become a casino and the chairmen are compulsive gamblers.

'Good managers these days are ones with a sense of humour, like Joe Royle and David Pleat. They talk well about the game and never rubbish other people. Joe Kinnear at Wimbledon is a great lad, laugh a minute. Alan Smith is passionate with a great feel for the game – yet Palace sacked him! But some managers come across as if they've never moved on from being arrogant little footballers. There are one or two who think they can do what they want, treat people with contempt, and, if they didn't happen to be blessed with the ability to play football, would be unemployable in any other industry.

'Football teams are always a reflection of the man that manages them. If you can combine that sense of humour with a rugged attitude, you've got a chance.'

THE FAN

Tim Crabbe supports Crystal Palace, which means he's seen more ups and downs than a bungee jumper. He is chairman of the Football Supporters' Association, the fans' organization which was founded after the Heysel Stadium disaster of 1985, a time when football supporters needed someone to speak up for them and found it via the FSA.

When it comes to the brief life-expectancy of the average football manager 'supporters are the villains of the piece,' he admits. 'Because we expect everything yesterday. Chairmen are criticized for sacking managers, but most of the time they're responding to the fans' demands.

'But the manager is the focal point of the club. When fans chant for "Dave Bassett's blue and red army" or "Alex Ferguson's army" it's always the manager they identify with – not the captain. The fans want more than success – they want entertainment as well. They will be the first to relate the failings of the team back to the manager. They expect him to set principles and establish a style. For example, Ron Atkinson is a footballing manager who tries to win things without resorting to a long-ball game.

'Fans expect a style which will fit in with the traditions of the club. After all, managers change clubs, as do players, but the fans stick with the same one for life. So managers who are held up as great managers are those who fit in with the club's traditions. Liverpool fans admire Roy Evans because he is running the club on the traditional lines established by Bill Shankly.'

Any new manager enjoys a honeymoon period. The chances are that he's only got the job because the previous man failed. So fans tend to be enthusiastic about a new appointment. Where the relationship breaks down, says Crabbe, is either through a run of poor results or the sale of particular players.

'Every club has its bad times, and when that happens the supporters look to see how the manager handles it. Whether he takes responsibility, how he handles the media – that's very important to the fans' perception as to whether he can turn things round. Quite often fans will give the manager time if they can see there's some method in the madness. They also look to the chairman to come up with some cash for new signings.

'But when peculiar things happen, like Paul Ince's departure from Manchester United, fans get resentful. If the manager doesn't explain what's going on, or if the fans think their concerns aren't being considered, that will kick things off.'

So how significant is it if the manager dutifully attends supporters' forums, like a prospective MP mingling with the electorate? 'It helps, but it won't really make that much difference in the bad times. Graham Taylor did a great job at Watford, taking players around factories and so on, but things were going well for the team at the same time. I'm not sure it would have helped him if things had taken a downturn.

'Managers do have a responsibility to go out and speak to fans, but at the end of the day it isn't the fans' top priority.

'Matt Busby was probably the ideal. When fans can see the

players genuinely respect the manager they feel the club is in good hands. It was the same with Brian Clough at Nottingham Forest. There's a mystique that surrounds football – every fan wants to be a great player, and if they can see that the manager is able to transmit that passion and desire into the players, and get them to perform the way the fans would like to perform, respect transmits from the fans to the manager.'

Crabbe doubts if most managers understand what motivates the supporters. 'Some do. But most don't know what makes them tick, or realize why they have such enthusiasm for a particular club. And there isn't enough respect for what the fans think, or for their knowledge of the game. In the 1994–95 season, when Palace played Forest and Chris Armstrong didn't perform, Ron Noades made the point that fans know when a player isn't producing the goods. But I can't remember another instance of someone in a position of authority at a football club giving the fans' opinions that sort of respect. Managers should have more confidence in the ability of the fans to recognize who really is performing for the benefit of the team – and who isn't.

'The real test is how the manager responds when the chips are down. Alan Smith is a good example. He seemed to share the fans' attitude towards football, and even though people knew he was going to leave Palace at the end of the season there was immense warmth towards the man. He would say things about players that were so refreshingly honest. To hear a manager saying that the fans had the right to know what was going on, and that the fans were as important to the club as anyone else, was very welcome.'

THE REFEREE

Neil Midgley blew his whistle on the fields of the football world for 18 seasons, including 10 years on the international panel, before retiring in 1992. He had a common-sense approach, allied to a sharp sense of humour that helped make him one of the most successful referees. He now attends matches as an observer for UEFA and the Premier League. He is a former president of the Referees' Association.

'The managers who ranked highest with me were those like

Brian Clough and Ron Atkinson who had good standards and allowed players to express their skills. I always had least trouble with their teams, from the moment I inspected the studs in the dressing room to the end of the game. They used to show you respect – or at least, it appeared that way!

'It was always the sides that played most attractively that gave the referee least trouble. Towards the end of my career attitudes changed. The rewards are greater now and that has a lot to do with the pressure managers are under. Mind, they always seem to get fixed up somewhere else when they're fired!

'Some of them will play games with you psychologically. They might send their assistant, or the next coach down the line, to bring in the team sheets instead of doing it themselves. It could be their way of making a point, or it could be superstition. There's a lot of superstition in football, and if a team has won when the manager didn't take the team sheet to the referee he'll stick with the same method next time. There are managers who will try to psych you out, either by what they say or by keeping silent. The older you get, the better you cope.

'It's a man-management thing. That's the manager's job and it's the referee's job too.'

Midgley has been on the receiving end of a manager's resentment after controversial matches but brushes such matters aside. 'It's ludicrous. It achieves nothing. Managers should be setting an example to the players. Nobody likes losing, but it's like playing golf. You only remember the bad putts and the shots that ended in the water. Managers only remember the bad decisions and fail to balance them with the good ones.

'The worst thing a referee can do is to send a manager away saying he won't speak to him. It's far better to say, "Go and cool off, then come and have a chat." When they're steaming they will only get themselves into bother. All they're trying to do is express their disappointment but sometimes they try to belittle the referee, and I don't like that.'

When the manager is fighting a losing battle against relegation, the fans are howling, the chairman is grumbling, and a referee's decision has cost a vital win in the last minute, is there any vestige of sympathy? 'No. It's the law of the jungle. You can't afford to feel sorry for them. It goes with the job. Anyway, I have pressure in my job. Do they feel sorry for me?

'It's very odd how, if one of their players is involved in an unsavoury incident, the manager never sees it. Yet they see everything else! Managers will accuse referees of only refereeing for the benefit of the League's assessor in the stand, not for the benefit of the game. But that's unfair. Our performances are also marked by the managers themselves. Each manager submits a report to the referees' officer. The referee himself doesn't get to see a copy, which I think is wrong. Of course, managers are against that because they think the ref might hold it against them for the next match. They can express their opinion of referees, yet they've never done the job themselves. They think they can do it but they can't – I've seen them handling practice matches, and I know they can't do it.'

THE UNION MAN

The Professional Footballers' Association is unusual among trade unions. Where most unions look to the management side to come up with financial solutions, the PFA has often loaned money from its own resources to keep failing clubs afloat. Gordon Taylor, once a professional with Bolton, Birmingham and Blackburn, is the union's chief executive. The closest he came to management himself was when he was asked to apply for the Newport County job. He didn't put his name forward, though he is a fully qualified coach and ran coaching courses for the FA at Lilleshall – once with Terry Venables as his assistant. He also did a stint as player-coach of Vancouver Whitecaps in the North American Soccer League.

'We have a good relationship with most managers because, having played the game themselves, they know where I'm coming from. But making that first transition from playing to managing is a problem for some of them. They have to become more of a loner and feel they must change their character, become tougher and harder. I don't know if that always works. Trevor Francis seems determined to respond to Brian Clough's criticism that he's too soft to be a football manager. Some become very authoritarian, like Stan Cullis in the fifties and sixties. Others, like

Joe Royle and Jim Smith, are more comfortable when it comes to handling people.

'We represent the rights of the players, and to some extent managers see that as a threat. But most, if not all, accept the role of the PFA and possibly wish their own Managers' Association was as strong.

'In this country we have fallen behind in international terms because we don't put enough into the training of managers and coaches. Whereas the likes of Spain, Italy and Germany put a lot of emphasis on the training of coaches, we appoint people on a hit or miss basis. There isn't enough attention paid to sports science, psychology, diet, and awareness of tactics and systems throughout the world. The FA is beginning to address that sort of thing now, having taken on board the views of UEFA, the Managers' Association and ourselves.

'I don't envy managers their job because so many times they can't win. They're caught between the directors and the players. They lose the camaraderie of the dressing room and although management is the next step after a playing career ends it can never replace it.'

THE AGENT

Eric Hall is a London-based agent who branched out into football in 1987 having previously concentrated on showbiz. It was hardly a coincidence; professional football was producing stars every bit as big as the glamorous names of rock and fashion. It was also producing equally complex contractual arrangements. Fast-talking and quick-witted Hall has clients at every club in the Premiership plus many in the Nationwide League. Some of them, like Steve Perryman and Terry Fenwick, have moved into management, which entails a remodelling of the relationship. Hall doesn't have managers under contract as such, but he does deal with them on a one-off basis. 'Or on a three-off or four-off basis,' he chuckles. No shady backstage manipulator, Hall has become a personality in his own right, familiar to the football public via regular appearances on TV and in newspapers.

'I sympathize 110 per cent with the pressures managers are

under,' he says. 'It's a night and day job and if you don't deliver you're out of work. It's just the same as showbiz. If your record flops the record company will cancel your contract. It won't get any easier, because the money is going to get bigger and bigger. We've seen £15 million transfers. They'll be up to £20 million eventually. People are throwing money into the game like crazy.'

Lawrie McMenemy, who handles salary negotiations on behalf of Southampton, made the point that, 'Managers come under pressure from four sources – players, press, public and directors. And now there's a fifth – the agent.' Fair comment? 'No,' says Hall. 'There is no pressure from agents. Well, maybe there is, up to a point. But who do the people want to watch – the managers and chairmen, or the players? It's the players who pull in the punters, so they should be rewarded. Players trust their agent more than they trust their manager. When it comes to negotiating a contract the club sends in their chief executive and their club secretary, maybe the chairman too. It's only fair that the player has someone he can turn to.'

Certainly the arrival of agents has disrupted many a club's wage structure. Managers like to keep salaries within certain boundaries so that the less glamorous performers don't become alienated. Hall dismisses the whole philosophy. 'Wage structures are bullshit. A star should be paid star money. If Sinatra was on the same bill as Vince Hill, would anyone expect Vince Hill to be paid the same?'

THE PHYSIO

Jim McGregor was one of the first of the new style of physiotherapist – a young, tracksuit-clad, streetwise enthusiast. McGregor and others who emerged in the late sixties and early seventies soon replaced the old brigade, men who wore white coats during the week and rarely got their shoes muddy on matchdays. McGregor began his football work part-time with Clyde, then moved south to Oldham Athletic, Everton and Manchester United, including a spell with the Northern Ireland team. He is now in private practice in Manchester, a role which includes freelance consultancy with a number of League clubs.

'Apart from the assistant manager, the physio is the closest person to the manager. This is because you travel away with them every other week, you work closely with them every day. The managers at all the big clubs have their little inner sanctum of assistant manager, kitman and physio, and these four are together all the time. In the dressing room before and after games, on the bench during games.

'Most managers react roughly the same when they start a losing run. Once they've lost three matches in a row you get reactions like making the lads do an extra half-hour's training, or bringing them in on a Sunday morning. Or not getting their usual day off. Small things, petty things, but nearly every manager I've worked with will do that. Because what else can they do? They lose a game and drop two players. Lose the next game and try a new formation. Lose again. By now they're running out of ideas so they blame the players. They always blame the players. It's rarely the fault of the manager's planning, selection of team, formation, training, fitness, etc. If a manager actually believes he has made errors he will very rarely say so to anyone. He always looks to make an excuse.'

McGregor believes managers are fully appreciative of the physical duress on players. 'Certainly Alex Ferguson is. A few times he's over-reacted. He would give younger players like Ryan Giggs a rest before they needed it. He's a great believer in making sure they are not subject to extreme physical demands.'

The suspicion that managers pressurize players to perform when less than 100 per cent is a widespread one. McGregor says: 'I've been lucky. If the physio is strong from day one and the manager realizes you know your job, he will respect you. If the players respect you the manager usually does, and he will then take exactly, word for word, what you say. He will, perhaps, in a gentle way put you under pressure. But I was never in 30 years put under direct pressure by a manager saying, "We must have Joe Bloggs fit for Wednesday night." He might say, "Do you think he'll be fit? Are you sure?" And that's as much pressure as I was under.

'But I know from speaking to colleagues at other clubs that there are some managers who I could never have worked with. For example, Brian Clough at Nottingham Forest. He had such a personality that he had to rule the roost even in the medical room. The man used to walk in and say, "You shouldn't be on the bed, you're fit." Totally undermining the physio. And if he is undermined in front of the footballers, he's dead. And I think that is still happening where the manager has a powerful personality and the medical man is not fully chartered or lacks a strong personality.

'To be a successful football manager, unless you're unusual, you have to be totally committed to football. It is the most important thing in their life. A lot of the wives won't want to hear this, but I know from the managers that I've worked with that the game is their lifeblood. The wife, unfortunately, comes second, and I don't even think it's a close second in most cases.

'A few years ago there was a controversial case when a QPR player, Malcolm Allen, was disciplined by his manager, Trevor Francis, for leaving the team hotel to be with his wife when his child was born. We had a big debate about that among the Manchester United staff. About 50 per cent of the players said they would do exactly the same thing. The other half said they wouldn't. But the manager and the coach were absolutely appalled that you could even think of your wife and your child. Football comes first.

'If you carry out a survey on days lost through illness among the senior staff at any club – manager, assistant manager, coaches, chief scout and physio – the results would be unbelievable. They don't miss a day. They are completely dedicated, especially the manager, and that's what he likes in his staff. He has to have, for example, a medical man who thinks nothing of getting home from Highbury at half past one in the morning and being back in first thing as normal. And I don't think you'll find anyone more immersed in it than Alex Ferguson.'

Jim McGregor has seen managers flounder, and he's seen them prosper. He has watched their reactions when things go from bad to worse. 'One well-known manager took his senior staff aside after another defeat and said, "I'm resigning." A year and a half later he was still in the job. The staff talked him out of it, and results improved. Other managers change routines dramatically, like Ron Atkinson. Whereas a lot of managers might say, "We'll get them in for extra running," not really believing that will help, Big Ron would do the opposite. He would say, "Four days in Marbella. Let's get the lads' arms round each other, have a few beers, improve team spirit." We did that a few times. Whether it worked or not I don't remember. I recall coming back to one match and doing well and another one when I thought they were still drunk! But Ron would try lots of things – including extra running on occasions.

'You can see them stressed. Alex Ferguson, after United lost 3–1 at Villa at the start of the '95–96 season, looked stressed. His throat was dry. It wasn't his normal voice. He had obviously been having a bit of a go in the dressing room. They are under unbelievable pressure, these guys.

'Managers like to feel secure. This is why, increasingly these days, the new manager brings in his own team. Even the medical man is at risk. That used to be unheard of – he was part of the bricks and mortar. But when a new manager comes in now, the entire backroom staff shake in their shoes. They bring assistant managers, youth-team coaches and even physios with them. Because they know they can trust them – they're not going to be stabbed in the back by a man who was there with the ex-manager.'

The physio occupies a privileged position in the club hierarchy. His place on the team bus is secure week-in, week-out. He is part of all the big occasions. He sits cheek by jowl with the boss while the action is at its fiercest on the pitch. And he has a vital role in conveying to the players the manager's latest thoughts (football regulations forbid managers actively to coach the team during a match). 'When the medical man runs on the park, eight times out of ten it's not necessary. Eighty per cent of injuries are knocks to the lower limbs or slight dazes where, in another 60 seconds, he'll be all right. But a lot of times when you run on it's to take a message – the manager wants the full-back to mark tighter, the wide man to make more runs, whatever.'

The physio sees the strain with a more practised eye than most. 'We played Southampton away, early one season. I think it was their second home game of the season, and the manager, Ian Branfoot, was already being booed by his own supporters. I walked along the touchline behind him – it's 60 yards from the tunnel to the dug-out at Southampton because the tunnel is in the corner of the ground. I thought, My God, is it worth it? He was hated by the supporters. OK, you expect animosity at away matches from the other supporters, but at home? Managers have to be hard-skinned, brave, or daft.

'Their life isn't their own, especially when they're doing well. It's a damn' hard job. All right, he might spend only an hour and a half working with the players in the mornings. But he's working from the moment he leaves home. Many of them are on the mobile phone as soon as the car leaves the front door, checking with their scouts, etc. Alex Ferguson would do that. Then he would arrive at the ground, talk to the laundry girls, go and see how the grass was growing – literally! Have a word with the groundsman, speak to staff, the physio, do a bit of training. A lot of managers go in the bath with the players afterwards, to get a bit of atmosphere and mix with them. Then there's the media, more interviews, and if you're manager of a club like Manchester United you can be out at dinners every night of the week if you want to be. It's an unbelievable job and I don't think it's overpaid. It is ridiculous money, but then it's a ridiculous job, and it doesn't matter whether you're manager of Manchester United or Rochdale, it's a ridiculous job.'

9

WHEN THE LAST FLOODLIGHT DIMS

Mid-afternoon and the bar is heaving. It's the heart of London's business sector and those who can make the right excuses have stayed away from the office to join the crush. TV monitors are emitting live pictures of England's rugby fifteen playing France in the play-off for third place at the World Cup in South Africa. Around the walls, scarcely noticed on this day when rugby commands all attention, glass-fronted showcases parade a host of mementoes from international days of another sport: caps, shirts, pennants and photographs recall the highspots of a great career in football.

Behind the bar a softly-spoken Irishman pulls the pints, tops up the wine glasses, and keeps an eye on the lively throng. Terry Neill, once manager of Arsenal, manager of Tottenham, player-manager of Hull City, player-manager of Northern Ireland, centre-half and captain of Arsenal and 59 times a Northern Ireland international, is no longer actively involved with professional football.

The bar is his. The name on the green awning outside is a dead giveaway: 'Terry Neill's Sports Bar and Brasserie.' The same identity is woven into the polo shirts worn by the staff. Business is booming.

The sports bar, within hailing distance of Holborn Circus, is Neill's brainchild. It's one of two which he runs, with more planned. Visits to the USA gave him the idea of transplanting the American sports bar concept to Britain. The walls display photographs and souvenirs of achievements other than his own, but the Irish theme is strong. The monitors provide a choice of viewing, with satellite sports channels as well as the terrestrial services.

It's 13 years now since the football industry, hurtling round one more sharp bend, allowed a passenger door to fly open and deposit Neill on the grass verge. He was in his eighth year as manager of Arsenal. The previous season the team had reached the semi-finals of both the FA Cup and League Cup, losing to Manchester United each time. He had taken them to three successive FA Cup Finals, winning one, and to the Final of the Cup Winners Cup, where they lost to Valencia in a penalty shoot-out. His tenure was no disaster but it didn't give the Gunners the consistent success they craved, and when poor form in the League was augmented by a home defeat against Third Division Walsall in the Cup, the lock on the passenger door was nudged undone.

For Neill, it was not simply the loss of a job. It was the end of a career.

The trouble with football management is that the job market is never going to expand. In England, there are 92 posts and that's it. So each year, a proportion of managers will be left high and dry, stranded without a chair when the music stops. Many stay in the game as coaches, either in Britain or overseas, working with footballers in the Gulf, the Far East or Africa. Some, by choice or by circumstance, become cut off from the game which has been their passion since boyhood. Terry Neill decided enough was enough, and claims he did so without a qualm.

How long did it take to adjust to NOT being a football manager?

'It took me about two minutes. If that. The time it took to walk from Ken Friar's office (the Arsenal secretary) to the main hall and out of the stadium. It wasn't a problem at all for me.'

Didn't he miss it? The involvement? No withdrawal symptoms?

'Not really. Occasionally I miss it. Round about July when the weather is nice and the grass is green, the thought of spending the next month working out with the players in pre-season training is appealing. You're not playing a game in earnest. You haven't lost to anyone. Everybody is still full of optimism. At times like that you do get the odd tug. But I have no complaints.'

Neill was dismissed by Arsenal shortly before Christmas. Within 48 hours he was offered the manager's post and twice his salary by Aston Villa, but declined.

'I decided to take a two or three-month sabbatical and enjoy the first real Christmas of my footballing life. The two or three months turned into two or three years and I thought, This is all right!

Neill was sought by charities looking for a personality to help with fundraising. He did more than help – he took part in an expedition to climb Kilimanjaro, the highest mountain in Africa. He went on the Beaujolais run, bringing back the first of the new wine from France. Professionally, the football contacts continued but without any pressure. He was at the 1984 Olympics in Los Angeles working for FIFA as a technical assessor, noting and analysing the tactics of the teams in the football tournament. There was work with television from time to time. 'All lovely, frivolous stuff, and I was making as much money as I did in football.'

When he decided to get serious again, it wasn't to professional football that he turned, but to the sports bar business. 'I had no background whatsoever in the trade. My CV for the job would have had nothing on it. I am not really a pub person. But I have always been confident enough to believe I can make a decent fist of anything I try. I had seen the success of sports bars through many years of travelling to the States.' Neill now has two in London, has ambitions for more, and plans to open three in Northern Ireland.

'The emergence of Sky and cable has made it the right time and I was surprised that none of the established pub chains were going down the same road.'

So the man who is still the only one to manage both the North London thoroughbreds, Arsenal and Tottenham, watches the development of the sport either from his position behind the bar, with a commanding view of the video monitors, or from the press box, through regular broadcasting and newspaper work.

Having had the destiny of both clubs in his hands makes him a unique figure. Given his long playing career in the red and white of Highbury it's hardly surprising that the Gunners come out better in any comparison of the managerial demands at the two clubs. But Tottenham fare notably badly – or at least, the Spurs directors of the day do.

'I walked out on Tottenham because I couldn't work with the directors. The board were of the old school. Rather mean and petty and I didn't think they were prepared to move into a more modern era. I'm talking mainly about their attitude to the staff.

Not the players – they come and go, but the unheralded heroes like coaches, scouts, kitmen. All sorts of people who can't be taken for granted. As a manager, you come to realize very quickly how much you depend on people like that – the backbone of the club.

'At Arsenal the atmosphere was totally different. I went back to a club where I had played for 11 years. The chairman, the late Dennis Hill-Wood, had been like a second father to me since I arrived at Highbury as a 17-year-old, and it was he who persuaded me to go back there as manager. I had nothing set up when I left Tottenham, and found myself having to earn to pay the mortgage.

'I had a lot of problems in my first year because there were a lot of players who I had played alongside, so it wasn't an easy transition. But we sorted it out. I was very lucky to have Dennis Hill-Wood there; we had always had a close relationship and I admired him more than most.'

Neill's managerial career started as player-manager of Hull City, where the chairman, Harold Needler, impressed him immensely. The Spurs board of the mid-seventies was clearly something of a let-down after Boothferry Park. 'It was quite different. I couldn't see the directors for dust in the first year when we were in trouble. I didn't arrive until the end of September '74 when they were already at the bottom of the League and, naturally, given my Arsenal history, I was not flavour of the month with the Tottenham fans. But I battled through that, and my Ulster background kept me going. If you come from that part of the world you have a pretty tight grip on reality.'

Under Neill, Spurs avoided relegation, improved to ninth the following season, and had a good run in the League Cup. But it was Arsenal who provided the greater moments, the peak being the 1979 FA Cup Final when the Gunners beat Manchester United 3–2 after a dramatic finish.

Brian Talbot and Frank Stapleton scored in the first half. With four minutes to go Arsenal still led 2–0. Then Gordon McQueen pulled one back for United, followed instantly by an equalizer from Sammy McIlroy. In one of Wembley's most sensational denouements, Arsenal recovered to nick the winner, Liam Brady and Graham Rix setting it up for an exultant Alan Sunderland.

'When we finally overcame Manchester United, the only thing

I wanted was to be on my own. Not to savour it – I just didn't feel I needed people around me. I enjoyed the atmosphere, but my first reaction on the final whistle was to seek out Dave Sexton and Tommy Cavanagh on the opposite bench. I had worked with Dave at the Arsenal and he is one of the people I most admire. Tommy Cavanagh had a year with me at Hull. I felt terrible for both of them. They in turn were both delighted for me, though disappointed for themselves.

'That was probably the nicest thing about the three consecutive Cup Finals. In the midst of the desire to win, the relations between the managerial and coaching staffs remained as strong as ever. In 1978 when we played Ipswich, you had two clubs who already had a close affinity because the two families in the two boardrooms – the Cobbolds at Ipswich and the Hill-Woods at Arsenal – were very close. Only a few weeks before the Final we were talking seriously about having a joint party after the game. The two boards of directors were First Division drinkers. They all enjoyed a good party. Never mind what you hear about some managers or players getting stuck into the amber nectar, those two boards of directors would have drunk any Football League team under the table. They were a different class.

'Then when John Lyall's West Ham beat us, I was delighted for him, and for Stuart Pearson who played for West Ham but started off with me at Hull. He came back to haunt me. You won't find nicer people in the game than Bobby Robson, who was at Ipswich then, Dave Sexton and John Lyall. But I still wish we'd stuffed the three of them!'

It all sounds far too chummy for the cut-throat world of professional football as we know it today, except that the vast majority of managers still maintain exactly that brand of matey togetherness that Neill describes. So long as no one expects any favours.

The 1980 FA Cup campaign saw his team take on Liverpool in four separate semi-final matches – the first meeting at Hillsborough followed by three replays, Arsenal finally edging it at Highfield Road. 'Those games were so important. They reflected everything that was great about English football, and we're talking about the age of Brady, Jennings, Dalglish and Souness. There were strong chairmen too, because there were mutterings from the FA about a penalty shoot-out to avoid the sequence dragging on. Dennis Hill-Wood and the Liverpool chairman John Smith resisted them. I understand the need these days for penalty shoot-outs, but back in 1980 all the players and staff only wanted to resolve it one way and that was by playing proper football. So the staff of both clubs were delighted at the strong lead provided by the two chairmen. Unfortunately now the days of great chairmen like them are over.

'In the four matches no quarter was asked or given, yet there were hardly any bookings – perhaps two or three – over the four games. When we finally managed to scrape through, the first people into our dressing room were Bob Paisley, Ronnie Moran and Joe Fagan. That said everything about the camaraderie.

'I remember in the first game at Hillsborough looking along the touchline at Bob Paisley and realizing that he had been at Anfield longer than I had been alive! If I had dwelt on that I would have ended up with a massive inferiority complex, so I dismissed it and tried to watch and learn as much as I could from the most successful manager in the business. After the game I dragged my heels out of the dressing room and let Bob deal with the press first. He took about 35 seconds to say nothing. I thought if it was good enough for him it was good enough for me, so I repeated it in an Irish accent.

'We started something that day that persisted throughout the four matches. All the members of the two clubs' backroom staffs went into the medical room at Hillsborough to have a drink. Of course, it was a neutral ground so no one had anything in stock as we would have done at a home game. All we had was some gut-rot brandy that we carried to mix with our tea on a cold afternoon. You would never drink it neat, but it was all we had and the place quickly looked like an alcoholics' paradise. We were drinking this stuff from plastic cups filled to the brim, everyone full of bravado and refusing to give in before the other side. At the next game the other side provided the gut-rot, and so on. It was all good-hearted stuff, but with a serious undertone because Liverpool's staff always looked for an opportunity to score points off you. Professional, competitive, crafty, and lovely people.'

Laid-back, urbane, articulate – Terry Neill was better equipped than many to withstand the twists of fortune that went with his job. In the First Division his best achievement was to take Arsenal into third place – this in an era when his drinking pals from Liverpool dominated the domestic game. Arsenal were always a force to be reckoned with and Neill's team made its mark in Europe too, reaching the Final of the Cup Winners Cup in 1980.

The match was staged in Brussels, the opposition Valencia, coached by one of the all-time greats of football, Alfredo di Stefano. After 90 minutes it was goalless. Extra-time failed to produce any goals. The trophy was decided on penalties. This was the same year as Arsenal's formation dance with Liverpool in the FA Cup semi-finals, a season in which the team played 70 matches, and a time when Neill and his coach Don Howe had forbidden the players from training, such were the demands from the fixture list. For it all to end on the execution of a series of single kicks under extreme pressure was typical of a cruel game.

Amazingly, Argentina's World Cup star of two summers previously, Mario Kempes, missed his penalty. So did Arsenal's Liam Brady. The sequence then progressed successfully until each team had completed its five-penalty quota. The score was 4–4. The competition moved to sudden death. So did Arsenal. The Spanish goalkeeper, Pereira, saved Graham Rix's shot. Valencia had won.

'One or two of the players shed some tears but they got over it, as players do. With all due respect I've no time for that. I'm not averse to shedding a few tears myself – I'm a soppy so-and-so when it comes to an old movie. But when you're working – and that's what I was doing – it's out of place.

'I felt for the fans. They had been absolutely magnificent that season. They had followed us faithfully all over Europe and behaved impeccably. I was so proud to be associated with them, and they were my first thought. Mind you, the team had played well, so it was a two-way street.

'Di Stefano came over. He was obviously delighted but he isn't the sort of person to gloat about it and dance about all over the place. He shrugged his shoulders. What else could he say? We hugged each other. We weren't bosom pals but we were old opponents. The nice thing about that season was the camaraderie with the other coaches. When Hajduk Split played us we looked after them, and they reciprocated when we went there. Myself, Don Howe and their coaches would spend some time together and we all knew what game we were in. Whoever won would be well aware of what it was like for the losers and would be thinking, There but for the grace of God go I. Someone is going to win this year and be a hero, somebody will hit the post, someone will get the bullet. It's our fraternity. Unless you've been at the sharp end and known the ups and downs you can't begin to understand it.

'It was the same with Giovanni Trapattoni, the coach of Juventus. We beat them in Turin – the first time Juventus had ever lost a home game in Europe. I had known Giovanni off and on for years – he was in the Italian team when I made my first appearance for Northern Ireland in Bologna in 1961. After we won in Turin he came into our dressing room and presented me with a Juventus shirt. It's still one of my proudest possessions. I wondered then if I could have been big enough to swallow my disappointment and act the way that man acted that night. Then, of course, we went back to our hotel and drank it dry!'

Neill ended his managerial career with only one major trophy – that FA Cup against Manchester United – and a host of close-run things. Looking back from his vantage point behind the bar in Holborn he reflects on the work he did with players, helping careers blossom. 'What gave me my greatest satisfaction was seeing players fulfil their potential. People like Frank Stapleton, a very raw-boned young lad when I first took over at the Arsenal. He worked and worked to make himself the great player he became. Taking Alan Sunderland for £125,000 from the right-back position at Wolves and linking him with Frank Stapleton in attack. Buying Willie Young twice, for Spurs and Arsenal. Buying Pat Jennings. That was no gamble. A lot of people thought when I brought him to Highbury at the age of 32 on a four-year contract that it was the old pals' act. The reality was that eight years later I was gone and Pat was still there. I loved to see young players make their mark – youngsters like Tony Adams, who I gave a debut to at the age of 16, Michael Thomas, Paul Davis, David Rocastle. I just like to see people do well.'

Being manager of clubs like Arsenal and Tottenham, each a

pillar of the football world, each a name known far beyond the boundaries of sport, is a special responsibility. That hasn't changed in the years since Neill's departure. 'You can either hack it or you can't. You either grow with the job or you don't. You are always aware that the club was there long before you and will be around long after you've gone. That keeps you sober. I just tried to be a credit to that club, and I wanted the fans to feel good about me being the manager. I wasn't the greatest manager in the world, but I was a long way from being the worst. I was comfortable with that.'

It was, perhaps, the right decision all round when Neill turned down Aston Villa's approach in the week that followed his sacking by Arsenal. It is hard to see him succeeding in the modern environment, in which the demand for absolute success is fuelled by big money and bigger expectations, and a ruthless wind has blown much of that cosy mateyness out of the boardrooms. 'Nothing can change the way the job is developing. Pressure will increase. The demands for success will increase. What we will see is a more dramatic fluctuation between being a genius and a bum. There won't be too many managers staying at a club for 10 years.'

The man uncorking the wine as the screens flit from terrestrial rugby to satellite golf is best off where he is, and knows it.

An Englishman who once had Pelé in his team, and another time had Johan Cruyff on his staff, lives quietly in the West Country, playing golf and keeping in touch with football solely via radio contributions to BBC Radio Devon.

Ken Furphy has been retired from management for more or less the same period as Terry Neill. Unlike Neill, he was far from content at being odd man out.

Furphy's managerial career took him from Workington to Watford, Blackburn Rovers, and Sheffield United before he moved to the USA in 1975. The NASL was still in business, and Furphy worked as coach to the New York Cosmos where Pelé was in the squad, winning the Soccerbowl in 1977, then enjoyed significant success with the Detroit Express, and wound up with the Washington Diplomats and Cruyff.

He came home to cash in that experience but found no takers. 'I was 52 and they all said I was too old, despite my record of doing well with clubs who had no money.' (Furphy had taken Workington to promotion from the Fourth Division and won the Third Division title with Watford.) 'I decided I would give myself a year to find a job. I didn't get one so I thought, Ken, that's football's way of saying you've been in the game for 32 years and that's long enough. Off you go.'

It was, he admits, a big wrench, and it took him time to settle into a different way of life. At first he went back to the States and worked as a car salesman in Cleveland with his son, Keith. Then he returned to England and took over a shop selling fishing tackle in the Devon town of Dawlish, converting it into a sports shop and running it on his own. He wrote to the BBC asking for work covering football, but without any luck until a new local radio station opened up in his area. 'The BBC asked if I was interested in working as a freelance for Radio Devon, and I have been doing that for 11 years now. I'd had a bit of experience with Radio Sheffield after I left Sheffield United – summarizing for the main reporters, but at Devon I am doing the reporting myself.'

Like many ex-professionals who move into the media, Furphy initially found the atmosphere of the press box somewhat alien. 'I didn't find it a problem doing the job itself. What I did find difficult was getting accustomed to the other journalists. They lived in a different world entirely. Lots of things they did or said, especially their criticism of players, annoyed me. They tend to be very cynical about players when they have no idea of how hard it can be to be a professional footballer. I found it very hard to keep a quiet tongue.'

But Furphy also learned quickly that the lot of the journalist is not all roses either. His criticism of the hacks was matched by criticism of the clubs. 'We are still well behind the USA in appreciating what the press can do for a club. In my early days with the radio I went to a match at Portsmouth and saw how the journalists were left to wait in the freezing cold for an hour and a half after the game, before the manager made himself available for comments. At Torquay you could wait an hour for the manager to give you a three-minute interview. But it is in the manager's own interests to have a good relationship with the press and to take the opportunity to put his views across to the public. Some managers are very good. Terry Cooper was always amenable at Exeter, and at Plymouth – win, lose or draw – Peter Shilton would never grumble at doing his thing for radio.'

You sense that there is still a well of frustration within Ken Furphy, that after amassing a wealth of experience he could make better use of it. He remains a champion of youth football, disapproving of those managers who follow what he calls the Ron Atkinson pattern – 'simply buying eight, nine or ten established players and trying to fit them together as a unit. Even Manchester United haven't got it right. How can a club like that fail to develop a striker or a centre-half of its own in 10 years? There's something drastically wrong at many clubs as regards the development of the right sort of player. The big drawback about the game now is that it is all about fitness and stamina, so what managers look for are players of strength, endurance and speed. So the ball players have gone. All those small men who were experts at controlling and using the ball have disappeared from the game.

'I saw it happening. When I was manager of Sheffield United I said to the scouts, "Bring me players for every position in the youth team who are quick and can dribble." I encouraged the players to run with the ball. The result was a very successful youth team. When I left and Jimmy Sirrel took over, he kicked three-quarters of them out.

'You could never get the clubs to pay an experienced youth-team coach. That's where I could have done a job. Instead, clubs tend to give it to an ex-player who has retired with a bad knee. That isn't a good investment for the future, because they lack experience. One lad who was in charge of the youths when I was at Watford developed a style of play which was unknown to me. He had been given full control and what he did was to instil in his team an attitude of unfair aggression. We have got to start developing our youth properly, or we will be in desperate trouble.'

Emlyn Hughes enjoyed a brief flirtation with management before deciding it wasn't for him. The former Liverpool and England captain was in charge at Rotherham United for the best part of two years in the early eighties, taking the team to seventh place in Division Two in his one full season. His dismissal following a change of ownership – admittedly with the team failing to reproduce its form of the previous year – left him disillusioned.

'The only time I miss the game is when I get together with other ex-players and managers for charity games and so on. Other than that, I never think about it.' Hughes, always effervescent, now runs a promotions company based in Brighouse, Yorkshire, while he busies himself with media work and after-dinner speaking.

'The job has changed now,' he says, echoing the observations of many others of his generation who thought they knew about stress until they saw what the present crop of managers have to cope with. 'There's a lot more pressure – pressure to win. The profession has become a merry-go-round. There are only so many managers about – one gets the sack and within a week he's appointed to a new job somewhere else.'

But that didn't happen to John Duncan when he was fired by Ipswich in 1990 after three years at Portman Road. He got a new job all right – but it was as a high school teacher specializing in P.E. and geography.

'If you have no job, you do whatever you can do,' he explains. 'I am a qualified teacher and although I had to go through a settling-in period I took to it and enjoyed it. I did get two offers to go back into football management but decided against them. I really needed a spell out of the game.'

Duncan started his professional career with his home-town club Dundee and went on to Tottenham and Derby before entering management as player-manager of Scunthorpe United. Things appeared to be going well for him until he was sacked three months from the end of a season in which the team gained promotion. Then came the Fourth Division Championship with Chesterfield before the Ipswich job became vacant.

The change from high-profile football manager, focal point of press, public and 15,000 paying spectators every Saturday, to teacher at Hadleigh in Suffolk was a tough one. Duncan concentrated on maximizing the qualities he knew. 'There are many similarities between the two professions. You have to handle people, organize them, and establish some sort of rapport. I wasn't completely cut off from the game – I did some radio and TV work and some scouting, so I was at a match every week.'

After two years came the scent of battle again, and Duncan began to fancy taking another trip to the topmost diving board. 'I felt drawn back to football. The teaching was going well and we were considering, as a family, moving back to Scotland. But if we did that it would have been harder to get back into the game at a later date. I was given the chance to go back to Chesterfield and by that time it was something I wanted to do again. I knew the people at the club and it seemed the right choice.'

Wilf McGuinness worked alongside many managers in his lengthy career. Starting with Sir Matt Busby gave him a notable benchmark against which to judge the others. So when he describes one of them as 'one of the smoothest guys in the game, someone who could have been a top-class manager', it's worth taking notice.

The man in question is Martin Dobson, McGuinness's boss at Bury from 1984 to 1989. 'Martin had a touch of class about him, he was good at bringing the right players into the club on free transfers, his teams played good football, and he had the qualities to make a big impact on the game.'

But instead of running a leading club, for which he seemed to be gaining all the right foundations, Dobson was, until recently, to be found on windswept playing fields coaching boys at schools in Lancashire. He has been out of the management business since 1991.

He won promotion from the Fourth Division with Bury but eventually became frustrated at the lack of financial backing at the club and was sacked after a disagreement over a new contract. He took over at non-League Northwich Victoria, but had made enough of an impact to tempt Bristol Rovers to offer him the job after Gerry Francis left for QPR. With Francis gone, half the team wanted to leave too and it was a difficult situation. After only 11 games Dobson and the directors decided things were not destined to work out and he left. He didn't realize it at the time, but he was also leaving the profession.

'I needed to get away from the game for a bit, and instead of waiting for opportunities I decided to go into the fashion business with my wife Carole.' The couple opened a shop in Burnley, the town which had rescued his playing career after a false start at Bolton Wanderers. But it wasn't long before the urge to be involved with football began to make itself felt. He went coaching in Cyprus, took on scouting work for Luton – and applied for managers' jobs.

The fashion business was sold and while Carole worked as a sales manager for a kitchen design company, Martin developed a new role as a freelance schools coach – travelling between Burnley, Clitheroe and Lancaster to work with the youngsters at their schools. It was a role he enjoyed, but, as he says, it lacked the day-by-day intensity of football management, at any level.

At Bury he had been through the usual eye-opening baptism of any manager descending to the lower divisions after a playing career at the top (with Burnley, Everton and England). 'One of the first things I had to do was sort out the training kit. It was an absolute shambles. Players just threw it on the floor. It was only washed once a week, so it dried from one training session to the next and the people who were in first got the best kit. I got in touch with suppliers and arranged for each player to have his own kit and towel, for which he was responsible himself.

'At the same time I got local companies to help us renovate the dressing rooms, so that the players felt they were being treated as professionals and would respond accordingly.

'Recruiting players all had to be done on free transfers, but the men I brought in were the likes of Lee Dixon, Andy Hill, Jamie Hoyland, David Lee and Liam Robinson, who all went on to play at a high level. When they first arrived they would come into my office feeling a bit down because some other club had given them a free transfer. I used to tell them, "I got a free from Bolton and within five years I was playing for England. If I can do it, so can you – and this football club is giving you a chance." Lee Dixon took his chance so well he did go on to play for England.'

But tough as the job may be, it still exerts an addictive grip. Martin Dobson broke away from the game, but through his coaching and scouting activities he retained contacts with it. In 1996 he was back in the professional environment, as youth development officer at Bolton Wanderers. The football bug was simply too deep to eradicate

Jimmy Armfield has no desire to return to a job he describes as one of the most dangerous there is. 'The three toughest jobs are football management, lion taming, and mountain rescue – in that order,' he says with a grin. Armfield, former captain of Blackpool and England, took Bolton Wanderers to the Third Division title in 1973 and Leeds United to the aforementioned European Cup Final in 1975. He left Elland Road three years later, rejected 12 offers from other clubs over the next few months while he assessed his options, then, convinced that life would be more enjoyable as an ex-manager, settled into a media role and opened his eyes to other opportunities.

'I missed football, but not management. I've never been one who needs power. I think people who like power are dangerous. What I missed was the game of football. I was one of the few managers who actually looked forward to the game on a Saturday afternoon. Some people are too much on edge to look forward to it. I enjoyed the matches and the training. It was the part after training, and all the travelling, that I didn't particularly warm to.'

These days Armfield is church organist at St Peter's in Blackpool, vice-chairman of the governors of his former school, a director of Blackpool Community Hospital Trust and vice-president of the local Outward Bound organization. The telephone in his house is almost as noisy as Blackpool's famous Golden Mile. 'I've got plenty to keep me occupied, eight days out of seven,' he comments. He drifted away from management with scarcely a qualm, convinced that life had more to offer. He has discovered he was right – yet he remains a self-styled 'football nut', devouring all the information on offer about the game. He is the sort of enthusiast who will get a buzz from watching any match, be it a kids' game on the park, Bury v Darlington, the Premiership, or the Copa America late at night via satellite TV.

Jimmy Armfield has never strayed from his native Blackpool. Even when he was manager of Leeds United he retained his family home on the Lancashire coast. To the public he became prominent when hired by the Football Association to headhunt the England manager in succession to Graham Taylor following England's failure to qualify for USA '94. But Armfield did not fade into obscurity once his selection, Terry Venables, was in post. With the title of FA Technical Consultant he has remained an articulate presence within the corridors of power, serving on four FA committees. As the game continues to progress through a period of intense upheaval, Armfield is one of the quiet but influential voices nudging the decision-makers in the direction of common sense.

The McAlpine Stadium in Huddersfield is eye-catching from afar – huge bowed arches ripple beyond the old grey streets and conglomeration of latter-day trading estates. On a warm summer's day there is almost a transatlantic feel to the place, with its smart paved approaches and backdrop of trees.

Brian Horton's efforts to continue the progress achieved by Town under their former boss Neil Warnock are watched with an unusual amount of informed interest from the directors' box. Trevor Cherry, once manager of Bradford City, has the title of associate director – a role which gives him the opportunity to advise the board and lend an ear to the manager, without the responsibility of investing any cash in the club.

Cherry turned his back on the management business, with a degree of regret but with total conviction, in the wake of his sacking by Bradford City in the opening weeks of 1987. He could easily have stayed around. There was a vacancy at Sunderland and he was offered the job but declined. Instead he went into business, building up a company in Huddersfield which supplies merchandise for promotional and marketing firms. He is now managing director and the company has been absorbed into the Conrad Group, a Manchester-based organization with various interests in the leisure market.

Trevor Cherry was manager of Bradford on the day of the Valley Parade fire. It should have been a day of celebration for the then 37-year-old manager. His team, rebuilt after a financial crisis which almost sent the club under, were Third Division Champions, and the last game of the season, against Lincoln, was preceded by the presentation of the trophy. But the day will always be remembered for the tragic fire which broke out shortly before half-time and cost 56 spectators their lives.

Like Kenny Dalglish after the Hillsborough disaster, Cherry found himself the focal point of attention which far surpassed anything the normal flow of football life could produce. Bereaved relatives, the media, fundraisers and sympathizers all queued up for his time. Children baking buns to sell for the disaster fund named them Cherry Trevors.

'I didn't leave the ground till 10 p.m. after the fire,' he recalls. 'I just felt I should be there. I had a responsibility to stay and do what I could. So many people were wanting one thing or another. I saw the fire brigade and the ambulance people at work, saw what they had to cope with. You could never pay those people enough for the experiences they go through.

'In practical terms, the aftermath stayed with me for the next 15 months. The players and myself visited patients at the burns unit, there were many fundraising events going on and they all wanted someone from the club to turn up. The town was brought much closer together. But while all that was going on, I still had a football team to run and that was quite hard.'

Unlike Liverpool post-Hillsborough, Bradford didn't have their historic home to retreat to. Valley Parade was destroyed. The team embarked on a nomadic existence, playing at Leeds, Huddersfield, Halifax, but mostly at the Odsal rugby league stadium. 'The pitch at Odsal was terrible. It wasn't fit to ride a horse on, never mind play football. But we had to make the best of it. Visiting managers couldn't believe the conditions there. Under normal circumstances they would have complained to the League, but they knew we were only there because of the fire and there was plenty of goodwill towards the club.'

The players responded well and despite the problems gave a good account of themselves the following season in Division Two. The next season, with the team again occupying a mid-table position, they moved back to the rebuilt Valley Parade, only for Cherry to be fired ten days later.

He blames a worsening relationship with the chairman, the late Stafford Heginbotham. 'He wanted to run the whole club. There was a suggestion to make me managing director, which would have been good, but the chairman probably felt that was a role he should fill.' The dismissal, after all the trials and tribulations, seemed particularly savage, even by football's standards. Cherry had played a significant part in keeping City going before the fire, when the club went into receivership. The grooming and sale of players like Stuart McCall and John Hendrie helped to transform the financial landscape. All of which counted for nothing in the end.

So when the chairman of Sunderland, Bob Murray, invited him to move in at Roker Park, Cherry's 'thanks but no thanks' was not just a rejection of Sunderland, it was a rejection of the whole game.

'I didn't fancy traipsing round the country getting the sack every three years.'

He had some knowledge of business. He had studied book-keeping and once ran his own waste-paper company. Life would be more rewarding, he decided, on the other side of the fence, and so it has proved, with his associate director's title at Huddersfield giving him an interest without the aggravation.

'I think my role can help the manager. When the heat is on you tend to blow things out of proportion instead of counting to ten. I can be a buffer between the board and the manager, smoothing things over where necessary. When you're not in the firing line yourself you can be a bit cooler about the problems.'

It's a position which he believes other clubs might be well advised to copy. 'Our game doesn't make enough use of older people. Ian Greaves, my old boss at Huddersfield, has so much to offer and should have more influence in the game. So should Brian Clough. A man with his knowledge shouldn't be completely lost to football. We are a great country for sacking people. Sir Alf Ramsey won us the World Cup and got sacked – I still can't fathom that one out.'

Trevor Cherry, capped 27 times by England, inspiration behind a Third Division Championship team and voice of a community in crisis, is now content to leave the manager's life to others. From his office he oversees the distribution of all manner of objects used by companies as incentives to persuade customers to buy their products. It is probably football's loss that he doesn't rate the job of the Boss as much incentive at all.

10

FOOTBALL PLC

You walk up the steps and explain yourself to a commissionaire. You continue through glass doors to a gleaming hall where a receptionist supervises the ebb and flow of visitors. Glass, metal and ceramics combine to give a cool, airy welcome, while shrubs surround an ornamental pond into which a small fountain splashes. It could be the headquarters of an upmarket, multinational legal practice. But the presence by the pond of a garden gnome, painted green and white, gives the game away. This is the home of Celtic Football Club.

No club better symbolizes the changes whipping through football's finances than the reviving giant in Glasgow's East End. Celtic began life in 1888, the inspiration of a religious monk named Brother Walfrid, who had two aims: to stage football matches to raise money for the poor, and to promote social integration – of immigrant Irish with indigenous Scots, and of Protestants with Catholics.

Today, a Mission Statement which enshrines Brother Walfrid's ideals is on display in that reception area. But Celtic are heading in a new direction. As one of the first clubs to be quoted on the stock market Celtic are at the forefront of the business revolution sweeping the game. So much money is flooding in from television, sponsorship and corporate activity that football clubs are being seen as attractive investment opportunities by City institutions – bodies which would normally view football down the length of their noses.

Clubs with a stock-market listing, like Celtic and Manchester United, have an obligation to make money for their shareholders – a situation which has implications for the manager of the team, Tommy Burns.

Burns is Celtic to the core. A former midfield player for the club, who earned eight caps for Scotland in the eighties, he has a deep appreciation of the club's principles and wonders about the direction in which it is headed.

'I feel very uneasy about the way football is so motivated by money. Ultimately greed will ruin the game. Here, we are moving away from what the football club was originally structured to achieve – a charitable club to help the people of the East End and a team which they could go and support. The whole thing now is based on winning or losing, and we're losing the moral fibre.'

Burns' office is awash with prayers – cards and notes sent in by supporters. Above the door is a framed blessing from the Pope. These are not mere gestures, they are a constant source of inspiration to the man striving to restore Celtic to a competitive level alongside Rangers. 'They're good thoughts. Considerate, genuine thoughts, and they make a difference to me because they come from ordinary people who are concerned about me.' Burns is himself a religious man. 'It's the thing that carries me in the job. It picks me up in the morning and gets me through my difficult situations each day.'

It was Tommy Burns who gathered up the pieces when Lou Macari had his acrimonious fall-out with Fergus McCann. The new board solved the club's financial problems by floating the business on the stock market, raising the money to secure its future and rebuild the stadium. But for the manager, flotation means more people owning the club – so more people thinking they own him.

'After we lost to Rangers 1–0 a newspaper headline the next day said that £10 million had been wiped off the value of the company because the share price had dropped. So now you've got all this to contend with as well. Shareholders' meetings are more high-profile. And these days people introduce themselves to you as a supporter and make the point that they're a shareholder as well. So they remind you that they own a little bit of you. It's a big thing. It takes everything to a higher level.'

As Alex Ferguson well knows. His desk at The Cliff, Manchester United's training ground, is covered with prayers of a different kind. Neat piles of correspondence from all manner of supplicants, all wanting a piece of his time – Manchester Children's Hospital, Woodhouses Cricket Club, the kit sponsors Umbro. 'Look at it,' he exclaims. 'This is all new this week.' And it's still Monday.

Like Tommy Burns, Ferguson is the one who holds the ring at a company which must blend sport with business. United floated in 1991. By happy coincidence the team started winning trophies at the same time. As the silverware arrived, investors moved in. Over half of Manchester United plc is now owned by City institutions ranging from the Abu Dhabi Investment Authority to the BBC Pension Trust. They are in it for one reason only: to make money. So a meaningful proportion of United's multi-million pound annual profit flows out of the club to reward its backers. Ferguson is reluctant to criticize but admits: 'Flotation has made a difference to the way we do business. You can't go out and sign a player just like that. There are financial restrictions. The Spanish and Italians handle it the best way because they are non profit-making. All their income goes back to the playing side. In England, football has taken a big step in the last couple of years but we are definitely handicapped when we come up against the Italians and Spanish. But at the end of the day we are expected to beat them.'

More than any other club United have seen the headlines describing huge rises and falls in their value after an important win or defeat. Ferguson keeps out of it. 'So long as I am working away at the things I want to do I can cope with it. I ignore the whole thing and just get on with my job.'

Even so, he couldn't ignore it when it was time to negotiate a new contract in 1996. Having completed his second Premiership/FA Cup Double Ferguson was in a strong position. Most clubs would have been happy to secure his signature after the formality of a chat with the chairman, but at Manchester United plc the Remuneration Committee fixes the top salaries and there was some unseemly argy-bargy before Ferguson got his new deal. 'Sometimes you have to put your foot down. Stand up for what you think is right, and I was in that situation. I felt I should be paid my worth.'

Alex Ferguson has travelled an astonishing distance. From the part-time manager of East Stirling, with a pub to run, to a key role in a publicly quoted company worth over £300 million is a huge achievement. His success as manager of the team enables him to take the business fluctuations in his stride. Tommy Burns still has to achieve the playing success of Ferguson, although the Scottish FA Cup in 1995 was a promising start. His definition of success will be to achieve victories on the pitch that enable the club to prosper financially, while maintaining Celtic's unique social commitments.

'The best part of my job,' he reflects, 'is to make people's dreams come true every day of the week. The boy who is handicapped, the terminally ill, the people who come here wanting to meet a player and have a photograph taken. We do that for them on a regular basis. We can literally make their dreams come true and give them a moment they will treasure for the rest of their lives.'

The breakaway from the Football League by the top 22 clubs, forming the FA Premier League in 1992, upped the stakes massively among the game's élite. Money flooded in as never before, attracting, as it tends to, even more money. From the £305 million investment on behalf of Sky TV and the BBC, to the £60 million ploughed into a single club, Blackburn Rovers, by a single individual, Jack Walker, the sport became the delighted beneficiary of riches beyond its wildest dreams. The coming years will see those figures dwarfed. Sky's latest deal more than doubles their previous investment, Carling's sponsorship deal has trebled, and the arrival of pay-per-view television will take the finances of the top clubs into even higher realms.

But, as one or two National Lottery winners might confirm, the arrival of the big golden finger from the sky brings not only big wealth, but also big problems.

The market leaders of professional football advanced through the nineties accompanied by accusations of profiteering, as admission prices rose and new replica kits were introduced with indecent haste. Transfer fees of more than four million pounds became commonplace, prompting some to wonder why the public purse had been used to fund stadium redevelopment (via a reduction in the pools betting levy) if the clubs themselves were so well-heeled.

The game's managers could take all of that in their stride. But the sight of one of their most respected colleagues, George

Graham, being arraigned before a tribunal at a hotel in Watford was serious stuff.

Graham, Arsenal manager for nine years, winner of two League Championships, one FA Cup, one Football League Cup, and the European Cup Winners Cup, was accused of accepting secret payments of £425,000 from a Norwegian football agent, Rune Hauge, linked to the purchase by Arsenal of two Scandinavian players, John Jensen and Pal Lydersen. Graham admitted receiving the money after the transfers had been completed but insisted it was an unsolicited gift. He had subsequently handed it to Arsenal – though not until after the payments had been exposed in the press. The FA Commission didn't contradict him but found him guilty of misconduct, ruling that he was wrong to have accepted the money, and handing down a 12-month suspension from any involvement with the game.

At the same time, court proceedings delving into unrelated matters threw up, in passing, accusations that other managers had accepted illegal payments, leaving the profession needing to clean up its image as a matter of urgency.

Howard Wilkinson, who Graham subsequently replaced at Leeds United, accepts that he and his colleagues could use some good PR. 'As a profession, being a football manager at times means nothing. It's something I'm very concerned about. You're on the same level of public esteem as a car salesman. Yet the professional standards required to succeed and survive over a long period of time in this job are of the highest order.

'I am 53 years of age. I have met a lot of people in the course of those 53 years, some of them very successful in other fields – business, the arts. Some of them inheritors of great wealth, some of them makers of great wealth. In my assessment, people who succeed in the job of the football manager should be ranked with the best.'

Was the George Graham case a one-off? Or are there more unsavoury smells waiting to be exhumed? 'At the turn of the century burglaries were only a fraction of what they are now. Does that mean there were fewer burglaries then and people were more honest? Or does it mean people report burglaries more these days, and the police catch more burglars? I tend to think the latter is the case. I know what is supposed to have happened in football recently goes on in other businesses. But because of the nature of those businesses you don't hear about it. The embezzler is fired but only occasionally does it go to court. There are solicitors who have done what some football managers are supposed to have done. Surgeons, accountants – it happens in all walks of life. If there's money there, it produces temptations and, unfortunately, sometimes people succumb. I would like to see standards improve so that the job acquires more respectability.'

It's a challenge that needs to be embraced by the whole managerial profession, but one man in particular had a heavy responsibility. By following in George Graham's footsteps as the manager of Arsenal, Bruce Rioch took on a massive task. Like Yeltsin trying to rebuild Russia, he had the weight of history pulling against him. Not only did he have to show that the new man at the top was above reproach, he also had to reverse a way of life that bequeathed him the drink and drug habits of Paul Merson, plus too many other embarrassing incidents involving Arsenal players for anyone but the gossip writers to find satisfactory.

History shows that Rioch's tenure at Arsenal ended prematurely. But as the man brought in to clean out the stables he performed a notable task, drawing heavily on his fierce personal philosophy.

'The balance between firmness and compassion is important. Listening to people's concerns matters. I treat players as if they were my sons. I look at them as people first and try to build a basis of faith and trust with them all. Good results help, but if you have good people and work honestly with them you ought to make progress.'

The thought occurs that the flaw in the doctrine is that while a son remains a man's son for life, a player is liable to depart through the first open door if it suits him and his agent. 'Yes, but that can happen with your sons anyway. Sons don't always have lifelong loyalty. They leave home for one reason or another and some families don't see them again. I look back on the players at Middlesbrough, and at Bolton, where it was perfectly possible to create a friendship and with it the right environment.

'There is a white line, a boundary, beyond which the players don't want me to intrude and beyond which I don't want them to intrude. But slowly you can integrate so we end up working together. I don't set out to be unpopular, but along the way I make unpopular decisions. To explain that in the most simple case, I can only pick 11 players on a Saturday, and I might have 33 in the club. So the 11 who play are happy and the 22 who are left out are not happy. So I'm unpopular. But that's no different to dealing with your own sons. They want something and you can't give it to them. You don't do it on purpose. You don't do it vindictively; you do it for a reason. So we face those issues as managers the same way we do as fathers, in our daily lives.'

It is a world crammed with temptations for young men with pocketfuls of cash, from casinos to designer drugs. The football manager has far more to worry about away from the playing arena than ever before. Rioch accepts that he has some degree of responsibility for the conduct of his players, but emphasizes that the responsibility has to be shared.

'Parents are responsible for their children. The club will take responsibility, it always does, but there is also a requirement for people to be responsible for themselves. If you look at the school situation, when a child misbehaves you can't always blame the teacher. There are parents who have a part to play.

'Because everyone is different, some can assume responsibility for themselves quicker than others. Some are led easier than others. But that's why they're all individuals. If they were all the same we would have a poor crop.

'It's a changed industry – in terms of finance, the youth of the players with good incomes, the amount of advice they receive, good and bad.

'The players must accept responsibility themselves. That's what happened in my playing days – the senior professionals would sit and talk to the younger ones and pass on advice and information. But the world has changed. There's far more out there for them than there was in my young days. Far more problems. Apart from pinching gooseberries off the tree or having a crafty cigarette, there was very little trouble for us to get into.

'Initially, players should have guidance from their families, but they don't always get it. So then they need the stability and togetherness of the football team, and the camaraderie of people around them. You need good people at a club. At Arsenal I signed

David Platt – a man who carries himself exceedingly well, not only on the field but off it. He was a tremendous ambassador for British football in Italy and at home. And yet, he got sent off in the quarter-final of a European tie which caused him to miss the two games in the semi-final against Arsenal! It can happen. But his character, attitude and appetite for football are spot on.'

Rioch is as keen as Howard Wilkinson to improve the image of the manager. 'The public profile hasn't been correct for many years. Because of the volume of terminations, sackings, people assume managers are expendable. But they have a huge role to play, and I'm not sure if the public fully appreciate that.

'When we see managers being sacked by clubs, and having to wait up to a year to get their outstanding salary paid, or when managers themselves walk out on their own contracts, the credibility of the profession is reduced. The reason why some managers walk out while under contract is because of clubs' records of sacking people over the years. People wonder who they can trust. So if you get another offer midway through your contract you may be inclined to jump ship. If there was some integrity about the job – as Middlesbrough showed when they paid up my salary within 30 minutes of terminating it – things would improve.'

Despite his abrupt dismissal Bruce Rioch did a sound job at Arsenal – not just for his employers but for the health of English football generally. When Arsène Wenger arrived at Highbury in the autumn of 1996 he inherited nothing like the mess Bruce Rioch encountered 18 months before. Rioch was stunned by his dismissal but kept his thoughts to himself. There was little comment from the directors, apart from vague references to inadequate communication between manager and board. Yet the team's performances had improved. Arsenal reached the semi-final of the Coca-Cola Cup (only losing to Aston Villa on the away goals rule) and went from 12th to sixth in the Premiership, qualifying for Europe. Considering the inauspicious circumstances at the start, it wasn't a bad effort.

Rioch does, however, believe that the modern trend in which chief executives or managing directors assume some of the manager's old powers is going too far, and this may be a clue to the problems he experienced at Highbury.

'For me the best manager is the hands-on manager – the man who likes controlling the day-to-day operations of the football side, coaching, training, transfers and salaries. There may be some modern managers who are not aware of how that worked. But now there are clubs who want to take away that hands-on operation. We now have chairmen and chief executives ringing their counterparts to enquire about players, and the more people who ring around, the less confidentiality there will be. Confidentiality is very important, but it's slipping out of the game. I prefer to be hands-on and I work best when I'm in control. I'm not against the director negotiating the salary or the transfer fee, but you've got to be sure that if someone else is making the phone calls they realize it's a full-time job. You don't ring the manager of a player you want once in a blue moon. It is a regular call.'

All managers are crying out for greater stability. More time to do their job, and if change proves unavoidable, a swift financial settlement.

The League Managers' Association attempted to take the initiative in March 1995. From his office in Leamington Spa the Association's secretary, John Camkin, circulated a six-page document headed: 'The time may have come to revise the manager's responsibilities.' The document made many of the points stressed by managers in *The Boss*, emphasizing the multiplicity of tasks expected of the contemporary manager and concluding: 'Even Superman might shake his head in disbelief.'

The document, mostly the work of Camkin, Howard Wilkinson (then Association chairman) and Steve Coppell (then the chief executive) called for the whittling down of the manager's involvement in 'peripheral' activities. The priority was to win the next match, or at least ensure the team played with style. The manager should, they said 'direct the great bulk if not all of his time and energy towards those purposes ... whilst the present situation remains it is difficult to escape the conclusion that, in too many instances, the administrative structures of English clubs are decades behind their counterparts in European or American sport generally. None would dream of throwing a dozen or more important jobs into the lap of one man.'

Most managers want their jobs to be redesignated to allow them more time working with the team. The Association's paper interprets this as a 'head coach' role, but stops short of calling specifically for that because the authors believe managers would object to the change of title. 'In all walks of life the British have a curious but fierce belief in titles as evidence of status.'

Nonetheless, regardless of title, the managers' representative body sees the way forward as being a more focused role for the manager/head coach, accompanied by the creation of the post of director of football to look after other football-related matters, while the wider responsibilities are devolved to other members of the club's management team.

So the future as sketched would see the man formerly known as the manager having control of: selection and preparation of the first team, the most influential say in the transfer of players, and the appointment of assistant coaches and physiotherapists. He would have more time to travel to Europe and elsewhere to study coaching methods and different styles of play.

The director of football would look after transfers, contracts, dealings with agents, possibly youth recruitment and development. Heads of other departments such as commercial, marketing, finance and administration would join the football director in reporting to the main board.

The desire within the game for constructive change is now so strong that developments along these lines are inevitable. The time scale may not be so clear-cut. British football is famously incapable of acting in unison, and it will be well into the next century before the redefined managerial role is commonplace. Some clubs are well on their way already – Crystal Palace being a prime example. Chairman Ron Noades' action in reorganizing the youth coaching, which angered his then manager Alan Smith so much in the summer of 1994, is in fact consistent with the League Managers' Association's own report.

At Southampton, Lawrie McMenemy's position as director of football could be the blueprint for Premiership clubs to follow. McMenemy handles contract negotiations, provides a link between team management and directors, advises the team manager when advice is sought, and maintains an overview of the way the club conducts itself.

His appointment coincided with the departure of Ian Branfoot and the arrival of Alan Ball. 'My role was not to show Alan how to play football. We both agreed on the principles anyway – one or two-touch football. Ian Branfoot had tried to introduce a long-ball game, but managers have to realize what their public wants. This club is a bit special. The people want to see a certain style of play, and part of my task is to remind the manager of that, and to show them what's required over and above the football itself. I have to ensure the club continues to run in the way it always has, maintains a good image, and plays the sort of football the crowd wants.'

One example of the input a director of football can have came after Southampton's first game under Dave Merrington, the opener to season 1995–96, which ended in a 4–3 home defeat to Nottingham Forest. McMenemy had a quiet word before Merrington faced his first post-match press inquest. 'We had a chat about what he might expect. It's a big thing if you're not used to it, being confronted by anything up to 50 people holding notepads and cameras.'

McMenemy describes himself as a buffer between boardroom and manager's office. 'Directors may not want to interfere, but it's human nature for them to want to know what's going on. When they get to their office or the pub, they're targeted as being someone on the inside. And whilst they mustn't be telling everything, it's nice for them to have some knowledge of what the manager is trying to achieve. You can't keep directors in the dark, because then you risk the taunts about who is running the club.'

The Managers' Association sums up the benefits of the changes it wants – greater efficiency, better budget control, more innovative thinking, improved quality of life for the managers, fewer sackings, and the prolongation of the manager's active career. 'Whilst few managers in this country continue beyond the age of 55,' they point out, 'it is not uncommon for successful head coaches in Europe and elsewhere to continue well into their sixties.'

Bruce Rioch, though, thinks the document was an own goal. 'It provided the opening for directors to take over part of the manager's job description,' he says. 'And it isn't necessarily for the best. You can't imagine Brian Clough taking his hand off the button, can you?'

But Lawrie McMenemy, 60 years of age at the start of season 1996–97, disagrees. 'In England,' he observes wryly, 'we shoot managers when they reach 50. Abroad they're very successful in their 60s and even 70s sometimes.' McMenemy himself was marched off to the firing range when his unhappy spell with Sunderland ended in 1987. He had three years out of the game, picking up what media work he could, before he received an unexpected call from Graham Taylor to become his assistant with the England squad. Now he has an important role to play at Southampton. 'We ask too much of our managers all the way along the line. I have been to Rome to watch Lazio train. Their coach, Dino Zoff, had different coaches to get the players organized, supervise the warm-up, ensure they're fully flexed – then he took over. He had other people looking after the admin. Here, it's coming full circle. Clubs are realizing that the other aspects of the manager's job are getting in the way of the football.'

Bobby Robson proves the point. The man who steered Ipswich to FA Cup success in 1978 and took England to the semi-finals of the 1990 World Cup turned to the Continent for his next employment – first with PSV Eindhoven in Holland, then with Sporting Lisbon and Porto in Portugal before landing the plum job at Barcelona. At the age of 63 he is still making an enthusiastic and effective contribution to the game.

The football world has never known quite what to make of Michael Knighton. Visionary? Or self-publicist? Football fan? Or opportunist? The man with the Midas touch? Or a latter-day Icarus who flew too close to the sun?

Knighton it was who pulled off the coup of coups, negotiating the purchase of Manchester United FC in 1989. Subsequently, with controversy rolling round Manchester like claps of thunder, he decided not to close the deal, accepting a seat on the board and playing a part in the successful flotation of United plc as a publically quoted company on the Stock Exchange.

But the ambition to create and control his own football club still burned, and in 1993 he took over Carlisle United, then in the pits and looking like staying there. Under Knighton, who has the title of chairman and works at Brunton Park as chief executive, the club has prospered beyond its wildest dreams – play-offs, then the Third Division Championship by several lengths, and a trip to Wembley for the Autoglass Final. Achieved, not by throwing money at the problem, but by a root-and-branch reorganization, careful recruitment – and putting the emphasis on coaching.

While the game's Establishment now talks of redesignating managers as coaches, Knighton has beaten them to it. There is no 'manager' at Carlisle. The man in charge of the team is Mervyn Day, director of coaching, a title he inherited from his predecessor, Mick Wadsworth. The newspapers refer to Day as Carlisle's manager, but Director of Coaching is the designation that appears in his contract.

'The system is working very well and I was the first chairman to introduce it,' claims Knighton cheerily. 'Mervyn can concentrate on what he's good at, which is the coaching side. The finances, transfers and contracts are the chief executive's domain, and I'm here 18 hours a day working on that side of it. All serious professional football clubs will end up doing exactly the same.

'The George Graham business further demonstrated the need to split the two roles. Quite apart from the temptation, how you can expect someone who is a footballer one day and a manager the next, to deal with budgets running into millions of pounds is stupefyingly nonsensical.

'It's astonishing how long it has taken the game to wake up to that fact. The George Graham case fast-forwarded the change. But it was inevitable. When you have companies turning over in excess of £40 million, as Manchester United do, with players who cost millions, you need someone who knows what he's talking about.'

According to Knighton, clubs should make the choice of chief executive with as much care as their choice of manager (or coach). 'The relationship between manager and chief executive is going to become the most important one at any club. If the chemistry is wrong, you've got a problem, because both parties will guard their territory jealously. But times have changed already, and within the next 10 years we'll see the system we operate at Carlisle become quite commonplace.'

So who will really make the big decisions? Who will decide on a major transfer bid? 'The chief executive will have the final say but he must always have confidence in his coaching staff. You have to believe they have recommended a deal which is a good one. But personally, I would always want to go and see what the money was being spent on.

'The arrogance that prevails among the coaching fraternity has to be stripped away. They all believe that they are right – but history shows they are often desperately wrong. That's why clubs go bankrupt.'

Well, maybe, but dodgy decisions by directors also play their part in taking clubs to the financial precipice. Knighton, however, is convinced that this is the way forward. 'The only safeguard for protecting the industry for all time is to make sure that the appointment of a chief executive is a good one. He should be accountable and judged by performance. That means, if the business is running at a loss, understanding whether it is a managed, budgeted loss. And where has the money gone? If the performance is poor, he should suffer the same consequences as the coach does if the team's performance is poor.

'We should do away with the term "manager". They are not managers – they are football coaches. But the traditional model is so entrenched. They will find it very difficult to lose the title, and they will fight tooth and nail to hold on to it. But they will cease to be referred to as managers eventually.'

Doug Ellis, chairman of Aston Villa, is adamant that things must change. 'The job will become more one of team management and coaching,' he says. 'Especially with the type of money involved these days. At Aston Villa we have spent £24 million on new players since November 1994, with £6 million coming back in. It's wrong to expect a manager whose background is that of a professional footballer – with the odd exception – to have that responsibility. In the old days they did – but that was when it was a shilling to stand on the terraces. It's all changed. It's market forces, I'm afraid.'

At Villa Park the intense personal involvement of Ellis means they are already well on the way. At a wealthy club like Villa, there would be no difficulty in hiring a specialist director of football if Ellis decided to step back and redefine the management structure there. But the League Managers' Association's vision has one major flaw. How could clubs in the lower divisions finance the extra post?

Many of them already lead a hand to mouth existence, reeling from the financial aftershocks of the Premiership breakaway which significantly redistributed the game's wealth away from the Nationwide League clubs. The prospect of funding another executive post is beyond many of them. Yet it is at these clubs that most managers start their careers. Here, surely, is where the re-focusing of the boss's role would be most relevant. The Association's document recognizes that, but beyond offering the hope that 'specialist financial directors' might offer assistance 'on a voluntary basis' has no solution.

Michael Knighton is swift to point out that Carlisle United were not exactly in clover when his system was introduced. 'In the lower leagues, someone on the board has to take on the role, preferably full-time. Every club should aim to have a full-time, well paid, qualified chief executive. That is the most important appointment at any club nowadays. You have to find the right animal, and they do exist, though it will be harder to find the right man for that job than for the coach's job.'

While the majority agree with the proposal to allow another executive to handle transfers and contracts, that is by no means true of everyone. Alan Smith, when at Wycombe: 'I wouldn't like all involvement with contracts to be taken away from me. There is a definite advantage in being the one who sorts out a player's contract – he knows that you are battling for him. If the manager earns £250,000 it is to accept responsibility. In transfers, someone who isn't intimately involved with the game might end up paying more for a player than is sensible. Yes, there is an element of PR work in the job, but the manager tends to be a bigger name in the community than the local MP, so why not? I don't see anything wrong with opening fêtes and so on – it's something I enjoy.'

Lennie Lawrence is very dubious about the developing trend. 'I don't want to be just a coach. I like the variety of the manager's job as it is at the moment, and the unpredictability of it. It's good to wake up in the morning not knowing what the day will bring.

I think I'm quite good at the buying and selling – my record proves that.'

Brian Horton is of a similar mind. 'I still want to be hands-on with certain things, but I think it's inevitable that more people will become involved in the manager's traditional area. More people want to be involved these days. It's more of a business than a sport.' David Pleat agrees. 'The manager still likes to feel he is the one in control of the player's destiny. When it comes to securing the best deal for the player from the directors, the manager should be prepared to "show" for the player. But it is getting harder to keep players happy because they are all owned by agents. Young players who the press elevate to superstardom read that they're worth £1 million and want to be paid £100,000 a year. The players are getting stronger and the manager is getting weaker.'

Brian Horton: 'With freedom of contract, allowing a player to move on at the end of his contract whether you want him to or not, it isn't the same situation as the days of the Busby Babes, when Manchester United knew that they could bring players through and keep them for the rest of their days if they wanted to. You've got them for, say, two years and if they want to leave after that, off they go. Forward planning is over a very short timespan these days.'

Howard Kendall experienced the Continental system at Athletic Bilbao and enjoyed it. 'If you look at the job specification of a top European coach, I think our game will work its way towards that. At the moment clubs change for the sake of changing, because of pressure from the media and the supporters, or because they've had one disappointing season. A coach abroad is responsible for the tactics and the results. He isn't criticized for a bad buy in the transfer market. He will make his recommendations and that's it. Next thing you know, the player has been signed or not. That would take a lot of pressure away from managers. What would also help would be a transfer embargo during the season, perhaps with a two-week window halfway through.'

And Wilf McGuinness finds it hard to believe that it has taken our game so long even to consider moving in the direction of the format he experienced with the Greek clubs Salonika and Patras in the seventies. 'In Greece, any problem – like a player not getting his wages, which happened a lot in Greece! – would be handled by a committee man. That is the right way of doing it. Over here, I've seen managers getting bogged down with minor matters like deciding which player rooms with who in hotels.'

Alex Ferguson believes that when the time comes for him to step aside Manchester United will need more than one man to replace him. 'General manager, director of football – call it what you like – the role has definitely got its attractions now. I don't think it's important at the smaller clubs. Maybe not even at the smaller Premier League clubs. But it is in keeping with a club of our size. We operate in the European context, particularly since the Bosman ruling. Assessment of players is more crucial, budgets have to be met. And the whole operation is so much bigger. Our full-time professional staff has increased by about ten players since I came. Plus an extra physiotherapist, and a nutritionist, and so on.

'Success brings its demands. There's always someone who wants a part of your time, and the arrival of a general manager or director of football will definitely help the team manager to maintain his focus on the job he's supposed to be doing.'

Football is moving gingerly in that direction. But not all those currently drawing a salary as director of football do the job that the title implies. A number of clubs are handing out the title as a reward for valued service in preference to the sack. Kenny Dalglish was the prime example. His role as director of football at Blackburn served little purpose. Dalglish drifted in and out of the club's training complex, a peripheral figure working mostly with the youth team. Yet if ever a club needed a strong, positive figure to head up their football operation it was Blackburn in that ill-fated 1995–96 season. The transfer policy was allowed to slump, and when team-mates Graeme le Saux and David Batty came to blows with one another during a Champions League match in Moscow, the club needed someone to make the right political noises, field the flak and shield Ray Harford from the heat. Dalglish could have played a role there, but the club gave him no clear brief about his responsibilities so he stayed out of it.

Genuine progress is being made towards resolving managers' other serious headache – the miserly attitude of clubs when it comes to paying up contracts following a sacking. 'Ninety per cent of clubs behave honourably,' estimates John Camkin, secretary of the Managers' Association. 'But the 10 per cent who do not are a problem. John Docherty had to wait nearly three years after leaving Bradford City before he received any money, and even then it only came after a High Court hearing. By that time it cost the club far more than if they had settled promptly.'

In June 1995 the Association struck a deal with the Premier League, setting up an arbitration system to avoid both delays in payment and costly legal action. If, after 28 days following a 'termination,' either the club or the manager is unhappy about the settlement of the contract, they can invoke the procedure. A three-man panel consisting of one representative from the Premier League, one from the Managers' Association and an independent chairman, hears both sides of the story and gives a ruling within another 28 days.

The system is also designed to prevent clubs suffering when a manager walks out in mid-contract. The Association accepts that cases like Mike Walker's exit from Norwich to join Everton are bad for the image, though Camkin points out: 'At times career enhancement makes it very difficult not to accept an offer.'

The aftermath of Walker's move was a public wrangle between the clubs over the amount of compensation Everton should pay. Under the new deal, a manager's registration is held by the Premier League and is not released until his new club has agreed compensation. If the clubs can't agree, the arbitration panel will again report for duty.

So far the deal only applies to the Premier League. Nationwide League clubs have declined to sign up, which was why David Pleat was able to walk out on Luton mid-contract and join Sheffield Wednesday. The Luton chairman David Kohler demanded £300,000 compensation, prompting Bobby Gould to comment: 'Managers these days have become a commodity for chairmen, something to be traded for the best price you can get.' Luton eventually settled for £150,000.

'Nationwide League clubs have got to come to terms with the way the game is developing,' says Pleat. 'They will always find that their managers are attracted into the top League. Even so, very few managers have actually walked away from their clubs compared to the number who are sacked. It's that fear of the sack that makes them move on.

'And when a chairman appoints a manager these days, he should ask himself what type of manager he really wants. A coach? Or a front man?'

Two men pedalling in the same direction is a sight no longer confined to the velodrome. Football clubs have begun to experiment with a two-man management team: not the old general manager/team manager combo, but two individuals with joint responsibility for team affairs.

The model was provided by Charlton Athletic, where the departure of Lennie Lawrence in 1991 led to two players, Alan Curbishley and Steve Gritt, being made joint managers. It looked a recipe for disaster, but the twosome reigned for four years – one of the most permanent appointments of the time, enjoying a degree of success along the way. In due course Reading followed suit, Jimmy Quinn and Mick Gooding succeeding Mark McGhee. Crystal Palace kicked off season 1995–96 with Peter Nicholas and Ray Lewington running team affairs, Rotherham paired Archie Gemmill with John McGovern.

But by this time the founding fathers had broken up. When Richard Murray took over in the Charlton boardroom he preferred a solo to a duet and Gritt was paid off.

'The chairman wanted one man to be accountable,' says the surviving Curbishley, 'and for my sins, that's me.' Curbishley and Gritt had their good times, taking Charlton into the thick of the promotion chase in 1993–94 when they also put together a memorable FA Cup run. They beat Blackburn Rovers 1–0 at Ewood Park before bowing out to Manchester United in the sixth round. But Curbishley is not an admirer of the system. 'Normally a club will only instigate it with two players who are nearing the end of their time as players, are already under contract, and are desperate to take it on. I can't see, say, Mike Walker and Jim Smith teaming up as joint managers.

'Chairmen see it as an easy way out. When Steve and I started, the entire outlook for the club was very black. Finances were tight, we didn't have our own ground – we were playing at West Ham. Probably they couldn't have afforded a manager in his own right. We lasted longer than anyone expected – in fact, we had the third most successful managerial record in Charlton's history, in terms of matches won.

'We had to sell our better players in order to fund the move back to the Valley, so it has been tough at times.'

Now running the show on his own, Curbishley admits to added pressure but believes that the job will be easier in many other ways. 'Several of the players have admitted they are more easy in their minds, dealing with just one person. Having joint managers made the job even more time consuming. We would sit for ages on a Thursday night, deciding on the team for Saturday, only for someone to pick up an injury in training on Friday and we'd have to start all over again. And it was always a compromise.

'If we wanted to sign a new player we would both have to go and watch him. Even if I saw someone on my own, Steve would have to check him out as well. Plus I would sometimes forget to pass on something that Steve needed to know. He would then hear it from a third party and things would get complicated.'

Having helped secure Charlton's future Curbishley quickly sensed a change in the fans' expectations. 'I used to think that simply keeping the club in the First Division constituted success, but the public wants more than that now. We have got our new stadium, and they think we have done enough selling of players, that it's about time we improved on the football side.' If it doesn't happen, there's only one man in the firing line now.

'Inevitably you're going to go at some stage. I've been 10 years at this club, but there isn't much loyalty being shown around football at the moment. Any manager whose team isn't doing well after 10 games is under pressure.'

The invention of the Premier League has already made life more difficult for managers in the Nationwide League, and will continue to do so. The rewards are so great, the requirement to get on to the gravy train is overpowering. 'The gap between the two Leagues is increasing at an alarming rate,' says Curbishley. 'The Nationwide League is suffering. Money coming into the game should be shared better. A lot of players in the Premier

League were in the lower divisions at one stage of their careers, but if the lower divisions suffer serious harm, what will happen to the development of those players in the future?

'But people want the best now, and the feeling is that you have to be in the Premier League.'

The signs are that the two-man team is a fad that has had its day. Crystal Palace brought in Dave Bassett to take principal responsibility for playing matters. Rotherham sacked Gemmill and McGovern and appointed Danny Bergara. With very few exceptions the manager remains alone in the front line.

The future is full of challenges for the football manager. So many strands contribute to the weave of football life and the boss has a needle in most of them. The nineties, for example, are witnessing the arrival of the financially-independent manager – men who earned huge sums in their playing days and so, as they move into management, are not dependent on their salary to pay the mortgage.

This in turn gives them the sort of clout few managers have had before, the power that allowed Kevin Keegan to walk out on Newcastle United when money he'd been promised to strengthen the team wasn't forthcoming. The money appeared and Keegan returned. Another time, he threatened to quit unless the fans stopped barracking his goalkeeper, Mike Hooper. 'Managers like Kevin have got enough money to live very comfortably without football,' says his former assistant, Terry McDermott. 'It makes them more relaxed and that spreads to the players. The manager can operate without his judgement being clouded; he doesn't have to do certain things to appease the chairman.' If, as David Pleat says, managers are in a weaker position regarding their players, an élite few are in a much stronger position regarding their chairmen.

'Managers who have been highly successful players have a head start because, financially, they don't need the job.' The summary is Peter Reid's. 'If you need the wage to feed the family, it's totally different.' Phil Neal agrees: 'There are managers in the game who will be stable for life, regardless. They've got a great situation when it comes to dealing with the chairman – ideal. I don't have that financial independence – I still need to work. But in ten years' time I can see there will be more managers in that enviable situation. So we have a situation where the manager is more at risk than ever, except for that small group of very well-to-do ex-players who basically don't need the job.'

Like Bryan Robson at Middlesbrough, who admits that his fulfilling career with Manchester United and England has left him free of financial worries. 'Yes, it does help if someone is not reliant on the job,' he says. 'They can relax and do the job the way they want to do it, and they know they can succeed or fail their own way. But whether or not the chairman interferes still depends on the chairman. I'm fortunate in having a chairman who lets me get on with it.'

Lawrie McMenemy, inevitably, has his personal definition of what he confirms is 'a new breed of manager'. He says: 'They have never had to take their team to the fish docks, as I did with Grimsby, to show the players how hard the people who support them work. They have been exceptional players who have made a lot of money from their talent. That's not to say they don't want to win. You could never accuse the likes of Kevin Keegan, Kenny Dalglish or Glenn Hoddle of that – winning is their hallmark. But they don't have to go round supporters' clubs, banging the drum and whipping enthusiasm as much as many managers do. And I can't see one of them wanting to go down the divisions and start their careers at the likes of Hartlepool and Doncaster, as Brian Clough did and I did.

'That's not to say they are worse for it, but it's difficult for anyone, no matter how good a player, to come straight into managing groups of people. The crucial element is to have good staff around you. If there aren't solid staff at the club, even Pelé would struggle.'

Terry Neill thinks that by the end of the decade the British manager will know and understand far more about tactics than he does now. 'He will be less involved with the physical side of training – he will let the coaches get on with it. The managers will deal with the players at the human level, will handle the PR and press side of things, and give directions to the coaching staff. The chairman or managing director will conduct the transfers.

'The managers today, all around the world, are under a greater spotlight than ever before. It takes a special kind of man to handle that and they all know, every one of them, that there are great rewards on the winning and losing of a game, on the kick of a ball. But nobody forces any of them into the game, so they must accept it for what it is. It can't be the worst way in the world to earn a living.'

As demand grows for men with the right experience to fill the role of director of football, one of the problems which gnaws at many managers might be resolved. As Trevor Cherry observed, the game is not good at making best use of those with the best experience. David Pleat echoes that: 'There has to be a role for people like Ian Greaves, Bertie Mee and Ron Greenwood, people who could act as advisers and mentors to the younger managers. Inexperienced young men get on the carousel and quickly fall off it because they get no meaningful advice.' The game just might be heading in the right direction to let those with hard-earned wisdom do just what they've been yearning to do – pass it on for the benefit of others and football in general.

Lawrie McMenemy was cast into the void after his unhappy spell with Sunderland but has found satisfaction in his post at Southampton. 'As the game gets bigger it's becoming very difficult for managers to retain the old relationships. I used to go and chat with the gatemen; it was important to make them feel they were part of the club. Managers now are touching so many people and they do need someone else to take the pressure off.'

Whether the recent influx of foreign players will be matched by the arrival of foreign managers is a good question. Doug Ellis made the bold move of hiring the respected Czech coach Dr Josef Venglos to replace Graham Taylor at Aston Villa in 1990. Venglos had coached throughout the world and went to Villa after two years in charge of the Czech national side. 'He was a revelation,' recalls Ellis. 'The players were thrilled – their eyes were like organ stops at the technical ability of this man. Managers came to watch what he was doing and the media were never away from our training ground. Unfortunately he was not in the western way of doing things so far as money was concerned. He couldn't handle that side of the business and that is part of the manager's job – he has to be entrepreneurial, to buy and sell.'

Jo Venglos called it a day after just one season, packing his bags for Turkey where he took over at Fenerbahçe. It was the best part of five years before English football looked again to the Continent. Then, in 1996, Holland's Ruud Gullit stepped up to become player-manager at Chelsea after Glenn Hoddle's appointment to the England job, and the Frenchman Arsène Wenger moved in at Arsenal. Each brought with him the Continental definition of the job – coaching being high on the agenda. Equally significant was Blackburn Rovers' unsuccessful attempt to recruit the Swede Sven Goran Eriksson from the Italian club Sampdoria. Colin Todd, speaking before Eriksson decided not to come to Ewood Park after all, saw that as evidence that the top clubs were changing the habits of a lifetime.

'Wenger and Eriksson have been called coaches wherever they've worked before. This tells me that Blackburn and Arsenal are changing their ways. They're going to let the coaches dictate the football side, while the admin people run the club and look for new players. The coach might recommend the players he wants but he's not going to be involved in scouting, boardroom meetings, finances or anything like that. Blackburn and Arsenal are looking for a European set-up. At Bolton we don't have a European set-up. Not many English clubs do. It's an old English trademark that so many tasks rest with the manager, but it's a sign of the times that Blackburn and Arsenal are adopting the European method.'

So determind, in fact, were Blackburn, that their response to Eriksson's rejection was to sign Inter Milan's Roy Hodgson on a three-year contract.

And the days of managers being chucked in at the deep end are numbered. The Managers' Association is campaigning for formal training because, as John Camkin points out: 'Within 12 months of getting a manager's job a young man is likely to have lost it, with little prospect of getting another, because he hasn't been properly prepared.'

Camkin is determined to bring to an end the situation in which 'we are the only country in Europe which does not have a training scheme for managers'. This is one of the areas the FA plans to address by setting up an International Football Institute. Its remit will include the training of coaches and physiotherapists as well as managers. It will, for example, tackle the outdated coaching scheme in which the same qualification covers a coach regardless of whether he wants to work with school kids or Premiership professionals.

'A judgement has to be made somewhere if a man is fit to run a club with 59 professionals plus coaching staff,' says David Pleat. 'It's about time we came into line with other nations. At the moment, once a player finds he can't kick the ball as hard or run as fast he thinks he'll turn to management. He's so naïve when he starts, yet he can't wait for two years to gain experience because he needs results straight away.'

From his privileged position within Lancaster Gate – or, to be more accurate, within his own house in Blackpool, with occasional visits to headquarters – the FA's Technical Consultant Jimmy Armfield is using his influence to assist progress. 'It will come through UEFA in the end. They have a statute saying managers – or coaches – should conform to certain standards. UEFA make it clear there should be a separate qualification for coaches working at a higher level – i.e. working with professional players. In most other countries you need a licence to coach. Here, players like Bryan Robson and Ray Wilkins can go straight into it.

'There should be some proper standard, because how do we know these people are giving out the right message? We don't. I'm not talking about their knowledge of football. They've got all that. But we should be testing whether they know about the development of young people – how they develop physically and psychologically. Do they know anything about nutrition and diet? Training programmes? Can they deal with people who have had problems in their club? They think they know all that, but I'm not totally convinced they're right.

'Why should anyone who wants to be a joiner or a plumber have to train for it, yet someone who wants to be a football manager not have to train for it at all? Teaching is a skill, isn't it? It has to be acquired through learning, and that's what the football manager's job is: teaching. People go to university or college for four years to learn about teaching. Football people don't.

'One of the problems in English football is that we're doing too many short-term things. Ninety-nine football clubs out of a hundred kowtow to the fans. Whatever the fans want for today is the immediate priority. There aren't enough visionaries about.

'The education of coaches is top of my list – that and the reorganization of schools' football. Everything is short term. It's all judged on the result of the last match, which is why, when we play Continental teams, we struggle. We need to expand the centres of excellence programme which the FA has been bringing in. The centres are run by youth coaches and the youth development officer. Both have nothing to do with the first team. The manager should be the only overseer of that. He should take an interest and provide encouragement, but otherwise leave it to the youth development officer, who should be trained to teach football to players under the age of 16. These days, he's got the youngsters from the age of nine. Liverpool and Manchester United have both got good programmes, because they've got the facilities and the money to do it. But we still don't spend as much on youth football as Continental teams. In 1994, Parma spent £1 million on development of young players, and Parma aren't the biggest team in Italy. They see the future as the development of their own players. Here I'd like to see more encouragement given to schools' football. We certainly need to bring through good English players.

'One of the most disturbing things is that, at this moment in time, there is not one teenage talent in the Premier League. Not one. Nobody thinks about it but it's a fact.'

Jimmy Armfield was speaking in early 1995. As football moved into 1997 there were signs that his theories were being heeded. Despite the cheap availability of foreign players, post-Bosman, clubs began to invest more money in their own youth schemes. Liverpool were among the pace-setters, declaring their intention to build a youth academy under the direction of their former player Steve Heighway. To those who feared the Premiership was becoming too cosmopolitan for its own good it was an encouraging development.

Having spent the best part of 15 years on the outside, writing about the game for the *Daily Express* and commentating on it for the BBC, Armfield is relishing his active involvement within the corridors of power. At the same time, access to the FA's contacts and research has opened his eyes to exactly how far the country he once represented has slipped. 'Other countries put a lot more into making themselves competitive at international level. It's almost a life and death attitude. Brazil, Argentina, Spain, Italy, Germany, Holland, Norway, and countries like Malaysia, Thailand, Egypt, Ghana – they get fantastic crowds for international football, and football is going to become more and more "international". That's why our big clubs need every bit of help they can get.'

Football in Britain has been notably conservative in its approach to new ideas. Other sports were well ahead in recognizing the benefits of sports science and sports psychology. Football is catching up and the expected changes in the manager's lifestyle will help. New influences are coming in – Ray Wilkins, when manager of Queens Park Rangers, took his players to Italy for a week's altitude training before the start of season 1995–96, putting the squad through a similar programme to that he experienced himself as a player with AC Milan. Times are changing, and the future is fascinating – particularly at the top level where they have the resources to make the most of new ideas. Further down, life will be the usual struggle, though even here managers will benefit from the better training on offer.

All-consuming though the job is, managers are quite capable of raising their eyes from the pitch and taking a good, clear look at the wider world. Howard Wilkinson wishes the rest of us would too. 'Something I would like to see, but I know I never shall, is the job being held in its rightful esteem. I am not a politician – I don't decide whether you or I should pay taxes or carry identity cards. I am not a clergyman – I don't make pronouncements as to what I think is right or wrong. I am not a general – I don't decide whether to bomb this or that target. I am working in part of the leisure and entertainment industry, and if football was abandoned tomorrow, within two years I doubt if we would miss it. Something else would take its place.

'Football is not one of the building blocks of life. It's a nice – I would say the best – leisure pursuit for performers and spectators alike, when viewed in its right perspective. Football is not life or death – that's rubbish. It shouldn't affect your marriage or the state of your mental health. I know it does, but, seriously, it shouldn't.'

Wilkinson has a soulmate in Everton's Joe Royle. 'The importance people attach to the manager has always amazed me. When teams win we get too much praise, when they lose we get too much criticism. But that's the job we're in, and managers will probably get an even higher profile as the wages within the business get higher. At the moment the thing is running away like a many-headed monster.'

Northern Ireland boss Bryan Hamilton: 'It's still a great game, for me the best in the world, but the opportunities financially for players have turned full circle and I'm not sure if it's all for the best. The game belongs to the people, and I think a game which used to be a real socialist thing has now become something from a very different spectrum altogether.'

Celtic's Tommy Burns: 'Football's profile is too high. It's no longer the pastime it used to be, when supporters really supported a team and went to watch whether they won or lost. People laugh at that now. But it's easy to follow a team that wins all the time, like Rangers, Celtic or Manchester United. But don't deny the guy who watches Ross County or Morton or Charlton the right to love his football club. He's supporting them for the right reasons. He doesn't call for the heads of the players, the manager or the chairman, every time the team loses, because that is his team.'

They are a special breed, football managers. They take the defeats, the public humiliations, the hopeless stress, the endless travel, and enough junk to keep Steptoe's yard busy for a year, and come back for more. Some earn a fortune. Most don't. But all would endorse Howard Wilkinson's explanation of why it is this sport, above all others, which has become so entrenched in the national way of life.

'To me it is the most difficult, complex, exciting, spontaneous, unpredictable, artistic, beautiful game. In the science of skills it is the most open – you can play it with any part of the body except the arm or hand, you can play it through 360 degrees, you can run forwards, backwards and sideways. That is why it's locked into our consciousness, and why worldwide it is the most popular sport.'

APPENDICES

i

DECISION DAY

Football management is no place for the indecisive. From making the right choices in the transfer market to deciding the best moment for a substitution, the trade is one which calls for the wisdom of the Lord Chief Justice and the timing of Rolex. If you can pre-empt by a few hours some of the good luck dispensed by Camelot every Saturday night, even better.

Decisive moments stick in the mind. At least, they do in the minds of the men who make the decisions and live with the consequences – for better or for worse.

What is the best decision you have made as a football manager in a match situation?

SAM ALLARDYCE (Notts County):
Tactical change versus Plymouth Argyle, when I was at Blackpool, putting Andy Morrison into midfield when we were 2–0 down. We came back to win 5–2.

JIMMY ARMFIELD (former manager):
Tactical approach to Leeds' European Cup semi-final second leg away to Barcelona in 1975. We had won at Elland Road 2–1, when Barcelona played man-to-man marking at the back. Their coach was Rinus Michels, rated one of the best in the world. In the away leg I told Peter Lorimer to start on the left and switch wings after ten minutes. He did so, and I was astonished to see the right-back going with him. Within five minutes Joe Jordan played the ball through and Lorimer caught the full-back on his wrong foot and

scored the goal that took us into the Final. So even a great coach like Rinus Michels could be caught out sometimes.

IAN ATKINS (Northampton Town):
A tactical ploy against Swindon when I was at Cambridge. We pushed Glenn Hoddle into areas where he wasn't comfortable, kept him deep in his own half, and won the match 1–0.

RON ATKINSON (Coventry City):
FA Cup sixth round, Manchester United v Everton in 1983. With ten seconds to go I threw Lou Macari on as sub. We had a corner. From the kick he got the touch which set up Frank Stapleton to volley the winner: 1–0. We went on to win the Cup. When we were getting Lou ready I remember Mickey Duxbury coming over to the touchline and saying, "Who's coming off?" I said, "You're nearest, you come off."

GRAHAM BARROW (Rochdale):
As player-manager of Chester, taking myself off at half-time in a match against Preston in the season we won promotion. It isn't easy to substitute yourself, but we went from losing the match to winning it.

IAN BRANFOOT (Fulham):
Tactical change in a home game for Reading against Plymouth in 1985–86, the season we won the Third Division title. We were 3–0 down with 20 minutes to go, and we were playing so badly it could have been 30–0. Kevin Bremner, normally a striker, was in midfield. I told him to go up front. We won it 4–3 and Bremner played a part in all the goals, scoring one himself.

CRAIG BROWN (Scotland):
Sending on Ally McCoist as substitute with 20 minutes to go in our European Championship match against Greece at Hampden Park. He scored with his second touch of the ball and that was the only goal of the game.

TOMMY BURNS (Celtic):

Not selecting John Collins for a game at Hearts in the 1995–96 season, even though we had three other senior players absent injured. John gave a TV interview the day before the game in which he unfairly criticized me. I had to decide what to do about it. I left him behind to play in the reserves and selected two of the younger players. We won 4–0.

TREVOR CHERRY (former manager):
Sending on John Hawley as substitute for Bradford City when we were 2–1 down in a home game. We drew 2–2.

STEVE COPPELL (Crystal Palace):
Formulating the style of play that enabled Palace to beat Liverpool 4–3 in the FA Cup semi-final in 1990.

ALAN CURBISHLEY (Charlton Athletic):
At half-time in a match against Newcastle, losing 3–1, telling the players to go out and attack. We did, and won 4–3, scoring in the last minute.

MARTIN DOBSON (former manager):
Substituting the substitute in a match for Bury against Chester at Gigg Lane. We were winning 1–0 but not playing well. I sent on Nigel Greenwood as sub but we got worse. Chester equalized. I pulled Nigel off and sent on the other sub. We won 2–1. It was nice to see something positive work out.

MICK DOCHERTY (ex-Rochdale):
The last correct one!

TOMMY DOCHERTY (retired):
A substitution and reshuffle for Manchester United when we were losing 2–0 to Wolves. I sent Jimmy Nicholl on, took Lou Macari off, reorganized the formation and we won 3–2.

TERRY DOLAN (Hull City):
Turning Dean Windass from a midfield player into a striker and seeing him score 41 goals in two seasons.

JOHN DUNCAN (Chesterfield):
Changing from a 3–4–3 formation to 4–4–2 for the play-off matches against Mansfield and Bury and winning promotion.

SAM ELLIS (ex-Bury and Lincoln City):
Making Matt Carbon, originally a defender, a centre-forward.

ROY EVANS (Liverpool):
Switching Steve McManaman to the left flank for a spell during the second half in the Coca-Cola Cup Final against Bolton. It was very important and caused them a lot of problems.

ALEX FERGUSON (Manchester United):
With Aberdeen, we were 2–1 down to Bayern Munich in the quarter-finals of the European Cup. I took off the right-back and central midfield player, sent on two attackers and we won 3–2.

DARIO GRADI (Crewe Alexandra):
When assistant manager of Derby County, pushing Archie Gemmill up front against the Manchester City centre-half Dave Watson. In the same game we took a gamble on goalkeeper Colin Boulton's fitness. Both selections were particularly successful.

BOBBY GOULD (Wales):
A tactical substitution for Coventry at Manchester City. I brought Lloyd McGrath off from midfield, pushed Leigh Jenkinson up front, and realized I got it totally wrong. We were left with a 4–1–5 formation with only Willie Boland in midfield. I was shouting to the others on the bench, 'I've cocked it up, I've cocked it up,' when Roy Wegerle scored! That was our equalizer in a 1–1 draw. Brilliant!!

BRYAN HAMILTON (Northern Ireland):
Selection of the goalkeeper to play Austria away. Both our top two keepers were out, so I had a choice between two part-timers. Paul Kee was the last of them to be called into the squad so by rights he should have been the substitute. But in preparation he looked good and I just felt he was right for the job. He played and was inspired.

BRIAN HORTON (Huddersfield Town):
Taking Garry Parker off at half-time in a match for Hull City against Grimsby. He was the best player in the club and the other players begged me not to do it, but the sub Andy Saville came on and turned the game.

KEITH HOUCHEN (ex-Hartlepool):
In the last game of season '94–95 playing young Steve Halliday wide on the right against Mansfield. He scored a hat-trick – we won 3–2.

EMLYN HUGHES (former manager):
Never selecting a defender as substitute.

HOWARD KENDALL (Sheffield United):
With Everton, a reshuffle against Luton in the FA Cup when we were 2–0 down. I brought Adrian Heath on as sub, and switched Kevin Richardson to left-back/left midfield. We got it back to 2–2 and won the replay.

ANDY KING (ex-Mansfield Town):
We were under the cosh against Lincoln with the score 1–1. They hit the bar. I sent on Stewart Hadley and switched to a three-man attack. Hadley scored twice and we won easily.

LENNIE LAWRENCE (Luton Town):
Bringing on two subs with 20 minutes to go in the final match of the 1991–92 season, with Middlesbrough away to Wolves. We needed to win to be promoted, but we were 1–0 down and we'd had a man sent off. I brought on Andy Peake and Andy Payton – we won 2–1. It was the sort of change you make many times, but this one brought us the big payday.

MICK McCARTHY (Republic of Ireland):
Moving Colin Cooper from left-back to centre-back in my first game in charge of Millwall. He made the position his own and was eventually sold for £1.7 million.

WILF McGUINNESS (retired):
A tactical switch away to Leeds United. I told George Best and Willie Morgan to switch wings. Paul Reaney was marking Best and changed sides to follow him, but the other Leeds full-back, Terry Cooper, stayed put. That left a gap and Morgan went through to score the winner.

JIMMY MULLEN (ex-Blackpool and Burnley):
Team selection for the second leg of Burnley's play-off match at Plymouth in '93–94. We won 3–1.

JOHN NEAL (retired):
An important Cup tie with Chelsea at Sheffield Wednesday. We were 3–0 down at half-time and I brought on Paul Canoville as substitute. He scored with his first touch. We took it to extra time, drew 4–4, and won the replay.

PHIL NEAL (ex-Manchester City, Coventry, Cardiff City and Bolton):
Deciding to retire as a first team player when player-manager of Bolton, and playing for two years in the reserves to bring on the kids.

TERRY NEILL (former manager):
Deciding to take the first penalty myself in the first shoot-out ever to be televised in this country. I was player-manager of Hull City against Peterborough in the old Watney Cup. As the boss I thought I had better take the first kick. Thank God it went in.

PETER REID (Sunderland):
Putting Craig Russell on as sub against Sheffield United at Roker in my first game. He scored the winner with 15 minutes to go.

BRUCE RIOCH (Queens Park Rangers):
Sending on Fabian de Freitas at half-time in the play-off final against Reading when I was with Bolton. He turned the game in our favour and we finished up in the Premier League. I was also pleased with a double substitution in the second leg of the Coca-Cola Cup semi-final against Swindon when we brought on Mixu Paateleinen and

Richard Sneekes at the same time. Again, it was effective.

BRYAN ROBSON (Middlesbrough):
Using a sweeper system in away games which we thought would be particularly tough, when we won the First Division. We got a result every time.

JOE ROYLE (Everton):
The semi-final of the League Cup against West Ham on the plastic pitch at Boundary Park, with Oldham. I wasn't sure which way West Ham would play, but laid contingency plans in case they played a sweeper. They did, so we pushed Ian Marshall up front from defence, only keeping three at the back. By half-time we were 3–0 up. At half-time we pulled Marshall back – and scored on the restart.

ALAN SMITH (ex-Wycombe Wanderers and Crystal Palace):
With Crystal Palace against Derby in our promotion year, 1993–94. We were losing 1–0. I pushed Dean Gordon up on the left. He got the equalizer in injury time. Once he scored I knew we would be promoted.

WALTER SMITH (Rangers):
The choice of substitute for the League Cup Final against Hibs in 1994. Ally McCoist had been out injured. There was a debate about whether to start him or not. I decided he couldn't handle a full game so put him on the bench. He came on after about an hour and scored one of his most spectacular goals. It won us the Cup, 2–1.

GRAEME SOUNESS (Southampton):
Signing Terry Butcher for Rangers. Not so much for what he provided on the pitch, but for what he gave me off it – his character and leadership. If you can get someone like Terry in your team, you're halfway to achieving what you want.

MIKE WALKER (Norwich City):
The tactical approach to Norwich's matches against Bayern

Munich in 1993. We won 2–1 in Munich and drew 1–1 at Carrow Road against one of the best club sides in the business.

MIKE WALSH (ex-Bury):
A tactical switch against Fulham. They played us off the park in the first half. At half-time we changed to a sweeper system and marked man-to-man. It was the first time we had played with a sweeper. We won 3–1.

STEVE WIGNALL (Colchester United):
Putting Niall Thompson on to the field in a match at Scunthorpe. We were 3–2 down with 15 minutes to go. Niall scored twice and we won 4–3. After 20 minutes of the match we had been losing 3–0. It was the best comeback in the club's history.

What has been your best decision away from a matchday situation?

SAM ALLARDYCE:
Persevering with James Quinn, a young striker, who became Blackpool's most valuable asset.

JIMMY ARMFIELD:
Signing Peter Thompson from Liverpool when I was manager of Bolton. The signing of Tony Currie for Leeds from Sheffield United was also a good decision – Currie was a sensation, arguably the best midfield player English football has produced since the war.

IAN ATKINS:
Leaving Birmingham City, where I was player-assistant manager, to join Cambridge United as manager in 1992. It wasn't something I had to do – just a rush of blood!

GRAHAM BARROW:
Signing Colin Greenall for Chester City from Preston North End.

IAN BRANFOOT:
Leaving Southampton, where I was reserve team coach, to join Reading as coach. I wanted to get into management and I couldn't have done so by staying at Southampton.

CRAIG BROWN:
Appointing Alex Miller, the former Rangers player, as my assistant. Neither of us has any international caps but it has proved a good partnership. It was also a good decision to continue using Alan Hodgkinson as goalkeeping coach.

TOMMY BURNS:
Signing van Hooijdonk from Holland for just over a million pounds.

TREVOR CHERRY:
Getting rid of one particular player within two weeks of taking over at Bradford City. He had such a bad attitude I wouldn't even play him in the reserves. Both Terry Yorath, who was my assistant then, and I had been brought up to believe that if you didn't try, you didn't play.

STEVE COPPELL:
Signing Ian Wright. Somebody brought him in for a trial. We took him for a fortnight and offered him a contract after only three days.

ALAN CURBISHLEY:
Going back to Charlton Athletic as reserve team manager when I had two years left on my playing contract at Brighton.

MARTIN DOBSON:
Giving David Lee a contract at Bury. He had finished a two-year apprenticeship and the coaches were doubtful about him. But he had a great attitude so I signed him on. He responded very well and within months we put him on an improved 18-month contract. He became a top-class player.

MICK DOCHERTY:
Persuading key players to re-sign for the club.

TOMMY DOCHERTY:
Dealing with a transfer request from Eddie McCreadie at Chelsea. He didn't want to play full-back any more – he wanted to be a centre-forward. I made him sweat for a few days, then told him we had had a bid from one club: Darlington. He withdrew his request.

TERRY DOLAN:
Selecting my own staff.

JOHN DUNCAN:
Enticing Steve Norris to go to Scarborough and VS Rugby on loan. We went on a 21-match unbeaten run and he scored valuable goals for VS Rugby.

SAM ELLIS:
Deciding to move from coaching into management in 1982, when I became manager of Blackpool.

ROY EVANS:
Selection of staff at every level.

ALEX FERGUSON:
Joining Manchester United. I had already turned down Tottenham, Arsenal, Wolves, and Rangers twice. But I knew Old Trafford was the right place to go.

KEN FURPHY (retired):
Making the decision to leave Watford and join Blackburn Rovers, even though Blackburn were a division lower at the time. I couldn't convince the Watford chairman that he needed to make more investment to continue making progress.

DARIO GRADI:
Persuading David Platt to sign for Crewe when he was freed by Manchester United.

BRYAN HAMILTON:
Bringing Tommy Cavanagh back as Northern Ireland coach.

BRIAN HORTON:
Persuading the Oxford chairman Kevin Maxwell not to sell Jim Magilton when the club was in dire straits financially. By keeping him we escaped relegation.

EMLYN HUGHES:
Signing Gerry Gow from Manchester City for Rotherham. He gave us vital experience in midfield.

HOWARD KENDALL:
Moving from Everton to Birmingham as a player. It turned out to be my first step towards management because of the way the Birmingham manager, Freddie Goodwin, involved me in the club's activities. If I had stayed at Everton my future career could have been very different.

ANDY KING:
Signing Ian Baraclough on a free transfer. Soon he was worth £200,000.

LENNIE LAWRENCE:
Joining Middlesbrough.

MICK McCARTHY:
Taking the player-manager's job at Millwall.

JIMMY MULLEN:
Agreeing to become manager of Burnley in succession to Frank Casper.

JOHN NEAL:
Going to the doctor after Chelsea won the Second Division title. He diagnosed serious heart problems and saved my life.

PHIL NEAL:
Buying Dion Dublin from Manchester United for Coventry City.

PETER REID:
Sending Gary Flitcroft on loan from Manchester City to Bury. It made a player of him.

BRUCE RIOCH:
Joining Middlesbrough after being out of the English game for two years.

BRYAN ROBSON:
Hiring a plane for the long away trips with Middlesbrough, instead of going by coach.

JOE ROYLE:
It was the right decision to come to Everton when I did. It was right for Oldham too.

ALAN SMITH:
Deciding to become a football manager.

WALTER SMITH:
Bringing in Archie Knox as my assistant manager at Rangers. His experience has been invaluable.

COLIN TODD:
Deciding on not going to Arsenal with Bruce Rioch when he left Bolton to become the manager at Highbury, and electing to take my chances here.

MIKE WALKER:
After being sacked by Colchester, deciding not to hold out for another managerial job but accepting the post of reserve coach at Norwich City. It paid dividends in the long term.

MIKE WALSH:
Setting up a youth policy at Bury.

STEVE WIGNALL:
Setting up Aldershot Town from the ruins of the old Aldershot FC which went out of existence. Putting into place the whole infrastructure, from first team to under-nines. They made a £25,000 profit in their first season.

Most managers had more difficulty identifying their best moments than their worst. The memory, for some awkward reason, seems reluctant to blank out the decisions that backfired!

What has been your worst decison in a matchday situation?

SAM ALLARDYCE:
Selecting the wrong side when we played Birmingham, losing 7–1.

IAN ATKINS:
Deciding to experiment in an away game for Northampton at Bury. I left out several regulars. Result: we lost 5–0. It was definitely the wrong game to do it!

RON ATKINSON:
Not changing a winning team for the FA Cup semi-final with West Bromwich against Ipswich (lost 1–3). We were on a good run even though Bryan Robson and Laurie Cunningham were out of the side. They were available for the semi-final but I stuck with the settled team. Perhaps if they'd played we would have got through to Wembley.

GRAHAM BARROW:
As player-manager of Chester, staying on the field too long when I picked up a hamstring strain in a match at Huddersfield. Because I didn't come off straight away I was out of action for three months.

IAN BRANFOOT:
Every decision you make that doesn't work out is a bad one.

CRAIG BROWN:
Playing a flat back four against Greece in Athens, instead of the three-man defence we had used before that game. They had two strikers of electrifying pace and got through us with one-twos far too easily.

TOMMY BURNS:
I have been too loyal to certain players.

TREVOR CHERRY:
Failing to inspect the pitch before Bradford City played Telford away in the FA Cup. It was January, there was frost everywhere, and we were convinced the game would be called off. I didn't go to look at the pitch. The referee ruled it playable. I went mad, complaining that it wasn't fit to take a duck for a walk on never mind play football. That transmitted negative vibes to the players. I should have been at the 11 a.m. inspection where I could have told the referee the pitch was unfit for play. Instead the game went ahead and we lost.

STEVE COPPELL:
In our relegation season we got a penalty away to Ipswich. We had missed the last two and no one wanted to take it. I sent on a message that Gareth Southgate was to take it, even though he wasn't feeling comfortable about it. He missed.

MARTIN DOBSON:
At Bristol Rovers bringing our leading scorer Carl Saunders on as substitute and playing him right-side midfield. It made him look a poor player and me a poor manager.

MICK DOCHERTY:
Sending a player on as substitute only to see him sent off two minutes later, leaving my options for the rest of the match nil.

TOMMY DOCHERTY:
Letting Alex Stepney take penalties for Manchester United (no one else wanted to).

JOHN DUNCAN:
Playing Dave Lancaster, a striker, at centre-half. We lost 3–0.

SAM ELLIS:
Too many!

ROY EVANS:
Substituting Jan Molby when we were drawing 0–0 and playing well against Manchester United away. The pattern of play changed and we lost 2–0.

ALEX FERGUSON:
Not picking Graeme Souness for the last group match of the 1986 World Cup Finals – Scotland v Uruguay – when I was acting-manager of Scotland. I thought he would not be strong enough after losing 12lbs in the previous game. I would never make that decision now.

DARIO GRADI:
Against Blackburn Rovers in the FA Cup we played a sweeper and were losing 1–0. I abandoned the sweeper system – we lost 4–0.

BOBBY GOULD:
With Coventry, going on to the pitch at Leicester to complain to the referee about a penalty decision. I shouldn't have gone on to the pitch. We lost the game 5–1. I still think it was a diabolical decision.

BRYAN HAMILTON:
Playing four men in midfield against the Republic in Dublin. I thought we could match them physically. We couldn't. I should have put an extra man in there and played a five-man midfield.

KEITH HOUCHEN:
Losing 2–1 in a home game I sent the centre-half up as an extra front man. The outcome was we lost 4–1.

HOWARD KENDALL:
Not playing Peter Reid in a Merseyside derby at Anfield. We only played with one striker and Liverpool hammered us.

ANDY KING:
Getting too worked up on the touchline, and not substituting a player early enough when it's obvious he isn't on form. I tend to leave them on too long – particularly strikers.

LENNIE LAWRENCE:
Not selecting at least one wide player as substitute for the Full Members Cup Final against Blackburn in 1987. We lost in the last five minutes.

MICK McCARTHY:
Playing three centre-backs against Derby County in the First Division play-offs in 1994. We were well beaten. The score was 2–0 but it could have been worse.

WILF McGUINNESS:
Dropping Denis Law and Bobby Charlton for the same game – Everton away.

PHIL NEAL:
Playing myself as sweeper at Chesterfield in an FA Cup tie. We went 1–0 down early in the game. Later I substituted myself and we won 3–2.

PETER REID:
Playing a sweeper against Coventry when I was at Manchester City. We were two down after 25 minutes and lost 3–1.

BRUCE RIOCH:
Striking a player, Colin Anderson, after an argument on the training ground at Torquay.

BRYAN ROBSON:
Selecting the wrong team to play Luton away. Lost 5–1.

JOE ROYLE:
With Oldham, at the FA Cup semi-final against Manchester United in 1990. We were one down. I pushed Andy Holden forward from defence and we equalized. I should have pulled Andy back at that point but didn't, and Mark Robins came on as sub for them and scored. I still wonder if I should have played safe and gone for another replay.

ALAN SMITH:
Letting players who aren't performing well stay on the pitch. I tend to think the team I send out is the best so I want to keep it intact.

WALTER SMITH:
The whole build-up to our European Cup tie against AEK Athens in 1994–95 was wrong. It was our first competitive game of the season. We weren't properly prepared. A lot of decisions in the period leading up to the game were not the right ones.

COLIN TODD:
When we were fighting to avoid relegation in 1996 we went to Middlesbrough and won 4–1. The next game was against Manchester United and I selected the same team. We lost 6–0. I should have made changes. It might not have made any difference but I should have changed it. I was tempted to do so but was loyal to the team that won 4–1.

MIKE WALKER:
Not picking a team good enough to win any of the first 14 matches of season 1994–95 for Everton.

MIXE WALSH:
We were 4–0 up at Huddersfield and ended up with a 4–4 draw. I don't know what I did wrong. Maybe I should have ripped into the players at half-time – but we were winning 4–0 at the time!

STEVE WIGNALL:
Not playing Niall Thompson from the start in a home game

against Scarborough. We needed to win to stay in a play-off position, but lost 2–0.

What has been your worst decision away from a matchday situation?

SAM ALLARDYCE:
Not walking into the boardroom after an undefeated run as caretaker manager of Preston North End and demanding the job, which went to John Beck.

JIMMY ARMFIELD:
Not asking for a longer contract when I was in a strong position at Leeds.

IAN ATKINS:
Not resigning earlier when I was at Cambridge, after being told I couldn't get rid of Gary Johnson and the chief scout John Griffin.

RON ATKINSON:
At Manchester United we had first option on buying Gary Lineker from Leicester. But we were well off for strikers so we decided to delay any move until we had moved on one of them. In the meantime Howard Kendall jumped in and took him to Everton. I learned a lesson then – if you can afford to do a deal, do it.

GRAHAM BARROW:
Not changing the Wigan team for an FA Cup tie against Altrincham in '94–95. It probably cost us a place in the third round, where Altrincham drew Spurs.

IAN BRANFOOT:
Taking David Speedie as makeweight in the Alan Shearer transfer to Blackburn Rovers. Speedie has an exceptional track record elsewhere, but it didn't work out for either party at Southampton.

CRAIG BROWN:
When manager of Clyde, selling Steve Archibald too cheaply to Aberdeen for £25,000, and not insisting on a sell-on clause. Eighteen months later he went to Spurs for £800,000. In my defence, sell-on clauses were not customary at the time, but I still think Clyde could have got more money out of the deal.

TOMMY BURNS:
I spend too many hours at work. I have created a routine for myself which is hard to break.

TREVOR CHERRY:
As player-manager of Bradford City I played in a 5–1 win at Swansea. When I came off I told Terry Yorath and our chief scout Maurice Linley that Swansea had one great little player – Dean Saunders. At the end of the season Saunders was given a free transfer. That evening I contacted him and offered him a year's contract. He said he was going on holiday and would think about it. When he got back he received a better offer from an old team-mate of mine, Chris Cattlin, at Brighton, so he went there. I should have had the courage of my convictions and forced the board to let me offer him a two-year deal. That way I think we would have got him.

ALAN CURBISHLEY:
Moving home from London to Birmingham and seeing house prices soar in London.

MARTIN DOBSON:
Taking the Bristol Rovers team captaincy away from Geoff Twentyman and giving it to Steve Yates. For all sorts of reasons it was a difficult situation and the decision didn't go down well with the directors.

MICK DOCHERTY:
Criticizing in public the way my club was being run. I lost my job two weeks later.

TOMMY DOCHERTY:
Taking the job as manager of Altrincham in 1987.

JOHN DUNCAN:
Releasing John Matthews, a good midfield player, thinking I could sign someone better.

SAM ELLIS:
Not signing Colin Clarke for £30,000 when I could have done in 1984–85. He went on to various clubs including Southampton and won a lot of caps for Northern Ireland.

ROY EVANS:
Letting things simply tick over when I first took over. I was happy to have a honeymoon period when I should have gone for the throat. We free-wheeled for the rest of that season ('93–94) when we should have got stuck in.

ALEX FERGUSON:
Not seizing the opportunity to sign John Barnes from Watford soon after I came to United. We had just signed Jesper Olsen on a new contract and I didn't think we needed Barnes. Mistake!

DARIO GRADI:
I have twice bought players for £50,000 (one a fee set by a tribunal) and after two years of disappointment have had to let them go for nothing. We can't afford that.

BOBBY GOULD:
Going to West Bromwich as manager.

BRYAN HAMILTON:
Rejoining Wigan Athletic after leaving Leicester.

BRIAN HORTON:
Selling Garry Parker from Hull to Nottingham Forest for £272,000 on the transfer deadline. We didn't win another game for the rest of the season and I got the sack.

EMLYN HUGHES:
Not leaving Rotherham when I had the chance to join a First Division club.

HOWARD KENDALL:
Signing Maurice Johnston for Everton. He was a proven international, but he didn't produce the goods for us.

ANDY KING:
We went to Fulham for a Christmas match. The pitch was frozen but we were on a good run and the players were keen to play. Fulham weren't enthusiastic but we said the game should go ahead. We lost 4–2. It hurt for a few weeks but taught me a lesson.

LENNIE LAWRENCE:
Selling Peter Shirtliff from Charlton to Sheffield Wednesday. The money was good but we missed him badly. And not signing Robert Lee when I was at Middlesbrough.

MICK McCARTHY:
Not signing Stan Collymore when I had the opportunity.

WILF McGUINNESS:
Selling instead of keeping good players at York City, including Gordon Staniforth who went to Carlisle for £120,000.

LOU MACARI:
Resigning from the job at West Ham.

JOHN NEAL:
Only offering £8000 to Scunthorpe for Kevin Keegan and a centre-half, Steve Deere. For only a little more I could have signed them both for Wrexham.

PHIL NEAL:
Signing Peter Barnes. I thought I could get something out of him where other managers had failed, and didn't.

TERRY NEILL:
Being swayed by players' emotions prior to the 1978 FA Cup Final, Arsenal v Ipswich. In my naïvety I allowed certain players to take part who weren't fully fit. Once the game got under way it was clear they couldn't do themselves justice. I wasn't strong enough on that occasion.

PETER REID:
Not buying John Aldridge when I had the chance.

BRUCE RIOCH:
Underestimating how isolated Torquay is from the rest of the football world.

ALAN SMITH:
After a 1–0 midweek defeat with Palace at Bolton, and getting back home in the snow at 4 a.m., I made the players report for training at 9.30 a.m. because I was upset with the performance and angry with them. But it was the wrong thing to do – it created a lot of bad feeling.

COLIN TODD:
Resigning as manager of Middlesbrough in 1991.

MIKE WALKER:
Expecting other people to treat me right because that is the way I try to treat them. I made up my mind to treat the people I work with as adults, but sometimes people who don't adopt that policy get on better. For example, I turned down money to write critical articles about Everton after I was sacked, but Everton still made me start legal action before they settled my contract.

MIKE WALSH:
I could have done more homework on one or two players I brought in from outside the area.

STEVE WIGNALL:
Not putting a certain youngster on contract earlier in the season

Aldershot. He was poached by another club and it cost me money to replace him.

ii

MOVING THE GOALPOSTS

Managers are always being asked their views on players, tactics, referees and the general development of the game. But what about their own profession? What would they most like to see changed about the manager's job?

Most have a clear idea of what needs fixing. Occasionally – as in the case of John Neal, the former Wrexham, Middlesbrough and Chelsea boss, or Graeme Souness – the answer is a complete surprise.

SAM ALLARDYCE:

Contracts should be more secure with termination payments made within 28 days. Managers should also be given the time to do the job properly.

JIMMY ARMFIELD:

There should be a proper training programme for managers before they take their first job. After that clubs and managers should both honour their contracts totally.

IAN ATKINS:

If clubs employ you for three years they must honour it, not sack you halfway through.

RON ATKINSON:

Managers should have the same status as players with regard to contracts.

GRAHAM BARROW:
The manager should have the responsibility for financial dealings lifted.

IAN BRANFOOT:
Security of tenure. The Nationwide League should follow the Premier League and have managers' contracts registered. At present managers get no help from anyone when they are dismissed while clubs use every trick in the book to avoid paying them what they are due.

CRAIG BROWN:
More job security for club managers, and no changing of managers during the season. Clubs should honour their contracts.

TOMMY BURNS:
Managers should see out their contracts. Changes should not be made on the back of a run of bad results. The people who appoint the manager should back their judgement.

TREVOR CHERRY:
More security and backing from the directors.

STEVE COPPELL:
Nothing. It has evolved into a job where the manager knows exactly where he is. If he loses too often, he gets the boot. Sometimes a manager might wish the chairman was more accountable.

ALAN CURBISHLEY:
There should be less insecurity. A manager should see out his contract.

MARTIN DOBSON:
Managers shouldn't be released from contracts until the close season. They ought to know they couldn't be sacked once the season is under way.

MICK DOCHERTY:
To be given *carte blanche* to run the club as I see fit, and then stand

or fall by my own decisions.

TOMMY DOCHERTY:
Full compensation for managers when they get the sack.

TERRY DOLAN:
Managers should have a lower profile.

JOHN DUNCAN:
Clubs should only be allowed to employ a new manager if the previous manager's contract has been fully settled.

SAM ELLIS:
Clubs should not be permitted to fill the job until they have agreed compensation with the previous manager.

ROY EVANS:
The manager's job has never been secure but now it's ridiculous. There should be some curtailment of movement during the season. People think if they change the manager their entire fortunes will improve, but it isn't just down to the manager – there could be other problems.

ALEX FERGUSON:
Managers should have more influence on the way the game is run. The PFA has more influence than the Managers' Association but Gordon Milne and John Barnwell have done a good job there and it is improving.

KEN FURPHY:
Contracts and salaries should be handled by a finance director – even though in the past you attracted loyalty from your players because you negotiated for them and looked after them. There's too much money involved now for that to apply.

DARIO GRADI:
Clubs and managers should both be made to honour contracts. It's ridiculous that managers have to fight for their money, but it's

also ridiculous for managers to walk out. It's wrong that they put public pressure on their club to be allowed to go.

BOBBY GOULD:
Proper Preparation Prevents Poor Performances.

BRYAN HAMILTON:
More stability.

BRIAN HORTON:
More stability; managers should be allowed to fulfil their contracts.

EMLYN HUGHES:
Managers should be allowed to give the chairman the bullet!

HOWARD KENDALL:
Change of responsibilities to that of coach. But it's vital the chairman and directors let the man they've hired get on with his job.

ANDY KING:
Managers should be allowed more time to prove themselves, and the lower divisions should receive a better share of TV exposure and revenue.

LENNIE LAWRENCE:
Contracts should be allowed to run their full course – if not, compensation should be settled promptly without managers having to go to court.

MICK McCARTHY:
The way in which managers can be so easily sacked and then held to ransom over their compensation is wrong. There should be a set period for payment – e.g. 30 days, 60 days or 90 days from the time he was sacked.

WILF McGUINNESS:
Managers should be allowed to concentrate on team matters.

LOU MACARI:
We should change to the European pattern and lighten the load on the manager.

STEVE McMAHON:
Things are OK as they are.

JIMMY MULLEN:
A set compensation figure to be paid to a manager when he leaves a club – the amount to be determined by the division the club is in.

JOHN NEAL:
Managers shouldn't expect too much when they fail. The way compensation is paid these days, they make a fortune out of failure. If anyone else fails in their business they don't get paid well for it. At the moment people are receiving a lot in compensation, yet their record is abysmal.

PHIL NEAL:
There should be equal media attention for all Premier League clubs.

TERRY NEILL:
Nothing.

PETER REID:
Contracts should be lodged with the FA. Then, if a manager is sacked, he knows he'll be looked after.

BRUCE RIOCH:
No relegation! If that isn't possible, there should be greater honour between managers and clubs when the time comes to part company. That would take the cynical aspect out of the manager's mind. At present, if you are treated badly once, it stays with you.

BRYAN ROBSON:
Handling contracts and wages should be taken away from the manager and done by the chief executive. If players are going to feel aggrieved over their pay it's better to fall out with the chief

executive than the manager who trains and plays with them.

JOE ROYLE:
I don't think any one change would dramatically alter things for better or for worse.

ALAN SMITH:
Managers should be forced to acquire proper qualifications before they take a job.

WALTER SMITH:
Not a lot. If you're with a good club, which I am, and it's run well from the chairman down, there isn't a lot wrong.

GRAEME SOUNESS:
The rewards are so enormous, managers have to accept everything that goes with the job. The intrusion into your private life and the criticism is a small price to pay, and I speak from experience. A newspaper story one day is in the bin the next. You have to remember the good lifestyle that football gives you.

COLIN TODD:
Change the day-to-day running of clubs. Far too much is put on to the manager, who should be left to concentrate on the team.

MIKE WALKER:
The job should be reorganized on Continental lines. Take away all the paperwork and let you get on with coaching.

MIKE WALSH:
Once you've proved you can do the job you should be given a reasonable length of time to carry it through.

STEVE WIGNALL:
No mid-season sackings, and less office work.

HOWARD WILKINSON:
The manager's job should be kept in the right perspective.

iii

PERSONAL CHOICE

Football managers are rarely short of an opinion. Their verdicts on the other professionals in the game are founded on years of observation and analysis. *The Boss* asked them:

a) Which manager – past or present – have you most admired?

b) What players – British and Overseas – would you most like to have bought, given the funds?

c) What club, apart from your own, would you most like to manage?

NAME	Manager	British Player	Overseas Player	Club
Sam ALLARDYCE (Notts County)	Bill Shankly	Alan Shearer	Ronaldo	Manchester United
Jimmy ARMFIELD (former manager)	Walter Winterbottom	Bobby Charlton	Johan Cruyff	Real Madrid
Ian ATKINS (Northampton Town)	Alan Durban	Peter Beardsley	Diego Maradona	AC Milan

Ron ATKINSON (Coventry City)	Brian Clough	Alan Shearer	Johan Cruyff	Real Madrid or one of the Milan clubs
Graham BARROW (Rochdale)	Kenny Dalglish	Mark Hughes	Eric Cantona	Manchester United
Ian BRANFOOT (Fulham)	Alan Brown	would have kept Alan Shearer	Roberto Baggio	Sunderland (I'm a lifelong fan)
Craig BROWN (Scotland)	Willie McLean & Bob Shankly, Bill's brother	Kenny Dalglish	Franco Baresi	If I lost this job I'd like my old job back as manager of Scotland under-21s
Tommy BURNS (Celtic)	Jock Stein, Walter Smith	Bryan Robson	Eric Cantona	Celtic
Trevor CHERRY (former manager)	Don Revie	Kevin Keegan	Rivelino	Leeds United
Steve COPPELL (Crystal Palace)	Bill Shankly	Gary Lineker	Diego Maradona	Manchester United
Alan CURBISHLEY (Charlton Athletic)	Ron Greenwood, George Graham	Ian Rush	Jürgen Klinsmann	Manchester United
Martin DOBSON (ex-Bristol Rovers & Bury)	Jimmy Adamson	Kenny Dalglish	Eusebio	Anyone at the moment!
Michael DOCHERTY (ex-Rochdale)	Jimmy Adamson	Alan Shearer	Roberto Baggio	Manchester United
Tommy DOCHERTY (Retired)	Kenny Dalglish	Tom Finney	Alfredo di Stefano	Manchester United
Terry DOLAN (Hull City)	Joe Royle	Alan Shearer	Franco Baresi	Hull City (with some money to spend!)
John DUNCAN (Chesterfield)	George Graham	Steve Bruce	Marco van Basten	Dundee FC (home town)
Sam ELLIS (ex-Bury & Lincoln City)	Alan Brown	Alan Shearer	Arthur Neumann (PSV)	They all have their problems

Roy EVANS (Liverpool)	Bob Paisley	I bought him – Stan Collymore!	Ronaldo	Liverpool
Alex FERGUSON (Manchester United)	Scot Symon, Jock Stein, Sir Matt Busby		Maldini, Maradona	Only this one
Peter FOX (Exeter City)	Jack Charlton	Matthew le Tissier	Roberto Baggio	Spurs
Ken FURPHY (Retired)	Matt Busby	Wilf Mannion	Alfredo di Stefano	Any club with ambition willing to let you have control
Dario GRADI (Crewe Alexandra)	Dave Sexton	Bryan Robson	Pelé	Crewe
Bobby GOULD (Wales)	Jimmy Hill	Trevor Peake, Steve Ogrizovic	Roberto Carlos	Anywhere where you can have a good relationship with the chairman
Bryan HAMILTON (N. Ireland)	Joe Mercer, Bill Shankly, Bobby Robson	George Best	Pelé	Real Madrid
Brian HORTON (Huddersfield Town)	Gordon Lee, Alan Mullery, David Pleat	Bryan Robson	Michel Platini	Real Madrid
Keith HOUCHEN (ex-Hartlepool)	John Sillett, George Curtis	Alan Shearer	Roberto Baggio	Middlesbrough
Emlyn HUGHES (Retired)	Bill Shankly	Kenny Dalglish	Don't know	Liverpool
Howard KENDALL (Sheffield United)	Alex Ferguson	Bryan Robson	Ossie Ardiles	Barcelona
Andy KING (ex-Mansfield Town)	Bill Shankly	Stan Collymore	Franco Baresi	Everton
Lennie LAWRENCE (Luton Town)	Alex Ferguson	Alan Shearer	Roberto Baggio	West Ham United

Lou MACARI (Stoke City)	Jock Stein	Bryan Robson	Lothar Matthäus	Don't know
Mick McCARTHY (Republic of Ireland)	Jack Charlton	Alan Shearer	Ruud Gullit	AC Milan
Wilf McGUINNESS (retired)	Sir Matt Busby, Sir Alf Ramsey	Malcolm Macdonald	Alfredo di Stefano	Manchester United or Newcastle United
Steve McMAHON (Swindon Town)	Kenny Dalglish	Alan Shearer	Marco van Basten	Liverpool
Jimmy MULLEN (ex-Blackpool & Burnley)	George Graham	Kenny Dalglish	Jürgen Klinsmann	Real Madrid
John NEAL (retired)	Bill Shankly	Kevin Keegan	Ludo Coeck (ex Anderlecht)	Sunderland (home-town team)
Phil NEAL (ex-Bolton Wanderers, Coventry City, Cardiff City & Manchester City)	Bob Paisley, Joe Fagan, Ron Greenwood	Alan Shearer	Zico	Any club in Premier or Nationwide League; just want to get involved again
Terry NEILL (retired)	Bob Paisley	George Best	Pelé	Wouldn't change the ones I managed
Peter REID (Sunderland)	Bill Shankly	Alan Shearer	Marco van Basten	Barcelona
Bruce RIOCH (QPR)	Ron Wylie (ex-Aston Villa coach), Bill Shankly, Bill Nicholson	Kenny Dalglish	Zico	Rangers
Bryan ROBSON (Middlesbrough)	Bobby Robson, Ron Atkinson, Alex Ferguson	Alan Shearer	Gianfranco Zola	Middlesbrough
Joe ROYLE (Everton)	Brian Clough	Kenny Dalglish	Marco van Basten	Everton
Alan SMITH (Wycombe Wanderers)	Alex Ferguson, Bill Nicholson, George Graham	Paul Ince	Pelé	Don't know

Walter SMITH

(Rangers)	Jock Stein	Bryan Robson	Franco Baresi	Barcelona or Real Madrid

Graeme SOUNESS

(Southampton)	Bob Paisley, Jock Stein	Alan Shearer	Zico	Have already managed the two I most wanted to in Britain

Colin TODD

(Bolton Wanderers)	Brian Clough, Jim Smith	David Beckham	Ronaldo	Am truly very happy where I am

Mike WALKER

(ex-Norwich City)	Bobby Roberts, Jim Smith, Terry Venables	Paul Gascoigne	Franco Baresi	Manchester United

Mike WALSH

(ex-Bury)	Ian Greaves	Alan Shearer	Marco van Basten	Anyone at the highest level

Steve WIGNALL

(Colchester United)	Bill Shankly	Ian Rush	Ruud Gullit	Liverpool

Howard WILKINSON

(England)	Alan Brown	George Best	Michel Platini	Real Madrid

iv

ACTION REPLAY

Walter Smith has won it all with Rangers yet he still regrets the final leg of the treble that slipped away. Bruce Rioch went through the mill at Arsenal, but one afternoon in May, when he was manager of Middlesbrough, still gives him the shakes. And Brian Horton reckons one particular game changed his football destiny.

If he could have his time again, what one match would the Boss most like to end differently?

(Note how many times Manchester United feature in the answers!)

SAM ALLARDYCE:
Blackpool losing 7–1 at Birmingham on 31 December 1994. What a way to celebrate New Year's Eve!

JIMMY ARMFIELD:
The European Cup Final 1975 which Leeds lost 2–0 to Bayern Munich.

IAN ATKINS:
Colchester United v Witton Albion in the FA Trophy, when I was manager of Colchester, in the club's non-League days. Witton scored in injury time to win the game.

RON ATKINSON:
Last game of the 1989–90 season, with Sheffield Wednesday. I wish we'd drawn with Nottingham Forest instead of losing – we wouldn't have been relegated.

GRAHAM BARROW:
Chester v Crewe, 1994 (lost 2–1). My last game as manager of Chester. We had already clinched promotion but we could have been Champions and it would have been nice to end with a win.

IAN BRANFOOT:
FA Cup sixth-round replay, Norwich v Southampton, in 1992. We had already beaten Manchester United on penalties at Old Trafford in the fourth round. Against Norwich we drew at the Dell, then played magnificently in the replay. We murdered them. Unfortunately we had Matt le Tissier and Barry Horne sent off for retaliation. That changed the game – Norwich won it with a flukey goal in the last five minutes. It changed the course of the history of my tenure at Southampton. If we had won we would have been in the semi-finals, which would have meant a lot to the club.

CRAIG BROWN:
Greece v Scotland, 1994–95 season. We lost 1–0 but if the game were to be played again the referee, Mr Blankenstein from Holland, would give us the penalty we deserved when John Spencer was upended, and perhaps he wouldn't give them one for a Colin Hendry tackle.

STEVE COPPELL:
FA Cup Final, Crystal Palace v Manchester United, in 1990 which ended in a 3–3 draw. I wish the game had been eight minutes shorter – we would have won.

ALAN CURBISHLEY:
Charlton's FA Cup quarter-final away to Manchester United in 1994 (lost 3–1). I believe we would have beaten any of the other teams left in the competition and reached the Final.

MARTIN DOBSON:
Bury's League Cup fourth-round tie away to Manchester United (lost 2–1). We took the lead but then Bryan Robson switched from sweeper to midfield and set up two goals.

MICK DOCHERTY:
Auto Windscreen Trophy, Area Final, Rochdale v Carlisle, 1995 (aggregate score Rochdale 3 Carlisle 5). Next stop would have been Wembley.

TOMMY DOCHERTY:
1976 FA Cup Final, Manchester United 0 Southampton 1.

TERRY DOLAN:
Bradford City 2 Ipswich 3 – the last match of the 1987–88 season. A win would have taken Bradford into the First Division automatically. We lost to Middlesbrough in the play-offs.

JOHN DUNCAN:
A 1–0 home defeat by Portsmouth. A win would have kept Ipswich in the promotion hunt.

SAM ELLIS:
Bury v Tranmere, Third Division play-off semi-finals, 1990. We only drew at Gigg Lane and Tranmere beat us 2–0 in the second leg.

ROY EVANS:
Manchester United 1 Liverpool 0, Premiership, March 1994. It was not long after I took over as Liverpool manager. I still think we deserved something from that game.

KEN FURPHY:
Manchester United v Watford in the FA Cup, 1969, when United were European champions. I took Watford to Jersey for a week to prepare. We worked very hard on ways to contain their stars – George Best and company. Stewart Scullion scored and we were 1–0 up with ten minutes to play. Then we left Law unmarked and he scored the equalizer. In the replay at Vicarage Road Matt Busby had the game postponed because it was so wet. The following week, on a bone-hard ground, we lost 2–0.

DARIO GRADI:
Chester 3 Crewe 0, May 1991. It was the year we were relegated

from the Third Division to the Fourth. If we had won our last six games we would have stayed up. The match with Chester, when they shared Macclesfield's ground, was the only one we lost.

BOBBY GOULD:
1–1 draw with West Brom at Bristol Rovers. If we had won we wouldn't have been relegated.

BRYAN HAMILTON:
Cup tie with Leicester City at home to Oxford United. They won with a goal following a handball infringement in the last minute. Also Northern Ireland's home defeat by Latvia.

BRIAN HORTON:
Crystal Palace 4 Manchester City 0, Coca-Cola Cup quarter-final, 1995. Getting City into a semi-final after a run which included winning at Newcastle could have changed the course of my football life.

EMLYN HUGHES:
Rotherham 2 Sheffield Wednesday 2, May 1982. If we had won, we would have only needed to win our last game of the season, away to Wrexham, to go up to the First Division. Instead we finished seventh.

HOWARD KENDALL:
FA Cup Final, 1986, which finished Everton 1 Liverpool 3. Then they wouldn't have done the Double, and we would have been spared the embarrassment of coming home on an open-top bus with nothing while they had both trophies.

ANDY KING:
3–2 defeat in the Coca-Cola Cup at Wolves, and losing to Chesterfield in 1995 play-offs.

LENNIE LAWRENCE:
League Cup semi-final, second leg, Middlesbrough v Manchester United, 1992. We'd drawn 0–0 at Old Trafford, but lost 2–1 in

extra-time at Ayresome Park having watched Peter Schmeichel make an impossible save from Willie Falconer to deprive us of the winner in normal time.

MICK McCARTHY:
Millwall's 1994 play-offs against Derby – we lost both legs.

WILF McGUINNESS:
FA Cup semi-final replay, Manchester United v Leeds United, 1970. It was a 0–0 draw but we played really well. However, we lost the second replay at Bolton 1–0.

LOU MACARI:
Losing 2–0 with Swindon to Crystal Palace in the second leg of the play-off semi-finals in 1989. We'd won the home game 1–0.

STEVE McMAHON:
Losing 3–1 at Bolton in the Coca-Cola Cup semi-final second leg, having led 2–1 from the home game at Swindon. Heartbreaking.

JIMMY MULLEN:
The 2–1 home defeat to Millwall in 1995, which meant Burnley were relegated.

JOHN NEAL:
Wrexham v Mansfield, last game of season 1976–77. We needed one point for promotion but lost.

PHIL NEAL:
Second Division play-off Final, Bolton v Tranmere at Wembley, 1991. Tranmere beat us 1–0 and Paul Comstive missed a good chance for us 10 minutes before they scored.

PETER REID:
Manchester City 2 Tottenham 4, FA Cup quarter-final at Maine Road in 1993. There was a lot of belief that we could get to Wembley but nothing went right in the match and the supporters

invaded the pitch. They had to bring on the police horses.

BRUCE RIOCH:

Sheffield Wednesday 1 Middlesbrough 0, 1989. The result which meant Middlesbrough were relegated after only one season in the top division. It was a bodyblow. The players were good enough to have progressed – they just needed time.

BRYAN ROBSON:

FA Cup tie, Middlesbrough v Swansea City. Lost 2–0 at home. We would have played Newcastle in the next round.

JOE ROYLE:

Manchester United 1 Oldham Athletic 1, FA Cup semi-final at Wembley, 1994. The match in which Mark Hughes scored the equalizer in the last minute.

ALAN SMITH:

FA Cup semi-final, 1995, Palace 2 Manchester United 2. We lost the replay.

WALTER SMITH:

Scottish Cup Final, 1994, Dundee United 1 Rangers 0. We were going for the Treble. The players had had two years of almost constant football and they weren't up for it – they were quite a tired team that day. If we had won we would have completed two domestic Trebles in a row, and no one has ever done that. I would have liked that team to go into the history books, because they deserved it.

COLIN TODD:

West Ham 1 Bolton 0, 1996. Bolton were fighting to avoid relegation from the Premiership. If we had won that game we would have moved out of the bottom three with two games to go – I am certain we would have stayed up.

MIKE WALKER:

Norwich 1 Manchester United 3, April 1993, in the Premier

League. It was the year we finished third. We had just beaten our other main rivals, Aston Villa, to go three points clear at the top. Had we beaten United I think we would have been Champions.

MIKE WALSH:
Bury losing the 1995 Third Division play-off final to Chesterfield.

STEVE WIGNALL:
Quarter-final FA Vase match with Aldershot Town against Atherton. After two 0–0 draws we lost 2–0 at home.

HOWARD WILKINSON:
FA Cup semi-final, Sheffield Wednesday, 1986 (lost 2–1 in extra-time). Victory would have afforded me the luxury of a great day out at Wembley.

V

IS YOUR CLUB IN THE DANGER ZONE?

The next time an out-of-work manager is offered a job, he might be advised to consult the following tables before accepting.

The way different clubs treat their team bosses differs dramatically. Some, like Port Vale and Crewe Alexandra, are amazingly loyal to their managers. Others, like Hartlepool, chop and change like yachts tacking in a westerly gale. Clubs like Sunderland and Bradford City fire managers as if they were the noonday gun. Others, like Exeter, seem to make a habit of being left in the lurch.

The following statistics analyse the fate which has befallen each manager of every club in the two English Leagues over the last decade. From this, we can deduce which clubs are the most stable, which are unlucky – and which constitute football management's Danger Zone.

HOW THE BOSS MET HIS FATE:

CLUB BY CLUB ANALYSIS

KEY:

s	sacked	**ret**	retired
r	resigned	**up**	moved 'upstairs'
mc	left by mutual consent		

Danger Zone points are calculated as follows:

+1 point	for each managerial change
+6 pts	for a sacking
+4 pts	for a resignation
+2 pts	for a move upstairs or mutual consent
+0 pts	for retirement

The higher the points tally, the more chance of a manager failing to pass the test of time. Symbols show if a club has a cut-throat attitude to its managers, whether it's plain unlucky and likely to lose a manager to another club, or whether it is a stable set-up which gives the manager a fair chance.

= This is the dream job, exceptionally stable.

= Take the job – you'll get a good run for your money.

? = Hard to predict how things will work out here. You'll get a reasonable chance but don't waste too much time before achieving something concrete.

= An unlucky club. Managers get time to prove themselves but the relationship tends to break down with either manager or club deciding on a change of direction.

= A very unlucky club, managers tend not to stick around for long, either because they are poached by other clubs or things just don't work out.

 = Watch your back. Liable to give the boss the chop.

 = Say your prayers before accepting a job here.

TABLES

ARSENAL

Manager	Years	
Don Howe	1983–1986	r
George Graham	1986–1995	s
Bruce Rioch	1995–1996	s
Arsene Wenger	1996–	
Danger Zone Points:	**19 –**	

ASTON VILLA

Manager	Years	
Graham Turner	1984–1986	s
Billy McNeill	1986–1987	s
Graham Taylor	1987–1990	r
Josef Venglos	1990–1991	mc
Ron Atkinson	1991–1994	s
Brian Little	1995–	
Points:	**29 –**	

BARNSLEY

Manager	Years	
Bobby Collins	1984–1985	s
Allan Clarke	1985–1989	s
Mel Machin	1989–1993	r
Viv Anderson	1993–1994	r
Danny Wilson	1994–	
Points:	**24 –**	

BIRMINGHAM CITY

Ron Saunders	1982–1986	r
John Bond	1986–1987	s
Gary Pendrey	1987–1989	s
Dave Mackay	1989–1991	s
Lou Macari	1991	r
Terry Cooper	1991–1993	r
Barry Fry	1993–1996	s
Trevor Francis	1996–	
Points:	**43 –**	

BLACKBURN ROVERS

Bobby Saxton	1981–1986	s
Don Mackay	1987–1991	s
Kenny Dalglish	1991–1995	up
Ray Harford	1995–1996	r
Points:	**22 –**	

BLACKPOOL

Sam Ellis	1982–1989	s
Jimmy Mullen	1989–1990	s
Graham Carr	1990	s
Billy Ayre	1990–1994	r
Sam Allardyce	1994–1996	s
Gary Megson	1996–	
Points:	**33 –**	

BOLTON WANDERERS

John McGovern	1982–1985	s
Charlie Wright	1985	mc
Phil Neal	1985–1992	s
Bruce Rioch	1992–1995	r
Roy McFarland	1995–1996	s
Colin Todd	1996–	
Points:	**29 –**	

BOURNEMOUTH

Harry Redknapp	1983–1992	r
Tony Pulis	1992–1994	s
Mel Machin	1994–	
Points:	**12 –**	

BRADFORD CITY

Trevor Cherry	1982–1987	s
Terry Dolan	1987–1989	s
Terry Yorath	1989–1990	s
John Docherty	1990–1991	s
Frank Stapleton	1991–1994	s
Lennie Lawrence	1994–1995	s
Chris Kamara	1995–	
Points:	**42 –**	

BRENTFORD

Frank McLintock	1984–1987	s
Steve Perryman	1987–1990	r
Phil Holder	1990–1993	s
Dave Webb	1993–	
Points:	**19 –**	

BRIGHTON & HOVE ALBION

Chris Cattlin	1983–1986	s
Alan Mullery	1986–1987	r
Barry Lloyd	1987–1993	mc
Liam Brady	1993–1995	mc
Jimmy Case	1995–1996	s
Steve Gritt	1996–	
Points:	**25 – ?**	

BRISTOL CITY

Terry Cooper	1982–1988	s
Joe Jordan	1988–1990	r

Jimmy Lumsden	1990–1992	s
Denis Smith	1992–1993	s
Russell Osman	1993–1994	s
Joe Jordan	1994–	

Points: **33 –**

BRISTOL ROVERS

David Williams	1983–1985	r
Bobby Gould	1985–1987	r
Gerry Francis	1987–1991	r
Martin Dobson	1991	mc
Dennis Rofe	1991–1992	s
John Ward	1993–1996	s
Ian Holloway	1996–	

Points: **32 –**

BURNLEY

John Benson	1984–1985	s
Martin Buchan	1985	r
Brian Miller	1986–1989	s
Frank Casper	1989–1991	s
Jimmy Mullen	1991–1996	s
Adrian Heath	1996–	

Points: **33 –**

BURY

Martin Dobson	1984–1989	s
Sam Ellis	1989–1990	r
Mike Walsh	1990–1995	mc
Stan Ternent	1995–	

Points: **15 –**

CAMBRIDGE UNITED

John Ryan	1984–1985	s
Ken Shellito	1985	r
Chris Turner	1986–1990	r

John Beck	1990–1992	s
Ian Atkins	1992–1993	r
Gary Johnson	1993–1995	s
Tommy Taylor	1995–1996	r
Roy McFarland	1996–	
Points:	**41 –**	

CARDIFF CITY

Jimmy Goodfellow	1984	s
Alan Durban	1984–1986	s
Frank Burrows	1986–1989	r
Len Ashurst	1989–1991	s
Eddie May	1991–1994	s
Terry Yorath	1994–1995	r
Eddie May	1995	mc
Kenny Hibbitt	1995–1996	up
Phil Neal	1996	r
Russell Osman	1996–	
Points:	**49 –**	

CARLISLE UNITED

Bob Stokoe	1980–1985	ret
Bryan Robson	1985	r
Bob Stokoe	1985–1986	ret
Harry Gregg	1986–1987	s
Clive Middlemass	1987–1991	s
Aiden McCaffrey	1991–1992	s
David McCreery	1992–1993	s
Mick Wadsworth	1993–1996	r
Mervyn Day	1996–	
Points:	**40 –**	

CHARLTON ATHLETIC

Lennie Lawrence	1982–1991	r
Alan Curbishley/Steve Gritt	1991–1995	s
Alan Curbishley	1995–	
Points:	**12 –**	

CHELSEA

John Neal	1981–1985	up
John Hollins	1985–1988	r
Bobby Campbell	1988–1991	r
Ian Porterfield	1991–1993	s
Dave Webb	1993	s
Glenn Hoddle	1993–1996	r
Ruud Gullit	1996–	
Points:	**32 – ?**	

CHESTER CITY

John McGrath	1984	s
Mick Speight	1984–1985	s
Harry McNally	1985–1992	s
Graham Barrow	1992–1994	r
Mike Pejic	1994–1995	s
Derek Mann	1995	r
Kevin Ratcliffe	1995–	
Points:	**38 – ?**	

CHESTERFIELD

John Duncan	1983–1987	r
Kevin Randall	1987–1988	s
Paul Hart	1988–1991	s
Chris McMenemy	1991–1993	s
John Duncan	1993–	
Points:	**26 – ?**	

COLCHESTER UNITED

Cyril Lea	1983–1986	s
Mike Walker	1986–1987	s
Roger Brown	1987–1988	r
Jock Wallace	1989	r
Mick Mills	1990	r
Ian Atkins	1990–1991	r
Roy McDonough	1991–1994	s
George Burley	1994	r
Steve Wignall	1995–	
Points:	**46 –**	

COVENTRY CITY

Bobby Gould	1983–1984	s
Don Mackay	1984–1986	r
George Curtis/John Sillett	1986–1990	s
Terry Butcher	1990–1992	s
Don Howe	1992	r
Bobby Gould	1992–1993	r
Phil Neal	1993–1995	s
Ron Atkinson	1995–1996	up
Gordon Strachan	1996–	
Points:	**46 –**	

CREWE ALEXANDRA

Dario Gradi	1983–	
Points:	**0 –**	

CRYSTAL PALACE

Steve Coppell	1984–1993	r
Alan Smith	1993–1995	s
Steve Coppell	1995–1996	up
Dave Bassett	1996–1997	r
Steve Coppell	1997–	
Points:	**20 –**	

DARLINGTON

Cyril Knowles	1983–1987	s
David Booth	1987–1989	s
Brian Little	1989–1991	r
Frank Gray	1991–1992	s
Billy McEwan	1992–1993	r
Alan Murray	1993–1995	s
Paul Futcher	1995	s
David Hodgson	1995	r
Jim Platt	1995–1996	s
David Hodgson	1996–	
Points:	**57 –**	

DERBY COUNTY

Arthur Cox	1984–1993	r
Roy McFarland	1993–1995	s
Jim Smith	1995–	
Points:	**12 –**	

DONCASTER ROVERS

Billy Bremner	1978–1985	r
Dave Cusack	1985–1987	s
Dave Mackay	1987–1989	r
Billy Bremner	1989–1991	s
Steve Beaglehole	1991–1994	s
Ian Atkins	1994	s
Sammy Chung	1994–1996	s
Kerry Dixon	1996–	
Points:	**45 –**	

EVERTON

Howard Kendall	1981–1987	r
Colin Harvey	1987–1990	s
Howard Kendall	1990–1993	r
Mike Walker	1994	s
Joe Royle	1995–	
Points:	**24 –**	

EXETER CITY

Jim Iley	1984–1985	s
Colin Appleton	1985–1987	r
Terry Cooper	1988–1991	r
Alan Ball	1991–1994	r
Terry Cooper	1994–1995	r
Peter Fox	1995–	
Points:	**27 –**	

FULHAM

Ray Harford	1984–1986	r
Ray Lewington	1986–1990	s
Alan Dicks	1990–1991	s
Don Mackay	1992–1994	s
Ian Branfoot	1994–1996	up
Micky Adams	1996–	
Points:	**29 – ?**	

GILLINGHAM

Keith Peacock	1981–1987	s
Paul Taylor	1987–1988	s
Keith Burkinshaw	1988–1989	r
Damien Richardson	1989–1992	s
Glenn Roeder	1992–1993	r
Mike Flanagan	1993–1995	s
Tony Pulis	1995–	
Points:	**38 –**	

GRIMSBY TOWN

Dave Booth	1982–1985	r
Mike Lyons	1985–1987	s
Bobby Roberts	1987–1988	s
Alan Buckley	1988–1994	r
Brian Laws	1994–1996	s
Kenny Swain	1997–	
Points:	**38 – ?**	

HARTLEPOOL UNITED

Billy Horner	1983–1986	s
John Bird	1986–1988	r
Bobby Moncur	1988–1989	s
Cyril Knowles	1989–1991	ret
Alan Murray	1991–1993	s

Viv Busby	1993	s
John MacPhail	1993–1994	s
David McCreery	1994–1995	s
Keith Houchen	1995–1996	s
Points:	**55 –**	

HEREFORD UNITED

John Newman	1983–1987	mc
Ian Bowyer	1987–1990	s
Colin Addison	1990–1991	r
John Sillett	1991–1992	r
Greg Downes	1992–1994	s
John Layton	1994–1995	s
Graham Turner	1995–	
Points:	**34 –**	

HUDDERSFIELD TOWN

Mick Buxton	1978–1986	s
Steve Smith	1987	s
Malcolm Macdonald	1987–1988	r
Eoin Hand	1988–1992	s
Ian Ross	1992–1993	r
Neil Warnock	1993–1995	r
Brian Horton	1995–	
Points:	**36 –**	

HULL CITY

Brian Horton	1984–1988	s
Eddie Gray	1988–1989	s
Colin Appleton	1989	s
Stan Ternent	1989–1991	s
Terry Dolan	1991–	
Points:	**28 –**	

IPSWICH TOWN

Bobby Ferguson	1982–1987	s
John Duncan	1987–1990	s
John Lyall	1990–1992	up
Mick McGiven	1992–1994	mc
John Lyall	1994	r
George Burley	1994–	

Points: **24 –**

LEEDS UNITED

Eddie Gray	1982–1985	s
Billy Bremner	1985–1988	s
Howard Wilkinson	1988–1996	s
George Graham	1996–	

Points: **21 –**

LEICESTER CITY

Gordon Milne	1982–1986	up
Bryan Hamilton	1986–1987	s
David Pleat	1987–1991	s
Brian Little	1991–1994	r
Mark McGhee	1994–1995	r
Martin O'Neill	1995–	

Points: **27 –**

LEYTON ORIENT

Frank Clark	1983–1991	up
Peter Eustace	1991–1994	s
John Sitton/Chris Turner	1994–1995	s
Pat Holland	1995–1996	s
Tommy Taylor	1996–	

Points: **24 –**

LINCOLN CITY

Colin Murphy	1978–1985	mc
John Pickering	1985	s
George Kerr	1985–1987	s
Colin Murphy	1987–1990	mc
Allan Clarke	1990	s
Steve Thompson	1990–1993	r
Keith Alexander	1993–1994	s
Sam Ellis	1994–1995	s
Steve Wicks	1995	s
John Beck	1995–	
Points:	**53 –**	

LIVERPOOL

Joe Fagan	1983–1985	ret
Kenny Dalglish	1985–1991	r
Graeme Souness	1991–1994	r
Roy Evans	1994–	
Points:	**11 –**	

LUTON TOWN

David Pleat	1978–1986	r
John Moore	1986–1987	s
Ray Harford	1987–1990	s
Jimmy Ryan	1990–1991	s
David Pleat	1991–1995	r
Terry Westley	1995	mc
Lennie Lawrence	1995–	
Points:	**34 –**	

MANCHESTER CITY

Billy McNeill	1983–1986	r
Jimmy Frizzell	1986–1987	up
Mel Machin	1987–1989	s
Howard Kendall	1989–1990	r
Peter Reid	1990–1993	s
Brian Horton	1993–1995	s

Alan Ball	1995–1996	r
Steve Coppell	1996	r
Frank Clark	1996–	
Points:	**44 –**	

MANCHESTER UNITED

Ron Atkinson	1981–1986	s
Alex Ferguson	1986–	
Points:	**7 –**	

MANSFIELD TOWN

Ian Greaves	1983–1989	mc
George Foster	1989–1993	s
Andy King	1993–1996	s
Steve Parkin	1996–	
Points:	**17 –**	

MIDDLESBROUGH

Willie Maddren	1984–1986	s
Bruce Rioch	1986–1990	s
Colin Todd	1990–1991	r
Lennie Lawrence	1991–1994	mc
Bryan Robson	1994–	
Points:	**22 –**	

MILLWALL

George Graham	1982–1986	r
John Docherty	1986–1990	s
Bruce Rioch	1990–1992	r
Mick McCarthy	1992–1996	r
Jimmy Nicholl	1996–1997	s
John Docherty	1997–	
Points:	**29 –**	

NEWCASTLE UNITED

Jack Charlton	1984–1985	r
Willie McFaul	1985–1988	s
Jim Smith	1988–1991	r
Ossie Ardiles	1991–1992	s
Kevin Keegan	1992–1997	r
Kenny Dalglish	1997–	
Points:	**29 –**	

NORTHAMPTON TOWN

Tony Barton	1984–1985	mc
Graham Carr	1985–1990	s
Theo Foley	1990–1992	s
Phil Chard	1992–1993	s
John Barnwell	1993–1994	s
Ian Atkins	1995–	
Points:	**31 –**	

NORWICH CITY

Ken Brown	1980–1987	s
Dave Stringer	1987–1992	r
Mike Walker	1992–1994	r
John Deehan	1994–1995	s
Martin O'Neill	1995	r
Gary Megson	1995–1996	s
Mike Walker	1996–	
Points:	**36 –**	

NOTTINGHAM FOREST

Brian Clough	1975–1993	ret
Frank Clark	1993–1996	r
Stuart Pearce	1996–	
Points:	**6 –**	

NOTTS COUNTY

Larry Lloyd	1983–1984	s
Ritchie Barker	1984–1985	s
Jimmy Sirrel	1985–1987	ret
John Barnwell	1987–1988	s
Neil Warnock	1989–1993	s
Mick Walker	1993–1994	s
Russell Slade	1994–1995	s
Howard Kendall	1995	s
Steve Thompson/Colin Murphy	1995–1996	s
Sam Allardyce	1997–	

Points: 57 –

OLDHAM ATHLETIC

Joe Royle	1982–1995	r
Graeme Sharp	1995–1997	r
Neil Warnock	1997–	

Points: 10 –

OXFORD UNITED

Jim Smith	1982–1985	r
Maurice Evans	1985–1988	r
Mark Lawrenson	1988	s
Brian Horton	1988–1993	r
Denis Smith	1993–	

Points: 22 –

PETERBOROUGH UNITED

John Wile	1983–1986	s
Noel Cantwell	1986–1988	up
Mick Jones	1988–1989	s
Mark Lawrenson	1989–1990	s
David Booth	1990–1991	s
Chris Turner	1991–1992	up
Lil Fuccillo	1992–1993	r

John Still	1994–1995	r
Mick Halsall	1995–1996	r
Barry Fry	1996–	
Points:	**49 –** ?	

PLYMOUTH ARGYLE

Dave Smith	1984–1988	r
Ken Brown	1988–1990	s
David Kemp	1990–1992	s
Peter Shilton	1992–1995	r
Steve McCall	1995	r
Neil Warnock	1995–1997	s
Points:	**36 –**	

PORTSMOUTH

Alan Ball	1984–1989	s
John Gregory	1989–1990	s
Frank Burrows	1990–1991	mc
Jim Smith	1991–1995	s
Terry Fenwick	1995–	
Points:	**24 –** ?	

PORT VALE

John Rudge	1983–	
Points:	**0 –**	

PRESTON NORTH END

Alan Kelly	1983–1985	s
Tommy Booth	1985–1986	s
Brian Kidd	1986	s
John McGrath	1986–1990	s
Les Chapman	1990–1992	s
John Beck	1992–1994	r
Gary Peters	1994–	
Points:	**40 –**	

QPR

Manager	Years	
Alan Mullery	1984	s
Jim Smith	1985–1988	r
Trevor Francis	1988–1989	s
Don Howe	1989–1991	s
Gerry Francis	1991–1994	r
Ray Wilkins	1994–1996	r
Stewart Houston	1996–	
Points:	**36 –**	

READING

Manager	Years	
Ian Branfoot	1984–1989	s
Ian Porterfield	1989–1991	r
Mark McGhee	1991–1994	r
Jimmy Quinn/Mick Gooding	1994–	
Points:	**17 –**	

ROCHDALE

Manager	Years	
Vic Halom	1984–1986	s
Eddie Gray	1986–1988	r
Danny Bergara	1988–1989	r
Terry Dolan	1989–1991	r
Dave Sutton	1991–1994	r
Mick Docherty	1994–1996	s
Graham Barrow	1996–	
Points:	**34 –**	

ROTHERHAM UNITED

Manager	Years	
George Kerr	1983–1985	s
Norman Hunter	1985–1987	s
Dave Cusack	1987–1988	s
Billy McEwan	1988–1991	s
Phil Henson	1991–1994	up
Archie Gemmill/John McGovern	1994–1996	s
Danny Bergara	1996–	
Points:	**38 –**	

SCARBOROUGH

Neil Warnock	1986–1989	r
Colin Morris	1989	s
Ray McHale	1989–1993	s
Phil Chambers	1993	s
Steve Wicks	1993–1994	s
Billy Ayre	1994	s
Ray McHale	1994–1996	r
Mick Wadsworth	1996–	

Points: **45 –**

SCUNTHORPE UNITED

Allan Clarke	1983–1984	r
Frank Barlow	1984–1987	s
Mick Buxton	1987–1991	r
Bill Green	1991–1993	s
Richard Money	1993–1994	r
David Moore	1994–1996	s
Mick Buxton	1996–1997	mc
Brian Laws	1997–	

Points: **39 –**

SHEFFIELD UNITED

Ian Porterfield	1981–1986	r
Billy McEwan	1986–1988	r
Dave Bassett	1988–1995	mc
Howard Kendall	1995–	

Points: **13 –**

SHEFFIELD WEDNESDAY

Howard Wilkinson	1983–1988	r
Peter Eustace	1988–1989	s
Ron Atkinson	1989–1991	r
Trevor Francis	1991–1995	s
David Pleat	1995–	

Points: **24 –**

SHREWSBURY TOWN

Chic Bates	1984–1987	s
Ian McNeill	1987–1990	s
Asa Hartford	1990–1991	s
John Bond	1991–1993	r
Fred Davies	1993–	
Points:	**26 – ?**	

SOUTHAMPTON

Lawrie McMenemy	1973–1985	r
Chris Nicholl	1985–1991	s
Ian Branfoot	1991–1994	r
Alan Ball	1994–1995	r
Dave Merrington	1995–1996	s
Graeme Souness	1996–	
Points:	**29 –**	

SOUTHEND UNITED

Bobby Moore	1984–1986	r
Dave Webb	1986–1987	r
Dick Bate	1987	s
Paul Clark	1987–1988	s
Dave Webb	1988–1992	r
Colin Murphy	1992–1993	s
Barry Fry	1993	r
Peter Taylor	1993–1995	s
Steve Thompson	1995	r
Ronnie Whelan	1995–	
Points:	**53 –**	

STOCKPORT COUNTY

Colin Murphy	1985	r
Les Chapman	1985–1986	s
Jimmy Melia	1986	r
Colin Murphy	1986–1987	r
Asa Hartford	1987–1989	s
Danny Bergara	1989–1995	s
David Jones	1995–	

Points:	36 –	

STOKE CITY

Bill Asprey	1983–1985	s
Mick Mills	1985–1989	s
Alan Ball	1989	s
Lou Macari	1991–1993	r
Joe Jordan	1993–1994	mc
Lou Macari	1994–	
Points:	29 –	

SUNDERLAND

Len Ashurst	1984–1985	s
Lawrie McMenemy	1985–1987	s
Denis Smith	1987–1991	s
Malcolm Crosby	1991–1993	s
Mick Buxton	1993–1995	s
Peter Reid	1995–	
Points:	35 –	

SWANSEA CITY

Colin Appleton	1984	s
John Bond	1984–1985	s
Tommy Hutchison	1985–1986	s
Terry Yorath	1986–1989	r
Ian Evans	1989–1990	s
Terry Yorath	1990–1991	s
Frank Burrows	1991–1995	r
Bobby Smith	1995	r
Kevin Cullis	1996	s
Jan Molby	1996–	
Points:	57 –	

SWINDON TOWN

Lou Macari	1984–1989	r
Ossie Ardiles	1989–1991	r
Glenn Hoddle	1991–1993	r
John Gorman	1993–1994	s
Steve McMahon	1994–	

Points: **22 –**

TORQUAY UNITED

David Webb	1984–1985	up
John Sims	1985	s
Stuart Morgan	1985–1987	r
Cyril Knowles	1987–1989	s
Dave Smith	1989–1991	r
John Impey	1991	s
Ivan Golac	1992	s
Paul Compton	1992–1993	s
Don O'Riordan	1993–1995	s
Eddie May	1995–	

Points: **55 –**

TOTTENHAM HOTSPUR

Peter Shreeve	1984–1986	s
David Pleat	1986–1987	s
Terry Venables	1987–1991	up
Peter Shreeve	1991–1992	s
Doug Livermore/Ray Clemence	1992–1993	s
Ossie Ardiles	1993–1994	s
Gerry Francis	1994–	

Points: **38 –**

TRANMERE ROVERS

Bryan Hamilton	1980–1985	s
Frank Worthington	1985–1987	s
Ronnie Moore	1987	r
John King	1987–1996	up
John Aldridge	1996–	

Points: **22 –**

WALSALL

Alan Buckley	1982–1986	s
Tommy Coakley	1986–1988	s
John Barnwell	1989–1990	s
Kenny Hibbitt	1990–1994	s
Chris Nicholl	1994–	
Points:	**28 –**	

WATFORD

Graham Taylor	1977–1987	r
Dave Bassett	1987–1988	r
Steve Harrison	1988–1990	s
Colin Lee	1990	s
Steve Perryman	1990–1993	r
Glen Roeder	1993–1996	s
Kenny Jackett	1996–	
Points:	**36 –**	

WEST BROMWICH ALBION

Johnny Giles	1984–1985	r
Ron Saunders	1986–1987	s
Ron Atkinson	1987–1988	r
Brian Talbot	1988–1991	s
Bobby Gould	1991–1992	s
Ossie Ardiles	1992–1993	r
Keith Burkinshaw	1993–1994	s
Alan Buckley	1994–1997	s
Ray Harford	1997–	
Points:	**50 –**	

WEST HAM UNITED

John Lyall	1974–1989	s
Lou Macari	1989–1990	r
Billy Bonds	1990–1994	r
Harry Redknapp	1994–	
Points:	**17 –**	

WIGAN ATHLETIC

Harry McNally	1983–1985	r
Bryan Hamilton	1985–1986	r
Ray Mathias	1986–1989	s
Bryan Hamilton	1989–1993	mc
Kenny Swain	1993–1994	s
Graham Barrow	1994–1995	s
John Deehan	1995–	
Points:	**34 – ?**	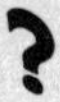

WIMBLEDON

Dave Bassett	1981–1987	r
Bobby Gould	1987–1990	r
Ray Harford	1990–1991	r
Peter Withe	1991–1992	s
Joe Kinnear	1992–	
Points:	**22 –**	

WOLVERHAMPTON WANDERERS

Tommy Docherty	1984–1985	s
Bill McGarry	1985	r
Sammy Chapman	1985–1986	s
Graham Turner	1986–1994	r
Graham Taylor	1994–1995	r
Mark McGhee	1995–	
Points:	**29 –**	

WREXHAM

Bobby Roberts	1982–1985	s
Dixie McNeil	1985–1989	s
Brian Flynn	1989–	
Points:	**14 –**	

YORK CITY

Denis Smith	1982–1987	r
Bobby Saxton	1987–1988	r
John Bird	1988–1991	s
John Ward	1991–1993	r
Alan Little	1993–	
Points:	22 –	

(NB Barnet and Wycombe Wanderers did not join the Football League until 1991 and 1993 respectively and are not included in the statistical review.)

PREMIERSHIP DANGER ZONE

Sunderland
Tottenham Hotspur

Coventry City

NATIONWIDE LEAGUE DANGER ZONE

Bradford City
Darlington
Doncaster Rovers
Hartlepool United
Lincoln City
Notts County
Scarborough
Swansea City
Torquay United

Blackpool
Bristol City
Carlisle United
Gillingham
Hull City
Northampton Town
Preston North End
Rotherham United
Walsall
West Bromwich Albion

PREMIERSHIP SAFE SEATS

(lowest points total signifies clubs where manager is least likely to lose his job)

1	Nottingham Forest	6
2	Manchester United	7
3	Liverpool	11
4	Derby County	12
5	West Ham United	17

NATIONWIDE LEAGUE SAFE SEATS

1	Crewe Alexandra	0
2	Port Vale	0
3	Oldham Athletic	10
4	Charlton Athletic	12
5	Bournemouth	12

(Neither Crewe nor Port Vale have had any changes in the review period. Crewe are given first place because their last managerial change was nine months before Port Vale's last change)

COMPLETE RANKING OF PREMIERSHIP AND NATIONWIDE LEAGUE TEAMS

Since the first publication of *The Boss* in 1995 Darlington have moved to the top of the table of clubs with the most unstable seat in management. The resignation of David Hodgson and sacking of Jim Platt in less than 12 months was enough to take the Quakers five places up the least auspicious table in the League. Hodgson, brave man, returned for a second stint at the end of 1996.

Conversely, Ronnie Whelan's survival into 1997 at Southend made Roots Hall look a little less like a managerial graveyard. Not surprisingly Notts County maintained their prominent showing – the Christmas '96 axing of management duo Colin Murphy and Steve Thompson saw to that. Hartlepool and Torquay also kept up their record of chopping and changing.

Among the clubs with the safest seats, Oldham dropped one place following the resignation of Graeme Sharpe. Despite a rare change at the City Ground – the resignation of Frank Clark – Nottingham Forest remained the Premiership's most stable base for managers – in marked contrast to their neighbours across the Trent. Liverpool and Derby improved their placings significantly, as did Bournemouth and Charlton, while Dave Bassett's departure from Sheffield United and Andy King's sacking by Mansfield brought uncharacteristic changes at those two clubs.

The full rankings follow, with clubs most likely to have a change of manager given the highest points, and the safest seats at the foot of the table.

Darlington	57
Notts County	57
Swansea City	57
Hartlepool United	55

Torquay United	55
Lincoln City	53
Southend United	53
West Bromwich Albion	50
Peterborough	49
Colchester United	46
Coventry City	46
Doncaster Rovers	45
Scarborough	45
Manchester City	44
Birmingham City	43
Bradford City	42
Cambridge United	41
Cardiff City	41
Carlisle United	40
Preston North End	40
Scunthorpe United	39
Chester City	38
Gillingham	38
Grimsby Town	38
Rotherham United	38
Tottenham Hotspur	38
Huddersfield Town	36
Norwich City	36
Plymouth Argyle	36
QPR	36
Stockport County	36
Watford	36
Sunderland	35

Hereford United	34
Luton Town	34
Rochdale	34
Wigan Athletic	34
Blackpool	33
Bristol City	33
Burnley	33
Bristol Rovers	32
Northampton Town	31
Aston Villa	29
Bolton Wanderers	29
Fulham	29
Millwall	29
Newcastle United	29
Southampton	29
Stoke City	29
Wolverhampton Wanderers	29
Hull City	28
Walsall	28
Chelsea	27
Exeter City	27
Leicester City	27
Chesterfield	26
Shrewsbury Town	26
Brighton & Hove Albion	25
Barnsley	24
Everton	24
Ipswich Town	24
Leyton Orient	24

Portsmouth	24
Sheffield Wednesday	24
Blackburn Rovers	22
Middlesbrough	22
Oxford United	22
Swindon Town	22
Tranmere Rovers	22
Wimbledon	22
York City	22
Leeds United	21
Crystal Palace	20
Arsenal	19
Brentford	19
Mansfield Town	17
Reading	17
West Ham United	17
Bury	15
Wrexham	14
Sheffield United	13
Bournemouth	12
Charlton Athletic	12
Derby County	12
Liverpool	11
Oldham Athletic	10
Manchester United	7
Nottingham Forest	6
Port Vale	0
Crewe Alexandra	0

vi

FOR THE RECORD

Life and times of the managers featured in the book:

Roy AITKEN

Capped 57 times by Scotland in an inspirational career mostly with Celtic, followed by Newcastle and St Mirren. Stepped into 1995 relegation crisis at Aberdeen, his first managerial post, and pulled off a rescue the SAS would have been proud of.

Sam ALLARDYCE

Born in Dudley but an adopted Lancastrian, having played most of his football as principal jailer of the Bolton Wanderers defence. His clubs also included Sunderland, Millwall, Coventry and Huddersfield. He suffered the indignity of being sacked by an imprisoned chairman – Blackpool's Owen Oyston, serving time for rape when Allardyce was dismissed after failing to win a play-off semi-final. Appointed manager of Notts County in January 1997.

Jimmy ARMFIELD

Like the famous tower, a landmark in Blackpool. Pipe-smoking, organ-playing guru whose position as a director of the local hospital makes him eminently suitable for the task imposed on him by the FA – to revive English football. Played in the same Blackpool team as Stanley Matthews, captained club and country. Manager of Bolton (Third Division Champions) and Leeds United (European Cup runners-up). Post-managerial career as *Daily Express* and BBC radio reporter.

Ian ATKINS

Born leader still seeking the right followers. Was made captain at most of the clubs he played for. Playing career embraced Shrewsbury, Sunderland, Everton, Ipswich and Birmingham – a long route to his home city. Management began with Colchester in their non-League days, then briefly to Cambridge United. Took over at Northampton in January 1995.

Ron ATKINSON

For a man much sought-after by football chairmen, it's a surprise that Atkinson didn't have any early ambitions for the profession. After a playing career mostly with Oxford United he was planning a future in business until persuaded to take over at non-League Kettering Town. Until arriving at Coventry enjoyed success at every club, including Atlético Madrid, who reached third place before Atkinson became a victim of Spanish football politics. Won the FA Cup twice with Manchester United, the League Cup with Sheffield Wednesday and Aston Villa. Manager of Coventry from February 1995 until becoming director of football in 1996.

Graham BARROW

Former central heating engineer who knows how to install boilers and plumbing in unpromising property, as fans of Chester City and Wigan Athletic will confirm. Playing career with non-League Altrincham, then Wigan and Chester both of whom he has now managed. Promotion with Chester in 1994, fired by Wigan in 1995, took over at Rochdale in 1996.

Ian BRANFOOT

Has something in common with Sir Alf Ramsey – like Sir Alf, who declined to select Jimmy Greaves for England, Branfoot is renowned for not picking a gifted forward – Matt le Tissier at Southampton. Playing days with Sheffield Wednesday, Doncaster and Lincoln. Added to Fourth Division Championship medal as a player by taking **Reading to Third Division** title, but found it tough going at Southampton, resigning in January 1994. Bounced back for more with Fulham and became general manager in 1996.

Craig BROWN

Former Rangers and Dundee player who launched his managerial career with Clyde while lecturing to student teachers in Ayr. Took Clyde from mid-table Second Division to mid-table First Division. Assistant manager of Motherwell before joining SFA. National team manager from 1993.

Tommy BURNS

Ex-Celtic player and Scotland international who took on the task of reviving his old club in 1994. Began managerial career with Kilmarnock.

Trevor CHERRY

Disappointed his mum by pursuing a career in football. She didn't believe it was the right profession for young Trevor, although when he captained Huddersfield to the Second Division title, played in two FA Cup Finals for Leeds and won 27 England caps he proved his point. Still, he was glad to have book-keeping qualifications and the experience of running a waste-paper business under his belt when Bradford City dispensed with his services as manager in 1987. Shaking the dust of football from his shoes, he went into business in his native Huddersfield, retaining links with the game as associate director of Huddersfield Town.

Sammy CHUNG

Son of a Chinese father and English mother, played for Reading, Norwich and Watford before moving into coaching with Watford, Ipswich and Wolves. Manager of Wolves when they became Second Division Champions in 1977.

Steve COPPELL

Brilliant winger with Tranmere and Manchester United whose career was curtailed by injury. Was youngest manager in the game when he took over at Crystal Palace at the age of 28. Had a good run for his money, serving nine years at Selhurst and recording a final placing of third in the First Division in 1991, an achievement which pips a Zenith Data Systems Cup Final win over Everton among topics to debate with his grandchildren in years to come. Resigned following relegation in 1993. A man on whom others like to depend, he was chairman of the Professional Footballers' Association, and later chief executive of the League Managers' Association. Returned to Palace as technical director in 1995, moving to Manchester City for 33 ill-fated days as manager in 1996, before returning again to Palace in early 1997.

Alan CURBISHLEY

Learned all the good habits as an apprentice at West Ham and displayed them in the colours of Birmingham, Aston Villa, Charlton and Brighton. Returned to Charlton as reserve coach and accepted the Mission Impossible of managing the team before the club self-destructed. In tandem with co-manager Steve Gritt created a successful team despite having no stadium and less money. Appointed sole manager in 1995, with Charlton, having defied destruction, back at the Valley.

Kenny DALGLISH

Brilliant playing career with Celtic, Liverpool and Scotland (record 102 caps, 30 goals), equally successful as manager, winning three League titles and two FA Cups, including the Double in 1986, with Liverpool, and Second Division promotion and the Premier League title with Blackburn. Spent an unsatisfactory year as director of football at Blackburn before leaving by mutual consent. In 1997 he stepped back into the limelight at Newcastle, following the sudden departure of Kevin Keegan.

Martin DOBSON

As a midfield player with Bolton, Burnley, Everton and England always had plenty of options; much the same away from football. Once considered opening a kennels, tried the fashion business, and did his time as manager of Bury (promotion from Fourth Division), Northwich Victoria and Bristol Rovers. Stunned his staff at Bury by telling them to take a week off in mid-season to recharge batteries. Had too long recharging his own batteries for his liking – returned to football as youth development officer at Bolton in 1996.

Mick DOCHERTY

Son of Tommy Docherty and as resilient as his dad, bouncing back from the sack when he took Hartlepool to last in the League in 1983. Worked as coach or assistant manager at Wolves, Blackpool, Burnley and Rochdale before taking over as Rochdale boss 1994. Playing days looked bright – skippered Burnley to FA Youth Cup 1968, became the club's youngest captain at 19 and collected a Second Division medal 1973. Serious injury disrupted his progress from then on. If learning the hard way counts for anything, Mick Docherty has all the qualifications. Sacked by Rochdale in 1996.

Tommy DOCHERTY

Incapable of leading a dull life, has experienced the sack more often than Santa Claus and collected clubs the way youngsters collect Panini stickers. Played for Celtic, Preston, Arsenal and Chelsea, winning 25 Scotland caps; as a manager won the League Cup with Chelsea, the FA Cup with Manchester United and the Second Division Championship, also with Manchester United in 1975. Notches on the managerial belt include eight English League clubs plus Oporto, Sydney Olympic, South Melbourne, Scotland and Altrincham. Not renowned for keeping his opinions to himself.

Terry DOLAN

Rochdale's claims to fame include being the birthplace of the Co-operative movement and Gracie Fields. The Lancashire cotton town also contains the one and only club to entice Terry Dolan away from his native Yorkshire. As a player Dolan wore the colours of Bradford City (two spells), Bradford Park Avenue, Huddersfield, non-League Harrogate (player-coach) – and Rochdale. As a manager he has controlled Bradford City, Hull City – and Rochdale. Major success has been elusive – closest calls were a play-off final in 1988, Bradford City losing to Middlesbrough for a place in the old Division One, and a good FA Cup run with Rochdale in 1990. Manager of Hull since 1991.

John DUNCAN

Qualified teacher who learned all the football lessons they don't include in the textbooks by managing Hartlepool United, though he spent only two months there. Scunthorpe taught him that getting good results doesn't necessarily keep you in a job; Ipswich taught him that not getting good results does throw you out of a job; but at Chesterfield he learned that success (Fourth Division Championship, 1985) is so sweet that the offer of a second chance (1993) can prove irresistible. As a player won a Scottish League Cup medal with Dundee (1974). Also played for Spurs and Derby.

Sam ELLIS

A sign on the dressing-room wall at Bury FC read: 'For Sale – apply to Sam.' Ellis was the unlucky man to be manager of Bury when financial crisis in 1990 caused the whole squad to be transfer listed. Moved on himself soon afterwards, joining Peter Reid at Manchester City. Made headlines as a player when included in Sheffield Wednesday's FA Cup Final team of 1966 after a handful of League appearances. Won Fourth Division title twice – with Lincoln (1976) and Watford (1978), and as manager won promotion from same division with Blackpool (1985). Manager of Lincoln, 1994–95.

Roy EVANS

Liverpool's only local-born manager post-war. Made the ultimate career move by quitting playing aged 25, having failed to gain a regular first-team place at Anfield. Preferred a job on the coaching staff to continuing playing career elsewhere. Progressed steadily upward and appointed assistant to Graeme Souness, then given full command when Souness quit in 1994. Key member of redoubtable bootroom team which chivvied successive Reds teams to four European Cups and numerous domestic honours. Crowned first full season as manager by winning the Coca-Cola Cup.

Alex FERGUSON

Passionate, volatile and a born winner. Ex-Rangers striker who made Aberdeen a European power, winning three Scottish Championships, four Scottish Cups, the Scottish League Cup and the European Cup Winners Cup. Manager of Manchester United from 1986, winning three Premier League titles and three FA Cups, the League Cup once and the European Cup Winners Cup. Those triumphs incorporated the League and Cup Double twice – Ferguson being the first manager to achieve this.

Peter FOX

Former goalkeeper with Sheffield Wednesday, Stoke City and Exeter. If it was hard work being the last line behind some dodgy defences it was even harder in his first managerial position – took over at Exeter when Terry Cooper resigned in 1995, with the club bottom and broke. Mid-table security in his first season was some achievement.

Ken FURPHY

Saw it all, from Workington to New York Cosmos – winning honours on both sides of the Atlantic. Knew how to make a silk purse from a sow's ear, achieving notable success at Workington (Fourth Division promotion, 1963) and Watford (Third Division Championship, 1969; FA Cup semi-finals, 1970). Also managed

Blackburn Rovers, Sheffield United, Detroit Express and Washington Diplomats, taking Detroit to the NASL Championship, and coaching New York Cosmos.

Bobby GOULD

Restless wanderer who played for nine clubs and managed four – two of them (Bristol Rovers and Coventry) twice. Greatest success was the 1988 FA Cup Final win as manager of Wimbledon against overwhelming favourites and League Champions Liverpool. Capacity for creating surprises never better illustrated than by unheralded resignation from Coventry immediately after 5–1 defeat at QPR – a twist matched by appointment as manager of Wales in 1995.

Dario GRADI

Began 1996–97 as the longest-serving manager with the same club in England. Secret of longevity has to be unique background – born Milan, never played League football, no wonder Crewe have never found anyone with right qualifications to replace him. Not that they would want to – Gradi's policy of nurturing young talent to be sold at huge profit, while playing attractive and often winning football, has been consistently successful. Played as an amateur for Sutton United (one amateur international cap; FA Amateur Cup Finalist, 1969), then FA coach followed by coaching position with Chelsea. Assistant manager of Derby and manager of Wimbledon (Fourth Division promotion, 1979) and Crystal Palace. In command at Crewe from June 1983 (Fourth Division promotion, 1989; Third Division promotion, 1994).

Bryan HAMILTON

Scorer of the great goal that never was, the 'winner' for Everton against Liverpool in 1977 FA Cup semi-final which was controversially disallowed. Linfield, Ipswich, Everton, Millwall, Swindon, Tranmere and 50 caps for Northern Ireland led to managerial posts at Tranmere, Wigan (Freight Rover Trophy,

1985), Leicester, Wigan again and the Northern Ireland job.

Brian HORTON

Might have made a good fireman, since he's often called upon to douse infernos which happen to break out when he's around – Maxwell crisis at Oxford, anti-Swales campaign at Manchester City. Outstanding midfield player who galvanized Brighton's push from Division Three to Division One (1977–79) and Luton to the Second Division title in 1982. Managed Hull City to Third Division promotion, 1985. Huddersfield Town manager from 1995.

Keith HOUCHEN

Made the right decision in 1987 when offered a choice between Coventry and Leicester. Signed for Coventry and scored memorable diving header in the Cup Final triumph over Spurs – Leicester were relegated. Travelled many miles to complete a full circle – started playing career at Hartlepool and advanced via Orient, York (giant-killing Arsenal), Scunthorpe, Coventry, Hibernian and Port Vale to complete the circle back at Hartlepool. Manager 1995–96.

Emlyn HUGHES

Effervescent enthusiast who captained Liverpool to two European Championships but enjoyed only a brief encounter with management, lasting less than two years at Rotherham before finding greater fame and better rewards as a TV sports quiz host. Viktor is the name of the promotions company he now runs, a victor he certainly was in a playing career that will linger longer in the memory than his stint at Millmoor.

Kevin KEEGAN

Among his many successes was victory in the TV *Superstars* competition in 1976, although a bad fall in the cycle race caught up with him later and he spent four days in Northampton General

Hospital. Apart from that, has always been firmly in the saddle. Player with Scunthorpe, Liverpool, Hamburg, Southampton and Newcastle; won numerous honours including European Footballer of the Year. Manager of Newcastle from 1992 before controversially resigning in January 1997.

Howard KENDALL

Few realize the significant part played by Shrewsbury Town in the career of one of Britain's best managers. The Stoke manager Alan Durban wanted to appoint Ritchie Barker as his assistant but Barker preferred to accept the managerial vacancy at Shrewsbury. Durban then offered Kendall, a player on the Stoke staff, the player-coach's role. Thus was born a managerial voyage which achieved landfall at Blackburn, Everton, Athletic Bilbao, Manchester City, Everton again, Notts County and the Greek club Xanthe. Two League Championships, one FA Cup and the European Cup Winners Cup in his first stint at Everton established undisputable credentials, embellished by his revival of Sheffield United after taking over in 1995.

Andy KING

Former Luton, Everton and Wolves midfielder who enjoyed his best times at Everton and married the girl next door – Barbara, a member of the commercial staff at neighbouring Liverpool. Took a drop in pay when leaving post of commercial manager at Luton to dip his toe in the managerial ocean at Mansfield in 1993; steered the club into the play-offs in his first full season but failure to do even better 12 months later cost him his job.

Lennie LAWRENCE

Never played League football, entered management as assistant, then caretaker at Plymouth. Synonymous with Charlton Athletic for almost a decade, winning promotion to First Division in 1986 despite having no home of their own (sharing Selhurst Park with Crystal Palace). Took Middlesbrough to the Premier League;

departed 12 months after relegation. Ventured into the Danger Zone by accepting Bradford City post in 1994. Halfway through contract City dismissed him after run of 13 games with only two wins. Quickly back in business with Luton.

Mick McCARTHY

Multi-national Yorkshireman who advanced from the Barnsley defence to play at the top with Manchester City in England, Olympic Lyonnaise in France and Celtic in Scotland, and won 57 caps for the Republic of Ireland. Millwall provided his only managerial experience before he succeeded Jack Charlton as manager of the Republic of Ireland in January 1996.

Wilf McGUINNESS

Cheerful Kojak look-alike whose humorous outlook on life was chiselled from the hard granite of disappointment following dismissal by the only club he ever wanted to serve, Manchester United. Coaching posts in Jordan and Syria barely kept him afloat financially before Bury came to the rescue with a staff post that lasted until retirement. Now a matchday host at Old Trafford.

Lou MACARI

Glasgow-born but spent part of his childhood in London's East End, a connection which made him particularly pleased to become manager of West Ham and particularly sore at deciding to resign. Very much his own man, he achieved notable success at Swindon (Fourth Division Champions, 1986; Third Division promotion, 1987). Playing career with Celtic and Manchester United, for whom he signed in preference to Liverpool when he became one of the few players not to be won over by the powerful personality of Bill Shankly. Helped United beat Liverpool in the 1977 FA Cup Final. After swings and roundabouts with Birmingham and Celtic began his second stint in charge of Stoke in 1994.

Steve McMAHON

Abrasive midfield commander who served in the trenches with Everton, Villa, Liverpool and Manchester City before becoming the surprise choice to take over at Swindon in 1994. Witnessed relegation and a Coca-Cola Cup semi-final in his first few months, topped by the Second Division Championship in 1996.

Lawrie McMENEMY

Director of football at Southampton, the club he turned into a regular contender for honours, winning the FA Cup in 1976. Has sampled the wide sweep of management, from the Fourth Division with Doncaster and Grimsby to the international stage as assistant to Graham Taylor with the England squad. Sums up the changing nature of the job: 'At Doncaster I was 95 per cent coach and five per cent manager. By the time I finished at Southampton I was 95 per cent manager and five per cent coach.'

Jimmy MULLEN

Served his managerial apprenticeship across Great Britain – assistant manager of Cardiff, player-manager of Newport County, assistant manager of Aberdeen. Fired by Blackpool after relegation but took Burnley from the Fourth Division to the new-style First Division, a record which was good enough to keep him in a job despite relegation in 1995 – though not to ensure his survival after more bad results 12 months on.

John NEAL

Milk-swigging, golf-swinging traditionalist who puts grit far ahead of glitz. Playing career with Hull, Kings Lynn, Swindon, Aston Villa and Southend was followed by a spell working in the Ford car plant at Dagenham. Returned to football and managed Wrexham, Middlesbrough and Chelsea, achieving success at the price of his health. Retreated to St Andrews, Scotland, to recuperate. Now burning up the fairways from his home near Wrexham.

Phil NEAL

Phenomenally consistent right-back with Liverpool in their greatest era, collecting four European Cup winners medals and becoming the most-capped Englishman in his position. Experienced fluctuating fortunes as manager of Bolton and Coventry, where good housekeeping behind the scenes wasn't always rewarded with comparable achievements on the big stage. Had a brief encounter with Cardiff City in 1996 before moving to Manchester City as number two to Steve Coppell. Temporarily took over the managerial role after Coppell quit.

Terry NEILL

Personable Ulsterman who anchored the Arsenal defence for 11 years and achieved the distinction of managing both north London giants, Tottenham and Arsenal, as well as Hull City and Northern Ireland. Steered the Gunners to an FA Cup triumph in 1979 and the European Cup Winners Cup Final 12 months later. Sacked in 1983, he decided the feeling was mutual and kicked the managerial business into touch as well.

David PLEAT

Outstanding as a young footballer but career was blighted by injury. Managerial career began with Nuneaton Borough, followed by success at Luton (Second Division Champions, 1982; FA Cup semi-finalists, 1985). Took Tottenham to the FA Cup Final in 1987 and third place in the League. Experienced cash-strapped restrictions at Leicester and Luton again, before returning to the big time with Sheffield Wednesday in 1995.

Peter REID

Ex-workaholic midfielder with Bolton, Everton, QPR and Manchester City who earned the loyalty of the Maine Road aficionados by declining to follow Howard Kendall on a sentimental return to Everton. Unable to establish City as a major power in the Premiership and paid with the sack in 1993.

Sunderland manager from 1995, winning the Endsleigh League Division One title in 1996.

Bruce RIOCH

Tough midfielder who presents a more mellow image as a manager, though anyone mistaking it for softness is in for a shock. Greatest achievements in management have been to revolutionize the status of first Middlesbrough, then Bolton Wanderers, whom he took into the Premiership in 1995. Fired by Arsenal after one season in which he steered the club back into Europe. Surprised everyone by making his next job assistant manager at QPR.

Bryan ROBSON

One of the most admired players in the history of British football. Record signing when Manchester United took him from West Bromwich for £1.5 million in 1981, he spent 13 impressive years at Old Trafford, collecting Cup medals at home and in Europe before playing a part in the return of the League title in 1993 and the Cup and League Double in '94. Won 90 international caps and was member of England coaching set-up while still a United player. Player-manager of Middlesbrough from 1994, winning the Division One Endsleigh League title in his first season.

Joe ROYLE

Unusually phlegmatic for a football man, Royle took Oldham Athletic to undreamed-of heights – the Premiership, League Cup Final, FA Cup semi-finals. His appointment as Everton manager in 1994 was a genuine homecoming – Royle's father is a shareholder. His playing debut for Everton at 16 wasn't greeted with universal approval – the manager, Harry Catterick, was jostled by fans angry that the revered Alex Young had been supplanted by an unknown. Royle's managerial debut – a home win over Liverpool – was received rather more warmly.

Alan SMITH

Four years as manager of Isthmian Leaguers Dulwich Hamlet proved valuable training for the big time. In their own environment, Dulwich were subject to proportionately as much pressure as a Premier League team. Replaced Steve Coppell as Crystal Palace manager following Palace's relegation in 1993. Achieved promotion, followed by relegation, followed by the sack. Manager of Wycombe Wanderers, 1995–96.

Walter SMITH

Playing career ended by injury at Dundee United. Coach and assistant manager to Jim McLean at Tannadice, then five years as assistant to Graeme Souness during a dramatic revival of fortunes at Ibrox. Manager from 1991, securing Premier Division title six times out of six plus Scottish Cup in '92, '93 and '96 and Scottish League Cup in '91, '93 and '94.

Graeme SOUNESS

Habitual winner who judged everyone by his own high standards until a triple heart bypass coupled with disappointing days as Liverpool manager forced him to view life and mankind in a new light. Player with Middlesbrough, Liverpool and Sampdoria, player-manager of Rangers, revitalizing the club after years in the doldrums. Mixed fortunes as Liverpool manager. Returned to football with Turkish club Galatasaray 1995. Southampton manager from 1996.

Paul STURROCK

Won 20 Scotland caps as a striker with Dundee United. Became coach of his old club before moving into management with St Johnstone in season 1993–94.

Colin TODD

As assistant to Bruce Rioch, Todd played a key part in securing Bolton's promotion to the Premiership in 1995. Then, as co-manager with Roy McFarland, he saw the club slip so deep into relegation trouble that not even a stirring revival when placed in sole command could save them. He was a classy defender with Sunderland, Derby and Everton, among others, earning two Championship medals with Derby. Underwent management experience with Whitley Bay and Middlesbrough before taking over at Bolton.

Mike WALKER

Stylish of appearance and likes his teams to play with the same attribute. Grounding at Colchester followed by fairytale adventures with Norwich – third place in Premier League, UEFA Cup triumph over Bayern Munich and heroic defeat to Inter Milan. Was appointed to the Everton vacancy 1993, a move which looked perfect but was blighted by boardroom in-fighting. Avoided relegation on last day of season 1993–94, sacked after three months with only one win the following season. Returned to Norwich in 1996 after his old foe, chairman Robert Chase, was ousted.

Mike WALSH

Stubborn defender with Bolton, Everton, Blackpool, Manchester City, Bury and the Republic of Ireland. Inherited a poisoned chalice at Bury, taking on a club in the depths of a spectacular financial slump. Success should be rated as much through keeping the club in business as taking them to the play-offs in '93 and '95. But Walsh became the first managerial casualty of 1995–96, then joined Swindon as assistant to Steve McMahon.

Steve WIGNALL

Liverpool-born centre-back who played for Darlington and Colchester. Made a significant mark by reviving football in Aldershot after the collapse of the football team, helping to form the new Aldershot Town FC. Appointed Colchester manager in 1995.

Howard WILKINSON

Thoughtful Yorkshireman who graduated from non-League football to League management with Notts County, Sheffield Wednesday (promotion to First Division) and Leeds United (Second Division Champions, 1990; Premier League Champions, 1992). Chairman of the League Managers' Association and was appointed technical director for the FA at Lancaster Gate in early 1997.

Tales From the Boot Camps

STEVE CLARIDGE
with Ian Ridley

Away from the glamour and wall-to-wall coverage of the Premiership lies the reality, for the majority of fans and players, of British football. From his early days in and out of the Bournemouth reserves and on loan at non-league Weymouth, to scoring the last-minute winner in a First Division play-off at Wembley, Steve Claridge has experienced life at every level of football.

Tales From the Boot Camps is the story of irregular salary payments and training sessions conducted on dog-fouled car parks at soon-to-be-defunct Aldershot; of repeated clashes with John Beck over his long-ball tactics and army-camp methods of preparation at Cambridge; of David Pleat's flimsy Luton who 'played too much passing football'; of Barry Fry's unorthodox reign at Birmingham; and of the flight to the Premiership with Leicester.

Controversial, itinerant, but popular wherever he plays, Claridge also talks frankly about his addiction to gambling, and of the consequences, both material and psychological, of his fifteen-year affliction. Part biography, part autobiography, Ian Ridley's narrative is full of insight and the dry wit of Claridge, and skilfully intertwines the story of a Midlands cult-hero with a portrait of life in the lower divisions of English football.

£16.99 Hardback   ISBN 0 575 06398 X   GOLLANCZ

Cantona
The Red and the Black

IAN RIDLEY

Ian Ridley's acclaimed critical biography of the visionary French forward – fully updated for this paperback edition – places Eric Cantona's actions in the context of an English season beset by hooliganism and allegations of sleaze. It assembles testimony and insight from the most influential figures in Cantona's career, both in England and France, and explores the character and motivation of one of the most charismatic and colourful characters in the world game – part Rambo, part Rimbaud.

'...masterful biography that will enthrall believers and heathens alike' *Loaded*

'A refreshing but sadly rare example of a well-written, carefully researched study of a controversial footballer, which never allows sympathy for a gifted player to fudge his obvious shortcomings' *Guardian*

'The whole truth about the man and his most turbulent times' *Observer*

£4.99 Paperback **ISBN 0 575 60021 7**